Author of the widely acc
winner of the 1996 *Yorks*
Award, Martyn Bedford was born in Croydon in 1959.
He worked as a journalist on a number of regional
papers before graduating in 1994 from the Creative
Writing MA Course at the University of East Anglia.
He lives in Yorkshire with his wife, Damaris.

Praise for *Acts of Revision*:

'A remarkable psychological thriller'
You Magazine, *Mail on Sunday*

'A uniquely British psycho . . . a moving début'
Independent

'A macabre and extraordinary début'
Daily Telegraph

'Very clever and highly polished . . . Dazzling'
Sunday Telegraph

'In Martyn Bedford, the University of Creative Writing MA (which gave us Ishiguro and McEwan) has spawned another star'
Guardian

'An accomplished first novel . . . On the surface, the novel is a chillingly clever variation, compellingly written and impressively structured, on the theme of revenge. Beneath that, it is a complex psychological portrait, painted with a subtle and instinctive hand'
David Horspool, *The Times Literary Supplement*

'Comparisons with Ian McEwan and Iain Banks are inevitable, but also justified, for this disturbing, powerful book could well be the best début novel of the year'
Dominic Bradbury, *Literary Review*

'Unsettling . . . gripping'
New Statesman & Society

'A terrific début . . . touching and sad and funny and spooky'
Campbell Armstrong

'The interleaving of past with present, of thought with action, of dictionary definitions with explanatory letters, of internal and external dialogue – all this is so skillful that the novel becomes ever more interesting in its complications as it becomes less and less obvious in its intentions. There is a similar devotion to detail – again and again some tiny piece of acute observation proves arresting. The whole amounts to a fast and exhilarating read with, at the end, a disturbing amount to consider and think about'
Margaret Forster, *Spectator*

'A brilliant portrait of a psychopathic breakdown . . . an exceptional first novel. He is a clever and stylish writer . . . This is a profoundly sinister work,

and all the more so for being wildly funny too'
Mary Loudon, *The Times*

'Chilling, disturbing, at times even funny, this is a tale of revolt against the written laws of the world. Gregory Lynn, 35 years old, bachelor and orphan, wants to rewrite, revise, the entire story of his life and education, and the reports the world has made on both. His tale of menacing triumph is a challenge both to the laws of society and the laws of writing. It's a brilliant, finely written and very contemporary book'
Malcolm Bradbury

'Thoroughly unsettling, this tale forcefully presents the workings of a deranged mind in all its complexity while retaining the page-turning pleasure of a genuine thriller. A riveting début'
Kirkus Reviews

'A chilling revenge fantasy . . . A mystery story turned inside out; you know whodunit, but not what. The narratives collide and bounce off one another like particles in an atom smasher. Mr Bedford's book is intellectual, even playful – a post-modern exploration of the nature of reality and the inability of narrative to record or interpret events without making them into something else . . . Compelling'
New York Times Book Review

'This is the perfect read. Not since Thomas Harris gave us Red Dragon have I experienced such a gripping tale – one that grabs you by the throat and won't let you go'
Atlanta Journal

'Bedford's taut language, strategic repetition and honed irony effectively underscore the narrator's obsessions, while the story's symmetry, suspense and strong central character hold the reader hostage'
Chicago Tribune

'Martyn Bedford's début novel makes us aware of what doesn't exist in Germany – excellent literary entertainment. he succeeds triumphantly in blending the various levels of storytelling from the psychological case study to thriller and guarantees increasing suspense until the very last page on a high literary level. Why don't we have writers like him?'
Die Woche (*The Week*)

'A thrilling and terrifying read . . . I was impressed by the detached delicacy with which Martyn Bedford controls his frightening material and found myself chuckling nervously at the treacly black humour. a novel to make any teacher's hair stand on end'
Lesley Glaister

EXIT, ORANGE & RED

Martyn Bedford

BLACK SWAN

EXIT, ORANGE & RED
A BLACK SWAN BOOK : 0 552 99675 0

Originally published in Great Britain by Bantam Press,
a division of Transworld Publishers Ltd

PRINTING HISTORY
Bantam Press edition published 1997
Black Swan edition published 1998

Black Swan Books are published by Transworld Publishers Ltd,
61–63 Uxbridge Road, London W5 5SA,
in Australia by Transworld Publishers (Australia) Pty Ltd,
15–25 Helles Avenue, Moorebank, NSW 2170
and in New Zealand by Transworld Publishers (NZ) Ltd,
3 William Pickering Drive, Albany, Auckland.

Printed and bound in Great Britain by
Cox & Wyman Ltd, Reading, Berkshire.

AUTHOR'S NOTE

The Hallam of this book is, and is not, Sheffield; the Urbopark shopping mall is, and is not, Meadowhall. I have used these real places as a basis for fictional settings, making whatever alterations suited my purpose. Similarly, in the historical sections of this book I have based my story on actual events while taking certain liberties with them. In the contemporary sections, all of the characters and organizations are invented; in the historical sections some are invented and some are not. This is a novel.

M.B.

Chapter One

SHOP TALK

It's like a maze, first time tha goes in theer. All t'thingummies – the arcades – look the same and tha dunt know wheer owt is, like. Then tha've to find t'way aht again.

Christine Mumby, 26, mother-of-two, housewife.

The road propelled her beneath the colossal brick arches of a viaduct and out through slabs of factory and wasteground. She sang in time to, though not in tune with, the car radio; her lyrics, sporadically inconsistent with those of the song. Leaving the city centre, its ski-slope-steep hills studded with high-rise flats and office blocks, she drove east towards a double-decker section of motorway. Twin cooling towers framed a fresh sun. The driver dunked the visor, reducing her field of vision to parallel strips of car bonnet and tarmac. The dashboard clock read 7.35. At a red light, she assessed an explosion of ginger hair in the rearview; no time to scrape and scrunchie before the signal switched to green. Right-angled turn. Half a dozen empty Lucozade Orange clinked in the passenger seat footwell, the bottles dishevelling dead crisp packets and Snickers' wrappers. Labouring away from the junction, she addressed the car by name – Fifi – coaxing, encouraging. *Come on, Feef, don't stall on me.* The young woman's accent, no longer Americanized by song, became flat-vowelled Hallam buffed smooth at the edges. When the record ended, she channel-hopped. Another junction, wheeling her in a long loop that swung the sun into dazzling reflection from the rear. She tilted the mirror out of alignment. Up with the visor, exposing a view now entirely occupied by the complicated interlocking edifice, the brightly coloured roofs, the glass domes and atria, the ceaseless grey swathe of car-parks of an immense shopping mall silhouetted against a bleached sky.

Green Zone Car-Park (Lower), Section 11, Area C, Bay 24. Constance Amory got out of the car, locked it, unlocked it, removed her handbag from the passenger seat, locked the car again, crossed the car-park, returned to the car, unlocked it, fitted an anti-theft device, locked the car. She walked once more towards the mall, across a concourse crazy-paved in pale green brick. Automatic glass doors, trimmed with chrome, were flanked on either side by wrought-iron hanging baskets like a pair of pendulous earrings. A sign above the entrance read:

URBOPARK: SHOPPING IS LIBERTY

She'd passed this sign so often its words barely registered, even now when the fluorescent characters were illuminated and the second P of 'shopping' blinked on and off. The doors, their sensors deactivated, remained closed as she made for an adjacent entrance. The door was wooden, olive green. She fumbled in her bag for her security card. It wasn't there. It wasn't there, it was at home. Shit, she'd left it at home in her other bag. Shit. Shit. She searched again, rifling the assorted junk – papers, pens, notebooks, keys, letters, make-up – with which the compartments were crammed. Why didn't she use a card-wallet like everyone else? Why couldn't she ever . . . there it was, that was it wedged between a bank statement and a trial sachet of honey-blossom conditioner, free with *Cosmo*, which she'd tucked away in her bag for some reason and which was now, she noticed, leaking. She swiped the card in a slot set into the wall and punched in her personal identity code: 2513 – which she had memorized as her age (25) followed by her initials (C.A.) reversed, when A = 1, B = 2, C = 3. Next birthday, she'd have to devise another mnemonic. The door clicked open.

'Morning, Connie love.'

'Spotless, Effie. Absolutely see your face in it.'

'I ant done this bit yet.'

The woman switched on an industrial vacuum cleaner, drowning out her next remark as Constance squeezed past. Effie. Not short for Euphemia, but a convoluted corruption of Frances. *Folk called me Eff, like F for Frances. Then it were Effie.* She had at least eight children, although confusion over names and nicknames, children and godchildren (combined with anecdotal inexactitude) meant there could be any number – several with offspring of their own. As far as Constance could tell.

At the end of the passage, a second door opened onto the arcade: Lower Mall, Green. A trough of potted plants divided the arcade along most of its length, leaves gleaming so perfectly beneath artificial lighting that a casual observer might incorrectly assume the foliage to be synthetic. Benches, which would later be occupied, were empty; a rank of payphones stood as though in patient anticipation of queues to come. This was a *sub*-arcade, a short slipway of retail units connecting the mall's main pedestrian thoroughfare with the nearest car-park. Enclosed not by a lofty glass roof, but by a low ceiling chequered with lime-green and white panels and diffused strip lights; the ambience was of a windowless, claustrophobic corridor in the bowels of a vast institution. Here, were the mall's *off-prime* plots: a financial services adviser, a building society, a cycle shop, a travel agency, a fax-and-photocopy point and the district office of the *Hallam Evening Crucible*.

The shopfronts were locked and unlit, the arcade's marble-effect floor shiny, deserted. The muzak had yet to be switched on, the silence broken only by a background hum of air conditioning and the distant drone of cleaning equipment as the overnight shift finished in time for Doors Open.

Constance's footsteps reverberated. She loved this, the early morning aloneness of being in a busy place that was not yet busy. She loved to drive on empty roads at dawn, imagining herself to be the only survivor in a post-apocalyptic world. How often had she done this? Once. She'd only once driven on empty roads at dawn – not even dawn, but 3.00 a.m. or something – so how could you say you loved to do something when you'd only done it once? You couldn't. You couldn't say that. It was the aloneness she loved, now she came to think of it. Being alone with her thoughts. Though, mostly, when she was by herself she thought about other people; or about herself *in relation* to them. She'd not want to be alone for long, for ever; but it was fine on mornings like this when her mood was ... what? Cheery. Cheerful. Bit of banter with Effie; the Virgin breakfast show. Her head was buzzing.

She stopped at the *Crucible* office and let herself in. She turned on the lights and crossed reception to the rear office, where she plugged in the fax, computer terminal, photocopier and Mall Link printer and checked her answering machine. One, from her mam, which filled the entire tape and took fifteen minutes to listen to while Constance made and drank a mug of coffee and flicked through the newspapers that had been left as usual in a bundle outside the front door. Yes, Mam, yes, Mam. How could anyone talk for so long without punctuation? Constance rewound the tape so subsequent messages would record over it. Although it was likely Mam herself would be the next to ring. She'd once overlaid one of her own fifteen-minute monologues with a second lasting only ten minutes, the two running into each other with such neatness of meter and meaning that the messages sounded as though they'd been expertly edited into one.

At eight o'clock, Constance rang Mall PRO's information tape, noted down the summary details and keyed in the i.d. numbers of the items that interested her. After a moment, the Mall Link printer chuntered into life, expelling press releases into a plastic tray. She fished out one of the pages, read it, and made a call to the police to cross-check. At 8.07, the phone rang. She fielded it on the answering machine before picking up mid-message.

'Hello . . . hello?'

'Morning, Gary.'

'What'ya got, Con?'

'*Morning*, Gary.'

'Yeah, yeah. Nice weekend and all that. Anyway.'

'Got a piece here might make something. From Mall PRO.'

'How come you'd got the answerphone on?'

'I thought you might be my mam.'

'Your *what*?'

'D'you want to hear about this?'

'We talking first edition?'

'Vandalism. Happened overnight. Someone daubed graffiti over all the entrances to the mall.'

'What sort of graffiti?'

' "Rage".'

'Rage?'

'Just that, one word. R-A-G-E. Over every set of doors. Actually on the doors themselves, I mean.'

'What's fucking "rage" when it's at home?'

'How should I know? Rage, as in anger. I don't know.'

'Make a pic?'

'They've already cleaned it off.'

'Who?'

'Mall Clean.'

'Bollocks. Police got any idea who dunnit?'

'No.'

'Kids? School holidays, an' that.'

'They've no idea.'

15

'Nib, then. Just bang out a couple of pars for first time.'

'I think it's worth more than a nib.'

'Look, Con, I'm going into conference in a minute – I'll ask the editor if he'll send you on a copy-tasting course.'

'I'm serious.'

'Yeah, yeah. Anyway, what else you got?'

'*Gary*, the letters were daubed in blood.'

The story made page three; single-column, top right. Constance tied up the details by 8.55, filed at 9.20 – ten minutes before the copy deadline. The page was schemed, sub-edited and typeset by 9.52; and by 11.15 thousands of papers were being dispatched to all parts of the city. In Urbopark, billboards spelled out the headline – its words echoed by a vendor with the dreadful shriek of a mortally wounded primate: *Blush Ocka Maar! Blah Shocka Mow! Blaschk ya Myah!*

'Blood' shock at mall

by Constance Amory, Urbopark Reporter

A worker made a gruesome discovery today after vandals used 'fresh blood' to daub graffiti over entrances to Hallam's giant Urbopark shopping mall.

Cleaner Bill Honey, 48, of Foundry Road, Brightcliffe, found the word 'RAGE' in red letters on the glass doors of the HypaCenta foodhall when he turned up for his shift at 1 a.m.

'The letters were still wet,' he said. 'At first I thought it was paint, but when I looked more closely I knew it was blood. I worked in an abattoir for ten years and I know blood when I see it.'

Mr Honey, a father-of-three who has worked for the Urbopark in-house cleaning firm Mall Clean for 18 months, reported the discovery to his supervisor. Meanwhile, cleaners in other parts of the mall found identical slogans daubed on other entrances.

Analysis

Police were notified and forensic officers took samples of the 'blood' for analysis.

A spokesman said, 'Until we have the results of the tests we cannot be certain about the exact nature of the substance.'

He added that there was no indication who had carried out the vandalism or the motive behind the attack.

Television

Closed-circuit television-film will be studied to see if the perpetrator was caught in the act by any of the mall's security cameras.

The graffiti was wiped off using a special cleaning agent before the shops and stores opened for business as usual this morning at 8.30.

Urbopark spokesman Warren Bartholomew said, 'The incident posed no health risk either to staff or to shoppers and caused minimal disruption to our cleaning teams.

'Nevertheless, it was an unpleasant incident and a quite mindless act of vandalism.'

Nothing to file for second edition or city final, there being no anticipated update to the graffiti story until the police released results of the forensic tests or CCTV analysis. Constance worked on 'overnights': fashion boutique opens in Upper Mall, Pink; Mall Admin's human resources director bemoans poor educational standards of young job applicants; HypaCenta ranked bottom in Hallam Metropolitan University regional survey of supermarket wages; party of civic dignitaries from Hallam's twin town in Czech Republic pays official visit to Urbopark. The HypaCenta pay story was awaiting the addition of a union reaction, being obtained by the *Crucible*'s industrial correspondent, William Boyce, based at head office. As soon as the add pars had been transmitted from his terminal to hers, she set to work – splitting the screen vertically to display her copy on one half and his on the other. It was then a matter of highlighting the union spokesman's more significant quotes and lifting them into the original story before sending the final version to Gary on the newsdesk. *Cut 'n' paste job, in t'old days*. The 'old days', in William's parlance, were the era of the manual typewriter – when a merger of copy would require scissors (to slice up the pages of text into separate paragraphs) and clear adhesive tape (to reassemble them in the appropriate order). *Like playing bloody consequences*. In the afternoon she prepared copy for Urbopark Digest, a weekly colour page of news and pictures, under a byline displaying her idiotically beaming face alongside the slogan: Constance Amory – Our Gal at the Mall. Awful mugshot. Made her look like a ghost,

17

or as though she'd just got out of bed. The original print was bad enough, but the grainily reproduced version at the head of the page was even worse. Washed out, baggy eyed, jowly. The colour was too vivid and slightly out of register, so that her red hair appeared not only to have been ignited but was slipping on her scalp like an ill-fitting wig. *Nice one of you, that,* according to her mam, who – despite daughterly protest – had procured an enlargement which now stood, framed, on the mantelpiece at 'home'.

With timing that would've been uncanny but for the frequency of her unannounced visits, Mam *popped in* to the office just as Constance was thinking of her. She heard her before she saw her, the unmistakeable voice audible beyond the connecting door to reception as Mrs Amory chatted to Sally, on front counter. Constance stopped typing. She saved the text she was working on and closed the document, leaning back in her seat and waiting for the door to open, unknocked.

The Inky Path
Journalism is a profession best suited to those of an inquisitive disposition. This is not to say that being 'nosy' is, in itself, tantamount to having the proverbial 'nose for a story', but it is a distinct advantage. For it is basic to the art of good reporting that the journalist should seek to answer the questions: who? what? where? when? and why? In this respect, the reporter's task is not dissimilar to that of a police detective or, for that matter, the neighbourhood gossip. Nor, in the slippery business of separating fact from fiction, is it by any means certain which of these three will establish the most reliable version of events.

'You're wearing your hair down.'

'Yeah.'

'Suits you better up.' Vivienne Amory kissed her daughter on the forehead, leaving lipstick. 'Neater. More professional. Down is for t'disco.'

'I've not been to a disco since my twenty-first. And my

18

hair was shorter then, in a bob. Jesus, I'm talking about my hair.'

'When your hair's like mine, is the time to stop talking about it.'

'Mam, quit the Maureen Lipman stuff, will you?'

'All those lovely curls.'

'It isn't curly, it's *frizzy*. My hair is frizzy.'

'You know your trouble, don't you?'

'Go on.'

'You work too hard.'

'And that makes my hair frizzy?'

Mrs Amory sat down heavily in a chair across the desk from her daughter, selecting one of her sighs – somewhere between *God, am I glad to tek t'weight off me feet!* and *What a blimmin day I've had!* Mam never swore, not even 'bloody'; not even 'blooming', though she permitted herself the approximation of 'blimmin' as an all-purpose adjectival expletive (conjoined, most often, to the words 'weather' 'government' and 'your . . . father'). She unbuttoned her coat – purple, quilted – and gave another of her expressive exhalations, coupled with a vague fanning motion of hand before face, that signified: *too blimmin warm in here.* The implication being that her daughter, somehow, was to blame for working in a cramped, windowless office with faulty air conditioning. Constance got up to make coffee.

'What's that smell?' said Mam, wrinkling her nose.

'What smell?'

'Oranges or apples, or summat.'

'Pot-pourri. Peach and apricot.' Constance indicated a book-shelf, where she'd stood a small wicker basket filled with tangerine-coloured wood shavings and dried leaves. 'I decided the room needed freshening up.'

'Stuffy enough in here as it is wi'out that pong.'

'You can always take your coat *off*, Mam. I mean, we're barely into September.'

'Could be Siberia out theer, for all you'd know cooped up in this place. No wonder you're so pale.'

'I don't tan.' She wheeled round from the drinks counter, kettle in hand. 'When've I ever tanned, with my colouring?'

'Anaemic. It were going vegetarian what started it.'

'I gave up meat for a *year*, while I was at university. Not even a year, more like nine months. And that was *five years ago*.'

'Nobody eats that much macaroni cheese and gets away wi' it.'

Constance filled two mugs with boiling water. Frothy – you put the milk in with the granules before adding water. *Mam's* method. *Milk in first*. Same with tea. Even with cereal, you were supposed to pour on the milk, then the sugar. Mrs Amory hauled herself to her feet; panicky, as though she'd mislaid something of vital importance.

'What've I done with me shopping?'

'You didn't have—'

'Oh, aye – I left it wi' wotsername out theer. Sandra.'

'*Sally*.'

She went back to reception, returning shortly weighed down by four bulging carrier bags – two suspended from the end of each arm. The carriers had been turned inside out, to conceal the names of the shops whose goods they contained. *I've paid them good money, they'll not get free advertising out of me*. You couldn't make her see that the stores' corporate logos – typeface, colour, design – were so distinctively familiar as to be unmistakeable even when the lettering was reversed. She lowered the bags to the floor, arranging them so they'd not topple over.

'*Mam*.'

Mrs Amory rummaged in one of the carriers, producing a paper bag which she placed on Constance's mouse mat – the only space amid the clutter of her desktop.

'Breadcakes, cheese-and-pickle. And one o' them custard slices you like.'

'*Why*, Mam?'

'You'll not've had any lunch, that I do know.'

Constance made room for the mugs of coffee, setting one down within reach of her mam and lifting the keyboard on top of the monitor, out of spillage range.

'No, why all *this*? I thought you'd . . .'

'Food.' Mrs Amory indicated one of the carrier bags, which had sagged – despite her precautions – tipping a four-pack of frozen meat-and-potato pies onto the floor. She pointed to the other bags in turn. 'Clothes, clothes, shoes.'

'How much?'

'There was a sale.'

'There's always a sale. How much?'

'This is your mother you're talking to, not some interview for t'paper.'

'Mam.'

'Three hundred and twenty-one pounds.'

'Jesus Christ.'

'It'll be going back, except t'food. I've kept all t'receipts.'

Constance pushed her hair back from her face, leaning her elbows on the desk and propping her head in her hands. Her forehead was greasy. Her eyes stung with impending tears. The older woman stared into her coffee, the fleshy skin around her throat and neck was mottled pink – like one of her heat rashes, or an allergic reaction to cats, or when she lost her temper or became embarrassed. When Mam spoke again her voice was softer, less defiant.

'Like I say, it's all going back.'

'This is getting out of hand, Mam. Don't you think?'

'Dr Singh says my condition is to shopping what bulimia is to eating disorders. Gorge missen, then up it comes. He's got ten yards of hair inside his turban.'

'He told you that?'

'No, Dorothy Davies did.'

'I mean about the bulimia thing.'

'Eat your breadcakes, love. I bought them special.'

Constance took one from the bag and peeled off the

clingfilm wrapping. White roll, processed cheese slice with the consistency of melted plastic; first bite, no pickle.

'Does Dad know?'

'She says they've to inhale water through their nostrils.'

'That's Muslims, isn't it?'

'Why've they to do that?'

'Something to do with cleansing themselves before prayer. And, anyway, it's *Muslims*. Dr Singh's a Sikh.'

'It's them store cards, credit an' that. You knew wheer you were wi' cash.'

There was no pickle in this breadcake . . . yes there was, there it was. Half a teaspoonful, right in the middle. Not Branston. You could tell Branston right away, and this definitely wasn't Branston. Jesus Christ, three hundred pounds. She wanted to speak to Dr Singh herself, but how could you do that? You couldn't. Mrs Amory sipped her coffee, pulling a face and replacing the mug on the press release which Constance had provided in lieu of a coaster. Not that the desk – chipboard concealed beneath panels of pine-effect veneer – warranted protection; force of habit, again.

'You get my message?'

'First thing in the morning, I don't have time to play back a fifteen-minute diatribe about Dad's eating habits or the fact that Mags hasn't phoned for two days.'

'You rang every day when you were at university.'

'*You* phoned *me*. I made the mistake of living in digs with a phone.'

'I send Margaret a bag of 20p pieces every week. She spends them on drugs, I shouldn't wonder.'

Constance got an inhaler from her handbag and took two squirts of Ventolin. *Polly Puffer*, Mam used to call it. *Give Polly a kiss*. If it was a really bad attack, Mrs Amory made her daughter lie on the bed and pummelled her ribs with the heels of her hands to *loosen the tubes*, working at her back and chest for an hour at a time.

'Wheezy, love?'

'I think I'm allergic to you.'

Mrs Amory pointed to a copy of that day's *Evening Crucible*, lying atop a pile of documents on Constance's desk.

'I read your thing about the blood.'

'Oh, yeah? What d'you think?'

'Very nice.'

'Not the story, what happened. The graffiti.'

'Animal rights.'

'But they used *animals*' blood. Possibly, anyway. I mean, they're doing tests – the police are – to find out what—'

'Dorothy's Bert – what does t'*Daily Mail* crossword every day – he says "rage" is French for rabies. Only, it's "raj" – like in India. Reckons t'blood were probably infected wi' rabies.'

'Why, for God's sake?'

'Veal.'

'What about veal?'

'They're selling veal again. Produce of France, it says. Last time, theer were folk outside handing out leaflets till they took it off o' t'shelves.' She shifted her position on the chair. 'Not very comfortable, these, are they?'

'Ergonomically designed,' said Constance. 'Supposed to be good for the posture.'

'Aye, well, feller what designed this 'un never 'ad to sit in it for long.' She finished her coffee. 'You mark my words: animal rights.'

'Yeah, but they did *all* the entrances to the mall, not just HypaCenta.'

'*Diversionary tactics*, Dorothy's Bert says.'

'What's the point of a protest if no-one knows who you are or why you've done it?'

'Here, you've lipstick on your face.' Mrs Amory produced a paper hanky from her coat pocket, moistened one corner on her tongue and leaned across the desk to wipe the smudge from her daughter's forehead. 'There.'

23

Constance grinned. 'C'mon then, Mam, show us what you've bought.'

She drove out of the Green Lower car-park. On with BBC Radio Hallam, to see if they'd picked up the latest on the graffiti story – a police statement expressing disappointment at the failure of the mall's CCTV system to *furnish the investigation with practical evidential assistance*. Puzzling, because how could anyone daub blood over the doors – all of which had camera points – without being caught on film? The police spokesman had declined to elaborate, Mall Secure had refused to comment. Red light. She braked, took a slug of Lucozade and bit into a Snickers. You could get lost, driving into or away from the mall; people did, frequently, despite the crop of direction signs at each junction. If anything, the signs contributed to the problem; so many arrows, so many options – you could overshoot a turning in less time than it took to decide if it was the one you wanted. And then you'd to find it again. Mall Drive published free plans of the *traffic system*, with its elliptical inner and outer orbitals interconnected by a radial pattern of smaller link roads – the whole resembling a spider's web. More drink, more chocolate. Green light. Shit. Handbrake, shit, shit. *C'mon, Feef.* In her haste, she failed to synchronize the raising of clutch and lowering of accelerator, causing Fifi to lurch. There was a scraping noise overhead and Constance glanced in the rearview mirror to witness her handbag scooting down the back windscreen. Jesus Christ. She pulled over, leapt out of the car and ran back to retrieve the bag. At least the clasp was fastened. Last time, the contents had been strewn along the road to be gathered up and returned – along with the handbag – by a van driver who'd pursued her for three miles before managing to catch her attention.

She got back behind the wheel and drove off, smiling to herself. How would she have reported this latest mishap in the *Amory Advertiser*? New Outbreak of Mad Bag Disease. The *Adver*, every copy of which was still stored in a cardboard box

beneath her bed at home – which was to s...
Dad's – was a personalized newspaper she...
week for nearly two years (free every Sun...
to record the goings-on in the life of a te...
journalist. Written in neat black biro on sheets of ...
into newspaper-style columns. The headlines were ...
felt-tip, the 'pictures' drawn by hand or cut out of magazines.
Editor: Miss C. Amory; Chief Reporter: Constance Amory;
Chief Photographer: Connie Amory. Some of the stories,
more than ten years old now, were as fresh in her memory
as if she'd written them yesterday. Dad In Last-Ditch Peace
Bid *Father-of-two Derek Amory acted as mediator this week in
an eleventh-hour bid to end hostilities in the 'battle of the
bathroom'. Mr Amory, 35, intervened after skirmishes between
the warring factions – Constance Amory, 14, and her sister
Margaret 'Mags the Hag' Amory, 10, who has an I.Q. of nil
. . .* It's Love, Says Duran Duran Star! *Pop superstar Simon
Le Bon stunned the showbiz world today when he announced
that he was 'head over heels in love' with Hallam schoolgirl
Connie Amory, 13. The couple, who have been carrying on a
secret affair for months . . .* No-one else had ever seen a copy
of the *Adver*, though she'd mentioned it during her interview
for the job at the *Evening Crucible* – leading the editor to
confide, with evident delight, that he'd done something similar
when he was a lad. After that, the interview – littered thus far
with the debris of self-doubt – had been a breeze.

No *Amory Advertiser* any more, but she still clipped her
bylined stories from the paper each evening and pasted them
into an album. Her portfolio. *The day you don't get a buzz out
of seeing your name on a story is the day you do summat else
for a living* – William Boyce (industrial correspondent, union
official, mentor). She'd shadowed him in her first week as a
trainee and he'd somehow adopted her as his protégé. In the
newspaper game for nearly forty years; contacts book as thick
as a telephone directory, and a stock of journalistic aphorisms
and philosophies which he bestowed on younger colleagues

garlands of flowers. He'd lent her a book, that first week *The Inky Path* – written in 1959 as a guide for cub reporters. The language seemed stilted to a 1990s reader and much of the information on journalistic practice and newspaper production was out of date; nevertheless, he revered it as a bible of the profession. *Basics*, he'd said. The basics of good journalism, like the basics of a good religion, remained unaltered by the passage of time or the vicissitudes of modern society. The book was still on her shelves three years later – read, reread and dipped into. He'd never asked for its return. Hallam born and bred, like Constance, William's reporting of industry and business affairs for the *Crucible* had earned him national renown as an authority on the products which were synonymous with the city: cutlery and steel. When he retired next year, Constance intended to have his job.

The tail-end of the rush hour delayed her progress through Hallam's one-way system and out towards the university side of the city, with its straggly hillsides of red brick and stone terraces. As the traffic came to a standstill, she removed an elasticated scrunchie from her wrist and fixed her heap of ginger hair into a long ponytail, scraping the sides and most of the fringe away from her face and clipping it in place. Inspecting the result in the mirror, Constance saw that the driver in the car behind was watching. Didn't even look away when her eyes made contact with his, but continued brazenly to hold her gaze. He was smiling. Nice smile, too: confident, relaxed, friendly. Not one of those sad and serious haunted expressions of desperate loneliness, nor a leer of threatened fuck. About her age; dark wavy hair, white shirt undone at the collar, flowery tie, hands resting on the steering-wheel, sleeves rolled back to mid-forearm. How much could *he* see, of her? Hardly anything. The back of her head, her hands – briefly, while she'd rearranged her hair – the rectangular section of her face (forehead, eyebrows, eyes, nose, cheeks) reflected in the mirror. Her initial annoyance, her embarrassment, at being observed was yielding to a spasm of sexual attraction. The

thing was not to move your head, just your eyes; and not to stare, but to flit back occasionally to steal another glance. The thing was *definitely not* to smile back. And what you'd do was store up enough of him, visually, from his reflection to recreate him in your mind later on; to concoct implausibly delicious ways in which you might meet in circumstances other than you-in-your-car, him-in-his. Because the fantasy would always be better than the alternative, which was to make your interest so obvious *now* that he'd be encouraged to – what? – *do* something. Get out of his car while the lights were still red and pass his name and phone number to you on a slip of paper; pull up alongside at the next junction and flirt with you through open windows; worse still, follow you home. *The ultimate in safe sex*, Milly called it when Constance had confided in her about this inclination towards surreptitious, unfulfilled arousal. There'd be a tug of disappointment when your cars went their separate ways – but, he was more perfect than he could ever be if you actually *met* him; and you remained indefinitely interesting, attractive, sexy and enticing to him. You were all the things you knew yourself not to be. The lights changed. She allowed herself a last lingering look. When the traffic eased at a section of dual carriageway, the driver – predictably – manoeuvred to overtake, turning to smile as his car passed alongside hers. No mirror now, just his face separated from hers by two panes of glass. Constance ignored him utterly.

'Any post?'
  'Nope.'
  'Any calls?'
  'Howard.'
  'Oh, right.'
  'Some query about a job you put in the . . . *picture diary*, is it?'
  'Does he want me to ring him?'
  'He said it could wait while tomorrow, no probs.'

'He didn't say anything else?'

'*Connie.*'

'OK, OK.'

' "Tough is my middle name," remember?'

'Yeah, well, we've not all been emotionally anaesthetized.'

'I love you too.'

Constance dumped her bag and jacket on an armchair and went out to the kitchen. Milly, still in her smart work clothes and cupping a mug of tea, followed her.

'There's some in the pot.'

'Great.'

'I ate one of your Snickers. You know, they go rock hard in the fridge.'

'That's how I like them.'

'Another couple of weeks of this and you'll weigh twelve stone, have spots all over your face and your teeth will drop out. That'll show him, eh?'

'Milly, I've had a long day.'

Constance poured tea and fixed herself beans on toast. She ate at the kitchen table, finishing quickly and stacking the plate and cutlery in the sink along with the debris of her housemate's meal. She turned on the tap, testing the temperature.

'Should be plenty of hot water if you want a shower,' said Milly. '*Leave* the washing-up.'

'You sure?'

'I wouldn't stand in the way of History.'

'It's an *evening class*. Hardly a momentous event in the life of womankind.'

'You never know who you might meet.'

'I'll be the youngest person there by thirty years. Anyway, if I wanted to cop off I'd join Dateline or put an ad in the Lonely Hearts.'

Constance showered and shaved in ten minutes, nicking herself just above the ankle and having to place a small shred of toilet tissue on the cut. She put on a fresh blouse and skirt, left her hair up – the ends of the ponytail dripping where she'd neglected to keep it out of the shower spray – and hurried up the road towards the adult education centre. Halfway there, she had to run back to the house, where Milly stood smiling on the doorstep with a shoulder bag containing a new notepad, pen, registration form, purse, inhaler, Snickers bars and house keys.

Milly and Constance had gone along to enrolment the previous week intending to sign up together for a class, but found nothing of mutual appeal. So Milly, whose job as a cataloguer in the university library left her with stiff shoulders and surplus energy, had opted for yoga on Wednesdays and aerobics on Fridays. Constance had considered pottery, briefly, before putting her name down for a non-examination course on The Industrial History of Hallam. Every Tuesday, for twelve weeks. By the time she arrived at the centre – a former school ten minutes' walk from home – and located the classroom, the tutor was into his introductory spiel. Constance apologized.

'Come in and park yourself.'

He waved at an empty place near the back. Some of the windows were open to admit a summery breeze and the room was drenched with the day's last sunshine. The angles of desks and plain white walls were given sharp definition by the light; its clarity, paradoxically, creating an illusion of gleaming modernity while harshly exposing age and ill-repair in all its shabbiness. Missing ceiling panels, scuffed skirting boards, a cracked window pane, damp-stained walls and peeling paint. Constance – breathless, blushing – made her way towards the vacant seat, conscious of being the centre of attention for the other students. Mostly women, mostly older than her.

'There's been a rather exciting handing-in-of-the-registration-forms ceremony,' said the tutor. 'Otherwise, you've missed nowt.'

Curious accent: educated northern English with a trace of something foreign and slightly nasal, Australian or South African. The last word, however, was pure, blunt Hallam;

29

emphasized, it seemed, not in mockery or affectation but as a genuine attempt at *bonhomie*, and – she saw, as she sat down – punctuated by a broad grin.

'I've got mine here somewhere.' The bag slipped from her shoulder as she searched inside it, still flustered by her late arrival. 'Bit crumpled, I'm afraid.'

The tutor took the form from her and carried it back to his desk, marking an entry on a register. He perused her details before slipping the sheet inside a buff folder. The older woman sitting alongside Constance smiled and mouthed 'hello'.

'*Amory.*' The tutor looked up. 'Good old Hallam name, that: Amory.'

She was arranging herself, searching out her pad and pen and hooking her bag over the back of the chair. The desk – apparently a legacy of the days before the school's conversion – was tattooed with marks made by pupils who must've long since grown up and had children of their own.

'Is it? I mean, well, I know my great-granddad – on my dad's side – he was from Hallam. I don't know about before then.'

'You'll not be a genealogist, then?'

'No. No, not really. I've never been . . . you know, I don't think our family has ever done anything . . . all that interesting. Far as I know.'

'There's more to history than kings and queens and prime ministers.'

The smile disarmed her, his expression and tone of voice offering reassurance that no criticism was intended, nor was it necessary for her to continue the discussion if it made her uncomfortable. Which it did, prolonging her ordeal-by-lateness. The tutor was not especially tall, but well-built, in his forties; his beard and collar-length dark brown hair were flecked with grey. He wore wire-framed glasses which he would remove from time to time during the course of the evening so that he might suck one of the ends, clicking it between his teeth like a pipe. His trousers were too large and too long, rucking up over his shoes in loose folds; suggesting, to her, either that he had an academic's stereotypical disconcern for his appearance or that he'd recently lost weight. On the lapel of his brown-and-beige check sports jacket he wore a badge with the slogan: 'Don't Mess with Essendon'.

'My name is Stanley Bell. *Professor* Stanley Bell,' he added with mock solemnity. 'Stan, to you; That Bastard, to my ex-wife.'

This raised a laugh. Constance smiled too, though she was preoccupied with trying to place his accent – the first 'a' in bastard had a distinct twang, almost a drawl; yet the flat 'a' in Stanley and the truncated 'ley', sounded local. As though anticipating her curiosity, he added: 'For those of you trying to figure out where the hell I'm from – it's mostly Hallam, mixed in with a smidgin of London and a heap of Oz. Plays havoc with your vowels.'

Out came the *potted biog*, reeled off with a familiarity of repetition. Prof. Bell had been born in London and moved north with his parents at the age of eleven, settling in Hallam – firstly as a student (undergraduate, Masters and Ph.D.), then as a lecturer – and had spent the last thirteen years teaching in Melbourne. Now, he was home again: a professorship at the university and a part-time lecturing post here at the ad. ed., as he called it.

'History is my kick. History, and Aussie Rules . . .' He indicated the lapel badge. 'So that's me, what about you lot?'

Throughout the introductions, Prof. Bell made notes – a sketch plan of the seating arrangements, he said, to assist him in remembering names and faces. *I forget things. God knows how I became a History professor when I've a memory like a . . . what d'you call it, one of those things for sifting flour?* As her turn approached, Constance worked herself up into a state of wheeziness – that frantic run up the hill, anxiety at being late, first-night nerves and, now, petrified of public speaking.

31

What she should do was use her inhaler, but how could you
– in front of a room full of total strangers? You couldn't. You
just couldn't do that. Name, age, job. Name, age, job. Easy,
half a dozen words or so, then it's someone else's turn and
everyone forgets about you. What could be simpler than that?
The woman next to her had been going for – how long? – five
minutes, at least. What was she saying? What *was there* to
say? Whatever it was, people were laughing, enjoying themselves; they were relaxed. Nobody else ever got nervous or
embarrassed in these situations, only her. Her turn. Short
sentences, disguising a repeated refuelling of the lungs as
pauses for thought.

'My name is Constance. Constance *Amory*,' she added,
smiling awkwardly at the tutor. 'I'm twenty-five. I'm a reporter
with the *Evening Crucible*. I did History at Birmingham. And
I chose this course, I suppose . . . because I wanted to learn
about Hallam's industrial heritage. For my job. And because
I'm interested, I mean.'

Introductions over, Prof. Bell distributed reading lists *for
those who wish to expand their studies beyond the scope of this
course*, then summarized the historical period and main topics
he intended to cover over the coming weeks. There would be
no essays or assignments, though students with a particular
area of interest were free to carry out their own research and
to raise any issues during the weekly sessions. In any case,
they were encouraged to question and challenge him at all
times.

'If you knock off the first two letters of "history", you're
left with "story". That's all I'm able to offer you: my story of
Hallam's industrial history; my version of events. It's not a
definitive history, because that – in my view – is a contradiction
in terms. And just because I'm standing up here at the
front of the class, doing all the talking, don't assume I can
differentiate between an arse and an elbow.'

He paused to allow a murmur of amusement to subside.

'Example: while I was in Australia, I spent one of the

holidays in Sydney. I went on a boat trip round the harbour – sightseeing, usual stuff: opera house, harbour bridge – and the guide was drawing our attention to some of the sights. Anyway, as we went past Point Piper – where all the rich gits live – she pointed out one of the big mansions up on the hill and said it was owned by some multi-millionaire businessman who spent half the year there and the other half on his estate in the Lake District . . . in *Scotland*. So, of course, I stick my hand up and tell her: actually, the Lake District's in England, not Scotland. And d'you know what she said? She said, "Mister, I've been doing this job for ten years – please give me credit for knowing my subject." '

Prof. Bell's grin encompassed the entire classroom. He checked his watch. 'Anyway. Any*road*, what say we break for tea now and get cracking when we come back? Say, fifteen minutes.' There was a scraping of chairs as the students began to stand up and move towards the door. Raising his voice to make himself audible, the tutor added: 'Turn left out of here and the canteen's at the end of the corridor, through two sets of doors. Oh, and a word of warning, the coffee is *truly* appalling.'

Notes

Iron smelted in Hallam since Roman times. Ref. to quarrying of ironstone in this area in Domesday Book (10??, I should know this!!); in 1161 Cistercian (sp?) monks smelted and forged iron here.

NB: 11th C. communities in H'shire came to H. to market their produce. Hallam, in those days, was a <u>marketplace rather than hotbed of manufacturing</u>; twice-weekly markets, annual fair etc.

Ironworking and smithying flourished in late-12th early-13th Cs; work essentially rural in character, workers part-time and seasonal. Smithying part of annual round of tasks from harvest to harvest.

Geographical factors:

- water (fast-flowing streams in hills to south & west of H. provided water-power)
- coal (H'shire an area of exposed coal measures; fuel for smelting)

- iron ore (basic raw material of iron & steel m'facture)
- clay ('refractory' clays for lining furnaces, crucibles etc)
- stone (local sandstone used for grindstones)
- woodlands (i.e. charcoal, for fuel)

Labour

QUOTE: (c.late-16th C) 'The manorial landowners' rents and the plant invested in the water-wheels, used to manufacture items at economic prices, forced craftsmen to go one of two ways: either to invest in plant and rents, or work for those who had invested. This is the start of the classic separation in capitalist society of the worker from the means of production. Instead of exchanging the products of their labour at the marketplace, their *labour itself was a product.*' – Prof. Stanley Bell*

(*Marxist?!)

Prof. Stanley Bell's Physical, Metaphysical & Philosophical Glossary of Metal

Iron: Iron is made from rock (as glass is made from sand, and paper from trees). Ore is extracted from rock and smelted in a blast furnace, the resultant molten metal is run into receptacles known as pigs. The pig iron is remelted and turned into castings; or it is forged – that is to say, heated and hammered into bars of wrought iron. These in turn are sent to slitting mills to be heated and passed through grooved rollers, drawing out the iron ready for cutting into rods. Each piece of metal may then be moulded, bent, beaten and edged to become, say, a scythe, a saw, a knife. The finished tool no more resembles the ore-bearing rock from which it originated than a pane of glass resembles sand, or a sheet of paper resembles a tree. Iron – as an end product – is therefore the result of a series of transformations, the turning of one thing into another and into another; it is manufactured. Man-made, from naturally occurring materials. It is created (i.e. brought into existence, produced or caused, designed or invented). Creation, in this sense, is not the making of something from nothing but the making of something new by transforming that which is already there.

*   *   *

A Tuesday evening in the Tongs & Dozzle, just after nine-thirty. The lounge bar – tastefully done out in a blue-and-gold colour scheme of mock-velvet upholstery and polished brass fixtures and trimmings – was moderately busy. The wallpaper was floral, William Morris. Constance sat with a small group of fellow students, discussing the metallurgical definition of 'creation'. The reappearance of Stanley Bell – bearded bespectacled, excessively betrousered and bearing a tray of drinks – terminated the conversation. The tutor distributed the glasses, pulling up a stool and sitting at the head of the table. He went round the group one by one, testing himself on their names. Five out of six. Constance, sitting at the end farthest from him, was 'Ms *Amory*', and – amid profuse apologies on his part – she had to remind him of her first name.

'Tell you what else I forgot – you asked for a pint, didn't you?'

'Doesn't matter, a half's fine.' She raised a hand to stop him from returning to the bar. 'No really, Stan, I'm OK.'

Despite her protests, he fetched her a second half and an empty pint glass, decanting both measures for her with a flourish that should've resulted in much spillage but, in fact, caused hardly any.

'It's me, assuming a woman would be drinking halves.' He set her pint down on a coaster. 'Too long in Oz, is my trouble. I've gone Neanderthal.'

Separated by a crossfire of multiple conversations, they didn't have another opportunity to speak until the group thinned out. Having departed to the Gents, Stan returned to occupy a newly vacated seat directly opposite Constance.

'You were taking a hell of a lot of notes in class tonight,' he said.

'Shorthand. I'll write them up later.'

'You can always have a copy of my lecture notes, if you'd rather.'

'I find I take more in if I write it down for myself. It's like,

35

I mean, you have to *concentrate* on what's being said. You know?'

They talked. Relaxed now, in a smaller gathering – and, within that group, just the two of them involved in this particular conversation. No longer the centre of attention, no public speaking. She'd sneaked off to the loo to use her inhaler. And, being with him, she became less self-conscious; he was older, he had the casual air of someone who'd long ceased caring what anyone thought of him. His conviviality, his loquaciousness, were infectious. Even so, she sensed herself seeking refuge now and again in journalist-mode – interestedly inquisitorial, her confidence fortified by faking professionalism. With strangers, or during an awkward silence among friends, or when *you* would otherwise be the subject under discussion . . . *If in doubt, ask a question.* She asked him how come he'd emigrated to Australia.

'If I told you it was 1983, would that give you a clue?'

Constance shook her head.

'What if I mentioned the name Margaret Thatcher?'

'Oh right, '83 – General Election, wasn't it?'

'You'd have been how old?'

'I don't know . . . twelve. Nearly thirteen.'

'Jeez that makes me feel ancient.'

. 'I don't remember much about it. Probably more interested in pop music in those days.'

'When she got in for a second time, I slung my hook. If I'd known she was going to win again in '87 . . . and the bastards got back in in '92! *Unbelievable.*'

She kept a straight face. 'There's more to history than prime ministers, you know.'

Stan lowered his pint, paused to gauge her expression, then let out a guffaw that drew the amused attention of other drinkers several tables away. 'OK, OK. The words "hoist" and "petard" spring to mind.'

He removed his glasses and began cleaning the lenses with a tissue. His hands were large and it was a wonder he didn't damage the wire frames beyond repair, he handled them so roughly. Every now and then he'd raise them to the light, breathe on one of the lenses and continue polishing. His hands were tanned, the nails appallingly bitten – which surprised her, because – despite the nervous habit of fiddling with his glasses – he seemed the least likely person to chew his fingernails. Reformed smoker, she speculated. Examining his fingers for tobacco stains, she saw that the third digit of his left hand bore a faint band of paler skin.

'Tell me, is – what was his name – Bill Boyce . . . still at the *Crucible*?'

'William? Yeah, he's industry correspondent. You know him?'

The tutor put his glasses back on and almost immediately removed them again so he could resume chewing the ends. Already, she could see, his fingers had smudged the lenses.

'I know *of* him.' He smiled. 'His coverage of the steel strike in the early eighties . . . absolutely required reading. Brilliant. You'd definitely be too young to remember that.'

'I remember my dad and my granddad being made redundant. Within a year of each other. At least, I don't know if I remember it, or whether I've heard the story so often from them it just seems like I do. Your memories and theirs get sort of . . .'

'They were steelworkers?'

'Granddad worked in one of the big rolling mills, Dad was an engineer in the machine-shop. Same place. Dad went in the first round of redundancies in . . . I was in the second year, so it would've been 1983. He did a retraining course – Dad this is – and used the redundancy pay-off to set up his own business. Builder and decorator. Granddad went the following year, when the whole works closed.'

Prof. Bell nodded. They both paused to take a drink. When he didn't say anything, Constance continued with her train of thought.

37

'Big shopping mall there now, where the rolling mill used to be. Urbopark.'

'They'd have worked at Bayfield's, then? Bloody big firm, that one.'

'You know, the thing I remember most about Dad's redundancy was him being out in the garden every day while we were on school holiday. Mags and me – Mags is my sister, Margaret – we thought it was great having him around. When he was working, what with overtime and that, we hardly used to see him except at weekends.'

The tutor was about to say something when one of the other students – who was getting up to leave – interrupted to ask a question about the following week's class. Constance finished her drink. She talked too much, that was her trouble. If anyone showed even the remotest interest in her she either became tongue-tied like a dizzy teenager or waffled on and on worse than her mam. Jesus, he'd not even *asked* about her family, specifically – that stuff about genealogy – it just came out. *My great-granddad was from Hallam* . . . And going on about her dad and granddad being made redundant. And *Mags*. She'd leave the pub, was what she'd do; now that her drink was finished and Stan was talking to someone else. She'd go home and have some jam on toast or something, because what she wanted to do more than anything was stuff her face. And she'd use her inhaler again. It was so smoky in here. Three of the other students at their table smoked. Professor Bell didn't. *Stan*. Too preoccupied sucking the ends of his glasses or stroking his beard with his stubby, nail-bitten fingers. It was nearly half-past ten and she'd to be up by six, Constance said, in response to the tutor's *going already?* expression. She retrieved her bag from beneath the table. As she did so, she saw that a piece of toilet paper was stuck to her shin, just above the ankle. The tissue, encrusted with blood, had been there all evening for everyone to see.

*   *   *

38

The Inky Path
It is incumbent upon the journalist to behave sensibly . . . wear
a hat by all means but do not invariably tilt it on the back of
your head.

It was a warm, airless September night. Constance couldn't
sleep. She kicked off the duvet, fetched a sheet from the airing
cupboard and remade the bed. She opened the window wider
still, knotting the curtains to prevent them from flapping if a
breeze got up during the night. She propped the bedroom door
ajar to create a through-draught. Still unable to sleep, she
clenched and unclenched each part of her body in turn – from
toes to scalp – in an effort to relax. The luminous red digits
of the radio-clock read 00.55. From the street below came the
sudden wailing of a car alarm and, in response, the barking of
a dog. Constance took off the oversized T-shirt (one of
Howard's) she used as a nightgown and dropped it onto the
floor. Still too hot, too restless. Despairing of falling asleep,
she resorted to a tactic which had – over the years – charmed,
initially, then ultimately irritated each of her lovers. She slid
round, so that her head was now at the foot of the bed –
beneath loose folds of untucked sheet – and her feet were
nestling on the pillow. In this position, she drifted into sleep;
still too warm, but comforted and, therefore, at rest.

The Life and Times of a Hallam Saw Grinder
(a Dramatic Reconstruction in Many Parts)

November 1857

The children were still asleep when Thomas Amory sat on his fireside stool to eat the breakfast his wife had made. He ate alone by the guttering light of oil lamps and the orange glow of an open hearth that warmed the front of him but left his back exposed. He yawned. From the kitchen came the scuff of his wife's feet on flagstones, the clank of pots and pans. It was raining, Frances had said. Not heavily, but enough to wet her clothes when she'd gone out to the yard earlier to fetch water. Still black outside, the day-room window dimly reflecting the interior as Thomas turned to inspect the panes of glass for evidence of fresh raindrops. He turned to the fire again, which Frances had laid and lit while he was in bed. He would have liked to take breakfast in the kitchen, with her. It was warmer in the kitchen, and they had little enough time to themselves. But she was usually irritable, first thing. He suspected that he made her so with his chatter; she had the urge to be up and doing, while Thomas was content to take stock. There would be enough clamour once the children were awake, without his bothering her with news of the previous night's Society meeting or some anecdote he had heard in The George. He could hear her singing to herself. Frances was a woman content with her own company, and he had learnt when to leave her be. It was sufficient to hear her moving around, to know she was there. Sometimes, though not this morning, he found himself softly humming in accompaniment to her songs.

Thomas finished his tea and placed the mug on the floor by the empty plate. He toasted his face and hands a while longer, inhaling air made humid by the washing which had been fetched in from the yard the night before and strung up on two lengths of twine over the fireplace. The clothes would smell of smoke and of the herbs hanging in bunches beneath the ceiling beam, but at least they would dry free of the smuts which the rains washed from the sky. He smiled at little Agnes's dress, and at the boys' trousers and shirts – like miniature replicas of his own. Daniel would be first to waken. It wasn't unknown for him to come into Mam and Dad's chamber at some ungodly hour and rouse them with his bouncing on the bed. And Thomas would feign annoyance, wrestling him out of the room before Frances had a chance to fetch the lad a clip round the ear. He reached up to test the clothes for dampness, rubbing the coarse material between thumb and middle finger. The movement brought on a coughing fit. He spat into the fire, the gobbet of phlegm hissing on the coals. Sometimes, when he breathed, his lungs made a noise like a set of old bellows. He inhaled deeply, twice, three times. Thomas carried his breakfast things through to the kitchen, placing them beside the large stone sink at which he had strip-washed earlier while Frances prepared his food. He rinsed his hands again, scooping water onto his greasy lips and swilling some in his mouth. His wife was watching him from the range. Her cheeks were flushed and her hair hung in dark curls made chestnut in the light cast by an adjacent lamp. She handed him a towel.

Royal Commission of Inquiry
(sitting at) Hallam Town Hall
Wednesday, 19 June 1867 (Twelfth Day)

Witness: Frances Amory (Mrs), No.11 Garden Street, Hallam.
    Q. Are you familiar with the term 'rattening'?
    A. I shouldn't wonder that every person in Hallam knows it.
    Q. What is your understanding of this term?
    A. Rattening is when a man is rolled up.

Q. What do you mean by that?

A. He has his bands rolled up so that he might not work his stone.

Q. The bands which drive his grindstone are taken away?

A. That is my understanding.

Q. How came you to know this term?

A. Every person in Hallam knows this term.

Q. Did you read of it in the newspapers?

A. I cannot read.

Q. You heard tell of it?

A. Yes.

Q. You knew of men who were rattened?

A. I heard tell of them, yes.

Q. And you knew of men who did the rattening?

A. Not only I.

Q. That was not my question. My question was, did you know of the ratteners?

A. Yes.

Q. Was your husband one such?

A. I cannot say.

Q. You cannot say or you do not know?

A. It amounts to the same.

Q. It does not.

A. I cannot say whether Thomas ever rolled a man up.

Q. Would he have told you of it, if he had?

A. No, I should say not.

Q. Was rattening common practice in Hallam?

A. It was.

Q. And you say every person knew of it and knew of those responsible for it?

A. Mostly everyone.

Q. Why then did not they name these men to the appropriate authorities?

A. Because of those who were rolled up.

Q. What do you mean by that?

A. The men who were rolled up had their deserts.

Q. This was a commonly held view in Hallam at that time?
A. By all decent folk, it was.

His bag and jacket were hanging up as usual on the front door. He put on his work boots, lacing them tightly and stamping each foot, a small rag-rug deadening the clump of the thick wooden soles against the stone floor. He shut the door behind him, shoving it hard until he heard the latch click into place. The rain had eased. Thomas nodded to two men – neighbours – who reciprocated as they passed, the metal studs in their clogs striking sparks from the pavement. He followed them briefly before turning down the jennel between numbers five and seven and into the courtyard at the rear of the terrace, startling two chickens. The ground was muddy, especially round the privies. He picked his way carefully in the half-light from the windows of those homes facing onto the yard. The stench was made more bearable by the cool morning air, nevertheless he relieved himself quickly and returned to the street without tarrying. The rain had ceased altogether now and the brisk walk warmed him. A trolley-bus trundled past as he turned out of Garden Street and down the hill. Where the road broadened at West Bar, he traversed the wide irregular-shaped junction and headed down Corporation Street. The route was so familiar he could have walked it with his eyes closed, if it wasn't for the horse dung, sewage run-offs, rotten fruit skins and an occasional loose cobble. He supposed there was as much debris in the street in spring and summer, though one was less inclined to look upon it.

He saw a figure emerge from a recess some way ahead. A cap pulled low on his head and wearing a long coat similar to his own, his whitened breaths escaping into the grey light of impending dawn. By his size and manner, and by his paleness of complexion – visible even at this distance – he knew him. The man waited for Thomas to draw near before falling in step alongside.

43

'If I'd a watch, I could set it by thee, Tom.'

''Ow do, Sammy.'

Thomas did not break stride nor turn to look at his companion. His breakfast was repeating on him, leaving a sour, doughy taste at the back of his throat. He coughed and spat into the gutter. Sammy, by virtue of his shorter stature, had to take three steps to every two of Thomas's, causing him to proceed along the street with a peculiar skipping motion. When he spoke, his voice was breathless from exertion.

'I've 'ad word on Linley.'

'Oh, aye.'

'Whenever it suits, Old Smite 'Em says.'

A man was walking towards them. Thomas waited for him to pass before resuming the conversation.

'I've work on, rest o' this week.'

'It shall not harm for keeping.'

They were nearly at Alma Street, and Thomas was anxious not to be seen with Sammy by any of his fellows at the Wheel. He slowed and came to a stop before the turning, looking up and down the road.

'Thou knowst where he's living presently?'

'Aye.' Sammy nodded in the direction of the end of Corporation Street, where Borough Bridge carried the road across the river. 'Not five minutes from here.'

'Nursery Street?'

The other man nodded. Thomas pulled his jacket tighter about him, shrugging his shoulder sack into a more comfortable position. His feet pained him. The boots were almost new, the tough leather uppers pinching at the heel and across the instep. For the first time, he met his companion's gaze. They were the same age, bar three months, but from his face you would have taken Sammy for the older by some years, despite him being no taller than an adolescent. It was his pallor, and a lifelessness of his eyes that could not be concealed by their alertness of movement.

'Sunday, then,' said Thomas. 'On t'bridge, fore it's proper light.'

Sammy gave another nod and they parted, Thomas continuing into Alma Street and crossing the road towards the squat block of the Union Wheel. Lamps were already lit inside the building and he could hear the pounding of the great water-wheel at the rear, where the river powered the paddles that rotated the shafts that drove the bands that turned the grindstones. He hurried inside, glancing along the road at the huge rolling mill occupying the upper half of Hallam Island and from which was issuing the relentless thud-thud-thud of the steam-powered presses and hammers.

Witness: Thomas Amory, saw grinder, No.11 Garden Street, Hallam.

Q. How came you to know Samuel Crookes?

A. I have known him since we were lads. Apprentices, I should say.

Q. You were both apprenticed to James Linley?

A. No, sir. I was apprenticed to my father.

Q. So how came you to know Crookes?

A. We were in the same Society.

Q. The Saw Grinders'?

A. Yes.

Q. You were friends?

A. We were known as Carrot and Cabbage.

Q. How so?

A. I was Carrot on account of my red hair, he was Cabbage for his face.

Q. He had a face the colour of a cabbage?

A. He had.

Q. A red cabbage?

A. No, a white one.

(*laughter*)

Q. What was the nature of your acquaintance?

A. We supped together. And we attended Society meetings.

45

Q. This continued up to the period with which this inquiry is concerned?

A. We were not supping together by then.

Q. When you and Crookes attended Society meetings, would they call over the names of those who were obnoxious to the trade?

A. They would.

Q. What did you take this to mean, 'obnoxious'?

A. It meant men who had not paid their natty brass, or who had broken the rules of the Society, or who were working out of union, or who were knobsticks.

Q. Natty money is a member's weekly subscription to the Society, is it not?

A. It is.

Q. And what is a knobstick?

A. A knobstick is a man who works where other men are on strike.

Q. What would be done to men whose names were called over?

A. Most likely, they would be rattened.

Q. What would happen to the bands of a man who had been rattened?

A. He would have to pay for their return.

Q. Pay whom?

A. The Society.

Q. And cease whatever behaviour it was which had made him obnoxious to the trade?

A. Yes.

Q. If rattening failed to have the desired effect, would stronger methods be employed?

A. Rattening was enough, mostly.

Q. Did you and Crookes ever ratten men?

(*witness hesitates*)

Q. I must remind you that this Commission of Inquiry has been granted the power to indemnify a witness for any criminal act he may admit to, but that this indemnity will be withheld if it transpires that he has not been entirely truthful in all respects. Do you understand?

A. Yes.

Q. Now, I will ask you again, did you and Samuel Crookes ever ratten a man?

A. We did.

Q. How many men?

A. I could not say exactly.

Q. Did you ever ratten James Linley?

A. We did.

Q. Why did you ratten James Linley?

A. Because he was obnoxious to the trade.

Q. Did you ratten him on more than one occasion?

A. We did.

Q. What else did you do to him?

(*witness hesitates*)

Chapter Two

SHOP TALK

OK, it breaks down like this: 'urbo', from 'urban', denotes a town or urban area; 'park', obviously, has connotations of parkland and country estates. Urbopark, then, transmits subliminal images of a rural oasis amid a concrete desert. It is also associative with bringing the fresh produce of the land to the people of the city.

Miles Merryweather, Corporate Image Consultant.
(from the minutes of a meeting of the Development
Sub-Committee of Mall Build UK Plc, 15/4/84)

Constance Amory grabbed a notebook and pen and headed out of the *Evening Crucible* office, slaloming among the shopper hordes (55,000 on an average weekday, according to Mall PRO). Impediments, as she negotiated a route through the marbled, garbled arcades: a bag-laden woman, a pushchair, a couple holding hands, a man eating fries from a paper cone. Familiarity and distraction of purpose dulled her sense of surroundings – noise, commotion, colour – reducing her to peripheral awareness of patisserie smells; sunlight shed whitely via glass ceilings onto brilliant benches; a rainforest of flower-boxes, hanging baskets, potted plants and giant palms in terracotta tubs; muzak, so subliminal as to be barely discernible above the general babble; pastel shades of avocado and lavender, peach and lilac, aquamarine and lemon; silvery sounds of fountain and waterfall. And, dominant, the illuminated shopfronts – phalanxes of vivid window dressings encased in sheets of plate glass shimmering with a collage of mirrored images. Stalled momentarily by a knot of people, Constance glimpsed herself – her translucent image superimposed over the display and fractured by the reflections of those folk milling around and behind and beside her. There too, in kaleidoscopic whirl, were reflected fragments of other shopfronts, their lookers-in looking out. Vertigo. She could become no more dizzy were she to spin on the spot, arms outstretched, until she staggered and fell in drunken genuflection.

When this mall was no more than a concept, its progenitors considered naming it Phantasmagoria. Phantasmagoria: an optical effect by which figures appear to dwindle into the distance or rush towards the observer with enormous increase of size; a constantly shifting, confused succession of things seen or imagined, e.g. in a dream or feverish state. But misgivings were expressed over the word's aural and etymological proximity to 'phantasm' and 'phantom', with their ghoulish connotations, their suggestion of illusion, fantasy and unreality; a superficial appearance of existence but devoid of form or substance. Phantasmagoria. A name better suited to a funfair, with its ghost train, haunted house and hall of mirrors, than a shopping mall. The creators of Urbopark – real, substantial, solid 'Urbopark' – were afraid of ghosts.

Constance, untangled, continued on her way; towards Hypa-Centa, with its two kilometres of shelving, fifty-four checkouts, eleven varieties of lettuce.

John Chapple, the store manager, was about to place an ushering arm around her shoulders, but thought better of it. The arm, half-raised, was lowered in a gesture disguised as a rearrangement of his suit jacket. Even so, he succeeded – without recourse to physical contact – in steering her away from the skip to a less conspicuous part of the service bay. The doors to the foodhall's delivery area were open. Half a dozen workers in white overalls, and carrying black plastic refuse sacks, were moving back and forth between the doors and the skip. Two men were inside the skip, only the humps of their backs visible above its rim as they loaded the bags ready for removal. The yard was yellowed by morning sunshine.

'Connie, your timing is impeccable. Uncanny, I'd say.'

'I'm sure you'd have got round to telling us.'

'But someone saved me the trouble.'

'I can't . . .'

'Reveal your sources. No, quite.'

His tie was decorated with a medley of Disney characters: Mickey Mouse, Donald Duck, Goofy, Bambi, Snow White and three of the seven dwarfs (the remainder, she presumed, concealed within the knot). He wore a gold-plated tie clip and matching cufflinks. Even at thirtysomething, his fine blond thatch was thinning – the scalp exposed pinkly at crown and temple, gleaming in the sunlight; what hair he had was dishelleved by the breeze. Constance pointed with her pen towards the skip, where the workmen – hands protected by disposable gloves of the type worn by staff on a supermarket cheese counter – were still busy.

'What're they doing?'

'Technically, you're trespassing.' His smile wasn't a smile at all, but an elastication of the lips. 'This yard is access approved for HypaCenta staff and authorized delivery personnel only.'

'I only want to know what's in the skip.'

'Can we put the notebook away, for a moment?'

She lowered her hand so that the spiral-bound pad was at her side rather than held in front of her beneath poised pen.

His tone softened. 'This may not be what you think, is all I'm saying.'

'And what do I think it is?'

'Look, I don't know what your mysterious informant told you, but I'd hazard a guess that you're assuming a connection with what happened the other night. The graffiti. Am I right, or am I right?'

'And the veal.'

'What veal?'

'You start selling veal; someone daubs blood on your doors . . .'

'*All* the doors. The graffiti was a mall-wide scenario, don't forget.'

'And now this.'

'You still don't know what "this" is, though, do you?'

'John, I can see the bloodstains on their gloves. And the feathers.' As she spoke, a mottled brown-and-white feather zigzagged a lazy path through the air and landed at their feet. 'What I don't know is how many, when they were dumped in your skip, who found them and who put them there. Oh, and why?'

'Off the record?'

'If *you* don't tell me, the Environmental Health people will.'

Mr Chapple pinched the tip of his nose between thumb and middle finger in an idiosyncratic gesture of deep concentration she recognized from previous interviews. 'Constance . . . let me ask you, how long have you been with the *Crucible*?'

'Three years, give or take. Why?'

'A year at the Urbopark office?'

'Just over.'

He let go of his nose, allowing his hands to swing heavily at his sides. He shrugged. 'All I'm saying is, don't jump to conclusions on this. I know you're hoping for – what d'you call it – a "splash". But . . .' He looked at her. 'Today's front page story could be tomorrow's correction, with apologies. Is all I'm saying.'

She raised the notebook again. 'How many, John?'

'Fucking hell, head office are going to love this.' He gestured at the skip. 'As you can see, we haven't finished getting them out.'

'I mean, roughly.'

'OK, a hundred. Maybe more.'

'Jesus.'

'One of our maintenance lads found them when he was binning some waste packaging. They couldn't have been there too long or the smell would be intolerable by now. Overnight, I'd say.'

Constance finished the note she was making and turned to a fresh page. Difficult to write standing up, the shorthand outlines would be imprecise and hard to decipher when she came to type the story.

'Any idea how they were killed?'

'Decapitated. At least, they're decapitated now – whether they were killed and then decapitated, I couldn't say. Either way, these are your proverbial headless chickens. No sign of the heads anywhere. Oh, and their feet have been removed.'

'Their *feet*?'

'All of them.' He made a chopping motion with his hand. 'I got our chief butcher to take a look, and he reckons they've been ritually slaughtered.' Noting her reaction, the manager added: 'Is what he says, is all I'm saying. Don't you go putting some tosh in the paper about black magic and voodoo.'

'What did he mean, you know, by ritually slaughtered?'

'Not just killed indiscriminately, is how I took it. Whoever did it, knew what they were doing – heads and feet lopped off and all the blood drained out of them.'

'Who else knows about this?'

'Police, Environmental Health; Mall Admin, of course. Some of the staff – well, most of them by now – including your anonymous source. And, by this evening no doubt, forty-five thousand *Crucible* readers.'

'Are the police linking this with the graffiti?'

'You'd better ask *them* that. Anyway, they've not turned up yet. Chicken murders aren't top of their list of crime priorities, I imagine.'

'And the veal connection?'

'You've three separate factors,' he counted them off on his fingers, 'one, veal; two, graffiti; three, dead chickens. OK, so the business with the blood might suggest a link between two and three, but there's no proof. The police haven't even confirmed it *was* blood. And as for the veal . . . all I'm saying is, even animal rights nutters aren't going to slaughter a hundred chickens to protest about the veal trade. Are they?'

They paused to watch another sackload of carcasses being hauled out of the skip and carried away. 'So it's just a three-way coincidence, you think?' said Constance. 'Nothing to do with HypaCenta.'

'You mention veal in your article and we'll have furry-lib loonies camped outside my store in wigwams and chaining themselves to the shopping trolleys.'

'John . . .'

'Constance. Remember that piece you wrote a while back about a handful of teenage motorcyclists using the mall car-park as an illegal racetrack on Sunday nights? What happened the Sunday after the article appeared? Eh?' He smiled. 'Half the bikers within a thirty-mile radius of Hallam turned up and staged a fucking grand prix, was what happened.'

She pushed her hair back from her face, only for it to become rearranged again by the blustery wind which had suddenly gained momentum in the goods yard, bearing a faint stench from the skip and creating a mini-snowstorm of bloodied feathers. What did she have by way of facts to stand up the veal angle? Nothing. Just coincidence; and her mam, quoting Dorothy's Bert, the crossword buff.

'OK, John, no veal.'

'Good.'

'How about a word with the lad who found the carcasses?' The manager hesitated. 'Fair enough. That's him over

53

there.' He placed a hand on Constance's shoulder. 'Hey, and *please*, no "Fowl Play" headlines!'

Hallam City Council's Environmental Health department confirmed the final body-count as 117. This figure had subsequently to be revised downwards, as one of the chickens turned out to be a dead pigeon, complete with head and feet. HypaCenta's chief butcher declined to be interviewed or photographed; nevertheless, his phrase 'ritual killings' would find its way into a strap over the main headline in that evening's paper. Gary had wanted the story to make an explicit link between the graffiti incident and the headless – bloodless – chickens, irrespective of forensic confirmation. Constance played down this angle in her original copy, only for the news editor to do a rewrite. *For fuck's sake, Con, how much fucking animal blood is swilling around out there if these two events aren't fucking connected?*

The Inky Path
Happenings, even the most prosaic and trivial ones, are like stones dropped into a pool – they set up a sequence of ever-widening ripples. The reporter's task is to chart these ripples. He will ask himself: 'If this happens, what happens next?' or 'If this has happened, what happened before?' Once he begins thinking in these terms, it will not be long before he realizes that news knows no boundaries. It is infinite.

With each bite, chunks of filling oozed from between the bread. His fingers and mouth were a mess of mayonnaise and moist fragments of unidentifiable foodstuff.

'What's actually in that?' Constance asked.

Howard took a laminated menu from the rack next to the condiments set and, drawing the back of his hand across the lower half of his face, he read aloud: ' "*Fowl*ing In Love Again ... a generous helping of roast breast of chicken, crispy bacon and fresh avocado with a delicious tarragon and mayonnaise dressing, served between two chunks of lightly toasted French bread." Worth four ninety-nine of anyone's money.'

'*Five pounds* for a sarnie?'

The Cocoa Foundry had been his suggestion. She would have preferred to eat at one of the cheaper snack diners in the galleried plaza at the other end of the mall. But Howard had only half an hour to spare before his next assignment, and this place was closer to the department store where they'd just finished interviewing and photographing members of the staff syndicate (Hosiery, second floor) who'd come up on the National Lottery. Ten grand each. When he'd asked her if she fancied *grabbing a bite* afterwards, the invitation had been so casual she'd agreed with barely a thought about motive. And now, witnessing his preoccupation with his food, and the amiable but inconsequential banter which accompanied it, Constance saw him set out the new terms of their relationship more clearly than ever: friends and colleagues. If he'd had any motive in asking her to lunch, it was to impress upon her that she should no longer seek motives in his dealings with her. Well, that was fine by her. That was just fine.

She took a sip of sparkling mineral water, her own sandwich – They're Playing Our Tuna – remaining untouched on its plate. They were seated at one of the alfresco tables; that is, outside the Cocoa Foundry proper, but in a small cordoned-off section of one of the mall arcades and, therefore, indoors. The furniture was wicker, painted white; the seating area – or *continental-style terrace*, as it was described in the café's publicity literature – enclosed within screens of potted ferns that shielded diners from the shoppers swarming by on all sides. The dining area was overlooked by the balcony of the mall's upper shopping deck and, occasionally, a glass-sided lift would glide silently into or out of view behind the shrubbery as it transported customers between levels. Here, Urbopark's omnipresent background muzak competed with the twenties American dance melodies issuing from within the open doors of the café itself and to which the younger, less inhibited, waiting staff were inclined to swing rhythmically as they weaved their way among the tables. The waiters and waitresses were in costume, dressed like characters out of *The Great Gatsby*.

'Talking of matters fowl,' said Howard, rescuing a chunk of freshly dropped chicken breast from his plate and pressing it between his lips, 'any news on the headless chickens story?'

Constance shook her head. 'Not since the piece that went in on Saturday.'

'Didn't see that.'

'Don't you read the paper?'

'Not if I can help it.'

Come to think of it, neither did she – other than to check her own stories to see if they'd been given a good show, or to make sure the subs hadn't rewritten her intro or ballsed up the copy in some way. In her first two years at the *Crucible* – while she was still a junior – she'd read the paper from front to back every night, even the sports pages. Even the *motoring* supplement. And, when she'd first started seeing Howard, she'd go through each edition trying to identify which pictures were his. He had a distinctive style – *arty-farty*, according to the editor – best suited to features work, but which turned even the most basic news photo into something eye-catchingly original. *He sees things differently to other people*, she'd remarked to Milly. *Don't we all*, her housemate had replied. Constance remembered hating her for that at the time, only now she recalled the comment with a smile of affection. Milly had a boundless capacity to be unimpressed by men.

'What's funny?' Howard asked.

'Nothing, I was thinking.'

'Fuck me, that's blown your chances of becoming a sub.'

Constance laughed, instinctively raising a hand to her face. He grinned. 'That brace still bothering you?'

One of his *in-jokes*. He'd never ceased to be amused by her habit of covering her mouth whenever she laughed, a throw-back – she'd confided in him – to her teens, when she was

56

embarrassed by the metalwork with which her dentist sought for two years to rectify her dental deficiencies. The trouble was, when you broke up with a feller you couldn't reclaim the things he knew about you. Your secrets. They were his as well now, his to keep and to flourish in front of you from time to time like the spoils of war. She didn't think that. She was just upset by the intimacy of his remark, and by the selectivity of his intimacy. Jesus, he probably didn't even realize he'd said it – *what* he'd said; just an insensitive, throwaway remark. It was her. It was her dwelling on things, making significance where there was none. As per.

She watched him while he ate. His hair was shorter, at the sides; and she hadn't seen that shirt before. Red-and-green check, open at the throat and patently unironed. She studied the pattern of hairs on the backs of his hands. Picking up her sandwich, she took a small bite and placed it back on the plate.

'So what was the story I missed?' he asked.

'They questioned Bill Honey – you know, the cleaner who found the graffiti.'

'Him? Why, apart from the fact that he's black?'

'Because of what he said about having worked in an abattoir.'

'Anything in it?'

'He'd been sacked. From his job at the abattoir, I mean. This was a couple of years ago. And the police – someone tipped them off – they thought he might've had some grudge against his former employers or something.'

'The chickens came from the abbatoir where he used to work, did they?'

'No, that's it – they didn't. The police don't know where they've come from. Besides, the graffiti turned out not to be chicken blood at all. So they let him go. It was crap, anyway, him being a suspect – I mean, even if he had some grievance with the abattoir, how would he have got hold of the chickens in the first place?'

'And why take it out on the mall?'

57

'*Exactly.*'

'Our boys in blue, putting two and two together and making five.'

'Well, I suppose they had this anonymous tip off and . . .'

'So the upshot of all this is, the chickens had nothing to do with the blood on the doors?'

'It wasn't even blood, as it turned out. Something synthetic. They're still carrying out tests.'

Howard laughed. 'Bet we buried that line way down the story after flying a kite on it the first time round.'

'Yeah, well. Good old Gary. I wouldn't mind, but it's never his byline that—'

'And the chickens? What's the story there?'

Constance shrugged. 'Police inquiries are continuing,' she said, making quote marks in the air with her fingers. She hated people who did that. So why did she do it? Sometimes you did things without knowing why. She was nervous, was what it was. With him. She was nervous being with him.

Howard had swivelled round in his chair and was trying to attract the attention of a waitress. Constance saw his neck, straining against the collar of his shirt, and – for the first time since they'd sat down to eat – she felt a twinge of lust. More than a twinge. That had always been her favourite part of his body, the silky black hairs at the nape of his neck; especially after he'd just come back from the barber's. The times she'd caressed them while he was driving, or while they were watching a film, or when they were making love. The times she'd nuzzled her face and lips and tongue into . . .

'Look, I'm going to have to get back,' she said, rising out of her chair.

'I was just going to order some pud.'

'Here's some dosh for my food, OK.'

'Con?'

'I didn't realize the time. Sorry.'

She gathered up her belongings – purse, notebook, handbag. The strap of her handbag was caught, and she had to lift the chair to free it. A waitress approached their table, smiling at them in turn, and Howard sent her away for the bill. Constance watched her go, sashaying in time to the music. Eighteen, at a guess. The girl was gorgeous in her costume; which, on her, would've looked ridiculous. She saw that Howard was watching too.

'OK?'

'Yeah, sure.' He checked his watch. 'I should be off too. Listen, good to see you again.'

'Yeah.'

'Anyway.'

'Right, OK.'

'See you.'

As she picked her way through the clutter of tables, she heard his voice calling her. Constance turned to see him unhooking a jacket from the back of her empty chair.

'Yours?' he said, smiling over the heads of the other diners.

On her way back to the office, Constance's attention was drawn to a cluster of people outside a shopfront. The Dashing Blade, Green Lower, specializing in high-class cutlery and silverware – she'd banged out a couple of pars on its official opening the previous week. Going over to investigate, she saw that the onlookers were watching a cutler at work at a wooden bench positioned in the window. A grey-haired man in brown apron and protective glasses, manipulating a table knife against a small electrically powered grindstone. Each time the blade came into contact with the stone a bright orange shower of sparks was emitted, to the delight of the young children watching. A sign in the window bore the same slogan which greeted motorists entering the city via its main approach roads: WELCOME TO THE HOME OF BRITISH CUTLERY – IF IT ISN'T MARKED HALLAM, IT ISN'T MADE IN HALLAM. Constance watched the man at work, the knotted purple veins on the backs of his hands reminding her of Granddad's, whose own delta of distended blood vessels – he insisted – matched exactly the pattern of rivers converging on Hallam. The cutler in the shop window didn't once glance up at the spectators while he worked, but now and then he'd send up an especially fierce cascade of sparks, causing the youngsters to leap back from the glass – their alarm dissolving immediately into gleeful squeals.

Her attention was distracted by the abrupt cessation of mall muzak followed by excessively loud doorbell chimes heralding a public address announcement. 'This is Customer Services reminding Urbopark customers losing family or friends to please meet them by the statues in Market Street.' Market Street. A parade of butchers, fishmongers, greengrocers and bakers designed to replicate the traditional street market atmosphere, complete with imitation cobbles and Victorian hawkers' cries piped over concealed loudspeakers. In fact, each stall was franchised by the neighbouring HypaCenta, their *country fresh produce* from identical suppliers to that on sale in the massive foodhall, minus the packaging. When Constance had discovered this she'd filed a piece for her weekly Our Gal at the Mall column, only for the editor to pull it. *No story there*, he'd said. When she'd suggested the decision might have had something to do with the superstore's status as a major advertiser with the paper, the editor told her she was too young and pretty to be so cynical.

Constance got out her notebook and scribbled a memo to herself, a reminder to set up a picture story about the performing cutler. Out of idle curiosity, she also jotted down the inscription, in Latin, on a sign beneath the shop name: *Deo Adamante Labor Proficit*. Not a clue what it meant, but she could always look it up or ask someone to translate. Howard would know. He'd attended the sort of school where Classics was on the curriculum. She wouldn't ask him. How could you ring him up to ask him to translate a piece of Latin? You couldn't. You couldn't ring him about anything at all. She stepped away from the window and continued on her way to the office via Snak Shak (Lucozade Orange, smoky bacon crisps, Snickers).

                      *   *   *

Tuesday morning. Constance hadn't seen Howard for a week,
she'd not thought about him for half an hour. She was not
thinking about him now as she prepared for a new day,
switching on her terminal and typing in her password –
CURLEW, the cursor moving in response to each keystroke
but leaving no characters on the screen. She didn't choose
'curlew', it was assigned to her by the *Crucible*'s senior systems
technician – an amateur ornithologist, who compiled a list of
passwords made up of birds' names. She typed in a Preliminary
News Schedule.

From: Constance Amory To: Newsdesk Time: 8.05
1. Customer gives birth in changing rooms at From Here to
   Maternity. [Pic of mum with baby being taken 9 a.m.]
2. Mall Admin to put Mall Secure contract out to tender.
   [Tip from contact. Putting call in this a.m. to Warren
   Bartholomew at Mall PRO to confirm.]
3. Mall Admin derecognizes trades unions in Mall Maintenance. [Gary, does William Boyce have this press release
   too?]
4. Staff at Enjoy Your Trip travel agency win award for
   customer service. With Pic.
5. Shoplifting rate rises for third quarter in a row. [Figures
   embargoed to 12 noon.]

'So what *can* I quote you as saying, Warren?'
   'OK, how's this: Mall Admin is always seeking ways to
improve efficiency and to find the most cost-effective means
of managing Urbopark without compromising our commitment
to total quality. Mall Secure, like every other department,
comes under constant scrutiny with regard to value for money.
The—'
   'Hang on, I'm taking all this down. OK, go on.'
   'The possibility of inviting bids for the Mall Secure contract
was only one of a number of options under discussion at a

recent management meeting. No decision has been taken yet and Mall Admin regrets that news of what was, after all, a confidential report should have been selectively leaked to the press. Still with me?'

'Just about.'

'Any decision to privatize would not be undertaken without full consultation with employees and supervisors at Mall Secure. In any case, the existing in-house security team would be perfectly entitled to bid for the contract. End of quote.'

'What about jobs?'

'What about them?'

'I mean, the thing with privatization is you make the cheapest bid by employing fewer people to do the same amount of work; or employ the same number at lower wages. Which has implications both for jobs and for quality of service, doesn't it?'

'You have a very cynical view of competitive tendering, Connie.'

'You can see why workers at Mall Secure are concerned, though, can't you?'

'Look, I don't really think there's anything I can usefully add to the statement I just gave you. I'm not going to speculate on the impact of a decision that hasn't even been taken yet.'

'OK.'

'OK . . .?'

'While you're on the phone, Warren, there *was* something else.'

'Another of your tip-offs?'

'It is, actually. You know the graffiti incident the other week?'

'Which graffiti incident?'

'Very funny. The thing is, I've been puzzling over why Mall Secure couldn't come up with any video evidence for the police. I mean, there are cameras all over the place here, certainly all the entrances and exits are monitored on CCTV.'

'What are you getting at?'

'Well, I can't believe whoever daubed this stuff on the doors wasn't caught on film. Even if he – or they – were wearing masks or balaclavas or whatever, you'd expect there to be *something* the police could use. You know, a clip they could show on TV – "Do you recognize the clothing being worn by these men etc. etc." '

'As I told you before, Mall Secure gave every co-operation to the—'

'Yeah, I know, but did they hand over any actual film?'

'That's something you should take up with the police, I would've thought.'

'The point is, my information is that there was no film. As I understand it – and this is a money-saving thing, from what I'm told – the CCTV cameras around the Urbopark site are dummies. Every single one of them. They're just for show – a visible deterrent; they don't actually *film* anything.'

'. . .'

'Warren?'

'My advice to you, Constance, is to tread very carefully indeed on this one. Ask yourself: who's telling me this, and why? If, as I suspect, it's the same source who leaked the privatization story, you want to think long and hard about his motives. You publish this, and get it wrong, we're talking shite creek sans paddle.'

'You won't confirm or deny, then?'

'You've got one story out of him – be happy with that, eh?'

She sat in front of the dressing-table mirror, choosing in turn from a selection of brushes and combs and tubs of goo. But no amount of teasing, flicking, clipping or moussing could compensate for the mess they'd made. Split Enz, Blue Lower; £19.99 for a wash, cut and blow-dry. A disaster. She gave up, began applying cleanser to her face – paying particular attention to the swathe of forehead newly revealed by a shorter fringe. She squeezed the largest of the spots, instantly regretting it as the resulting blemish was even more livid.

Twenty-five years old and she had the complexion of a teenager. The lighting in her bedroom didn't help. She tilted the mirror. Better. No, it wasn't. It was her jowls she didn't like. The new hairstyle emphasized her jowliness in a way that it hadn't in the photograph of the model she'd shown to the stylist. Models didn't have jowls. They were jowlless. And there she was, pouch-faced like a fucking squirrel with its cheek full of nuts. Chipmunk, Howard called her. *Used* to call her. His little chipmunk. Chippie for short. She puffed out her cheeks at the mirror. She'd skip the evening class. Knackered – look at those *eyes* for Christ's sake. A night in, in front of the telly, then early to bed with a book and mug of tea. She stared at her reflection again. Sod it, she'd go. What the hell. If you missed one week it became harder to go the next, you'd get out of the habit and end up dropping the class altogether. She dressed hurriedly. Two puffs on the inhaler. Bag: purse, notepad, pen. Keys. Where were her *keys*? Shit, shit. Downstairs, on the hall table. At the last moment she opted to wear her hair up instead of down, spending five minutes searching frantically for the scrunchie she'd been wearing earlier. Finally, she found it – looped round her wrist like a bracelet.

The Inky Path
As someone setting out on the inky path, you will find that the more you efface yourself and merge into the background, the more information you will collect and the better your stories will be.

Professor Stanley Bell started the video and switched off the lights. The television was perched on a stand fixed high up on the wall. The closing credits of a costume drama scrolled up the screen on fast-forward, followed by an advertisement for high-fibre, low-fat breakfast cereal. The tutor, silhouetted against a translucent blind, pointed the doofer and the picture slowed to normal. He clicked up the volume as the next commercial began. Men in grubby vests and jeans, heavy workboots and hard hats – their muscled arms coated with a sheen of sweat – were shovelling fuel into the mouth of a blast furnace. With each shovelful a fresh burst of sparks flared within the flaming orifice as the coals were engulfed. The workers' shoulders and backs strained with the effort; now and then one of them would use a grimy rag kerchief to mop his face. The end of the shift, the camera cut to a scene of the men, still in workclothes, gathered round a table in a tavern, raising glasses of cold beer to their mouths. A full pint was superimposed over this scene, its maker's name on the glass. A voiceover, gruff, flat-vowelled, no-nonsense: *Hallam Bitter, brewed in Hallam – home of British steel. Hallam: the finest steel, the finest ale. Nowt else will do.*

The advert ended, the video clicked off; lights on, blinds up. Prof. Bell addressed them. 'I saw this on the telly and I thought: "Stan, here's your kick-off for this week's class." I've videoed every commercial break for three nights waiting for the ad to come on again. Anyone know why, apart from the fact I'm a sad bastard?'

Laughter. Constance raised her hand.

'Hey we're not in school, you know!'

She lowered her arm self-consciously.

'Well, I suppose we're in what *used* to be a school,' the tutor said. He smiled at her. 'Constance, isn't it?'

'The advert wasn't filmed in Hallam,' she said.

'Right! Spot on. So *what's the story* here, if I may borrow a phrase from our Antipodean cousins?'

'Wasn't it filmed in East Germany, or somewhere?'

'Czechoslovakia. Czech Republic, I should say. The brewery wanted to film men at work in a traditional blast furnace – or, at least, what coincided with Joe and Joanna Public's perception of a blast furnace; only they haven't made steel that way in Hallam or anywhere else in Western Europe for a decade or two. All high-tech now. You go inside a modern steelworks, you could be in a dairy. So,' he jerked his thumb in the direction of the blank television screen, 'they'd to traipse

65

over to a plant in Prague, where they still melt steel like this. Those weren't Hallam steelworkers, they were Czech. Drinking Czech beer, for all I know.'

Prof. Bell surveyed the room, removing his glasses and clicking one of the ear-pieces between his teeth. The students were silent, faces upturned towards him. One or two had laid down their pens when they realized he was telling an anecdote rather than dictating information. Finally, a man sitting at the front cleared his throat and said: 'I don't understand your point.'

'Ah, my point. You want a message. You want this to *mean* something.' That disarming smile, a tone of amused affection which pre-empted the possibility of anyone taking offence. 'It doesn't mean a thing. It's just a story, make of it what you will.'

'*South Pacific*,' said the woman next to Constance. 'You know, the film. It weren't filmed in t'South Pacific at all, it were filmed on an island in t'South China Sea. Me daughter went theer when she were backpacking. Lovely musical, that.'

Someone else chipped in. 'You know *Gorky Park*, with William Hurt. They couldn't make that in Russia, like, because t'cold war were still on in them days so they had to do t'filming in Finland. The bits that were s'posed to be Moscow, they was Helsinki. Bit o'snow, people in fur coats – who's to know?'

'He were in *Elephant Man*, him. William Hurt.' It was the woman next to Constance. 'I like him.'

'No, that were *John* Hurt. He's English. T'other one's American.'

'Oh, aye. John Hurt.'

The tutor spread his arms, smiling expansively, glasses in one hand and a shirt-tail protruding from beneath his red chunky-knit sweater. Different trousers to the ones he'd worn before, Constance noticed, but just as baggy about the ankles. 'You see? You talk history – that's to say *representations* of actual events – and you inevitably end up telling stories. We live in an age when fiction is often more authentic than fact.'

He let that comment sink in; smiling, placing his glasses back on his face. The man at the front, who'd earlier sought a point to Prof. Bell's anecdote, cleared his throat once more and declared with indignant satisfaction:

'So it *does* mean summat.'

Notes
'Steel City' can be said to date from 1709 when Samuel Shore began to make steel on a commercial basis in H. by encouraging co-operation between metal manufacturer (i.e. steelmaker) and metal user (i.e. cutler or craftsman). The cutlers' demand for high-quality metal to work with brought steel (orig. imported from Europe) then steelmaking to Hallam.

Labour
1786: H had 52 cutlery unions (aka 'trade societies'). At first, activities of organized labour tolerated by Church and landed gentry. Pay strikes in 1777, 1787, 1790 & 1796 by file, table-knife, scissor and spring-knife workers were decreasingly successful yet increasingly political.

QUOTE: 'What had begun as a quest for reasonable employment conditions ended as a perceived threat against the state.' (S. Bell)

Prof. Stanley Bell's Physical, Metaphysical and Philosophical Glossary of Metals

Cast iron: An alloy of iron, carbon and silicon cast in a mould and characterized by its hardness and brittleness. A simple example of the production of a casting is that of making a hole in sand and filling it with molten metal. The metal, once solidified, retains the form of the hole. From this process we derive the adjective 'cast-iron', signifying that which is strong (e.g. a cast-iron constitution) or that which cannot be disproved or falsified (e.g. a cast-iron alibi).

Wrought Iron: Iron worked into shape, e.g. by being beaten, while the metal is hot rather than molten. The change in form, therefore, is not so marked. Wrought iron is tough but, because of its low carbon content, malleable and tensile rather than brittle.

Thus both metals possess an inherent strength, yet both are susceptible to alteration by external factors during the production process (i.e. the mould or the hammer). It is the nature of that strength and the degree of alteration which distinguishes them. In this sense, it is possible to be both strong *and* yielding; and for this combination of qualities to manifest itself in more ways than one.

Constance was in her office – typing, anticipating the weekend, sipping coffee, oblivious to the imminence of a more important story than the one she was writing. *The times they are a changing for staff at a Hallam clock and watch shop* . . . Cliché. She deleted the intro, started again. Meanwhile, a telephone call was being routed to Mall Admin. Urbopark's administration suite was a sanctuary of ergonomically sculpted serenity: thick-pile lavender carpet symmetrically pricked with a corporate pale blue 'U' motif, cherry-veneer desks, pot-plants and Impressionist prints, spot-lighting, a background hum of computers with their clackety-clack keyboard accompaniment, and a pervasive air- conditioned scent of synthetic upholstery and mineral water. In a room adjoining the reception space, two telephonists in matching cream blouses and chocolate-brown skirts operated a computerized switchboard. A notice on the wall urged: PUT A SMILE IN YOUR VOICE! One of the operators pressed a touch-sensitive pad and – smiling – singsonged without punctuation into the mouthpiece: *Good afternoon you're through to Mall Admin my name's Trish I'm pleased to help you*. A man's voice, slightly muffled, replied:

'There is a bomb in the mall. It is timed to go off in exactly one hour. This is not a hoax. The codeword is "rage", Roger Alpha Golf Echo.'

'Hello? Who is this? Hello?'

The line went dead. Trish – pale, her scarlet lipsticked lips not quite closed – slipped the headset onto her neck and, after a moment's hesitation, turned to her colleague. This conversation was the prelude to the implementation of the rehearsed procedure, as yet untested in an authentic emergency, for safely evacuating large numbers of people from the 250 retail units and six kilometres of arcades which comprised Urbopark.

Thousands of shoppers evacuated in bomb alert

by Constance Amory, Urbopark Reporter

Thousands of people were evacuated from Hallam's giant Urbopark shopping complex after a bomb warning.

Shop and security staff ushered an estimated 7,000 customers out of the mall following a public address announcement late yesterday afternoon.

The evacuation – completed in less than 15 minutes – was orderly and almost without incident, although two elderly shoppers were taken to hospital suffering from suspected heart attacks and a youth was arrested for alleged looting.

Teatime

The decision to clear the site was taken by mall manager Roy Dobbs – in consultation with the police and Mall Secure – after a switchboard operator took a call from a man claiming to have planted a bomb.

Police, fire and ambulance crews rushed to the scene and the area was cordoned off. Roads surrounding Urbopark were closed, causing long tailbacks in the teatime traffic.

A team of Army bomb disposal experts from the Hallamshire Regiment used sniffer dogs in a bid to track down and defuse the device, which was supposedly timed to explode an hour after the warning. The caller did not say where the bomb was hidden.

5 p.m.

But at 5 p.m., ten minutes before the bomb was due to go off, a caller to Hallam Central police station – using a codeword, and believed to be the same man who made the earlier call – said the warning was a hoax.

The security alert was not scaled down until a precautionary search had been completed, and it was nearly two hours before staff and customers were allowed to return to the mall.

Police said it was 'mere speculation' to link the hoax to two recent incidents at the mall – when graffiti was daubed over the entrances and more than a hundred headless chicken carcasses were dumped at the HypaCenta foodhall.

Mall manager, Mr Dobbs, described the bomb warning as a 'stupid and dangerous prank'.

He added: 'Two people have been taken ill because of this idiot, our retailers have had their business disrupted and several thousand folk have had a pleasant day's shopping ruined.'

A police spokesman said, 'It really is an irresponsible and criminal act. The emergency services have wasted a great deal of time and resources when we could all have been better deployed elsewhere.'

Radio

A tape recording of the hoaxer's call to the police station is to be analysed by voice experts and will be broadcast over local television and radio news in a bid to identify the culprit. Police have no idea of any motive for the hoax.

The two people taken ill during the evacuation, who have not been named, are reported to be comfortable in Hallam Royal Infirmary.

●●●Turn to page 6 for more pictures and our reporter's eye-witness account.

The editor sent an electronic message to Constance's mail directory (spelling her name 'Armory') in which he praised her skill *in pulling the story together under difficult circumstances*. She'd had to file from a public payphone half a mile from the Urbopark exclusion zone, dictating directly from her shorthand notes. The colour piece on page six, in which she described first-hand the evacuation of the mall – working in quotes from staff and customers – was *especially well written, conveying the full drama of the situation*. Constance ran off a print-out of the memo, to show her mam.

The Life and Times of a Hallam Saw Grinder
(a Dramatic Reconstruction in Many Parts)

November, 1857

Thomas Amory entered the wheel building, exchanging terse greetings with the other men as he made his way through the ramshackle labyrinth of wooden partitions and doorways to the hull he shared with four other workmen. He hung his jacket and bag on a peg and rolled up his shirtsleeves beyond the elbow, tucking the blue cotton into tight folds that pinched the flesh of his upper arm. He took a cloth cap from his jacket pocket and placed it firmly on his head. Thomas, unlike most men, was not in the habit of wearing a cap or hat about the streets, but used one at work to prevent his hair from becoming clogged with dust. Two of the troughs were already in use, their occupants pausing briefly to acknowledge his arrival with nods of the head. Conversation was impossible above the screech of saw blades against stone and the rhythmic clatter of bands and pulleys, creating a breed of workmen skilled at communicating in signs and gestures. Thomas's younger brother, Victor – busy at the glazing stone – gave him a wink. The air was patterned with dust, fine white particles dancing in the first light that seeped into the hull from the windows along one wall. Thomas's nostrils filled with familiar smells of dust, hot metal and leather; and of the emery, suet and beeswax concoction Victor rubbed meticulously onto the surface of his stone each morning like a farmer grooming a prize bull for show.

Thomas checked over the equipment, then fetched a scoop of water from the standpipe in the yard to top up his trough. He started up the grindstone, testing the surface with the palm of his hand for wetness. A good stone, purchased from the quarry at Wickersley – a great rough-hewn block of sandstone

71

as tall as a man. He had had it fetched by cart and hung it himself, hacking and dry-grinding until it was true. The dust when running wet was bad enough, but while trueing a new stone it had to be seen to be believed. He had not ceased coughing for two days. If his father had been alive he would have told Thomas to be thankful he was not a sheep-shear grinder, none of whom made old bones. Sheep shears had to be dry-ground on softer stone – not wet like saws – with no moisture to damp down the millions of particles of metal and stone. Even in the wet-grinding trades, some of the men – mostly outsiders from Birmingham and Derby, with their talk of factory laws – had been agitating for better ventilation, and for covers over the stones. But the hulls were cold and draughty enough in winter as it was without having the windows open, and you could not work properly at a stone with a cover. As for installing fans . . . well, the wheel owners would not pay for anything unless they had to. Thomas looked around the workshop: window panes cracked and broken, walls that had not seen a lick of whitewash in the six years he had been there, holes the size of a man's fist in the floorboards, and the floor filthy and unswept. Too hot in summer, too cold in winter. Vast damp patches on the walls and ceiling that sprouted blueish-white mildew at certain times of the year.

· He worked standing up, straddling the wooden horse, knees bent and using the strength of his back and arms to press the blade against the whirring grindstone. A thin strip of wood, gripped between the saw and the palms of his hands, protected his skin from the sharp edges and from being burnt as the metal heated up. The stone revolved upwards, away from Thomas, emitting a shower of sparks – white at its centre, fierce orange at the periphery. Each vivid flare illuminated the hull. The wall at the head of his trough had been scorched black over the years, and those sparks that fell short would fizz and die in the thick grey dust coating the floor. He was working on a batch of saws returned to him for regrinding after having the toothed edge die-cut. He selected each blade in turn from a wooden box, manipulating the metal with care and precision against the rapidly revolving stone – pausing now and then to check the quality of his workmanship. When he was satisfied he laid the finished article in another box, ready for glazing. This batch would keep him busy for the rest of the day and most of the next. Trade was good lately, no thanks to the likes of Linley. Thomas chafed his thumb against the grindstone, shaving off a layer of flesh. He let out an oath. Droplets of rich red blood dripped into the water in his trough, dispersing into filmy strands of pale pink before becoming altogether diluted. He sucked at the wound, inspecting his hand by the pale light from the window. Using his teeth to tear off a strip from his handkerchief, he wound the material tightly around the joint and fastened it with a crude knot. The thumb would not bend now. However, this temporary impediment had its advantages – compelling him, as it did, to attend all the more closely to his work by way of compensating for the loss of dexterity. In concentrating on nothing but the quality of the contact of metal against stone, all distracting thoughts were dispelled. A grinder's best work, his father would say, is done with the head as much as it is with the eye or the hand. Sunday was three days hence and there was nothing to be gained by thinking on it.

Royal Commission of Inquiry
(sitting at) Hallam Town Hall
Wednesday, 19 June 1867 (Twelfth Day)

Witness: Samuel Crookes, Unemployed Saw Grinder, No.28 Furnace Hill, Hallam.

Q. Had any person set you to do anything to Linley?

A. I asked Old Smite 'Em one day what he was doing with him.

Q. Old Smite 'Em is a man by the name of Broadhead, Secretary of the Saw Grinders' Society, is he not?

A. He is.

Q. What did he say?

A. He asked what I could do with Linley.

Q. What did you say?

A. I told him I would make him so as he would not work for a goodly while.

Q. What did Broadhead say to that?

A. He asked what I should want for doing it.

Q. What did you say?

A. I asked him if £20 would be too much.

Q. What did he say to that?

A. He said no, he should think it was not.

Thomas worked methodically, reducing the pile of blades with an intensity of purpose that was interrupted only by a familiar discomfort – the consequence of remaining in one position for too long. He broke off, at last, from his labours; standing upright, he arched his back and stretched his arms above his head. Taking what remained of his handkerchief from his trouser pocket, he mopped his face and neck and dried his hands, careful of the bandaged thumb. His new boots – for ha'pence he would take them off and work barefoot. He sat on the horse and removed each boot in turn, massaging his feet through the woollen socks. The toes felt gnarled and misshapen by bunions. Frances always said if she had seen his feet beforehand, they would never have married. Given her father's attitude to matters of romantic impropriety, Thomas would invariably reply that if she had seen his feet during courtship they would *have* to have become wed. He smiled to himself, fastening his boots and flexing his arms once more before reaching into the box for the next blade.

Witness: Thomas Amory, Saw Grinder, No.11 Garden Street, Hallam.

Q. Were you in the habit of shooting with Crookes?

(*witness hesitates*)

74

A. No.

Q. When you were apprentices?

A. We did, when we were apprentices.

Q. Where did you shoot?

A. At Ecclesall Woods. We would shoot rabbits, mostly.

Q. And pigeons?

A. We never shot pigeons.

Q. You never went to Ecclesall Woods on race days and brought down birds with a shotgun as they came over?

A. We never did that.

Q. What did you shoot with?

A. An air rifle.

Q. To whom did the rifle belong?

A. It was Sammy's.

Q. Samuel Crookes?

A. Yes.

Q. Did you ever shoot the air rifle?

A. I used it to shoot at rabbits, when we were apprentices. Then Sammy would not let me, for he said it was a waste of pellets.

Q. What did he mean by that?

A. He meant I would not hit anything.

Q. You were not able to shoot a gun as well as he?

A. I can shoot as well as the next man. It is only that my rabbits are not so good at catching the pellet.

(*laughter*)

The other men had already ceased work when Frances came with his snap. She was the last of the wives and daughters to visit the hull that morning – a wicker basket over her arm, containing bread and cold meat and a tin flask of tea. She exchanged greetings with Victor, her brother-in-law, who was seated by the fireplace with Thomas's fellow grinders, as was their custom in the colder months.

'Hast thou to go back?' Thomas said, so that he would not be overheard.

She shook her head. 'Our three are with next door's.'

He went to say something further but was interrupted by a series of coughs that left him flushed and watery-eyed. He took out his handkerchief and, turning away from his wife, expelled a mouthful of phlegm into the grubby cloth. She was rubbing the centre of his broad back with smooth, circular strokes while he regained his breath.

'Thou should learn to grind wi' thy mouth shut, Thomas Amory.'

'What dost thou know about keeping thy mouth shut?'

They went outside, to the rear of the Wheel building, and sat on a low wall overlooking the river. Thomas spread a square of sackcloth over the damp brickwork. It must have rained again during the morning, though it was dry now and the sky had whitened. The current beneath them was turbulent from its passage through the giant water-wheel, the foaming surface discoloured by discharge from the rolling mill a hundred yards upstream. Thomas found the yard a restful place – inhaling air fresher and cooler than that inside the hull, allowing his eyes to follow the mesmeric patterns created by the river; even the commotion of the water-wheel had a persistent, hypnotic quality that he found pleasantly lulling. On the occasions when Frances joined him they would sit for minutes at a time with barely a word exchanged, adjusting to one another's company again after the hours consumed by their separate preoccupations of work and home. And – if they had quarrelled, or if there were worries about money or work or one of the children – the passage of time by the river would dissolve their anxieties. Their voices, when silence finally yielded to conversation, would be softer, less harsh, less urgent. The men ribbed him about these visits and would no doubt do so again today when he returned to his trough. He did not like to be ridiculed – what man does? – but he liked less to be denied his wife's companionship.

Frances poured the tea while her husband pressed a wad of bread and meat between his lips. She enquired about his thumb and, speaking through a mouthful of food, he told her of the accident. He neglected to confess the cause of his distraction, merely stating that he had been clumsy. Displaying his handiwork, he saw that the binding was stained reddish-brown where blood had seeped through. When his wife asked whether he had washed the cut before strapping it, he shook his head. She would clean it for him at home that evening, she said, and make up a poultice. As Frances held his hand in hers, inspecting the bandaged thumb, Thomas was surprised to find himself wondering about Linley's wife. How was it possible for her to abide a man of his sort, to live with him and to bear his children? Was she not ashamed even to look at him? And what of the men who were content to be his supping companions in the taproom of a Saturday night? It did not do to dwell too long on such matters, for the conclusion – an uncomfortable one at that – was that it could be possible for a man to be at once the object of contempt and of respect, of both enmity and affection. For this to be so, that man must have aspects to his character which mitigated against an absolute assessment of him in either extreme. And, in this, Linley was not exceptional; he was merely a man. Thomas withdrew his hand and resumed eating.

'Wouldst thou stay wed to a man what had been rolled up?'

'What a question!'

'I'm not speaking of thee and me, but in general.'

'And why would he be rattened, this man?'

'You know as well as I that a man is rolled up for harming his fellows. And if he's to be done many a time, what then? Would you stay wed to that kind of man?'

Frances sat quietly for a moment, gazing into the eddying river a few feet beneath them where their legs dangled over the wall. At last she replied, 'I would not love him as well as I might.'

Thomas looked at her, then at the river. His wife's wisdom sometimes made him afraid of himself and of his own

77

ignorance. He knew in that instant he did not hate Linley enough to do him, as Crookes and Broadhead wished; but that he would do so nevertheless. And if anyone ever was to ask him the reason, he would say it was because you do not have to hate a man to loathe what that man does.

Chapter Three

SHOP TALK

Me, I used to work for an engineering firm out on t'Brinsley Road industrial estate. Closed down, now. Whole site's been turned into one o' them out-of-town places. You know: multiscreen cinema, DIY megastore, drive-in Burgerland an' that.

Jim Stott, 51, car-park attendant

His bespectacled eyes were indistinguishable behind the reflective patina of the lenses as he stood, pooled in the sodium lighting of the adult education centre car-park. *Three-one to you, Constance.* His conversational gambit had intrigued her sufficiently to draw her away from a gradually dispersing group of fellow students. As though sensing her bemusement, he'd elaborated, *You got your name in the paper three times last night, I only managed it once.* At home, Constance retrieved the previous day's copy of the *Crucible* from the recycling stack. The article on Stanley Bell was tucked away on page sixteen, in Folk in the News. Four pars, no quotes. He was referred to as a *history boffin*, the piece belatedly recording his return to Hallam – after thirteen years in *Austria* (sic) – to take up a *prestigeous* (sic) *professorship* at the university.

79

In the second paragraph his new post was described as having been *confirmed* rather than *conferred* upon him. His age was given as forty-three. Wrong. The university's press release, he'd said, had correctly stated his year of birth as 1953 – but the reporter's mistake had been simply to subtract from 1996. *My birthday's in December, so I'm still forty-two for another three months, thank you very much!* This had prompted a discussion between Constance and Stan about the mathematical conundrum of $96 - 53 = 42$. *You are in your forty-third year, though*, she'd pointed out. Stan had laughed. *Dates were never my strong point*. She smiled as she examined the report. The head-and-shoulders photo made him appear to be wearing a false beard. On an impulse, she fetched a pair of scissors and cut the article from the page. She pinned it to the cork board on her bedroom wall, among postcards, holiday snaps, cartoons, old theatre, concert and cinema tickets and various money-off coupons. As she made space, she noticed some of the coupons were out of date and spent a moment weeding them out. This led to a general reappraisal, removing pins and dropping items into a wastepaper basket; items dating back several years and which, in many cases, she was at a loss to recall the reason for pinning them up in the first place. She was so absorbed in this exercise that she gave a start when Milly bumped the door open and entered the room backwards carrying two mugs, a packet of chocolate digestives under her arm.

Constance sat cross-legged at the head of the bed, Milly lay sprawled on her stomach across the foot. The biscuits passed back and forth. Now and again, one of the women would yawn. The bedroom was warm, the heating on so that a batch of laundry draped over radiators around the house would dry by morning. The only illumination came from a bedside lamp, its shade casting a dim orange glow over the room's magnolia walls and white laminated wardrobe and matching chest of drawers. The curtains were drawn, the door was closed; the Cranberries played softly.

'I do the job, right? I cover a story and file the copy on time and I think: "That's OK, that's fine." But I don't know if it's any good or not. What I've written, I mean. Like with the bomb hoax thing – the colour piece, the eye-witness account – as I'm writing it, I can tell it's good stuff; you get a kind of buzz, you know?'

Milly nodded. 'Sure.'

'Then you send it, and you see it in the paper, and you're not so sure any more. It seems stale, somehow. Pretentious. Who am I to say these things, describe these things? Then the memo arrives from the editor and the buzz comes back. Not a buzz, a glow. It's like I need someone else to say "well done", to pat me on the back, before I really believe that what I've done is worth anything. That I'm any good.'

'Men, you mean. Like a label they pin on you – "self-esteem". Like it comes from them.'

'No, it could be anyone. Women as well. Other *people*, not just men.'

'What you were saying the other week about Howard, though. Him setting out the way the relationship is from now on – *just good friends*. It's . . . both of you are involved in the situation, *two* of you, and yet one of you – him – is in control of deciding the way things are going to be.'

Constance dunked a biscuit, watching a smear of melted chocolate form at the rim of the mug. She raised the biscuit to her mouth, dripping crumbs and hot tea onto her T-shirt. Shit, clean on this evening.

'That's different,' she said. 'That's not the same as what I'm saying. If it was the other way round, if I was the one who'd finished with Howard, I'd be the one setting the conditions and he'd be feeling the way I do.'

Milly raised her eyebrows. 'Would you? Would *he*, for that matter?'

'Yes. Yeah, I think so. It's not so tied up with this self-esteem business.'

'Suppose the editor never sent you that memo. The story's

the same, isn't it? It's the same story you've written – your story – whether or not he sends you a memo to tell you how good it is.'

'So?'

'So, according to what you're saying, the story's merit isn't inherent, it's determined by others – the editor; it's *attached* to the story. Like, your worth is also decided externally. Out of your control.'

'Don't let me have any more biscuits, Mill.'

'Don't let *me*.'

They looked at each other. Constance smiled. 'Go on then, just one.'

The two women listened to the song – a melodic, haunting ballad that seemed to soften the room's hard edges as though the music itself were issuing from the peachy light of the bedside lamp. Milly took another slurp of tea, placing the half-empty mug precariously beside her on the bed. Constance envied her friend's short-cropped dark hair – quick to wash and dry and requiring minimal fuss. Milly had the face for it, the bone structure, the colouring, the strong black eyebrows and full lips. An androgynous quality, smooth and sensuous. When they'd first met – three years earlier, after Constance had answered an ad for a 'n.s. prof. fem. to share house in H6 with one similar' – she'd assumed the other woman's self-assurance derived from her appearance, from years of experiencing the impact of her attractiveness. But, as they became close, she discovered her housemate to be as insecure about her looks as anyone else. Late one evening, after a session at the Tongs & Dozzle, they'd each compiled a list of their own physical imperfections. Milly filled an entire sheet of A4.

'Like, when I had my hair done – I felt reasonably OK about it and then one word out of place from you . . .'

'I said I *liked* your hair!'

'Mill, I saw the way you looked at me.'

'What look? I didn't . . . Con, it really suits you.'

'*Thanks.*'

'*Con.*'

Milly laughed, which made Constance laugh too. They each had another chocolate digestive and broke the last one in half to share. Constance's tea was tepid, almost cold, the dregs swimming with fragments of soggy biscuit. The tape ended with a plastic snap of the play button that effected a rude silence in the room.

'So, tell me, how was Stan the Man tonight?' asked Milly.

'He offered me a lift home.'

'Sounds promising.'

'No, we were just chatting outside in the car-park – he was being polite. Anyway, I walked. He's forty-three . . . *forty-two*, I should say.'

'Never mind his age – is he emotionally post-adolescent and does he have a nice bum?'

'Milly's two-step guide to choosing the right man.'

'Hasn't failed me yet.'

'I've only been to – what? – three classes. So I don't know about the post-adolescence. He likes football, Australian Rules . . .'

'Bad sign.'

'. . . and he wears baggy trousers, so no bum definition to speak of.' Constance smiled. 'He's funny, he makes me laugh. And he's intelligent.'

'Oh, spare me.'

'What?'

'Nothing.'

'*What?*'

'*Nothing.*'

Constance brushed the debris from her T-shirt. 'He makes me talk, about myself. I mean, I find myself burbling on to him – which is unusual for me.'

Milly raised her eyebrows.

'I don't mean with *you*, I mean generally. I spend so much of my time getting other people to talk, in my job, I find it hard to switch out of *journalist mode*. Howard reckoned that, in the first few weeks we were going out, a conversation with me was like being interviewed for a story.'

'Two words, Con: "defence" and "mechanism".'

'Yeah, yeah, I know all that. But it goes deeper. It's like, sometimes, I have this basic assumption that what the other person has to say is more significant or interesting. Self-effacement, I suppose. Comes with the job.'

'That's not journalism, that's called womanhood. It's conditioning. You just happen to be a woman *and* a journalist, so you're doubly fucked.'

'Now *there's* a thought.'

'*Connie.*'

She pressed the eject button on the radio-cassette player and flipped the tape over. 'The funny thing is, I really fancied going for a drink tonight, after class – some of the others were going. Only, they asked Stan and he said he couldn't. Then, when they asked me, I said "no" as well.'

'Because he wasn't going?'

'I was disappointed he wouldn't be there, I suppose. I mean, it's the dictation-of-terms thing again – me letting someone else decide what I'm going to do. And it's not just him or because he's a feller – it's me. It's in *me*. I'm like the blank screen on a word-processor, just waiting for someone else to type in the text.'

On returning to work from her daily dash to Snak Shak, she found her mam displaying – item by item – the contents of a carrier bag to two men, seated alongside her in the front office. One was examining a pair of beige sling-backs, the other held a red cabbage in his hands like a goalkeeper clutching a football. The former, Urbopark's press officer Warren Bartholomew, was attending to Mrs Amory's explanation of her buy-and-return syndrome. Constance didn't recognize the other man – charcoal-grey suit, bald, heavy eyebrows, thick fingers splayed around the cling-filmed cabbage – though he looked vaguely familiar. All three glanced up on her arrival, Mam breaking off in the midst of recounting Dr Singh's diagnosis of shopper's bulimia.

'Mam, was there summat you wanted?'

Summat. She hadn't said 'summat' since high school. *Don't know who put that plum in your mouth, but it weren't me or your dad, that I do know.* A familiar refrain when she'd moved back home, briefly, after university. Her accent, she'd argued, had simply become neutralized by being away and mixing with folk from other parts of the country. She still rhymed 'glass' with 'mass' rather than 'farce', didn't she? Jesus, Mam was removing a bra from her bag. It took several minutes to extricate the two men, ushering Mam out. Constance's embarrassment was complete when, in the sanctuary of the editorial room, the press officer introduced his companion as Detective Chief Inspector Paul Pink of Hallamshire CID. The policeman was still in possession of the abandoned cabbage. She relieved him of the vegetable, placing it on top of a sheaf of press releases in her in-tray so it wouldn't roll off the desk.

'Handy paperweight,' said the detective, straight-faced.

She smiled at him. 'You think, by making a joke of this, my humiliation will be somehow reduced?'

'My mother died two years ago,' he said. 'I'd willingly have her around to show me up at work.'

Constance didn't know what to say. She inspected his face more closely. Grey eyes, a thin white scar bisecting his right eyebrow. He was the sort of man who would appear to be in need of a shave even after he'd just had one. In returning her stare he neither smiled nor flinched nor seemed in any way disconcerted by her stunned reaction to his remark. His breath smelled distinctly of peppermint. She managed another smile, breaking the awkward silence by inviting the two men to sit down. Busying herself at the drinks counter, she exchanged work-related chit-chat with Warren while the detective sat quietly, legs crossed, hands clasped over one knee. His socks, like his tie and a matching handkerchief in the breast pocket

85

of his suit jacket, were pale pink. Milk and sugar requirements were established, and by the time the three of them were sitting round the desk – coffees to hand – she had managed to compose herself.

'I recognize you now, from your picture,' she said. 'You've made the headlines quite a bit over the years.'

' "Police in the pink after crime crackdown", "Pink sees red over court ruling".' The detective's face remained blank, no hint of amusement. ' "Pink perky as burglary rate drops",' he added, 'that one was a particular favourite with my children.'

Constance took a sip of coffee. Shoes, OK, you could understand someone showing off a new pair of shoes – even to two total strangers – but a *cabbage*? Perhaps she'd taken the cabbage out of the bag to get at something else, the shoes. That would be it. She put the mug down. The policeman had removed a half-consumed mint from his mouth and was wrapping it in a twist of paper. He slipped the paper in his pocket and reached for his drink.

As though prompted by the fascination with which she watched him do this, he explained: 'Excuse me, I find Extra Strong Mints and coffee incompatible.' He patted the pocket. 'And I've to save this one for later – I left the packet in the car.'

She laughed, covering her mouth with her hand. He was in his forties, she guessed; heavily built, and with a nose evidently misshapen by fracture. In his hand, the coffee mug was made to resemble a cup from a child's toy teaset. His softness of speech, delicate manner – the gentle way he cradled his drink – combined with the pink-accessorized foppishness of his attire to make his bulk all the more incongruous.

'I believe you've been in conversation with Patricia McVitie,' said the inspector, startling Constance by coming abruptly to the point when he'd so far exuded an air of interminable patience.

'Patricia . . .?'

'McVitie. Trish.'

86

'Oh, *her*. The girl on switchboard.' Constance hesitated.
'Yes. Is there a problem with that?'

'That depends.'

'On what?'

DCI Pink uncrossed his legs, crossed them the other way.
'On what information she imparted to you, and on what you
propose doing with that information.'

'She told you I'd spoken to her?'

'One of our officers . . . ascertained this fact earlier this
morning, during the course of a routine interview with Miss
McVitie.'

Turning to the other man, she asked, 'What's all this about,
Warren?'

The press officer exhaled loudly through his nose, a habit
which she'd learnt to decipher as an attempt to disguise anxiety
as indifference. *Connie, it's no big deal, but . . .* This occasional
mannerism apart, Warren Bartholomew was consummately
adept at *managing* information to Mall Admin's best advantage without alerting reporters to the fact he'd steered them
away from a more fruitful line of inquiry. Having recently
returned from a Mediterranean holiday – Greece? Malta?, she
couldn't remember – his boyish broad face was freckled and
the eyebrows were bleached blond, lending him a startled
expression. Until now, he'd been picking with his thumbnail
at a scabby graze at the base of his left wrist. He leaned forward
in his chair, nodding to himself as though confirming the
validity of the words he was assembling for utterance. His
southern accent sounded bland and insubstantial after DCI
Pink's Hallam.

'Constance, we're worried . . . that is, the police – the chief
inspector – and we in Mall Admin agree . . . that you might
be on the point of publishing a story based on something Trish
McVitie told you.'

'Is she in trouble over this?'

The press officer shook his head. 'No. Absolutely not.'

'You've sacked her.'

87

'She's been given a verbal warning.'

'Jesus, Warren . . .'

'She's employed to operate our switchboard, not to divulge sensitive information to the readership of the *Crucible*.'

DCI Pink, who had remained almost motionless in his chair during this exchange, reached forward and replaced his coffee mug on the table with a loud clunk.

'Miss Amory,' he said, merging the two words into one, 'did Patricia McVitie reveal to you the codeword used by the hoax caller?'

'I know the codeword, yes.'

'You know the codeword.' He paused. 'Do you intend to . . . publish it?'

Constance gestured at the computer terminal on her desk. 'The piece is more or less written, I've just got one or two points to check before I file.'

Warren Bartholomew interjected. 'You haven't sent the copy yet?'

'No, not yet. They're holding space for it in city final. Page two.'

The detective addressed her again, deadpan, his quiet voice betraying no emotion. 'What line are you taking?'

'The obvious one. The codeword is the same as the one daubed over the doors of the mall. I'm making – my story makes – the link. So far it's been speculation, but this means, you know, we can say for certain that these aren't two unrelated incidents. I was about to call one of your colleagues to get a quote to firm this up.'

DCI Pink nodded. He'd removed his pink handkerchief and was blowing his nose noisily, releasing a faint aroma of menthol into the cramped office.

'The fact that you're here,' she continued, 'more or less confirms what I'm saying, doesn't it? I mean, telephone pranksters and graffiti artists are right up there with TV licence dodgers on CID's list of most wanted criminals. Not to mention chicken murderers.'

'The . . . incidents to date, connected or otherwise, would not be enough in themselves to guarantee my involvement.'

'So why are you? Involved, I mean.'

The detective glanced at Warren, who gave another of his nasal exhalations. 'We received a letter today, addressed to the mall manager,' said the press officer. 'A ransom note, of sorts. A sum of one million pounds was mentioned, though there was no indication of the arrangements by which any money should be handed over. Nor was there a threat to carry out further acts against the mall if we failed to comply.'

'Can we use this?' asked Constance. She looked at her watch, calculating how much time she had to pull a story together before deadline.

DCI Pink answered. 'Ordinarily, we wouldn't release this as a matter of course; but the note – remarkably – is handwritten, and we believe it would be . . . helpful for the *Crucible* to publish a facsimile. In case anybody recognizes the writing.'

From the inside pocket of his jacket he produced a sheet of paper, unfolding it and handing it across the desk to her. It was a photocopy:

RAGE!
Who wants to be a millionaire?
I do!
Make me one.

'Not exactly explicit, is it?' she said.

'As I say,' said the detective, 'with the proviso that the codeword is blacked out, a copy of this is being made available for your use.'

'You still haven't told me why we can't publish the codeword.'

'Mr Bartholomew and his colleagues here at Urbopark are, naturally, concerned that any suggestion of a vendetta against the mall might be damaging to business . . .' He stilled her interruption with a raised hand. 'Personally, I couldn't give a flying fuck about their concerns.' He adjusted his tie, looking at Constance and Warren in turn. ''Scuse me, I used to play in the scrum for Pontefract.'

Shared laughter brought relief, a safety-valve releasing the tension which had accumulated over the preceding minutes. Warren caught her eye. She looked away. The detective, smiling self-consciously, placed a hand on the press officer's knee.

'No offence, Mr Bartholomew.'

'None taken.'

'Besides, the . . . ransom note, if that's what it is, makes such a consideration virtually academic.' Addressing Constance again, he added, 'My point is that *my* concern is professional rather than commercial. If you publish the codeword in your newspaper, my officers' investigations could be seriously compromised.'

'Copycat hoaxes?'

DCI Pink relaxed, extending an upturned palm as though implying her observation made any embellishment by him superfluous. Constance drew the keyboard towards her and called the story up on screen. After scanning the text, she swivelled her chair to bring the two men into view again beyond the monitor.

'I'm going to have to rejig the story anyway, to nose it off on the ransom note. But I can't keep out the vendetta angle. If anything,' she added, indicating the photcopy, 'this firms up the theory that the graffiti and the bomb hoax are the work of the same person, or group.'

Warren, who'd been fretting at his grazed wrist again, looked up. 'Came off a moped in Crete,' he said, catching the direction of her gaze. 'Itches like mad.'

Turning to DCI Pink, she said, 'We've already mentioned the word "rage" in the paper – three weeks ago, when we carried the graffiti story.'

'Can't be helped,' replied the inspector. 'What's imperative is that we – that is, you – don't make it public knowledge that this is the codeword. That has to be between us and . . . whoever is behind this.'

Constance nodded. 'OK, no "rage". But I don't see how making it public knowledge that the incidents are connected can interfere with your inquiries.'

He shrugged. 'As I say, my concern is purely a professional one.'

The flat finality of his tone suggested that, irrespective of what anyone else thought, a fair compromise had been struck. His features – impassive as ever – had softened sufficiently to hint at his satisfaction with the outcome of their discussion. He'd begun smoothing the few remaining wisps of hairs in the centre of his pate.

The press officer spread his hands. 'OK. OK, you're an independent newspaper, you have to cover stories as you see fit – without fear or favour, and so on. I accept that. Connie, I've served my time on local papers, as you know.'

'Yeah, I know.'

'What I'm asking is, play down any suggestion that these incidents might be the first of a series. You don't *know* they are. The police aren't saying that. Even the bloke who wrote the ransom note doesn't say it – not in as many words.'

Constance looked at him.

'You've still got your angle,' he said. ' "Million quid ransom demand", "police have reason to believe there is a connection . . . etc. etc.". Just go easy on the "madman with a vendetta who could strike again at any moment" line. Eh?'

The detective chief inspector did not leave the *Crucible* office with Warren, remaining behind to concoct a few quotes for Constance's article. As they talked, it occurred to her that he might be sporting pink socks, tie and handkerchief because his surname was Pink, and for no other reason. He struck her as the sort of man who would do that and not tell anyone, leaving them to puzzle it out for themselves or labour under a misapprehension. She closed her notebook and thanked him.

'Did you know Urbopark's monthly magazine is called

Arcadia?' He waited for her nod of affirmation before continuing: 'A play on the word "arcade", no doubt – as in "shopping arcade". But d'you know what Arcadia is, or rather was?' He answered his own question. 'Arkadia, with a "k", was a pastoral region of ancient Greece – the word, as we use it now, is taken to mean an . . . idealized rural area or a scene of simple pleasure and tranquillity. Next time you wander out into the mall, take a good look around and ask yourself: where's the Arcadian idyll in Urbopark?'

'You do crosswords, right?'

'It's a cliché, I know.'

DCI Pink removed the twist of paper from his pocket, unwrapped it and popped the piece of unfinished peppermint in his mouth.

'And the point of all this?'

'Off the record?'

'Wow, *two* clichés.'

He almost smiled. '*Not* for publication, I sense an Arcadia/ Urbopark contradiction here. A spot of graffiti; headless chickens; a hoax bomb warning; an obscure codeword the meaning of which eludes us, for now; an oddly worded handwritten note that may or may not be a ransom demand. Something and nothing. Summat and nowt. Well, it's the *summat* that interests me, being of a cryptic bent.'

'You think there's more to come?'

Paul Pink produced a calling card, placing it on the desk. 'That red cabbage is pathetic,' he said, indicating Constance's in-tray. 'I grow bigger and better cabbages than that on my allotment. Broad beans, carrots, Brussels, lettuce, onions, beetroot.' He tapped the calling card. 'Send your mother to me next time she's after vegetables.'

The Inky Path
The reporter is often dependent on information culled from eye-witnesses, those involved in an event or those dealing with its aftermath. An essential lesson for the young reporter is that

anything which is obtained in this second-hand fashion must be clearly attributed as such. 'Three shots were fired' may be a true statement or it may be false, but the reporter has no business uttering it unless he heard the shots for himself; whereas, 'a neighbour said she heard three shots being fired' is a true statement irrespective of whether or not three shots were fired. It is a paradox that, by taking a step back from certainty, the journalist moves closer towards veracity. Thus, the term 'story' – with its fictional connotations – becomes an appropriate description of a journalistic article of factual account. However, what the reporter comes to regard as his story is not his story at all but a composite of other people's accounts, assembled and edited by him. Without their stories he has none of his own to tell.

Sunday. Constance, who'd been floating on the periphery of consciousness, was finally and fully awoken by the sound of a church bell striking the hour. She counted the tolls. Nine. Or had she missed one or two? She yawned so widely her jaw clicked. Maybe it was ten. Her bedroom had a ten o'clock brightness to it; not sunny, but a garish morning that transformed her thin cotton curtains from gold to anaemic yellow. A neighbour was DIY-ing, the persistent drone of a drill reverberating through brick and wood. The drilling noise seemed lodged more deeply in her mind than her sudden awareness of it; perhaps it was this, rather than the church bell, which had woken her? She was lying on her right-hand side, as usual, but there was something about her position, as she came to, which was disorientating. Then she noticed the softness of pillow beneath her feet and the unyielding mattress under her head, the location of the window in relation to her angle of vision; reminders of another of her topsy-turvy attempts to defeat insomnia. *A retreat into the womb*, according to Howard. *You entered the world head first, you're escaping from it in the same way – trying to bury yourself in warmth and protection.* She'd related his theory to Milly, who'd dismissed it as a typical male fantasy about one female penetrating another. Whatever, it must've worked this time – she'd slept solidly for ten hours. Constance pushed the duvet away and lifted her head to squint at the digital radio-alarm on the bedside table, reaching with outstretched toes to nudge the clock-face towards her. The luminous red figures read 8.02. Shitting crap. *Eight o'clock.* Jesus. She let her head fall back heavily onto the bed. She'd never get back to sleep. Not now. Not now she'd woken up. Not with all that drilling going on next door.

Constance woke again at half past eleven. Her neck was stiff from where her head had been lolling over the end of the mattress; her feet were cold, the duvet having become partially dislodged. Puffy eyes, she could tell. Probably bloodshot. And she had half an hour to get showered and dressed and drive over to Huxworth for Sunday dinner. Nice leg of lamb, Mam had said. Sauce made with freshly picked mint from the garden. *Your father's garden.* Granddad would be there, but not Mags, who'd rung – using Mam's latest relief parcel of 20p pieces – to say she was going potholing with her university mates. Potholing. Certain death, to Mam's mind; or disappearance in some dank, pitch-black subterranean labyrinth – search parties, Mags trapped and barely alive beneath collapsed rock, Mam weeping at the mouth of a cave. Constance stretched, spilling the duvet altogether from the bed. Cool air on her skin. Hallam exerted no hold over Mags. 'Home', to her, was wherever she happened to be living at the time. *You're the homing pigeon of the family*, Mam liked to remind Constance. Mam this, Mam that. Howard called his mam 'Mum'. *A Hallam lass, through and through.* Yes, Mam. But hers was a different Hallam. When Stanley Bell talked of the city's history, when Dad and Granddad reminisced about their years in the steelworks, she felt herself to be an observer, an outsider. Journalist, white-collar worker; one of the new professional classes descended from the men and women of the factory age.

Where did all the words come from, in your head?

Sometimes your head just filled up with words and you'd no idea where they came from or where they went to, because they weren't there when you tried to speak them or write them down. And they *sounded* better – eloquent, coherent, articulate, sensible – when they were in your head; there wasn't anyone to contradict you, to make you sound foolish. Constance yawned, rolled over on to her stomach. Have to hurry. She didn't want to work *in industry*, she wanted to be an *industrial correspondent*. Industry was an abstract concept, something you wrote or read or heard about. Something that didn't happen much any more, and when it did it was done by other people. This wasn't true. You were always being reminded that Hallam produced more steel today than it ever had done in its heyday; only, fewer people were employed to do it. Which was why you lost any *sense* of it still happening. Factories were buildings you drove past, not really knowing what went on inside. Words again . . . Because, her Hallam was not that of the producer but the consumer; the *service sector*: shops, offices, restaurants. What had she ever produced that would last beyond the lifespan of a daily newspaper?

She drove away from the house. At the crest of a steep incline was the church whose bell may or may not have woken her, the first time, that morning. A hoarding displayed the words in blue capitals: GIVE YOUR LIFE TO JESUS AND YOU SHALL LIVE FOR EVE . The last letter had been obliterated by white spray paint. Constance smiled at the notion that even the word 'ever' didn't last for ever.

'What did you think o'them roast potatoes, duckie?'
  'Fine. I mean, they were nice. Crispy.'
  'They were from that Mr Pink's allotment.'
  'Chief Inspector Pink?'
  'Aye, that's him.'
  'You actually asked him for some vegetables?'
  'He said I should.'

'*Mam.*'

'He gave you his card.'

'But I never gave the card to *you*. It was just a throwaway remark, about the vegetables. His idea of a joke. The reason he gave me the card was so I could keep in touch with him about the Urbopark investigation.'

'Well, I rang him anyroad and he said he'd be delighted to let me have some potatoes. *Only too pleased, Mrs Amory*, that were what he said.'

'You rang him? Where?'

'He brought them round.'

'I don't believe this.'

'Onions an' all, and some plum jam his wife had made. Christina, she's called. They live over at—'

'Mam, where was he when you rang him?'

'At work.'

'The police station? Please don't tell me you dialled 999?'

'That's uniform, duckie; he's plain clothes. You ought to know that, being a reporter.'

'Jesus, Mam.'

'I looked t'number up in t'book, if you must know.'

'And he didn't mind?'

'Very nice man. Your dad's doing his gutters for him a week next Monday.'

They were washing up, Mrs Amory at the sink while Constance dried. Dad and Granddad were in the front room watching football, only the newly installed satellite dish was playing up and Dad had spent most of the match at the top of a ladder. *Tinkering*, Mam called it. Every now and then they'd hear Granddad call out: *Aye, that's it, you've got it now . . . no, it's gone again.* Through the kitchen window, Constance watched a chaffinch perch on the branch of an apple tree which stood in her parents' small, rectangular garden. The lawn was bordered by narrow flower-beds and enclosed by a wooden fence overgrown with cotoneaster. *Poor man's holly*, Mam called it, though the leaves would be gone by Christmas and

96

the fruit faded to dull orange. The chaffinch appeared to be scrutinizing Constance, its head twitching from side to side. A plate clinked against another in the draining rack and the bird flew off. Constance remembered when the tree was just a thin willowy thing, planted in the place where a gnarled old plum tree had stood before being rotted by disease. She'd have been eight or nine when Dad uprooted it, leaving a rich black crater alive with bugs and worms. He'd brought her and Mags indoors to watch from this same window as birds came to pick over the newly exposed soil.

'Heard from that Harold chap lately?'

'*Howard.* We see each other at work now and again. Nothing more.'

'That's a shame.'

'Yeah, well. And before you ask, no there isn't anyone else at the moment.'

Mrs Amory gave one of her sighs: *pardon me for asking*, combined with *you and your menfolk troubles – I don't know, I'm sure.* As soon as the washing-up was done, Mam made a pot of tea and poured two cups and two mugs. Handing the mugs to Constance, she asked her to *fetch them through to those two lummoxes.* Granddad was in front of the telly, Dad was outside again – being obscene to the satellite dish. She stood at the foot of the ladder, shielding her eyes as she looked up.

'Tea up!'

'Good timing, lass – I need a second pair of 'ands.'

'What?'

'All you've to do is cop 'old o' this a minute.'

'Up *there*?'

'Aye, just while I tighten t'bolts on this bracket.'

'D'you want me to fetch Granddad?'

'Oh aye, your mother'd love that.'

Constance put the mug down. She gripped the sides of the ladder, eyes fixed on her feet as she stepped painstakingly from one rung to the next. The ladder was made of aluminium.

It creaked as she climbed, flexing with her weight and chinking against the point of contact with the wall. Jesus. Halfway up, her legs jellified and she knew that if she let go with any of her hands or feet she'd plummet headlong onto the crazy paving that seemed to lurch beneath her like the deck of a ship.

'I can't do this.'

'You've only another—'

'*Dad!* Please, just get me down.'

'Aye. Aye, all reet, 'old up.'

'Don't!'

'How can I get you down if I've not to step on t'bloody ladder?'

'It's all right. I'll manage by myself. Just don't come down.'

One foot, then the other. One hand, then the other. At last, she felt the ground solid beneath her feet. Her heel jogged Dad's mug, spilling tea everywhere.

The two women were in the dining room – Constance flicking through the Sunday paper, while Mrs Amory continued with a partially completed jigsaw puzzle that spread across the table and had caused the family to eat in the kitchen to avoid disturbing the pieces. She had the lid of the box propped up on a metal stand designed to hold a recipe book. The picture was a Monet; 500 pieces. Mam liked nice pictures. She hated too much sky or trees. Her puzzle collection, an extensive one, consisted entirely of Impressionist prints which – when completed – she would fix into place with a sheet of adhesive plastic film and insert into a clip-frame. Each room in the house, including the bathroom, boasted jigsaw puzzles; the hallway, stairs and landing were similarly adorned. If you stood close enough, or when the light was at a certain angle, you could make out the interlocking pattern of individual pieces. Otherwise, it was difficult to tell the puzzle apart from an ordinary print.

'If you like the paintings so much why don't you just buy

prints and have done with?' Constance had asked her, in the early days of Mam's fixation.

'They'd not be mine, would they?' Mrs Amory had replied.

'These aren't yours either.'

'They're *mine*. I made them.'

'But it's not like you actually *painted* them or anything.'

She'd taken up jigsaws after Dr Singh suggested a hobby might distract her from the compulsion to shop. An unfortunate consequence being that, unless the puzzles were presented to her as gifts, she had to go out to the shops to buy them – exposing her to fresh temptation. Moreover, this new pastime was a bone of contention between Mam and Dad. Disruption to Sunday dinners apart, his prime source of annoyance was her habitual description of them as 'jigsaws'.

'They're jigsaw *puzzles*,' he would insist. 'A jigsaw is a machine for cutting patterns in wood.'

Her reply, typically, would be: 'If *I* know what I mean, and *you* know what I mean – then there's nowt to argue about.'

Constance put the newspaper aside and picked up the previous day's *Crucible*, idly turning the pages. There was a piece by William Boyce about a threatened reduction in council funding for the Hallam Island Heritage Centre – a museum dedicated to the city's industrial history. Her granddad, who worked there part-time in the admissions kiosk and as a tour guide, had taken up most of the dinner-time conversation with talk of the centre's uncertain future. *First they close t'factories, then they close t'pretend factories. There'll be nowt left soon.* It had been his tip-off to Constance – passed on in turn to William – which had brought the story to light. Not that these reciprocal favours between reporters were always so fruitful. The *Crucible*'s crime correspondent had spent the previous week trying to confirm Constance's information that the CCTV cameras at Urbopark were dummies. But his discreet approaches (beer, curry) to police contacts had drawn a blank. All he'd managed to unearth was further rumour – that the cameras *were* dummies, and that senior police officers were furious with Mall Secure for failing to invest in adequate security monitoring. But a deal had been struck: the absence of CCTV at the mall would be kept from public knowledge provided a working system was installed as soon as possible. None of this was on the record, no-one would be quoted; and the editor wasn't prepared to rely on hearsay and unsubstantiated, unattributable tips from a disgruntled Mall Secure union official and a couple of drunken coppers.

Even Constance's newfound ally and supplier of potatoes to the Amory family – DCI Paul Pink – had declined to be of assistance. *The positive approach*, he'd told her, *is to focus our energies on the facts we do have rather than those we don't*. Fact: no film evidence of the graffiti attack. *Can't be helped*. The detective had then proceeded – strictly not for publication – to outline various hypotheses: 1 – the cameras were dummies, the vandal knew this; 2 – the cameras were dummies, the vandal didn't know this. If No.2 was the case, then: a) the vandal's disguise was sufficient to make cameras irrelevant; b) the vandal was reckless about being captured on film; or c) the vandal hadn't considered the possibility of cameras, and had got away with it. However, if hypothesis No.1 was the case, then the vandal was privy to security information which wasn't widely known within the mall. *An inside job, you think?* Constance had asked. *It's just one hypothesis*. His tone of voice had implied, it seemed to her, that she'd been foolish to seek conclusions at a stage of an investigation when you ought to be content merely to accumulate random scraps of information.

The newspaper lay open on her lap, neglected. She gathered it up and resumed browsing, turning to the classified section. Sunday dinner had made her sleepy, and she yawned as she scanned the columns of Lonely Hearts. How did people compose these? *Insecure jowly-faced asthmatic scatterbrained*

chocoholic redhead, 25, seeks man who will love her for herself.
Another yawn. She turned to the pages of second-hand cars,
wondering if she could afford to replace Fifi. The room
was soporifically still, only muffled football commentary and
an occasional snap as her mam pressed a piece of jigsaw
into place. Mam never spoke while she was *puzzling*, nor
could you speak to her. In the category of social *faux pas*,
interrupting her in the middle of a jigsaw session ranked
second only to phoning during *Coronation Street*.

The Saturday edition of the *Crucible* was crap, Constance
decided. Fewer pages, fewer decent stories, fewer ads. She was
on the point of closing the paper and settling in her chair for
a snooze when her attention was arrested by a small notice
– set in a decoratively bordered display box – in the In
Memoriam section:

> HYDE, Constance – dearly beloved of
> W.B. Nothing shall destroy the memory.
> 'Rage, rage against the dying of the light.'

The Life and Times of a
Hallam Saw Grinder
(a Dramatic Reconstruction in Many Parts)

Royal Commission of Inquiry
(sitting at) Hallam Town Hall
Wednesday, 19 June 1867 (Twelfth Day)

Witness: Elizabeth Linley (Mrs), widow, No.42 Norwich Street, Hallam.

Q. Your husband was a saw grinder by trade, was he not?

A. James was a scissor grinder, then a saw grinder.

Q. In which was he apprenticed?

A. Scissors.

Q. While he was employed at saw grinding was he ever rattened, to your knowledge?

A. He was.

Q. How came you to know of this?

A. He told me.

Q. Was he rattened more than one time?

A. He was, many times.

Q. He told you so?

A. Yes.

Q. When his bands were taken, would he apply to the police for their recovery?

A. He would not.

Q. Why was that?

A. He dared not.

Q. Why dared he not?

A. In consequence of being worse off if he had.

Q. What do you mean by that?

A. He should either have been rolled up again, or have been done himself.

Q. What did he expect would be done to him?

A. I do not know.

Q. He did not tell you?
A. No.

November 1857

Boro' Bridge, at first light on a Sunday morning. Samuel
Crookes was wearing a long overcoat to conceal the air rifle
which, Thomas knew, he carried in a home-made harness
fashioned from lengths of twine. His straight brown hair,
normally hanging in unkempt strands about his ears and over
his eyebrows, had been slicked back beneath his cap; the pale
expanse of forehead lending his face an even more ghostly
complexion than was usual. The two men greeted one another
then lapsed into a silence which remained unbroken as they
made their way past the locked wrought-iron gates of the coal
depot and along Nursery Street. If their mood had not been
so sombre, the pair would have cut a comic spectacle – the
taller striding forth, the shorter skipping beside him in a gait
made the more peculiar by a necessary accommodation of the
rifle. The streets were deserted at this hour, the manufactories
and workshops ranged along the opposite bank lay dormant.
Even the river, muddied and swollen by recent rainfall,
appeared sluggish. The sky made a vast slate bank that seeped
into yellowy pink above the imposing arches of the Wicker
viaduct, just visible over the rooftops to the east.

Thomas had told Frances he was going to the allotment, and
was dressed, therefore, in work clothes rather than Sunday
best. His trips to the Society gardens were frequent enough,
even on the cusp of winter, not to arouse suspicion. And she
had said not a word to suggest that she doubted the explanation of his whereabouts, nor had her face betrayed any distrust.
Indeed, she had fed him his breakfast at an earlier hour than
was their custom on a holy day and had helped him to ready
himself. Not that the Amory household observed the sabbath
in the manner that some of their Christian neighbours might
wish, but – as Thomas liked to remark – it did not do to cause

103

offence to others' faith by rising too early of a Sunday morning. No, he was sure she had not suspected him. His actions were accountable – a prompt start was necessary, at this time of year, if a gardening man was to make the most of the daylight – and he had been careful to speak and behave ordinarily. If he was troubled by guilt, it was of his own making. Nor did it arise from the crime he and Sammy were about to perpetrate. Doubtless there would be many who disapproved of such acts; but, for Thomas, by far the worst of his misdemeanours this day – and one for which he would willingly submit to harsher judgement – was the deceiving of his wife. He would have to take care to muddy his boots and hands before returning home.

As they neared their destination, Sammy steered Thomas into a snicket which afforded an oblique view across the road to the front of Linley's house. Good range: six, perhaps eight, yards. The other man knew what he was about where shooting was concerned, assuming a confident authority that made his fellows deferential where, in other circumstances, they might not have been. Thomas listened to the whispered instructions without comment. Sammy's breath, as he leaned close, reeked of raw onion and chewing tobacco. Thomas waited for him to finish, then turned away and approached the house in long, easy strides. His footsteps alarmed him as he crossed the street, each strike of wooden sole against cobble resounding in the quiet of the after-dawn. He imagined his accomplice, behind him in the mouth of the passage, unhooking the rifle from inside his overcoat and slotting a pellet into the breech.

Witness: Frances Amory (Mrs), No.11 Garden Street, Hallam.

Q. Did you know of other punishment meted out to men who would not be brought to heel by having their grindstones rattened?

A. I heard tell of such things.

Q. Of what did you hear tell?

104

A. A woman in our neighbourhood saw her husband burnt.

Q. How so, burnt?

A. They put powder in his trough.

Q. Powder?

A. Gunpowder. That is what she said.

Q. Where did this take place?

A. At the Tower Wheel, I believe.

Q. And what was the effect of putting gunpowder in a man's trough?

A. When he started up his stone, the sparks from his grinding would explode the powder.

Q. With what consequence for the man?

A. This woman, she said they fetched him home black all over with his hair singed off and his face and his bosom burnt. He was blinded, too, I believe.

Q. He lost his sight?

A. For a time.

Q. Did you see this for yourself?

A. I did not. I only heard of it from the man's wife.

Q. Of what other things did you hear tell?

A. I cannot say.

Q. Did you hear of men being shot at?

(*witness does not respond*)

Q. Was it a view, commonly held by all decent folk, that a man who was blown up at his trough had his deserts?

A. I cannot say.

Q. Or that a man who was shot at got his deserts?

A. I cannot say.

James Linley's house occupied the middle of a short terrace of brick-built back-to-backs giving directly onto the pavement. The red paint of his front door had faded to mottled pink, flaking in places to reveal irregular patches of bare wood. The knocker, in the style of a horseshoe, was made of cast iron. No lights showed at the edges of the brown curtains drawn across the upper and lower windows. Thomas rubbed

105

a palm across the bottom half of his face, which was smooth and smelled of shaving soap. He had nicked himself in several places that morning and the base of his middle finger came away moist where he had reopened one of the cuts. He glanced along the road in both directions. Somewhere, a horse was drawing a cart – a distant clash of hooves and rumble of wooden wheels reverberating off the cobbles. Thomas inhaled deeply, raised the knocker and clapped it three times against the door. The noise seemed disproportionately loud and, for a moment, he envisaged half the occupants of the terrace being roused by it and peering out of their windows to discover its cause. On the third knock, he stepped back from the door without further ado and strode along the pavement, turning at the corner into Joiner Street. Sammy had told him to depart without delay but under no circumstances was he to run; he was to walk away and to keep walking. Shortly after the turning, the sound carried to him of a door shuddering against its frame; the creak of unoiled hinges and the rattle of a stubborn latch reminded him of his own front door. There were no footsteps – Linley would be barefoot or in nightsocks – but Thomas pictured him emerging onto his front step, puzzled to discover no caller. He would be standing in the doorway, hands on hips, hair ruffled and face baggy with disturbed sleep. He would be looking right and left, right and left, along the street; it would not occur to him to direct his gaze to the shadowy mouth of the snicket across the way.

Thomas was turning into Nursery Lane when he heard the shot. A harsh crack – louder than the report the rifle made when they used to hunt in the woods, where trees and the soft earth blunted any sudden sounds. The sharp snap, here, was amplified by the blank walls of the buildings; its echo pursuing him. He began to run, then checked himself, slowing once more to a brisk walking pace. He regulated his breathing. If Linley gave a cry, Thomas did not hear it. Nor did he hear Sammy's footsteps as he escaped along the snicket. By the time Linley's wife reacted to the commotion and hurried downstairs to investigate, the pair would be far removed from the scene. Two men innocently abroad of a Sunday morning, their separate and diverging paths carrying them deeper into the maze of narrow streets where an occasional passer-by nodded good morning and walked on without giving his fellow pedestrian a second thought. Mrs Linley, meanwhile, would be stooped over her husband as he sat slumped, Thomas imagined, against the door jamb. Neighbours, in various states of undress, would have gathered to enquire into what had occurred, and to offer assistance. No doubt one of them, or one of the Linley children, would have been dispatched on foot to fetch a doctor. Linley, dazed and in great discomfort, would be spattered with his own blood; clutching a hand over a wound to his right arm, just beneath the shoulder. For their instruction, Sammy had said, was to 'injure and incapacitate'. And if Samuel Crookes – able to pick off a moving rabbit at twenty paces – took aim at a man's upper arm, then that was where the pellet would strike.

Chapter Four

SHOP TALK

When the first British supermarkets opened in the 1950s, it was believed they induced a state of hypnotic trance in customers – many of whom would bump into things and pass by friends without noticing them. The eye-blink rate was found to fall from a normal 32 per minute to 14, rising again only at the checkout. The studies of the day concluded that this was a result of bewildered wonderment at the array of produce on offer. Current thinking, however, is that 'shopping hypnosis' is caused by boredom.

> *I Shop, Therefore I Am: Essays in Mall Culture*
> eds. Jeremy Nicholls and Barbara Cutteslowe
> (Hallam Metropolitan University Press, 1991)

The police were busy at Red Leather, Yellow Leather – a shop named after a popular tongue-twister and located, with ill-regard for colour co-ordination, in Blue Upper. When the eyewitnesses' statements had been taken, Constance and Howard were permitted to talk to them and to take photographs. Three people claimed to have seen the man responsible for the damage. One customer said she'd observed him *holding a shoulder bag in a funny way and running his hand up and down the side, like this.* She demonstrated. At the time, she'd assumed him to be testing the zip, or something; whatever, she hadn't thought anything of it until a few minutes later when the alarm was raised. When Constance asked if the woman was certain any of the damaged bags was the one she'd seen the man handling, she replied, *Well, it must of been, mustn't it?* The second witness was a young male sales assistant who'd seen someone *acting suspiciously* behind a display of leather overcoats. He'd been about to investigate, when he was distracted by another customer. Subsequently, several coats on the rail where the suspect had been loitering were found to have been vandalized. He gave an extraordinarily comprehensive description. *Part of our training, that, memorizing folk.* At which point he shut his eyes and reeled off a description of Constance that was accurate in every detail. A third witness had been walking past the shop when a man – emerging in a hurry – collided with her before making off towards the Blue car-park. *No apology or owt.* Her description of the suspect was at variance in several key respects with that of the sales assistant, and that of the first eyewitness.

Constance rejoined DCI Pink in the shop manager's office, which had been made temporarily available for his use. He was sitting at a desk, staring into space; a sequence of moist clicking noises testified to the sucking of what she assumed to be an Extra Strong Mint. Seeing her in the doorway, he broke off from whatever train of thought he'd been pursuing and stood up.

'Get what you wanted?' he asked.

When they compared notes, she discovered that the eyewitness accounts she'd recorded not only conflicted with each other but contradicted those the same three people had given the police just moments earlier.

'We get this all the time,' said the detective. 'People don't register things. The more they try to remember what they've seen, the more . . . distorted it becomes. Ten people see the same incident, you'll have ten different versions of what happened.'

'Who'd be an investigator?'

Without reciprocating her smile, DCI Pink continued: 'Eyewitness Syndrome, I call it. The three 'E's: Error, Embellishment and Exaggeration.'

Constance recounted a piece she'd written about a lad who helped a mother rescue her baby from a car that caught fire in one of the mall car-parks. *It were nowt really . . . anyone'd do t'same as what I done . . . tha dunt really think about t'danger, like . . .* The *Crucible* ran the story that afternoon. In the evening, on regional television news, the same lad adopted the role of have-a-go hero: *I thought I were gonna die, but I knew I'd to put missen at risk to save that little baby.*

The inspector nodded. 'And when you went to work the next day your editor wanted to know why *you* hadn't got those quotes.'

'Major bollocking.'

'Who'd be a reporter?'

Constance laughed. DCI Pink had moved over to the door, looking out into the shop – closed while staff assisted police in making sure all the vandalized stock was identified and removed from display, ready for forensic examination. She stood beside him, watching them at work. The manager was outside – she could see him through the glass frontage, posing for Howard. Noticing the security cameras mounted at strategic points around the store, she directed the detective's attention to them.

'Anything on film?'

He coughed, raising his hand to his mouth.

Constance looked at him. 'Jesus, is every camera in Urbopark a dummy?'

DCI Pink didn't say anything.

'So all you've got is three inconsistent and unreliable eyewitness accounts.'

'Aye.'

'What about the sales assistant? He seemed pretty clued up on memorizing people's descriptions – more reliable than the other two, anyway.'

The detective lowered his voice. 'The manager tells me the lad went on a crime-in-shops awareness course last week. Since then, he's . . . challenged eighteen customers on suspicion of shoplifting. Not *one* of whom was found to have any stolen items in their possession.'

They went back out into the store. Showing her some of the vandalized stock, DCI Pink indicated the small, ragged capitals cut crudely into the leather with evident haste. The enclosed parts of the letters – the semicircle in the upper half of the 'R' and the triangular segment of the 'A' – were missing, the small scraps of material having peeled off. With the fur garments, the damage had been done to the linings.

'I wanted to thank you for the tip-off,' Constance said, looking up from her notes. 'We wouldn't have picked this up in time for city final if you hadn't phoned.'

The inspector seemed embarrassed by her expression of gratitude, relieved to step aside so she could interview the newly returned shop manager. Pictures taken, Howard departed for head office. The manager ushered Constance out of the way of the police officers who had begun to carry the damaged goods outside. As they talked, her gaze fell on a promotional slogan on the wall above a rail of heavyweight jackets:

> **When it's so cold you have to hide your tan,**
> **Why not let us tan your hide?**
> **Get leathered this winter at Red Leather,**
> **Yellow Leather**

She caught up with DCI Pink in the Blue Upper arcade. They stood a couple of feet apart, forced into close proximity by the press of shoppers passing by on either side. His bald pate was luminous with the glare from a neon-lit shopfront, lending his face a waxy pallor. The chunky mobile phone he held in one hand appeared as small as a calculator in his banana-clump of fingers. How did he dial without hitting more than one number at a time? She was breathless from running after him, made awkward by his perplexed reaction at finding her by his side in the throng of the mall. He asked what was the matter. She told him about the In Memoriam advert in the previous Saturday's *Crucible*, with its dedication to Constance Hyde.

Police probe animal rights link after latest mall attack

by Constance Amory

Police say hard-line animal rights activists may be behind the spate of vandalism at Hallam's giant Urbopark shopping mall.

In the latest attack, goods worth £10,000 were slashed by a man wielding a razor at Red Leather, Yellow Leather – a fashion boutique selling leather and furs.

The incident, at around midday today, is believed by detectives to have followed a cryptic message containing a codeword used in connection with previous attacks. Details of the warning have not been released.

Skip

It comes less than a month after blood-red graffiti was daubed over entrances to the mall, including the HypaCenta foodhall where veal recently went on sale – a traditional target for animal welfare protests.

Other incidents since then have included the gruesome discovery of more than 100 headless chicken carcasses in a skip outside HypaCenta and a bomb hoax which caused Urbopark to be evacuated. There has also been a coded ransom demand for £1 million to Mall Admin.

No individual or group has claimed responsibility, but Det. Ch. Insp. Paul Pink of Hallam CID believes the attacks are linked.

Staff

He said he was 'keeping an open mind' on the involvement of animal rights extremists.

'This is just one of a number of lines of inquiry we are pursuing and I'm certainly not ruling anything out at this stage,' he said.

Staff and customers at Red Leather, Yellow Leather have been helping police compile a detailed description of the man suspected of

turn to page three

Constance swore down the phone at Gary, her news editor. She called him a shit. *Connie, Con . . . Don't you Con me.* She itemized her grievances: 1 – police did not say animal rights extremists may be behind the vandalism, they said they may or may not be – which wasn't the same thing at all (*Splitting hairs, Connie*); 2 – it was stated, as a fact, that a man was 'wielding' a razor – no-one *saw* that razor, all the police said was that damage was consistent with having been caused by a razor-type implement; 3 – Red Leather, Yellow Leather sold *faux* furs, not furs (*Those hairs again, Con*); 4 – she'd mentioned the veal angle in a background briefing to news-desk, there was no reference to it in her original copy (*Fair point*); 5 – DCI Pink believed *some* of the incidents were linked, not necessarily *all* of them. Gary blamed the subs. Nothing to do with him. Anyway, the story – the essential substance of the story – stood up. Maybe not accurate in every minor detail, but a *fair account* nevertheless – taken as a whole. Cracking good yarn, actually. If she'd done a decent job in the first place, he added, the subs wouldn't have needed to tickle her copy.

The irregularly shaped finger of land known as Hallam Island was not an island in the strict sense of the word, being bounded on only its longest sides by water – a river, and a man-made cut. Alma Street and Corporation Street provided the other boundaries, their junction defining the island's tapering point. In the nineteenth century this area was thronged with steel-works, rolling mills and blocks of craftsmen's and toolmakers' workshops (commonly referred to as 'Wheels'). Today, its chief feature was an industrial museum – the neighbour-ing streets forming an officially designated 'tourist trail' the route of which was plotted on glossy leaflets, informatively annotated. On the one-way system skirting the city centre, the turning to the island was indicated by a brown-and-cream sign of the kind employed to draw daytrippers' attention to historic ruins, ancient monuments, theme parks and stately homes. A coach, carrying a party of school children, followed this turning into Alma Street and onto the 'island' proper before entering the large cobbled courtyard which served as a car-park for a cluster of red-brick buildings – Hallam Island Heritage Centre. Behind the coach came a white Ford Fiesta 1.1 with poor bodywork and the word 'Fifi' finger-written on its dusty bonnet. The dot above each 'i' in Fifi was an open circle. The car's flame-haired driver parked, climbed out, let herself back in, got out again and approached a wooden kiosk. The kiosk had a square window made up of sliding glass panels, one of which displayed a notice listing the museum's admission prices and opening times. The other panel was open, a man in black uniform with red trim was seated at a high stool inside the hut, leaning forward slightly so that, in profile, the only parts of him protruding from the window were his nose – veined, bulbous – and the shiny peak of his cap.

Fred Amory looked pale, Constance thought. The hammocks of flesh beneath his eyes bore a blueish tint and the creased skin of his cheeks and forehead was the colour of dirty snow. *Face like an unmade bed*, as he habitually described it. His eyes, watery and slightly bloodshot, became animated on registering her presence.

'Thought I recognized your car, ducks.'

' 'Lo, Granddad.' She decided against leaning in through the window to kiss him. Children were disembarking noisily from their coach and, despite his expression of affection, the uniformed figure – *on sentry duty* – was a discouragement to informality.

He checked his watch. 'I'll not get me break while afe one.'

'I know, sorry.'

Constance stepped aside for one of the teachers with the school group. He purchased a block of tickets and strode back towards the children, his voice echoing in the courtyard as he ushered them through the museum entrance, arms spread wide like a shepherd steering sheep into a pen. When they'd gone, Granddad winked at her.

114

'I'll 'ave that kiss now!'

She pressed her lips against his cheek, inhaling a sharp scent of aftershave lotion and hair oil. His breath was briny from his lifelong habit, she knew, of brushing his teeth with salt instead of toothpaste. Say what you like about scratching the enamel, at sixty-four years old he still possessed a full head of teeth and hadn't sat in a dentist's chair since 1989. As they kissed, the peak of his cap nudged her hair so that – when they withdrew – his hat was tilted back at a jaunty angle. He made no move to adjust it. With the press of a button on the kiosk's stainless steel counter, a salmon-pink ticket was dispensed with a metallic chunk through a slot. He handed it to her.

'Here, 'ave a potter around and I'll see thee in t'cafetiere in twenty minutes.'

Constance smiled. 'OK, see you in a bit.'

Cafetiere. If Mags was here she'd correct him. *It's a cafeteria, Granddad; a cafetière's something you make coffee in.* Constance let it go, given less easily than her sister to exasperation with the idiosyncrasies of older relations. Except where Mam was concerned. She went through a double set of glass doors into the museum, meandering aimlessly among the exhibits and display boards. Glass cases of tools, cutlery and mechanical components; enlarged photographs and drawings of industrial landscapes, bewhiskered entrepreneurs; lifesize models of men at work: grinding, forging, smelting; noisy, clattering machinery with its smell of hot metal and engine oil; white panels of neat black text; video screens with their background burble of narrator's voice, of tinny taped music. Constance browsed with the disinterest of familiarity, killing time. The heritage centre held few surprises for her. Apart from occasional lunch dates with her granddad, she'd been there twice before – once, aged thirteen, as a bored school pupil and again two months ago. During the more recent visit she'd spent an entire day filling a notebook with jottings, coming away laden with books and pamphlets from the souvenir shop. Part of the strategy to succeed William Boyce when he retired. To be a specialist correspondent, he'd advised, you must acquire a certain expertise in your chosen field. He'd also warned her that, traditionally, industry was not regarded as an appropriate speciality for female reporters. The editor would expect her to go for health or education, *summat soft like that.* Constance became an industry buff – honing her newfound knowledge on Dad and Granddad, amusing and infuriating them by turns with her tendency to lecture them about the work to which they'd devoted most of their adult lives. Granddad, deadpan but with a mischievous glimmer in his eyes, would typically interrupt her with: *D'you know, I never realized how bloody* complicated *my job was.*

A rowdy group of schoolboys found its way into the section of the museum where Constance had wandered. She sought refuge in a quieter alcove where the essentials of Hallamshire's industrial past were arranged about the walls in words and illustrations. She scanned a potted history of the Company of Cutlers (founded in 1624) then moved along the display, travelling in the contrary direction to the arrows that guided visitors chronologically from panel to panel. As she stepped from seventeenth century to sixteenth, her eyes alighted on a quotation which she remembered noting down during her previous visit:

> Women's wittes are like Hallam knives, for they are sometimes so keen as they will cutte a hair and sometimes so blunt that they must goe to the grindstone.
>
> The Cobbler of Canterbury, 1590

She checked the time: one-thirty. One twenty-eight, actually; her watch was fast – a trick she'd learnt from *The Inky Path*, which advised that the good journalist, by deliberately setting his timepiece a couple of minutes fast, would never be late for an appointment nor miss a deadline. Turning away from the Cobbler of Canterbury, she retraced her steps through the museum and made her way to the cafeteria. A pot of tea for two, two plates of assorted sandwiches, a Danish pastry for Granddad and a Snickers bar for herself. *Make that two*, she said, smiling at the serving assistant.

'D'you miss working?'

'I'm working now. What d'you think this is, voluntary work?'

'I mean before. The steelworks.'

'Long time ago, that. Many moons.'

'Yeah . . . but, you know.'

'All changed, anyroad, what's left on it. *High tech*. No place for t'likes of me.'

'What about your mates, the men you worked with?'

'I still see some on 'em, down at t'club, like. Not the same, though, when you're not working together. Summat goes.'

They'd finished lunch, crockery and cutlery lay strewn about the formica-topped table. Granddad was smoking a Woodbine, holding the cigarette away from the table between puffs and aiming each exhalation of smoke ceilingwards, in deference to Constance. She finished her second Snickers, crumpling the wrapper into an empty teacup. The cafeteria was less busy now. The waitresses' pink-and-white check uniforms clashed horribly with the bright yellow decor, a scheme of buttercup and daffodil that gave the room a sunny, spring-like ambience even in the grey of autumn.

'Know what I remember most?' Granddad answered his own question, indicating the glass ashtray into which he'd tapped another speckled silvery turd from the tip of his cigarette. 'That stuff.'

'Ash?'

'Up to our bloody ankles in it afe the time. Dust, mostly, I s'pose – from t'insulation tiles. And the air were always thick wi' smoke an' that. It'd all settle on t'floor, this deep.' He held his hand flat, six inches above the surface of the table. 'Like walking through snow – only dry, like.'

'Didn't anyone ever clean up?'

117

'Oh aye, there were a gang of lads on overtime. They'd sweep it out once a week, but wi'in a few days tha'd be up to thy ankles again. Get through a pair o' boots in a fortnight.' He grinned. 'I don't bloody miss that!'

Constance dabbed at her mouth, leaving a smudge of chocolate on the serviette. Her granddad – she knew, because he'd told her often enough – had been a steelworker for more than thirty years. *Even t'Great Train Robbers never got that long.* Five quid a week, when he started; 'pit' labourer – general dogsbody – working with a gang whose job was to clean out the moulds ready for casting. Later, he became a charge-wheeler in the blast furnace, then a trainee foreman, finally ending up as shift supervisor. *Owt were better than working pit-side.*

'Where was it you worked?' she asked, tracing a pattern with her finger in a puddle of spilt tea. She knew the answer as well as he by now; she also knew he was glad to be offered an excuse to reminisce, however contrived. 'Browning's, wasn't it?'

'Browning and Greene, aye. Out on Leeds Road to start wi', then moved ower to t'East Winsley site, next to t'motorway – you know, wheer *you* are now. Same company, like, only it'd been taken ower by Bayfield's.'

She nodded towards the museum. 'As in Robert Bayfield, steel entrepreneur?'

'*Sir* Robert, aye – only he were long dead bi'then. I were on eight grand per annual by t'time I were made redundant. Good money, that, in them days.' He took a last drag on the Woodbine, crushing its glowing tip between thumb and finger and dropping the buckled stub into the ashtray. He laughed. 'Come to think on it, I'm not getting that now!'

Per annual. She'd have to remember that one for Mags. The thing she'd begun to notice about Granddad's anecdotes, was that – increasingly – he would interweave phrases and details she recognized from the heritage centre's exhibition material. It was as though, in his years as a tour guide, he'd assimilated

118

so much of the 'official' history he could no longer differentiate between his own memories and those of historians and other steelworkers whose words were enshrined among the displays. She'd heard it said that your mind tended to shrink as you grew older, but Granddad's was expanding to accommodate other pasts as well as his own. He was no longer Fred Amory, ex-steelworker; he was transformed into a clichéd composite of every Hallam steelworker there'd ever been. Crap, as per. He was just *Granddad*, in a memory muddle. *Bein' intellectual int the same as bein' intelligent*, he was fond of saying, whenever someone came out with a long word or a *university notion*. And, with a contemptuous sniff, he'd add: *Most o' them boffin-types couldn't find their backside wi' both 'ands*.

She glanced at the clock on the wall behind the serving counter. Time to go. For half an hour, at least, work – her own work – had been nudged to the edges of her mind while she and Granddad chatted: family gossip, the funding crisis at the museum, Granddad's bad back, Hallam United's latest defeat (the decisive goal described with the aid of salt and pepper pots, a plastic bottle of tomato ketchup and a sugar cube). There'd been a polite inquiry into how her job was going, followed by one of his well-worn jibes at out-of-town shopping complexes in general and Urbopark in particular. It was his proud boast that he must be the only Hallamite not to have visited the mall in all the years it had been open. *I'd sooner watch City than go to that bloody place*. They stood up, Constance assembling the debris from their table and carrying it to the counter. Granddad was already outside, making his way over to the admissions kiosk, when she caught up with him. She drew up alongside, slowing to his pace and reaching across to brush away a speckling of crumbs from his lapel. He returned her smile. A gust of wind ruffled his grey hair and he promptly put his cap back on, as though the breeze had served to remind him his head ought not to be uncovered while on duty.

'Back to t'salt mine, is it?'

' 'Fraid so.'

The click-click of her heels echoed off the walls of the courtyard, like the sound of someone two-finger typing. The cracks between the cobbles underfoot were green with moss, the bricks themselves the colour of pewter – chipped and scuffed, seemingly ground down with the passage of time. If she didn't know better, she'd have assumed the courtyard to date from the island's Victorian industrial heyday. But she'd discovered, from Granddad, that the car-park had been relaid with new cobbles when the museum was refurbished a couple of years ago and deliberately 'distressed' to appear old. *Like the staff*, he reckoned. *I'm only twenty-one, me.* She raised her head and breathed in deeply through her nose. A distinct wheeze, brought on by the sudden cold air after being indoors. She inhaled again. They'd reached the kiosk. The attendant who'd covered for Granddad during his break slipped out and, after a brief exchange of greetings with Constance, headed back into the museum.

'He's on guided tours. Same spiel six times a day, five days a week. Tha gets to sayin' t'same thing ower and ower, after a while the words stop meaning owt.'

Constance nodded. 'Still, only another year to retirement, eh?'

'Aye, then what? Sit at home all day talking to your grandmother's ghost, God rest her.' He gestured at the museum. 'At least, working 'ere, I get to meet folk what're still alive.'

'What, you mean people like Benjamin Huntsman, Henry Bessemer, *Sir* Robert Bayfield . . .?'

'I mean t'visitors – tourists and that, and folk I work with. Not a bunch o' waxwork dummies wi' daft hats and mutton-chop whiskers.'

They stood by the kiosk, Granddad tidying his uniform in readiness for the resumption of admissions duty. The position of the sun had altered, the museum building casting them in its shadow. Constance regretted the decision to leave her jacket in the car. She spoke almost before realizing what she was going to say.

'Did you ever court anyone else – before Gran, I mean?'

He chuckled – seemingly taken unawares by her question, though not displeased by it. 'I should say I did.'

'Anything, you know, *serious*.'

'Not really.' He paused. 'Well, one lass – aye, I suppose. Then I met your grandmother.'

'And she was the one for you.'

'Aye.'

'D'you ever think about the other girl – what might've happened if you'd married her instead?'

'Used to. First few years we were wed, I used to think on t'other lass from time to time. 'Ad I made t'right choice, an' that. Not that I'd 'ad the choice, mind, 'cos it were she what threw me ower on account of her 'aving met some other chap.'

Constance shivered, hugging herself against a gusty breeze and turning her head slightly to hide her face from him.

'You're all goosebumps, ducks.' Granddad put an arm round her shoulders, the coarse material of his jacket tickling her neck. His voice was made gentle. 'Eh, some other lad'll come along.'

'Did you hate her, for going off with someone else?'

'Aye, I did. I still do, an' we're talking forty-odd year ago now.'

She leaned into his hug. 'But you missed her.'

'Aye. Aye, I missed her.'

'So when does that stop, the missing?'

'I can't say that it ever does.'

Constance laughed, despite herself. 'Well thanks, Granddad – that's really cheered me up!'

'Aye, well, if tha wants to forget the past, tha haven't to ask advice from a maudlin old sod like me. Not one workin' in a bloody museum, anyroad.'

They kissed goodbye, Granddad squeezing her shoulders firmly through the thin material of her dress. Once again his

121

cap was dislodged. This time he straightened it, giving her a mock salute before entering the booth and shutting himself inside.

The Inky Path
The journalist must develop an appreciation of what his readers want to read, in the way that the good tradesman cultivates an understanding of the market for his wares. If the tradesman is he who supplies commodities to the customer, the journalist's function is to supply news to the reader. In each case, the intermediary would do well to remember that he is subservient both to product and to consumer. The journalist, then, ought not to set himself above that about which he writes; most importantly, neither should he look down upon those for whom he writes. In this sense stories belong to the reader, not the writer.

With Milly at her yoga class, Constance had the house to herself all evening. She unplugged the phone and shut herself away in the kitchen, where the dining table provided room for her notepaper, biros, coloured pens, pencils, ruler, newspaper clippings, a pot of tea, a carton of semi-skimmed milk, a teaspoon and a plate bearing an arrangement of refrigerated Snickers sliced into neat slabs. Alanis Morissette occupied the radio-cassette, with an assortment of other music on standby for intermittent changes of atmosphere. (As it happened, Constance was so absorbed by her work that long periods of silence would elapse before she realized that a tape had played out.) She began by taking a blank page and dividing it in half, vertically, with the words 'Suspect' and 'Motive' at the head of each column. Now and then she'd put a number in the margin and jot down an idea alongside it under one or other of the headings, pausing in between these flourishes of activity to sip tea, suck the end of a pen, eat a segment of chocolate or simply gaze into space. After an hour, the sheet was filled with untidy notes and crossings out. On a separate page, she'd sketched a plan of Urbopark annotated with asterisks to mark the location of each sabotage. Good word, that: 'sabotage'. She made a mental note to incorporate it into her next story about the spate of vandalism at the mall. A further sheet of paper was filled with a chronological list of the sabotages, along with a brief description of the corresponding incident.

On yet another page was a resumé of the saboteur's (*Yes, yes – use it!*) known 'public pronouncements', the occasions when – in the words of Paul Pink – he'd *stuck his head above the parapet*. The bomb warning to Trish on the Mall Admin switchboard; the tape-recorded call to Hallam Central police station to reveal the warning was a hoax; the handwritten 'ransom' note (a photocopy of which was among her auxiliary documents); the in memoriam advertisement in the *Crucible* (on a copy of the ad, she'd circled the words 'Hyde', 'Constance', 'W.B.', 'destroy' and 'rage', adding a double question mark after the initials W.B.). The word rage itself warranted inclusion in the 'above the parapet' section, she decided, having been variously used in written or spoken form, either as an identifying codeword or as an integral part of a sabotage. So far, the occasions when the saboteur went public had yielded little to assist the police investigation. The tape of his voice, indistinct and evidently heavily disguised, had been broadcast on local radio and television – prompting scores of phone calls to the inquiry hotline. These were still being followed up by CID, though none of the men (and one woman) interviewed to date came remotely close to resembling the speech patterns of the recording. Authorities on accent and dialect concurred that the rhythms and vowel sounds were so neutral or deliberately falsified as to make it impossible to get a geographical fix on the caller's origins. The sample of handwriting, similarly, contained so many inconsistencies as to defy conclusive expert analysis; and the response to the ransom note's publication in the *Crucible* had resulted in an over-whelming number of false leads.

Attempts to discover who'd placed the In Memoriam advertisement had also drawn a blank – it had been dictated over the phone by a customer (male, as far as the telesales operator could recall) giving a false name and address; unsurprisingly, no payment had been forthcoming. As for the ad's cryptic wording – and that of the ransom note – more questions were raised than answered. Why 'Constance' being chief among these. *Why me?* She sat back in her chair. It made her queasy to think the saboteur had placed a clue *naming* her, with the apparent intention that *she* should find it. *Saw your byline on the stories, I shouldn't wonder*. Paul Pink, in reassuring mode. *Publicity ploy on their part to target the local paper through its mall reporter – don't take it personally*. The DCI talked as though the perpetrators were a group. To Constance, the saboteur was distinctly male, singular. It was *he*. It was *him*. And, whoever he was, he'd singled her out.

She resumed her notetaking, compiling an entry under the heading Physical Evidence. This consisted primarily of a note to the effect that none of the fingerprints found on the damaged leather goods matched those obtained from the mall doors or around the HypaCenta skip. The ransom letter bore no prints other than those of the secretary at Mall Admin who'd opened the envelope. The 'blood' used in the graffiti attack, at least, was a more fruitful source of information. It had been found not to be blood at all – human or animal – but a synthetic substance whose chief constituents were water, artificial food colouring, glycerol and gelatin. However, it remained unclear whether the saboteur had obtained it in made-up form (if so, from where?) or had blended it himself from the various ingredients.

The tea was stewed and tepid, the colour of whisky. Constance made a fresh pot, put on another tape and sat down to redraft the first page of notes, having fished it out from among those others that now lay windswept across the kitchen table. This one had to be neat, legible; it had to make sense. Ten-thirty. Milly must've gone for a drink after yoga, which meant she'd roll in, squiffy, any time now. Constance threshed her hair with her fingers then refastened it to keep it from irritating her while she worked. She caught a glimpse of her greasy complexion in the kitchen window. With the rough copy beside her, she tore off a fresh page and began the revised draft.

Suspect	Motive
1. Animal rights group	Protest over animal products (e.g. veal, leather)
2. Shoplifter	Revenge on stores/mall over prosecution
3. Ex-Urbopark worker	Revenge after being sacked/made redundant
4. Environmental group	Protest over out-of-town developments
5. City centre shopkeeper	Anger over impact of mall on small retailers, maybe own business just gone bust
6. Developer/architect	Revenge after failing to win contract to design and build Urbopark
7. Builder	as above
8. Terrorist group	Uncertain
9. Nutter	Uncertain, maybe motiveless

At the foot of the page, she wrote: Query nos. 4, 6 & 7 – why wait so many years after mall opening to take revenge? Query no.4, Urbopark built on disused industrial land, not 'green field' site; maybe other environmental factors. She reread the list and tucked it inside an envelope, then composed a covering letter on a separate sheet. She addressed the envelope to DCI Paul Pink, c/o CID, Hallam Central Police Station, and went out to the postbox at the end of the street. In her slippers.

A bright, dry afternoon; mild for October, despite the billowy winds which seemed perpetually to sweep around the perimeter of Urbopark like a disgruntled customer buffeting

125

the doors and walls after being refused admission to the air-conditioned, temperature-controlled, climatically anaesthetized interior. Further away from the building, on the cerise macadam path beside the river, a border of shrubs, trees and grassy mounds offered protection from this wind-tunnel effect. The sun was low in the sky, to the rear, casting their shadows elastically ahead of them as they strolled side by side and infusing the afternoon with a peculiar lemony light. The river ran parallel to a road skirting the vast, misshapen oval that constituted the mall site. For all the artificially landscaped greenery, it remained an urban waterway – a narrow, sluggish, brown channel hemmed in on one side by the blank expanse of the shopping centre's outer walls and on the other by the huddled square blocks of a new-looking industrial estate. A large hoarding on the opposite bank listed the units To Let, their floorspace in sq.ft./sq.m. Constance drew his attention to the hoarding.

'Been open a year, that place. My colleague, William Boyce, rang the letting agents last week to ask if they could confirm whether all the units were still empty. Their spokesman would only be quoted as saying the site was "fully available". So we ended up with a news story as well as a diary piece on euphemistic PR-speak.'

Paul Pink bit into the first of his breadcakes, ham-and-mustard on white (one ninety-nine from Bake n Take, Yellow Lower). Still chewing, he said, 'D'you have an organized mind, would you say? Or disorganized?'

At school, at university and in the three years she'd been working, Constance had grown accustomed to not being attended to – conversationally – by men of all ages; her observations interrupted or ignored, her words (ideas, opinions, anecdotes) ill regarded or swept aside in an abrupt change of subject. During an especially raucous discussion among friends in a student union bar, she'd accused the males in the group of not listening to anything she and the other females had to say; *typical male mode of discourse, discourse*

126

by exclusion and intimidation. How she'd relished that phrase, mouthing it like a kiss. Then one of the men – she could picture his smug expression now, through a veil of cigarette smoke – had replied with a dismissive wave of the hand: *If the water's too choppy*, love, *swim in a different pool.* And here, five years later, was DCI Pink; ignoring her last remark, switching subjects – from hers to his. She considered the irony that his question implied an interest in the workings of *her* mind, while the conversational discourtesy indicated a preoccupation with his own.

'Neither and both,' she said. 'I organize myself – write reminders to myself – because if I didn't I'd forget. I mean, I organize myself *because* I'm disorganized.'

'I'm organized,' the detective replied, finishing the first breadcake and removing a second from the paper bag. Egg mayonnaise and cress. 'I have a disciplined mind. Mathematical . . . logical. I get very irritated with myself if I mislay summat, because it shouldn't happen. It just shouldn't happen.'

His mobile rang. He removed it from his jacket pocket and, swapping hands so he held the breadcake in his left and the phone in his right, he spoke into the mouthpiece. Four words: Pink. Yes. Yes. No. He clicked the phone off, put the half-eaten sandwich in his pocket.

'Bollocks.'

Constance masked her laughter with her hand as the detective – unsmiling as ever – retrieved the food, slopping gluey snots of chopped egg down his dark suit. He slipped the phone into another pocket, licking his fingers clean one at a time and slapping the worst of the debris from his jacket. Still grinning, she said, 'You were saying?'

'Aye, well.'

They walked on in silence while DCI Pink finished his lunch. He was the one to resume their conversation, coinciding his remark with the last mouthful of food.

'Your list . . .' he swallowed. 'See, that – to me – smacks of an organized mind. Do it myself all the time in my work, draw

127

up lists. Organizing my thoughts. But you have imagination as well – you came up with a longer list than me, some suspects and motives I'd not considered. And imagination, I reckon, is creative rather than manufactured. The product of a *dis*-organized mind. Why I asked.'

'You don't think a mind can be both organized and disorganized?'

'Anyroad, it's my turn to thank you. My officers, as we speak, are checking out some of your. . . lines of suspicion.'

Constance stepped aside, onto the grass verge, to allow a teenage boy to pass on a skateboard. She checked her watch. She'd to go back soon, an interview with a shopworkers' union official at Home Zone department store, Red Lower, about management plans to reduce Sunday pay rates from double time to time and a half.

'Are you in a union?' she asked.

'Police Federation. Not really what you'd call a union. You?'

'NUJ. I take the minutes.'

'Ever been on strike?'

'Once. The company was trying to push through a load of compulsory redundancies without seeking volunteers or following the statutory consultation period. One journo, been at the *Crucible* thirty-four years – since before the MD was born, actually – came in to find a letter on his desk telling him he was being made redundant. Editor didn't even have the decency to tell him to his face.'

'What happened? With the strike, I mean.'

'First day, they told us if we weren't back at work by the following morning they'd sack us all for breach of contract.'

'And?'

Constance shook her head. 'We went back.'

They lapsed into silence again, the only sounds those of their footsteps on the path and the drone of traffic on the double-decker elevated section of motorway looming up in the middle distance. They'd reached a point where an enclosed glass-walled footbridge connected the mall to a combined tram and rail station across the river. Urbopark Interchange, slogan: Here To Get You There. The path forked. While she hesitated, the inspector continued without losing momentum and she found herself following him to the left, down a gradient where the track narrowed beneath the footbridge. A strumming drumbeat of footsteps overhead, reverberating along the metal walkway. An extract from a Mall Promo history leaflet sprang to mind:

'. . . 12,000 tonnes of British steel were used in the
construction of the mall,
and 7,000 jobs created with its opening.
The cable-stay suspension bridge
link to Urbopark Interchange was built by
a local steel firm . . .'

A mudbank bisected the river here, a hummock pockmarked with drinks cans and litter and a partially engulfed shopping trolley. A wagtail, alarmed by the two pedestrians, flitted from a sapling up ahead and crossed the channel of water in swift dipping swoops. Constance watched it go, peripherally aware that her companion had also observed the bird's flight.

'Animal rights still top of the list, d'you think?' she said. 'The veal connection at HypaCenta, a shop selling leather and fur.'

'What about the bomb hoax? The chicken carcasses?'

'The bomb thing may be part of a . . . you know, a general protest against the mall for having shops that sell animal products or allow animal testing or whatever. I don't know. As for the chickens, well OK – I can't see the cruelty lobby actually killing animals to make a point.'

'You see, apart from a couple of . . . cryptic messages from our Mr Rage, no-one's claimed responsibility for any of these incidents. You're a journalist, what good's a protest without the attendant publicity for your cause?'

'Sure. I see that.'

'The ransom note, for example.'

'What about it?'

'The ambiguous wording, the absence of any follow up . . . it doesn't ring true. I wouldn't mind betting this wasn't a genuine attempt to extort money so much as a ploy to have the series of incidents taken more seriously.'

'Thereby guaranteeing more prominent news coverage, you think?'

'Aye. And anyone that publicity conscious would be happy to have us know their cause.' The inspector paused. '*Unless* the "why?" and the "who?" are too closely connected for comfort.'

'And animal rights is, I don't know, too non-specific – too broad a movement – for any one group or individual to be easily singled out for suspicion. Is that what you're saying?'

'Besides, *despite* what you read in the press, the fur coats and whathaveyou at Red Yeather L . . . Red Leather, Yellow Leather aren't made of real fur. Not a genuine mink, fox or sable in sight. They're . . . what's the word? There's a word for it.'

'*Faux.*'

'*Faux. Faux* fur. As in *faux pas*, meaning – literally – "false step".'

'*Faux naif.*'

'Yes. False naivety. An . . . affectation of innocence.'

'But the leather is real leather, isn't it? Most of it, anyway. And it was the leather goods that were vandalized, predominantly.'

DCI Pink scrunched up the paper bag which had contained his lunch and tossed it into a rubbish bin. One of his shoelaces had come undone. He stopped beside a bench, using it as a footrest while he retied the lace. For the first time on their walk she hadn't to crane her neck to look up at him. How tall *was* he? Six four, six five? As she watched him fasten his lace, she saw that the slats of the bench were scored with graffiti, with names and initials carved into the wood; a heart, indelibly arrow-pierced, inscribed by lovers (J.D. and K.W.) who – for all she knew – had long since fallen out of love. John and Karen? Joanne and Kevin? Justin and Kim?

'I'm not saying these incidents *aren't* to do with animal rights,' said the detective, straightening up. His bald dome was flushed with blood from where he'd been bending over, though his forehead was blanched white and deeply furrowed. 'I'm just not convinced that they are.'

'Police are keeping an open mind.' She noticed the small scar bisecting his eyebrow, wondering to herself how he came by it. Rugby injury, probably. Another player's stud, perhaps, or a flailing fist in a mid-match brawl. 'Can't rule anything out, can't rule anything in.'

He looked at her. 'If I were you, I'd not be so keen to hurry off in search of answers until you've worked out all the questions.'

131

The Life and Times of a Hallam Saw Grinder
(a Dramatic Reconstruction in Many Parts)

January 1859

On the morning of the sixth, when Samuel Poole opened up his butcher's shop for business, he found an envelope pinned to the front door. The envelope was addressed to JAMES LINLEY ESQ., the name inscribed clumsily in red block capitals. Linley, his brother-in-law, had been lodging with Poole's family in The Wicker for most of the winter – since the rattenings had flared up again. His whereabouts were supposed to be known only to close family and friends and, until this day, he had been in receipt of no correspondence. Poole was sufficiently intrigued to consider opening the envelope before handing it over, but the flap had been securely gummed down and would not reseal without evidence of tampering. In any event, he would discover the contents soon enough. Linley, being no scholar, would doubtless feign to read the letter then complain of poor eyesight, or some such, and pass it back to be read aloud. Poole went through to the living quarters, climbing two flights of stairs to Linley's chamber in the garret. He entered without knocking, caring little about disturbing him at an hour when most working folk were already long since at their trades. The man was sitting up in bed smoking, the room cloaked in semi-darkness and musty with the odour of tobacco and stale bedclothes. There was such a chill – Linley having neglected to lay or light the fire, nor even to have raked out the previous day's ashes from the grate – that Poole's breath was made visible. He opened the curtains, causing his brother-in-law to shield his eyes against the sudden daylight. Freshly fallen snow lay thick on the window-sill. As he gave over the letter, Poole – who had been butchering a calf's carcass prior to opening the shop – noticed a bloodstain in the form of a thumbprint on the envelope, partially obscuring the 'Y' of Linley.

'What's this, our Samuel?'

' 'Ow should I know? It's for thee.'

'Aye, but who brung it?'

'Nobody. It were just theer, stuck on t'door.'

Linley placed the cigarette between his lips so that both hands were free to open the envelope. He removed two sheets of coarse paper, tilting them towards the light from the window. Squinting at the first for a moment, he held it closer then farther away from his face before tossing both pages on to the bedspread.

'Read it for us, wilt thou, Samuel?'

'Read it thysen, I've a shop to think on.'

'I've woke up wi' one o' me 'eads. Like someone's in theer wi' an 'ammer.' He gestured towards the letter. 'All them words . . .'

Poole gave him a look, then took the letter over to the wooden chair by the window and sat down. The handwriting was in the same red ink as that on the envelope. Although he could read better than his brother-in-law, he had no great faculty for the practice. The undertaking was made the more irksome by virtue of the letter being penned by hand, the butcher being more accustomed to deciphering the neat columns of print in the *Hallam Telegraph*, either for his own benefit or on those evenings when Linley pressed him to broadcast some item or other of news. Thus it was that he read in a deliberate monotone, stumbling over unfamiliar words or those so poorly written as to be barely legible. Linley said nothing, simply continuing to sit up in bed with a pillow at his back, from time to time drawing on his cigarette.

Royal Commission of Inquiry
(sitting at) Hallam Town Hall
Thursday, 20 June 1867 (Thirteenth Day)

Witness: Frances Amory (Mrs), No.11 Garden Street, Hallam.

Q. Can you say how you came to discover the gunpowder?

A. I was about the household chores.

Q. Where were you?

A. In the chamber. I was putting on fresh bedding.

Q. And what did you find there?

A. I found three cans.

Q. Where did you find them?

A. In between the bed and the mattress.

Q. Did you make known this discovery to your husband?

A. I did.

Q. And what did he say?

A. He told me it was gunpowder.

Q. Did you ask why he was keeping gunpowder?

A. He said it was for his plot at the Society gardens.

Q. Your husband is a gardener?

A. He is.

Q. Did he say for what purpose he might require gunpowder at his plot?

A. He said there was an old oak stump that wanted blowing up.

Q. And he required three cans of gunpowder for this purpose?

A. Not all of it. He said he would mix up some with smithy slack and sell it on.

Q. To whom would he sell it?

A. I do not know. A man who shot pigeons.

Q. Was that man's name Samuel Crookes?

A. I do not know.

Q. Did your husband sell on some of the gunpowder?

A. He did.

Q. How much was he paid for it?

A. I believe it was seven shillings.

Q. You can recall how much he was paid for the gunpowder yet you cannot tell us the name of the man to whom he sold it?

A. I did not ever know his name.

Q. What did your husband do with the remainder of the powder?

134

A. He blew up the oak stump.

Q. He told you that?

A. He did.

Q. Did you not wonder why he found it necessary to conceal three cans of gunpowder beneath the mattress if he intended to use them for innocent purposes?

A. He said he did not want the children to come across them.

Q. How many children have you?

A. Three. Two boys and one girl.

Q. Was there not another place where the powder might have been kept from them?

A. I imagine there was.

Q. Yet you accepted your husband's explanation as to its concealment?

A. I do not know what you are asking.

Q. Did you believe him when he told you why he hid the gunpowder where he did?

(*witness hesitates*)

A. I asked if he was going to do any harm with it.

Q. What did he say?

A. He said he was not.

Q. Did he tell you from where he got the powder?

A. From Old Smite 'Em, he said.

Q. From Broadhead?

A. Yes, that is what he told me.

Q. Knowing this, you persisted in your belief that the powder was to be used to blow up a tree stump?

A. That is what Thomas told me.

Q. And you believed him?

A. I told him I hoped he would not do any mischief with it.

Q. What did he say?

A. He said he would not.

Q. Did you hear at or about this time of an explosion in The Wicker?

A. I believe so.

Q. Did your husband cause that explosion?

A. It was not my husband.

Q. You are sure of that?

A. My husband was at home in bed that night.

Q. You recall that?

A. I do.

Q. Is it possible, do you think, that he supplied the powder to another man? And it was that man rather than your husband who caused the explosion?

A. I cannot say.

Q. But it is possible?

A. Yes, it is possible.

Sir,

Thou shalt not know the name of thy correspondant, nor is it of consequence wether thou doest or thou doest not. Have a mind on what is said, not on who is doing the saying of it. Only knowest that if thou chooses to pay no heed to the words, those who do the saying have more than meer ink and paper to make thee look lively. We have given thee a flaver of this 'other medicine' over the years and thou seemst to want more doses than most to bring about a cure.

Look upon the following as a diagnosis by a kindly Physician of what it is that ails thee, and thou wilt see what tinctures and balms thou canst aply to restore thysen to good health, if thou wishest others not to administer a more seveer dosage.

1) Thou art a scissor grinder by trade, thou wert not aprenticed at the grinding of saws (tho' the coins are to be had in greater abundence at the one than the other).

2) Thy workmanship brings dishonour to the good name of the Hallam saw grinder.

3) What work thou canst not obtain by skilfulness of hand, thou obtainest by cheapness of price per piece. And what are others to do then?

4) Thou hast a Wheel full of aprentices taken with thee from the scissors trade, who thou instructs – if thou canst be

trobled to impart knowledge at all – in the trade of saw grinding (in the manner of 'the blind leading the blind').

5) When trade is good these lads of thine wilt take the work off other men and bring thee a pretty coin into the bargan.

6) When trade is poor they will go on the box, drawing scale from the pockets of others tho' thou hast paid not one ha'penny in natty brass to the society.

7) Thou speakest (oft times in one ale house or another) against the union of working men, tho' thou hast left one trade that were poorly paid for being out of union to join another where its members benefit from such combination.

All this, dear Sir, is to make no mention of the lads in thy Wheel who many a time get no pocket money from thee of a Monday morning because thou hast supped it all of a Saturday night. Nor of those lads who must find thee and give thee a ducking in the water trow to get their due wage. Nor to say anything of a man, brought up amongst us, who takes the bread from another man's mouth – not because he himself wants for bread, but because he's got a tooth for lazy roast meat. Nor of the sort of man grown fond of parading his idelness at working hours, a man loud at the drinking bar, a man with a habbit of jingling what money he hast in his pocket.

When a man hast broke the Laws of Trade and the Laws of Man as thou hast, James Linley, he cannot wonder at the aplication of 'strong medicine' by those concerned about the health of more men than one. For what is one man without his fellowes?

Your obediant servant,

A Kindly Physician.

Linley did not go to his work that day. And, when he arrived at the Wheel the following morning, he expected to find the bands missing from the grindstones and his apprentices idle for want of money to buy replacements or to pay the Society for the return of those that had been taken. But his hull had not been harmed and his lads were busy at their troughs.

Rattening held no fears for him, having been done more times than he could count. But the livid scar on the upper part of his right arm, and the occasional stiffness of movement in his shoulder on damp winter days, served to remind him that his enemies had more means than one to prevent him from working. In the days following receipt of the letter, Linley took care in his comings and goings from his brother-in-law's house, using the rear entrance to the shop yard and taking circuitous routes to and from work and the ale house. The surreptitious visits home to his family ceased and he discouraged them from calling on him in his 'exile'. When he was indoors at Samuel Poole's he never lingered at a window, nor would he answer the door to unexpected callers should he find himself alone. Even an attack on the house itself could not be discounted, for Poole – in harbouring him – would have adopted Linley's enemies for himself.

In the early hours of the eleventh of January, a figure approached the butcher's. Linley – who had been drinking – was soundly asleep in the upper chamber of the house above the shop, while Poole and his wife and children slept in the lower. The intruder's footsteps were deadened by a fresh covering of snow, his features – should an insomniac observer have chanced to peer out of an overlooking window – were partially obscured by the upturned collar of a poacher's overcoat and a cloth cap. What little could be seen of the man's face reflected with a sickly greenish-white pallor the pervasive luminescence of the moon. He neared the house with stealth, proceeding along the deserted, wintry street by the conceal-ment of whatever shadowy nooks and crannies it afforded him; hurrying from one to another when no such hiding place was to be had. At the front of the shop, he paused to ensure there was no likelihood of imminent disturbance. Satisfied, he knelt down above the grating to the cellar, producing a short bar from inside his coat and using it with care to lever off the grate. The metallic noise of this action was too fleeting, too in-substantial, to have roused even the lightest of sleepers. He drew the grate onto the snow-clad ground. Stowing the iron bar within his coat, he reached into another of its compartments to bring out a box of matches and a can that gleamed dully in his hand. The first two matches failed properly to ignite. The third, shielded by his cupped hand from the bitterly cold night air, caught alight; its flame immediately touched to the length of fuse protruding from the lid of the can. When the man was sure that the fuse was lit, he dropped the device into the gaping mouth of the cellar. The clatter it made within coincided with the thudding footsteps of his hasty retreat along the street. His legs had carried him to the safety of the corner by the time of the explosion.

The blast caused an avalanche from the slanting roofs of several houses in the terrace and blew out the downstairs windows of the building directly opposite Poole's premises. The cellar was destroyed, the butcher's above it severely damaged both by the force of the explosion itself and by the small fire which ensued. In the bed chamber directly over the shop, a number of floorboards were dislodged and ornaments toppled from the mantelpiece. Poole, it was, who went downstairs in panic to investigate – smothering the flames with a blanket before they took hold, while his wife pacified the children in their frightened state. In the garret, Linley – entirely unharmed – was fetched from snoring, inebriated stupor not by the blast but by the heavy scraping sound of several hundredweight of snow shifting from the slates overhead.

Chapter Five

SHOP TALK

A survey of member states by the European Union found that, when stress levels rise at home or in the workplace, 53% of women cope by shopping. The same study reported that when women choose clothes, make-up, jewellery, shoes, etc., they are not dressing to *please* – they are dressing to *please themselves*.

The Gender Spender
by Poppy Granola
(Sisterhood Press, 1994)

Constance parked in a pay and display within walking distance of head office, the *Crucible*'s own small car-park being reserved for executives. It had just started to rain. A newspaper vendor sheltered beneath a multicoloured golf umbrella, touting copies of the city final which lay stacked on a metal stand. Unshaven, fingerless woollen gloves grubby with printing ink; between drags on a roll-your-own, he cried, YINCREDIBLE! ING-RED-A-BALL! His voice – shrill, slightly nasal – rose in volume and pitch at the beginning and end of each call. Constance was struck by the reduction of '*Evening Crucible*' into an incoherent eruption of syllables seemingly fused to form an entirely new word. How often – over how many days, weeks, months, years – had he uttered this cry? YING CRABULE! YINCREDIBLE! *Tha gets to sayin' t'same thing ower and ower again, after a while the words stop meaning owt.* The erosion of language by repetition; depreciation of meaning. No, not depreciation of meaning – museum visitors would still comprehend the tour guide even if his words ceased to mean anything to *him*, passers-by would know what the newspaper vendor was selling even if his words had ceased to cohere. Was that a word, 'cohere'? She made a mental note to look it up. So, words did not necessarily need to make sense to convey meaning; language was a tool in the creation of meaning, not to be confused with meaning itself. *University notion.* Smiling to herself, Constance ascended the steps of Crucible House and awaited a vacancy in the revolving doors.

Dougal Aitken-Aitken closed the window, using a Kleenex to mop up the spattering of raindrops on the wooden sill. He compressed the sodden tissue and bowled it overarm across the room. As it splatted against the inside of a metal bin he gave a clenched-fist *yesss!* The fist unclenched, became an extended palm aimed in the direction of a chair. The tight lips expanded into a smile.

'Please.'

Constance sat down, knees together, hands on lap. Prim and proper. *If you want folk to see your knickers, wear them on t'outside.* Mam. She looked at the editor, who'd remained standing and was rotating his head. She could hear the bones click.

'Posture,' he said, massaging the base of his neck with both hands. He gestured at the computer terminal on his desk. 'Turning me into a hunchback.'

Mr Aitken-Aitken was wearing a blue-and-white striped shirt with a white collar, pale green tie and red braces. His suit jacket hung over the back of his chair. The expanse of desk contained the computer, a telephone, an A4 notepad, a

141

maroon fountain pen, a three-tier documents tray and a framed photograph of a woman and two toddlers of indeterminate sex. The picture was angled so that it could be seen by both the occupant of the desk and whoever happened to be sitting opposite him.

'And how's our *Urbo*charged hackette?'

Constance imitated a smile. The editor greeted her with this quip each time they met. He sat down at last, leaning back in his chair and pulling out the bottom drawer of his desk to use as a footrest. Hands behind his head. He'd recently returned from holiday – *Caribbean* – and his complexion bore the same tan hue as the desktop, his wavy mop of brown hair tinged with honey-blond. At thirty-two, he was the youngest editor in the group. He'd cut editorial staff by 10 per cent, cracked down on expenses claims and closed two district offices – earning him the nickname Frugal Dougal.

'Happy, Con? Busy? Bringing home the bacon?'

'Oh, you know.'

'Where does that expression come from?'

He ignored Constance's shrug; ignored Constance, addressing his remarks to a point on the wall somewhere above her head. The walls were bare apart from an enlarged aerial photograph of Hallam city centre – black and white, taken on a rainy day – and a poster bearing the words: THINK LIKE A READER. Similar slogans adorned the open-plan newsroom, his office being the only enclosed space in its midst. Even here, the prefabricated panels dividing editor from staff gave way to glass at shoulder height so that – simply by standing up – he could see them, and they could see his disembodied head. *Like a fucking periscope*, William Boyce had once remarked.

'Ask your Mr Whatsisname at HypaCenta,' he continued. 'They sell fresh bacon. Had some for my breakfast this morning.' He switched from his usual accent, neutral southern England, into thick northern. 'Bacon butty.'

'John Chapple.'

'Chapple, that's him. Spoke to him last week. Rotary bash.

Singing your praises. In fact, your ears must've been burning lately.'

Constance raised her eyebrows. 'How come?'

'Had a call today from Mr Pink. *Detective Chief Inspector Pink.*' The editor frowned. 'Said one of the crossword clues in last night's paper didn't make sense. Nine across.' He looked at her, as though expecting her to account for the error.

'I think he's a bit of a crossword buff,' she said.

'Bound to be. Appeal of the cryptic, solving riddles – goes with the job.'

Mr Aitken-Aitken was preoccupied with picking specks of lint from his tie. His fingernails, she noticed, were long and perfectly manicured.

'Bought this tie at Urbopark,' he said. 'Silk. Twelve ninety-nine. We take the little ones and dump them in the crèche. Did you know,' he added, affecting a Michael Caine cockney twang, 'they've got a pretend supermarket there – in the crèche – where the kids push miniature trolleys around and buy things with toy money? *Incredible.*'

'I know, I wrote a feature about it.'

The editor looked across the desk at her. 'Did you? So you did, so you did. I remember the headline now: "Trolley Good Fun at the Mall", wasn't it? Marvellous. Load of guff from some child psychologist, as I recall, about indoctrinating a new generation of consumers.'

'Couple of pars, that's all. I put in a lot more of her quotes – but the subs . . .'

'Ah, the subs. Bane of your life, pruning your precious words and, horror of horrors, *rewriting* your copy.'

Constance returned his smile, but made no reply. He'd stood up again and had his back to her, staring out of the rain-speckled window. Compact bum; briefs, not boxers, to judge by the visible panty line. She pictured him undressed; imagined licking him: the back of his neck, his back, his buttocks, parting them and nuzzling into the silky-haired, soap-scented cleft. She shuddered. There was a perverse thrill in fancying a man you

143

disliked so much. Sometimes, with Howard, she'd fantasized that it was Dougal making love with her. When the editor turned to face her again, the flush of sexual excitement evaporated as suddenly as it had begun; she assumed what was intended to be an expression of steady dispassion.

'Anyway, *anyroad* – we digress. Mr Pink, crossword fan and anagramatic DCI at CID.' He sat down once more, leaning forward and placing his palms face down on either side of the notepad, aligning it with the edges of the desk. 'D'you make of him?'

'Paul?'

'First-name terms. I like that. Good for a local hack – hackette – to be on friendly footing with the major players.' The editor tapped his fingernails on the desk, continuing to address his remarks to the notepad. 'Do you think he's telling us everything he knows?'

'I wouldn't have thought so. I mean, they don't – do they – the police? Not everything. They have to keep certain things back because . . .'

'He wouldn't, for example, reveal the codeword used by whoever's behind these attacks on the mall? Or let on – strictly off the record – that he thought there'd be more incidents to come? Things like that.'

. She hesitated. 'Some things, we couldn't print even if we knew about them.'

'Another example: a coded warning – about, say, a vandalism spree at a leather and fur boutique – being made through an ad in *our own newspaper*.'

Her mouth was dry. She watched him search among the papers in the top tier of his tray, producing a back issue of the *Crucible* folded open at her story on the sabotage at Red Leather, Yellow Leather.

'Here we are, third par,' he said, then reading aloud: 'The incident . . . blah, blah, blah . . . "is believed by detectives to have followed a cryptic message containing a codeword used in connection with previous attacks." This is the best bit:

"Details of the warning have not been released". Bloody right they haven't!'

'Paul Pink is anxious for us to keep the codeword—'

'I bumped into the classified advertising manager at the coffee machine today, and he mentioned in passing that the police had interviewed one of our telesales girls.'

'I . . .'

'Be nice to *know* these sort of things were going on in a newspaper, wouldn't it, Con? If you were the editor, for instance.'

Constance made no reply. Mr Aitken-Aitken put the news-paper down and picked up what she took to be a photocopy of the In Memoriam ad.

'Does the DCI have any idea why this contains what appears to be a reference to you, by name?'

She shook her head.

'Do *you*?'

'No.'

'But he'd tell you if he did. And, of course, you'd tell me.'

She exhaled. 'We think . . . that is, *he* thinks, the saboteur might be trying to maximize the publicity for what he's doing. Maybe, I don't know, whoever's responsible for the sabotages knows I'm covering the story and is targeting the newspaper through me. Keeping us interested.'

The telephone rang, startling both of them and punctuating the tail-end of her remarks. The editor waited for her to finish before picking up the receiver. He told the caller he'd ring back, then hung up. Continuing to stare at the phone for a moment, he finally looked up – some of the earlier annoyance having seeped from his expression in the few seconds it had taken to deal with the call. At least, he seemed annoyed by the distraction now rather than with her.

'I've been talking to DCI Pink, and to John Chapman for that matter—'

'Chapple.'

'*Sorry?*'

'Nothing, it's just . . . it's John *Chapple*. At HypaCenta.'

'Right, Chapple.' He glared at her, apparently exasperated at being interrupted yet again. 'The point is, he and the chief inspector are unhappy that certain things you've been told in confidence are appearing in the paper, and – no, let me finish – and other facts, they say, are either being misrepresented or given undue emphasis.'

'Like what?'

'They *like* you. Don't get me wrong, they're impressed with you as a person *and* as a journalist.'

'Like *what*, Dougal?'

'Veal. Animal Rights. Razor blades.'

'Jesus, I don't believe this!' Constance's eyes smarted and she found herself making tight fists. 'These were written into my copy by newsdesk or by the subs. I mean, stuff I'd only mentioned as background or not even included in the first place.'

'Which brings us full circle.'

'How d'you mean?'

'Gary. He's concerned by this habit of yours of keeping back information that would be useful – *important* – for us to know in planning our coverage, even if we didn't publish it. We're a team – all rowing in the same direction. He's worried you're going solo on us.'

'Is it any wonder? I mean . . . for Christ's sake, we *do* publish it! I've got my contacts accusing me of breach of confidence and now you telling me I'm . . .'

'I know, I know. Middle of a tug-of-war syndrome. Can't win. Can't do right for doing wrong. Terrible, isn't it – you leave the womb and, by the time you discover what a nasty world it is, it's too late to crawl back inside.'

'Dougal, this . . .' She stopped herself from saying *this is really unfair*. Childish. She felt childish enough as it was. 'Are they really complaining about me, Paul Pink and John Chapple? Formally, I mean.'

The editor shook his head. 'They trust you. That's what

they told me. What they don't trust is what happens to your copy once it leaves your terminal, and that – hang on, hang on – and that means our coverage is being compromised, because once contacts start withholding . . . well, goes without saying.'

'But it's hardly my fault, is it?'

'What I don't like, Con,' there was an edge to his voice, 'is having outsiders threatening me with non-co-operation because one of my own reporters has gone to them with sob stories about the way her copy is handled.'

She didn't say anything.

He paused, as though allowing that statement to sink in, before adding, 'Nor do I like one of my reporters deliberately falsifying a story; and lying, by omission, to her newsdesk. To *me*, effectively.'

Constance leaned back in her chair. Don't blink. Don't blink and don't break off eye-contact. She wanted to say something but didn't trust her voice not to betray her. Neither of them spoke for a moment. The silence had almost become embarrassing when Mr Aitken-Aitken, moderating his tone, said, 'I'm sending William Boyce out to Urbopark.'

'William?'

'His suggestion. His *request*.'

Constance smoothed the hem of her dress, the material having become puckered from being balled up in her fists. Her palms were clammy.

'So, what are you saying, I'm off the story?'

'Con, you're still Our Gal at the Mall.' Talking over her interruption, he added, '*And* you're still heading up our coverage of this story. If there's more to come, the impact on the mall could be significant. I want you two in tandem on this one: you on the crime and human interest angle, William on the business aspects.'

She looked at him.

'And before you take umbrage,' he continued, 'I'll let *you* in on a secret – if it'd been up to Gary, the police side of the

147

story would've been hived off to crime desk and covered from here. He thinks you're too inexperienced to handle this – first year as a senior reporter; big, running story.'

'Oh, fine – I mean . . .'

'So, prove him wrong.' The editor smiled, the whiteness of his teeth too perfect against his tanned face. 'Prove *me* right in pulling rank on him over this.'

The Inky Path
Words are precision instruments. If you use words recklessly you not only blunt your own meaning, but you are also helping to spoil the priceless heritage of the English language of which you are one of the natural custodians. Words are the tools of a journalist's trade and, in common with any craftsman, he should keep them keen and well-polished, using them appropriately; he will cherish them. The true wordsmith, however, is not inclined to show off his prowess, for – paradoxically, it may seem – the man with the broadest vocabulary can express his thoughts the most succinctly – able, in an instant, to select just the word or phrase that will exactly hit off his meaning.

A toilet cubicle: the best and the worst place in which to weep, few locations being at once so private and so utterly depressing. Constance would have saved her tears for the car or the bedroom, but they came of their own accord before she reached either sanctuary. She made it out of the editor's office, at least, and had negotiated her way across most of the newsroom before having to quicken her pace. Like someone succumbing to a sudden and irresistible urge to vomit, she burst into the staff toilets – hand clasped to mouth – and shut herself away. There, she wept. She wept briefly but copiously; she wept as silently as possible – for fear of being overheard. Her body shook with unarticulated sobs. And, when it was over, she sat wet-faced and swollen-eyed for a long time before dabbing at the evidence with a swab of loo roll. She completed the repairs at one of the wash-basins, then fixed her hair –

how does your hair become such a mess when you cry? – and reapplied her make-up.

By the time she returned to the newsroom, Gary was in conference with the editor and other section heads; just as well, because Constance couldn't face him. She left an expenses claim form on his desk and was collecting post from the 'Urbopark – By Van' tray when William Boyce approached her. His impending secondment wasn't mentioned, instead he handed her an agenda for an NUJ meeting. He couldn't stop to chat, as he'd to attend an Employment Sub-committee at the town hall. She glanced at the paper he'd given her, main items: derecognition; falling membership; multiskilling. Union meetings had become demoralizing, with fewer members and fewer of those bothering to turn up. The company – without formally banning the union or prohibiting membership – virtually ignored the NUJ and its elected officials on issues of pay, conditions of employment, staffing levels, disciplinary proceedings or health and safety. And now there was a plan to train reporters, photographers and sub-editors in one another's jobs, to create teams of journalists with inter-changeable skills – an increase in ability, flexibility and productivity *not* to be reflected in higher wages. William, father of chapel, had annotated this item on the agenda with a characteristically political footnote: *Management call it multi-skilling, we call it a way of employing fewer people at less pay to do more work.*

On her way out of the newsroom, Constance heard her name being called. The chief librarian was standing in the doorway to the cuttings library, waving a sheet of paper. Something about a Latin translation she'd requested a couple of weeks ago; which puzzled her, momentarily, because she'd no recollection of having asked for any such thing. It was only when she took the note from him that she remembered the inscription above The Dashing Blade silverware and cutlery shop at the mall, where she'd watched a cutler at work in the window. *Deo Adamante Labor Proficit.*

' "Deo," ' said the librarian, leaning over her shoulder to point at each word in turn, 'is the dative or ablative singular, meaning "to God" or "by God"; and "adamante" is the adjectival ablative of a third-person declension . . .'

'Well, I knew *that*.'

'OK, point taken – anyway, it means "hard" or "unbreakable" or "steel-like", as in the English words "adamant" or "adamantine". Yeah?'

'Go on.'

' "Labor", somewhat obviously is "labour" or "work" or, I suppose, "endeavour"; and "proficit" – present indicative – means "makes progress" or "advances" or "succeeds".' He indicated a phrase at the foot of the page, beneath the word-by-word breakdown. 'So the whole thing – and this is a rendering into modern idiomatic English rather than a literal translation – is: "We progress through God and hard work".'

'Right, thanks,' she said. 'Thanks very much.'

'Very Victorian. Protestant work ethic.'

She smiled. 'They'll be putting signs like that up in here before long.'

'Know what it reminded me of?' said the librarian. '*Arbeit Macht Frei*, on the gates of the concentration camps. "Freedom Through Work" or "Work Brings Freedom", or words to that effect.'

She nodded, muttering – to herself as much as to him: 'Shopping Is Liberty.'

'Sorry?'

'Nothing. Ignore me, I'm rambling.'

He looked at her, inspecting her face with concern. 'You OK?'

'What? Oh, it's hayfever. I get really bad hayfever. You know, my eyes . . .'

'If you're like this when it's raining in *October*, I wouldn't want to be within sneezing distance of you on a sunny day in August!'

William Boyce made the splash in the following day's first edition, having been smuggled pages from the confidential part of the agenda for the Employment Sub-committee. Under a headline Living in a Land of Make-Believe!, the article revealed – exclusively – that Hallam City Council planned to build 'factories' on derelict former industrial sites alongside the motorway and rail routes into the city. The new units would be empty shells – employing no-one, manufacturing nothing – intended to create the illusion of a vibrant, revitalized local economy in an area renowned for industrial decline. Business folk visiting or passing through the city would gaze out of their cars and trains and be impressed by these smart new sites with their indication of urban regeneration. Hallam would become known as a happening place, companies would want a slice of the action. In the short term, jobs would be created in making and erecting the sham units; long term, the council hoped the city would become a focus for investment and relocation by real firms producing real products in real buildings, located on the very sites where the fake factories had stood.

A Tuesday. Sticky-backed yellow notelets were gummed in a radial pattern around the perimeter of Constance's computer screen when she returned from lunch, creating the effect of a square-headed, stunted sunflower sitting squat in the centre of her desk. She hung up her coat and made herself a coffee before sitting down to peel off the rectangles of paper. *He loves me, he loves me not* . . . Several of the messages were in her own handwriting, reminders to herself; one, from William, said he was 'out on his rounds' – a schedule of introductions to key people at Urbopark: Mall Admin officials, shop managers, store executives. Contacts. *A reporter is only as good as his sources of information*. His desk, transported the previous day from head office and installed with some fuss opposite hers, had a locked drawer which, she knew, contained a fat, dog-eared contacts book. He had his own terminal, but

151

they had to share a phone – an arrangement which was already proving awkward, especially close to deadline. As well as becoming more cramped, the back office – windowless, stuffy at the best of times – now bore a permanent reek of fishpaste that overwhelmed even the most strongly scented pot-pourri. This was a consequence of the half-dozen rounds of sandwiches, cut diagonally into neat quarters, which her new colleague had brought to work on each of the two mornings in a huge tupperware container; the sandwiches to be eaten at precise twenty-minute intervals throughout the day. So far, the filling hadn't varied: fishpaste and cucumber. Twenty-four triangular sandwiches, three an hour for eight hours. When he went out on his rounds he took some with him, foil-wrapped, to maintain the quota. It was healthier for the stomach always to have something to digest rather than having a heavy meal to contend with followed by several hours of gastric inactivity. *Never full, never hungry*, he said. *Keeps you alert.*

Two of the remaining memos were also in his looping, swooping handwriting – both reporting messages from Constance's mam. Mam left another (not urgent) with reception – presumably after William had gone out – and Sally had also taken details of other callers: Gary, on newsdesk (no message); and Howard. This latter note contained no message either, just the words 'Howard rang (!?!?)'. Sally's last memo, timed at 2.05 p.m., was to inform her that a Prof. Stanley Bell had called to ask whether she'd be 'free for a bevy' after that evening's class; she couldn't phone him back because he'd be in lectures all afternoon. This note – missing a 'v' from 'bevvy', Constance noticed – was similarly peppered with the receptionist's exclamation and question marks.

Notes

Geographical concentration of the means of production – i.e. the vast (manu)factories and huge workforces of the industrial revolution – gathered momentum following the intro of the first steam engines (instead of water-wheels) geared to iron & steel m'facture. Tall brick

152

chimneys (Stan pronounces it 'chimbleys'!) – the outlet for steam
engine boilers – became a feature of H's skyline.
[Query: steam comes from water, so is water or steam the actual
source of power?!]

Labour
'Strikes among the workmen are very numerous at Hallam . . . the
unions are opposed to the introduction of machinery in the [tool]
trade and prejudice against it is so strong that I have known an
instance of a man being obliged to leave that town because he
substituted a bellows for the ordinary blowpipe used for soldering. I
was once obliged to leave a place in consequence of not belonging
to the union of the trade in which I worked at the time; it was not
the trade to which I had been brought up, and the men took care to
inform me that I was looked upon as an interloper. I had been out
of work for some time before entering that business, but was obliged
to leave it. In Hallam, I have known the children hoot a workman
in the streets who did not belong to the union of his trade.'

Anonymous edge-tool maker
(*Morning Chronicle*, 20 January 1851)

Prof. Stanley Bell's Physical, Metaphysical & Philosophical
Glossary of Metal
Crucible Steel: In 1740 Benjamin Huntsman introduced the crucible
process, a technological development that turned steel manufacture
from a craft into a science. Huntsman, a Hallam-based Quaker
clockmaker, was experimenting to find improved material for clock
springs and pendulums. His efforts resulted in the devising, by chance,
of a process for making purer and more uniform steel by remelting
blister steel at high temperatures in clay crucibles (using coke instead
of charcoal) and casting the molten steel in moulds. Inadvertently,
he had made the technological advance that would allow mass
production of steel. This discovery can be likened to the manner in
which the medieval alchemists – in attempting to transform base metal
into gold – stumbled across other practical but unexpected benefits.
Glauber's Salts, Dresden porcelain, the composition of gunpowder

and the properties of acids were all chanced upon by alchemical experiment. A lesson to be learnt from this is that in seeking to solve one problem we may discover the solution to another. The thing is, to seek.

Stan was at the bar, Constance was seated at a glass-strewn corner table refastening a plaited friendship bracelet given to her by Milly. Thin wrists, *knobbly*; long narrow forearms; dimpled elbows; flabby flesh at the backs of her upper arms. How was it possible, anatomically, to have arms that were both too fat *and* too thin? Light from a wall-lamp picked out the gingery-blond hairs. White and freckly in winter, pink and freckly in summer. Stan had a tan, legacy of Oz. She watched him set down two fresh pints on their respective coasters.

'Cheers!'

Frothy beard. A fleeting image of Santa Claus: red-sweatered, rosy-cheeked joviality, only not so bulky. Not fat so much as chunky, like his chunky-knit woollen pullover. Constance, swollen with alcoholic *bonhomie*, allowed the beer to settle before smilingly, belatedly, acknowledging his toast. She'd begun telling him about her summons to the editor's office, but now he'd returned from the bar she was disinclined to resume the airing of her grievances. Shop talk. Not even the newsgathering aspect of her job that he'd enquired about, but off at a tangent into in-house bickering. They hadn't come here to discuss her problems at the paper. Why *had* they come here? Because he'd asked her, because of *him*: why else? Not the familiar surroundings of the Tongs & Dozzle, but a pub she'd not been to before – sneaking off together while others headed for the usual post-class watering hole. Nothing for Sally to have got so punctuated about. Which, incidentally, was not on – making *a date* via the receptionist. Embarrassing. She hadn't said that to Stan, she'd just thought it. She'd . . . She was tipsy, was what she was. Somewhat under the affluence. Constance sipped her drink, placed it back on the beermat and reached beneath the table for her bag.

'Something to show you.' After rummaging unsuccessfully in two zippered compartments, she finally produced a paperback – slightly buckled – and handed it to him. Dickens, *Hard Times*. She'd begun it the previous day.

'I read this *years* ago,' said Stan, smiling. He turned the book over, flipping the pages. 'Am I s'posed to be looking at anything in particular?'

Concentration. By concentrating on what you were saying and doing and you could *think* yourself sober. Less squiffy, anyway. The thing was to focus: eyes, hands, speech. 'See the picture on the front?' she said, pointing.

'Smoky chimbleys. An iron foundry beside a river, by the looks of it.' He looked up. 'Why, what's the story?'

'Now read where it tells you what it's a picture of. On the back just above the thingy, the bar code.'

Stan spoke in his throaty tutor-reading-aloud voice. ' "The cover shows a detail from *The Nant-Y-Glo Iron Works*, a watercolour by George Robertson in the National Museum of Wales, Cardiff".' He smiled at her. 'Enlighten me.'

'Where's *Hard Times* set?'

'Jeez, now you're asking. Up north somewhere. Coketown, wasn't it?'

'Coketown being a fictional name for Preston,' said Constance. 'And what's the industry in the novel?'

'No, hang on . . . Preston . . . textiles. Textile mills. Got to be.'

She beamed at him, his face – puzzled – became infected with her smile. 'So what you've got here, courtesy of Penguin Classics,' she said, 'is a book about a mill town in Lancashire with a cover illustration depicting an ironworks in Wales.' She raised her pint. 'Brewed in Hallam, advertised by Czech steelworkers.'

The professor laughed loudly, patting the edge of the table with one downturned palm by way of applause. 'That was how many weeks ago, that class? D'you mean to say you actually *remember* the stuff I spout forth about?'

155

Constance accepted the book back from him and re-placed it in her bag. 'Fellow journalist, Dickens. Reporter, ironically, for the very newspaper you quoted from this evening – the *Morning Chronicle*. Taught himself shorthand, apparently.'

'Mate of mine went to Albania – years ago, this was, when it was still strictly communist – and he had a few paperbacks with him, and they confiscated all but one. The only one they'd let him bring into the country was *The Old Curiosity Shop*. The tour guide told him: "Mr Dickens is good socialist, champion of the people".'

'Really?'

'Personally, I've always found him vaguely patronizing towards the working classes; that pervasive Victorian sense of ... of a distinction between the *upper* and *lower* orders. Only with Dickens there's this notion of a social conscience, a belief that the nobs should behave more humanely – more *decently* – towards the oiks.'

'But no breakdown of the underlying social order, you mean?'

'Right. He was no revolutionary, our Charlie. *Hard Times*, from what I can remember of it, is ... has this distaste, if you like, for the idea that working folk might seek to take control of their own condition, yeah? Empowerment. He had no time for trades unions or radical political movements.'

'But, for his times, he was way ahead of current thinking,' said Constance. 'I mean, you can't blame Dickens for not having a 1990s perspective on social issues.'

'Chartism was around in his day. The Combination Acts.'

'The Chartists were reformers, not revolutionaries. And, anyway, most working people at that time couldn't read or write – so who was going to champion their cause if it wasn't the educated middle classes?'

Stan smiled. 'Well, there's a typical middle-class journalist's response: that social change is engineered only through the medium of the written word.'

156

'As opposed to the *spoken* word used by, say, History lecturers?'

They laughed. This at once relaxed them and, she sensed, drew a line under their discussion. They drank in silence for a moment, Stan picking at the edges of his beermat and creating a small pile of powdery cardboard fragments. As she watched, Constance realized he was sculpting the mat into a rough outline of Australia.

'So you do shorthand, do you, like Dickens? Pitman, is it?'

'Teeline. Pitman is phonetic – the characters, I mean, are based on the way the words sound – whereas in Teeline the outlines are made up of symbols based on the shape of the letters. It's like speed writing rendered into shorthand, more or less.'

Taking a biro from her bag, she demonstrated on the blank reverse of her own beermat: drawing the symbols for the letters s, t, n, l and b, then writing his name, Stanley Bell, in Teeline. He got her to write her own name, in shorthand, alongside his.

'What's Teeline for "You have a lovely smile"?'

Constance flushed. Unable to think of anything to say, she wrote the sentence down. Still avoiding eye contact, she said, 'You've to be careful how you transcribe that one because it could be misread as "You have a lively smell".'

'Yeah?'

'L-V-L-Y; S-M-L. The outlines are identical.'

'So, what, it's down to context?'

'Yeah. It all comes down to context.'

Stan reclined in his chair, tilting it on to the back legs and raising his hands behind his head in a mannerism disconcertingly reminiscent of Dougal Aitken-Aitken. Triceps. That was it, the name of the muscle (flabby, in her case) at the back of the upper arm. Biceps at the front, triceps at the back. Constance wished she'd worn a long-sleeved top instead of a T-shirt. Or kept her cardie on, she should've kept her cardie on. But it was so warm in the pub.

'Aren't you hot, in that?' she asked.

157

Stan's bearded chin doubled as he looked down at himself, seemingly surprised to find that he was, indeed, wearing a thick woolly jumper. For him, she imagined, dressing would be a haphazard matter of grabbing blindly in cupboards and drawers; a putting on of layers. No full-length mirror, no tucking in or fastening, no consciousness of cut or colour co-ordination, no last-minute changes of mind. No *anxiety*.

'England's so bloody cold after Oz,' he said. 'And it's not even winter yet.'

'Wait till you've sat in the stands at Hallam United of a snowy evening in February.' *Of*. Another thing she did when she'd been drinking – slip into dialect.

'Hallam United. That brings back memories. I've still got my red-and-white scarf somewhere.'

'You're a Unitedite as well, then?'

'Oh, aye. Wouldn't catch me at City. How about you, d'you go?'

'Now and then – you know, the big matches; not that there's many of them these days. My granddad's got a season ticket.'

'We should go to a game. If you fancy.' He removed his glasses, slipping one of the earpieces between his teeth and sucking on it. Smiling, he added, 'Or is Saturday when you join the faithful in their worship at the temple of consumerism?'

'If you mean Urbopark, I'm there every other Saturday – *working*.'

Why was she being defensive about the mall? It was him, his tone of voice. Nothing blatant, just an edge to his words; that slight smirk. Also, she was confused. Irritated that one moment he was suggesting they go to a football match together and, in the next sentence, having a subtle dig at . . . At what? At shopping, at Urbopark, at where she worked? At her? It felt, somehow, as if he was having a dig at her. Crap, she was just being over-sensitive. As per. Constance drank some more beer.

'Anyway, Mam's the shopper in our family. If shopping was an Olympic event, she'd—'

'My ex was the same. I swear our kids grew up thinking a pushchair was a wire trolley with food in one end and them dangling their legs out the other. Must've thought they had a frozen chicken and a box of cornflakes for sisters.'

'I didn't know you had children.'

Stan hesitated. 'Two boys. Eight and ten. Both with her now, in Oz.'

'That must be hard, not seeing them.'

He put his glasses back on and lifted his pint to his lips. He drank deeply, this time dabbing away the froth with the rolled cuff of his jumper. He was about to say something, then appeared to check himself. Constance detected a diminishment of frankness in this process, a withdrawal. The raised glass, the replaced spectacles with their reflective opacity, were a physical reinforcement to the emotional barricade.

He said, 'They'll be coming up for ten days or so at Christmas. And I plan to fly back in the summer holidays for a few weeks. *British* summer, that is.'

'Even so, it's a long time apart.'

The professor shrugged, had another drink. He switched subjects clumsily, inviting her to continue what she'd been saying earlier about her bollocking from the editor. Their conversation became stilted, disjointed. The smoky atmosphere in the pub was beginning to affect her breathing. A quick squirt of the inhaler would do the trick, but she was embarrassed to use it in front of Stan. And sneaking off to the loo would require her to rescue the inhaler from her bag without drawing his attention to it. Jesus. What she should do was just get the inhaler out of her bag and *use it*. Puff, puff. Right there in front of him. She took shallow breaths through her nose to lessen the discordant bagpipe swirls in her bronchial tubes that, surely, were as audible to him as they were to her. What was it with her? She'd been seeing Howard for months – *sleeping with him* – before he even knew she was asthmatic, never mind finding out about the inhaler.

'Excuse me.'

159

She took the bag with her. When she returned, her breathing had eased and her mouth tasted of Ventolin – a gaseous, faintly bitter tang. A familiar headachy sensation, too, a tightness at the back of her skull. Deep breaths, no wheezing. Approaching the table, she saw that Stan's glass, half full when she'd gone to the loo, stood empty in front of him. He'd put on his coat.

She phoned Howard because of Stan – because Stan said she had a lovely smile and because he invited her to go to a football match with him. Because he had a dig at her, because he put his coat on while she was in the ladies', because he said goodnight to her, in the street, with no further mention of lovely smiles or of football.

She phoned Howard because Milly was away and she had no-one to talk to.

She phoned Howard because she couldn't face phoning her mam.

She phoned Howard because *he'd* phoned *her* at the office.

She phoned Howard because she was lonely.

She phoned Howard because she missed him.

She phoned Howard because of her job.

She phoned Howard because she was drunk. Drunk *enough*.

She phoned Howard because it was tough to keep being strong and sassy and sophisticated – with Dougal Aitken-Aitken, with Paul Pink, with Gary, with Stanley Bell – and now she just wanted someone to hold, someone to *hold her*. Because she'd been hard and now she wanted to be soft, for a while. For a night.

She phoned Howard because she didn't know what she wanted.

She phoned Howard.

Eleven o'clock. He answered on the penultimate ring of the ten she'd imposed on herself as the hanging-up limit. They spoke for less than a minute. He arrived at her house at twenty past: red wine, chocolate biscuits, packets of Twiglets. By eleven-thirty they were sitting naked in her bed, with the light off, eating and drinking. No music. The curtains were open, a street lamp casting angular shadows on the walls. In the gloom, the wine in their glasses looked black against the ghostly white of the laminated bedside units. Constance's fingers were sticky, savoury with the taste of yeast extract and salt; she'd spilled wine and crumbs on the duvet, which was pulled up as far as their waists. Their bodies touched at shoulder and hip: his right, her left. Howard was listening, without interruption, while she explained (some of) the reasons why she'd phoned him. Urbopark, the editor, Gary. She'd needed to *talk* to someone. When she'd finished she asked why he'd phoned her at work, why he'd come round right away when she returned his call. And it was crap. What he told her was just so much crap. It was also what she wanted to hear. He said he couldn't get her out of his head. Those were his words: *I can't get you out of my head, Con.* Which meant *body*, she decided: he couldn't get her out of his body. Because, with men – with men like Howard – the body and the head became confused, interchangeable. He wanted sex. He wanted sex with her. And – this, a private admission to herself – she wanted sex with him. She also wanted *him*, but she'd settle for sex; she'd console herself with any residual emotional comfort that derived from a fleeting physical (re)union. It was implicit from their manner, as much as from what they said, that this was to be for one night only. In the morning, she knew, Howard would go back to the woman for whom he'd left her all those weeks ago; Constance would go back to Constance.

At first he tried to fuck her conventionally: manual and oral foreplay of increasingly breathy intensity followed by copulation, him on top. But she was dry, unaroused; distracted by the sensation – after so many weeks apart from him – of how his body was, at once, strange and familiar to her. He was bruising her. She coaxed him off, steering him onto his side so that her front was pressed against his back. Better. Her mouth on his neck, her hand reaching between his buttocks. This was better. But as soon as he rolled over and tried again

161

she became impenetrably tense once more. Even by closing her eyes to shut him from sight, which had worked on occasions, she was unable to make it possible for him to ease inside her. Soon he would begin to lose confidence, blaming himself for what he'd regard as his failure to arouse her; he would become clumsy with frustration and depleted self-esteem. And then he'd turn it on her: *How can I do this if you won't tell me what you want, if you just lie there and let me blunder away?* He would slump to the other side of the bed and she'd have to coax him back with manipulations and whispered reassurances. How many nights had they spent in this way? But the thrill of the forbidden – of him being here at all, with her – was just enough to save them from succumbing to old habits of sexual behaviour. Constance, in a moment of inventive inspiration, led Howard to the foot of the bed where – kneeling on all fours – she was able to watch their performing shadows on the bedroom wall while he licked and then fucked her. It was this more than the physical sensation of him that finally aroused her, an odd and irresistible sexual charge of being being both voyeur and participant; anonymous male and female forms projected onto the blank screen of the wall acting out her erotic fantasies. Even so, Constance was far from orgasm when she sensed a heightened urgency in Howard. So she faked it. Breathless moans and childlike whimperings, sighs and groans, a violent bucking of her buttocks against the persistence of his thrusts, coarse cries and a shrill crescendo of yesyesyes. She faked it. Not for his benefit, but for hers. Because she'd discovered, long ago – before Howard – that the very act of faking an orgasm almost invariably aroused her sufficiently to have one for real. *Reality engendered by imitation*, according to Milly. *What you are actually doing is fucking yourself.* So Constance faked an orgasm, bringing herself to climax a moment before Howard shuddered sweatily to a halt.

Among the miscellaneous items affixed to her cork notice-board was an article clipped from a newspaper column. She .

thought of this cutting as she watched the shadows slowly uncouple. She remembered the quote, attributed to Courtney Love: *I fake it so real I am beyond fake.* And she smiled, to herself, in the dark.

The Life and Times of a Hallam Saw Grinder (a Dramatic Reconstruction in Many Parts)

August 1859

From afar, the Friendly Society gardens appeared to be aflutter with flags, flapping in the breeze and brilliant with sunlight. A curious spectacle to a stranger on a morning when the allotments shimmered in the heat haze as though viewed through a liquid veil. But, to Thomas Amory – approaching on foot down Brook Hill, with his eldest son Daniel – the sight was too familiar to be noteworthy. The flags, mere scraps of rag bound to fenceposts to keep birds off the crop. To him, the most remarkable feature in prospect was the blessing of yet another glorious summer's day. Thomas had been laid off at his union's expense for two weeks, during which time his face had been restored – Frances said – to the ruddy hue she recalled when they were first courting. His arms were reddish-brown and freckled, the thick ginger hairs bleached blond by the sun. And he coughed less often and less harshly, his breathing made easier for being out of the damp and dusty hull. Sleep, too, was more refreshing – the exertion of working his plot each day being sufficient to ensure sound slumber, without reducing him to the state of accumulative exhaustion consequent upon his usual labours at the grindstone. Even the loss of earnings was not an immediate concern, the scale he drew from the Saw Grinders' being better than that received by men laid off from other trades. The Amorys had meat on their plates – though a cheaper cut – and Thomas was thankful the slackening off in work coincided with his allotment yielding the bulk of its harvest.

Father and son went through the wrought-iron gate and along the track to the shed where Thomas kept his implements. He unfastened the padlock and fetched a metal pail and a small fork which had to be held by the tang, the handle having long since split and become detached. Few other men were about, and none within hailing distance. He was keen to make good progress in the morning – for Frances would bring the younger children with her when she fetched the snap, and Jasper was sure to clamour to be allowed to remain for the afternoon. Being 'helped' by a boy of six was more hindrance than assistance, so it was necessary for Thomas and Daniel to accomplish the bulk of the work beforehand. He gave the fork to his son – eleven years old, coppery haired, and built like four beanpoles tied together with string.

'Tek care o' that un,' said Thomas. 'It's new.'

Daniel looked at the fork and then at his father. 'It ant got no 'andle.'

'Eh, thou'st not broke it already?'

'It were . . .!'

Catching on to Thomas's expression, the boy's indignant protestation gave way to laughter. He pushed his father, who pushed him back – dumping him on his posterior in a raised bed of comfrey.

'Thy mother's dolly-peg hast more meat on it than thee, son.'

The first task was to finish picking the crop of broad beans, a bucketful of which they had taken home the previous day for salting. The pair worked along opposite flanks of the double row, each bush waist-high and supported by lengths of twine stretched between stout stakes at either end of the strip. They stooped to search among the leaves, twisting off one pod after another and tossing them into one of the pails. This summer's was a good crop, unlike the previous year when the bushes had been ravaged by blackfly. This time Thomas had taken the advice of Robert Smith, who had the adjacent allotment – pinching off three inches of stem as soon as the first beans started to form, ensuring an earlier harvest and less likelihood of pests. When Thomas had sought an explanation, his friend had merely winked and told him, 'If it works, it works.' And it had. When father and son had harvested all the pods, they set about removing the upper leaves from the bushes and adding them to the contents of the pail. Poor man's spinach, Frances called it. Neither of the pickers spoke while they toiled, though from time to time Daniel would rise up on his haunches, as if stretching, in order to monitor which of them had made the greater progress.

The pair had worked up a sweat by now and broke off from their labours to take turns dousing face and neck at the standpipe and to rinse their mouths with the cold, metallic water. As Thomas stood up, dripping down the front of his shirt, he saw two men walking along the track towards him. One was Robert Smith. The other, who had his head lowered and his face partially obscured by his cap, would not have been immediately recognizable had it not been for the marked disparity in height between the two men and the singular manner of his gait. On drawing nearer, the second man raised his head to expose his cabbage-like complexion to the full whitewash glare of the morning sun. Thomas instructed Daniel to take the pail of pickings home.

'But we've not finished,' said the boy.

'I said, go home. Now do as I say.'

Royal Commission of Inquiry
(sitting at) Hallam Town Hall
Thursday, 20 June 1867 (Thirteenth Day)

Witness: Thomas Amory, saw grinder, No.11 Garden Street, Hallam.

Q. Do you recollect the second time when Linley was shot?

A. Yes.

Q. Was it you who shot him on this occasion?

A. No.

Q. Do you know who it was who fired the shot?

A. I know it was not I.

Q. That is not what I asked. I will ask you again, do you know who fired the shot?

A. Yes.

Q. Who was it?

(*witness hesitates*)

Q. You know if you tell the truth you have nothing to be afraid of. You will be entitled to your certificate of indemnity from prosecution if you tell the whole truth.

A. I will tell the truth if I may have my certificate.

Q. You shall have your certificate, and if the man whom you are going to implicate will come forward and ask for his indemnity, he shall have it also so long as he tells the whole truth. So you need not fear for anyone. I ask you again, was there anybody associated with you in shooting Linley the second time? Answer the question.

A. There was.

Q. Who was it?

A. (*after some hesitation*) Samuel Crookes.

Q. Who shot him? Did you or Crookes shoot him?

A. Crookes shot him.

Q. Had you any quarrel with Linley?

A. I did not know him to speak to.

Q. Had you any malice against him in any way?

A. Only for being obnoxious to the trade.

Q. And Crookes it was who shot him, you say?

A. Yes, Crookes shot him. (*witness hesitates*) I compelled Crookes to shoot him.

They met on the following Saturday evening, as arranged, in the public bar of the Royal George Hotel, in Carver Street. The George was not Thomas's local, but it was no more than a few minutes' walk from his home in Garden Street and, with the Society's secretary as proprietor, it was a popular ale house with saw grinders. For many of the men – particularly during times of poor trade – a weekly visit was necessary, if only to collect their scale; though few would do so without paying back over the bar a proportion of what they had drawn. Broadhead was not behind the counter when they arrived and, on asking after him, they were given to understand that he was upstairs. Saturday was not the customary night for committee meetings, but the barman gave no encouragement to their further enquiries. He merely drew off a couple of pints and set them down, clumsily and with much spillage. Thomas and Sammy sat in a corner farthest from the door, occupying what had been their usual table in the days when they remained in the habit of drinking regularly in one another's company. They supped without speaking for several minutes, Sammy taking small swift sips while Thomas consumed his beer in great gulps that left a rim of froth on his upper lip. Old Smite 'Em was renowned, among other things, for keeping good ale – warmish, sweet at first, then leaving a delicious bitter aftertaste in the back of the throat at each swallow. Thomas habitually mopped his lips on the cuff of his workshirt.

Sammy grinned at him. 'Tell thee summat, Tom – by night's end thou could wring thy sleeve and fill a pint pot.'

'Aye,' said Thomas. 'And these sods'd want payin' ower agen for it.'

The two men laughed. Being early in the evening, the pub was not yet full and the pair saw only a few men of their acquaintance, with whom they exchanged nods or raised their pots by way of greeting. The large inglenook fireplace lay empty and unlit, the frosted-glass panes ranged at head height along one wall of the room admitting the last of the day's sunshine. Thomas inspected his hands, moistening them with saliva and rubbing away ingrained soil from the creases of his palms. The broad beans were all in, and the beets – some of them as big as a baby's head. He took another sup, the ripe scent of hops briefly masking a general odour of sweat, smoke and beer slops.

They were into their second pint before Sammy broached the subject that had been the purpose of their meeting. Keeping his voice low, eyes alert for anyone who might eavesdrop, he said, 'If we cannot see Smite 'Em tonight, what'll we do with Linley? Will we do him even so?'

168

'There's nowt we can hear tonight as'll change what we've heard afore,' replied Thomas.

'Aye, but we could 'ave some brass in us pockets for t'trouble.'

'We'll 'ave us brass sooner or later if Smite 'Em hast owt to do wi' it.' He took a long draught of ale then set the pot down firmly on the rough wooden table, as if by way of punctuation, before drawing a cuff across his mouth.

Thomas had met Broadhead two days previously outside the Eagle works, where the secretary had been on his rounds collecting members' natty money. He was stepping out into the street, contributions book in hand, when Thomas approached. The other man folded the book away into a worn leather pouch, fat with clinking coins, and stowed a pencil stub behind his ear. He was taller than Thomas, though less broad of build; his dress that of any working man: cap, thick cotton shirt, corduroys held up by braces, heavy clogs. However, his clothes appeared cleaner and less frayed than those of his fellows, with only an ugly scar among the stubble of his lower lip as physical testimony to the days – many years ago – before he gave up saw grinding for full-time union work. An exploding grindstone had been the cause of this blemish; the grinder had been killed instantly, while Broadhead and two other men in the same hull were variously injured by flying fragments. With a stone at full speed and as tall as a man, it did not do to be in the vicinity when one broke up, as they were wont to do from time to time. Broadhead's face creased into a smile upon seeing who it was waiting on him outside the works. He placed a hand on Thomas's elbow as they walked along the street, exchanging hallos and enquiring after one another's health and the well-being of their respective families. After some hesitation, Thomas asked what was to be done about Linley, to which the secretary replied, 'Whatever is necessary.' Broadhead was similarly enigmatic when Sammy Crookes called on him at home the following day. The sum of twenty pounds was discussed and deemed to be appropriate

169

remuneration, but the man was no more specific about the manner in which the task was to be executed. His concern, he said, was not so much method as effectiveness.

This was a relative term where such as James Linley was concerned, Thomas and Sammy agreed – few men being more persistently obnoxious to their trade in the face of whatever punishment might be meted out. Sammy took another sup, then set his pot down while he reached into his pocket for a small rectangular tin. From within it, he produced a plug of tobacco which he placed in his mouth and began to chew. He offered the tin to Thomas, who shook his head – withdrawing his outstretched feet beneath the table for fear of having them inadvertently spat upon in due course.

'Could mean owt,' said Sammy. Imitating Broadhead's gruff voice, he added, 'Effectiveness.'

Witness: William Broadhead, Secretary, Saw Grinders' Union.

Q. You have heard what they have said, what do you have to say?

A. I am prepared to endorse the whole of their statements. Some of the details, I think, they are mistaken in, but the substance is correct.

Q. Am I to understand from you then, that you did hire Crookes and Amory to shoot at Linley in the first instance, in November, 1857?

A. I regret to say that I did.

Q. And did you pay them £20 for it?

A. That I cannot say. My impression is that it was £15, but I will not be certain.

Q. Did you hire Crookes and Amory in August, 1859 to shoot a second time at Linley?

A. Yes.

Q. Did you pay them the sum of £20 for the second shooting?

A. My impression is that is was £15 on both occasions.

*   *   *

170

Thomas Amory was not drunk when he left the George. As a consequence of being joined by a group of grinders of their acquaintance, he and Sammy had stayed longer and consumed more ale than had been their intention. However, supping did not affect him easily as it did some men, Sammy for instance. Even so, the fresh night air caused his head to swim as he walked alone along Carver Street in the direction of home. The clear sky was replete with stars, a three-quarter moon illuminating the buildings and making silver streams of the streets. A few folk were about, mostly drunken men – harmless, for the most part; more a danger to themselves than to anyone else. One such had been hauled out dead from the river only the previous week, fallen off Lady's Bridge and too stupefied to save himself. It was the gangs of lads – the apprentices – who were to be avoided; new to ale and always greedy for fisticuffs. Thomas passed a night-soil collector, two large pails supported by a wooden yoke across her shoulders. The pails were full, swinging from side to side and slopping their foul contents. He held his breath as the woman went by. Half-past eleven, and they were already out on their rounds. It occurred to him, with a beery snicker, that the day was not far distant when a night-soil collector would be in the privy with a man, holding the bucket beneath him.

From the turning into Garden Street he could see the house, an upstairs window dimly lit by the oil-lamp which – despite his objections about unnecessary expense – Frances kept alight for him to see by whenever he returned home late. Indoors, he undressed quickly and quietly so as not to disturb his wife, whose shallow breaths were in contrast to his own wheezy rasps as he recovered from the long walk and the steep climb upstairs. As he went to extinguish the lamp, he glimpsed a figure in the doorway. Daniel's pale face loomed out of the shadows. Father and son looked silently into one another's eyes for a moment, then Thomas shut off the light and climbed into bed. Frances stirred as he looped an arm round her, but did not waken.

Chapter Six

SHOP TALK

If customers ate a meal before going shopping, they'd be less inclined
to raid the fresh food and bakery sections; if they wrote a shopping
list – and stuck to it – they wouldn't load their trolley with things
they didn't need. Impulse buying. Splurchasing, we call it. If it wasn't
for splurchasing, supermarkets would go bust. But whose responsibility is it to ensure customers only buy what they require? Ours or
theirs?

John Chapple, Manager, HypaCenta.
Hallam Evening Crucible, 10 October 1996

Howard left before breakfast. He'd intended to leave without
disturbing her, he said, but she'd been woken by the sound of
taps being turned on and off, of the toilet being flushed.
Wearing robe and slippers, Constance intercepted him on the
landing. Sorry, he didn't have time for a cup of tea. He really
didn't. She yawned. Her mouth was gummy and had a stale
taste of wine and Twiglets. She followed him downstairs
and helped him with the double-lock on the front door,
once familiar but which now reduced him to ineptitude. On
the doorstep, in the milky morning air, he squeezed her

hand. But they didn't hug or kiss or say goodbye; they didn't speak at all. She closed the door. On her way to the kitchen she heard the loud fart of the engine, the characteristic and – even now – irritating series of revs as he gunned the accelerator.

It was cold in the kitchen, the central heating hadn't come on yet. The fluorescent strip-light was too bright, too garish; she switched it off almost as soon as it had flick-flick-flickered into life. The room became grey again. She sat on a high wooden stool, cradling an unfilled kettle. Tired. Her eyes felt gritty, puffy; how was her breathing? Fine, her lungs were OK considering the amount she'd drunk last night and the smoky pub and the lack of sleep. Headache? A little. She felt hungry and slightly nauseous, also aware of an impending need for the toilet. Sometimes, in the mornings, Howard used to drape an arm or a leg across her middle as they lay semi-awake in bed and she'd push him off because of the pressure on her bladder. *Don't, I want the loo*. And, predictably, he'd place a hand on her belly and press down. Or she'd get up to go to the bathroom and he'd pull her back into bed, holding her until she squealed to be freed before she wet herself. Widdle. Tea and toast. Shower. She'd advance the timer so the water would be hot by the time she'd finished breakfast, then have a shower and that would wake her up and she'd be fine.

Constance sat, empty kettle cradled like a sleeping baby. She raised a hand to her face, pinching her nose to stifle a sneeze. Rubber. Her fingers bore the distinctive lingering odour of rubber. Had Howard gathered up the used condom or would she find it – shrivelled, cold, clammy – among the debris around the bed? Her hand moved upwards, finger-combing the tangled fringe. She tugged, hard. Her hair, Jesus: dry and stiff with yesterday's mousse. She'd have to wash it. Maybe coffee, instead of tea, to wake her up; a big mug of black coffee. Constance pulled the robe more tightly around her. She went on sitting alone in silence in the gradually lightening kitchen, not once loosening her grip on the empty

173

kettle nor showing any inclination to take it over to the sink
and fill it with water.

The Inky Path

*The young reporter learns to judge and weigh up character, to
sift truth from falsehood. He soon comes to realize that one
cannot judge by appearances, that the world is a hard place,
that it does not do to be too trustful of one's fellows. A healthy
scepticism is the watchword of sound reporting practice. If
someone expresses an opinion to you or supplies you with
information, you must ask yourself 'why?'. What is the story
beneath the story? Beware not only of outright lies but also of
lies of omission – truth may be corrupted as much by the
information which is withheld as by false information per se.
Do not believe everything you are told. This is not to say that
you should, therefore, believe nothing you are told. Scepticism
lies between the two extremes of gullibility and cynicism; the
good journalist is he that learns to discern between what can be
believed and what cannot.*

William Boyce was eating a small triangular sandwich, an
aroma of fishpaste filling the room. White bread, ready sliced.
He was reading aloud in an American accent from a paperback
edition of *Death of a Salesman*. When Constance entered the
office he looked up over the book and said, 'Hi, howya doin'?'

'You're playing Willy Loman, not Popeye.'

'Aye, well, I'll admit the accent's not quite there yet.'

She hung up her coat and went to the coffee-maker. 'Any
messages?'

'Your—'

'Apart from my mam.'

'No.'

William lay the book face down on his desk. He'd confessed
his anxieties about this latest production – a marked departure
for him, and for the drama company, after fifteen years of
Gilbert and Sullivan. New director, new direction; if *Death of*

174

a Salesman was a success, rumour was he planned to follow it up with a stage version of *Reservoir Dogs*. Several veteran members had resigned already.

'Must be a quiet morning if you've time to learn your lines.'

He gestured at the radio. 'They've had me monitoring that bloody thing.'

One of the tasks assigned to early duty reporters was to tune in to the half-hourly news bulletins to make sure the local stations weren't carrying stories the *Crucible* had missed. *It's not 'news' unless some other bugger says it is*. He thought it farcical that while he was monitoring the local radio station, his opposite number there was going through the latest edition of the *Crucible* in a similar search for follow-ups. *I don't know why we don't just fucking ring each other up and swap stories*.

'Anyroad, with the flap at head office, they'd not notice if we didn't do owt all day.'

She carried a mug of coffee over to her desk and sat opposite her colleague, peering at him through the gap between their computer monitors. He was, as usual, wearing a maroon V-neck sweater, plain white shirt and a green tie patterned, in yellow, with a series of acorn motifs above the initials NUJ. The tie had been presented to him by the chapel to mark twenty-five years' unbroken membership of the union. That was five years ago, his proud claim being that he'd worn the tie to work every day since then. Unable to find a coaster among the mess, Constance placed the mug on a folded copy of the previous day's city final.

'What flap?'

'Those pictures, "magic eye" or whatever they're called. You know the ones I mean, the psychedelic patterns you hold up to your face and you're supposed to see summat – an image or summat – concealed in the pattern. You know?'

'Yeah. Mam's into them.'

'Aye, my missus an' all. Well, Trading Standards reckon we've stopped taking the syndicated pictures – the authentic ones – and are running our own. To save costs.'

'We did, didn't we? I mean, that's common knowledge.'

'Aye, but our pictures haven't got owt in them – no concealed image, nothing. Just pretty patterns – totally random – drawn by a computer graphics program.'

'But how long is it since we switched from the syndicated ones? A month? Five weeks? And my mam still swears she can see things in them.'

'So do lots of folk, apparently. When we knew Trading Standards were on to it, we conducted a survey: a hundred people were shown t'same pattern. Thirty-one said they couldn't see a hidden image and sixty-nine said they could.'

'And there was nothing *there*?'

'It gets better. The sixty-nine came up with forty-seven different images.' He finished his sandwich, clapping his hands to release the crumbs into a wastepaper bin beside his desk. 'Like I say, they're filling two pages with this crap – so if you've got owt worth a decent show, I'd hang on to it and file for tomorrow's paper.'

The phone rang. William took the call – from one of his business contacts, judging by the conspiratorial tone. Good tip-off, too, if the hurried manner in which he scrabbled for a fresh page in his notebook was anything to go by. His face, as he made notes, bore the expression of an angler landing a ten-pound salmon.

'Mall Madman' spree triggers slump in sales

Exclusive Report by William Boyce

Hallam's giant Urbopark complex is suffering a slump in trade following a spate of attacks by a mysery saboteur they call the Mall Madman.

Sales figures are down at many of the 250 retailers as shoppers stay away for fear of further incidents.

A confidential report, details of which have been leaked to the *Evening Crucible*, reveals that takings have fallen by nearly 10 percent across a representative spread of shops and stores since the attacks began in early September. Food and leisure outlets at the mall have also been hit.

Weeks

The number of people visiting Urbopark – closely monitored by Mall Admin – has dropped in each of the last four weeks and figures are sharply down on the same period last year, the report shows.

Uniformed

These worrying statistics emerged at a monthly meeting of retailers and mall managers this week and have occurred despite Mall Admin's attempts to play down the series of attacks.

The leaked report from that meeting also reveals that tighter security and increased patrols by uniformed Mall Secure officers, rather than reassuring shoppers, have had the opposite effect.

The incidents, which are being investigated by the police, include:
● blood-like graffiti daubed on doorways,
● the dumping of more than a hundred headless chicken carcasses,
● a mass evacuation caused by a bomb hoax, and
● the razor slashing of leathers and furs.

A £1m ransom demand has heightened fears that these may be the first in an escalating campaign of violence against the mall. So far there has been no indication of who is responsible, or why Urbopark is being targeted.

Something

One shop manager, who asked not be identified, told the *Crucible*: 'If the intention is to damage trade at the mall, then this madman is succeeding – customers are being driven away in their hundreds.

'Unless something is done soon to stop him, I fear that
turn to page 3

William was reading his own story when Constance returned from lunch. He tilted the paper towards her to display page one – his first splash since he'd been seconded to the district office. Constance congratulated him. He said Mall Admin and Mall PRO had both been on the phone, trying in vain to wheedle out of him the name of his source; they were furious, too, that the *Crucible* was *playing right into the perpetrator's hands* by raising public anxiety and publicizing the damage caused to business. As for the 'Mall Madman' *nom de crime* . . . William declared, with evident relish, that he was *not exactly flavour of the month* at Urbopark.

'Dougal say anything?' she asked, hanging up her coat.

'Oh aye, they've been on to him an' all. He gave them short shrift, so I hear.'

'The editor standing up for one of his reporters? There's a turn-up.'

177

'Apparently, he said to them, "If the story is *factually accurate*, what is there to complain about?".' 'Course, they'd no answer to that.'

Constance sat down at her desk. She said: 'I bet it's only a matter of time before one of us is assigned to write a follow-up – *It's safety first at Urbopark as mall bosses launch a campaign to woo back the missing shoppers*, or something similar.'

William looked at her, then at his screen, then back at her again.

'*Already?*' she said.

He hesitated. 'Tomorrow, page six.'

'Jesus.'

'Actually, that wasn't a bad intro – d'you mind if I . . .'

They laughed. Constance screwed up an old press release and threw it at him. She wouldn't have done *that* three years ago, when she shadowed him during her first week as a reporter. Nor would she have come up with an intro worth pinching. Her resentment at having to accommodate a hack from head office – one who'd then scooped her for a splash in her own patch – evaporated in a wave of fondness for the man. She watched him for a moment, as he resumed his reading of the paper, then turned her attention to the messages that had been left for her while she was out. Nothing urgent. Remembering her mam's morning call, Constance – yawning so widely her jaw clicked – pulled the answering machine towards her.

'Did Mam fill the entire tape again?'

'Aye, I'd say so.' William continued reading. 'I listened to t'first thirty seconds or so then fast-forwarded to near the end and it was still her talking.'

'Typical.'

She rewound the tape to the beginning and inserted the earpiece so as not to disturb her colleague. She pressed 'msg/rew'. What she heard on the tape was not one message from her mam, but two. The first, lasting almost ten minutes, was taken up with family chit-chat (Mags, Dad, Granddad, the

178

latest shopping acquisitions, house next-door-but-one up for sale, commemorative Charles and Di wedding mug broken in washing-up accident. Oh, and *that nice PC Pink* had fetched another batch of vegetables. She itemized them.) Constance didn't listen to the second message, presumably comprising various matters of gossip Mam had neglected to mention in the first call. She didn't listen to the second message because, in the interlude between Mam's two monologues, there was another call logged on the answering machine. This consisted of one sentence: *For Ms Amory, from the Man in the Moon: visitors should let Ruskin put them in the picture with regard to the nature of truth.* The caller was male, accent neutral, nondescript; the words slightly muffled and stilted, as though he was trying to disguise his identity. She recognized it immediately as the voice of the man who'd orchestrated the Urbopark bomb hoax, and whose call to the police was recorded for broadcast on the local radio and television news. She rummaged hurriedly in her bag for a notebook and replayed the new message, taking it down verbatim. When William Boyce broke off from his newspaper to direct an enquiring glance, she told him nothing. It would have been easy – natural – for her to play him the message or read it out, to share her excitement with a fellow journalist; but her instinct was to withhold the information. Not from *him*, as such, but at any rate to keep it to herself. Rereading the note she'd made, she broke the sentence down into its component parts and wrote each word or set of words on a separate line. She circled 'Ruskin' and 'Man in the Moon', placed question marks by 'visitors', 'in the picture' and 'nature of truth'. After staring at the page for a moment, Constance ejected the tape and slipped it, along with the notebook, into her handbag. A surprise present for Paul Pink, but not yet. First, there were inquiries of her own to be made. She retrieved her coat from its hook.

'Not bad news, I hope?' asked William.

'Bad news?'

'Your mother.'

'Oh, no. It's not Mam. Just something that might make a story.'

The bank of telephones outside the *Crucible* was in full view of Sally, on front desk, who would wonder – aloud, to William, probably – why Constance was using a payphone rather than the office phone. And what reason could she give? *It's a secret. Not telling.* She didn't even understand, herself, the exact nature of this urge towards subterfuge, other than a vague sense that her secrecy was spawned by his, the anonymous hoaxer's; that his cryptic message to her – to *her* – was as private and intimate and personal as a love letter from an unknown admirer. It gave her a thrill to be privy to a secret. Made her apprehensive, too, because here was further evidence that the saboteur – the Mall Madman – had opened up a direct line of communication. First the In Memoriam ad, now this. He knew her name, he knew her phone number; he had heard her voice on the answering machine tape, asking callers – asking *him* – to leave a message. And he had *spoken* to her. If there was a grand design in what he was doing to the mall, she was now incorporated into it – which filled her with excitement and dread and an irresistible exhilaration of plunging into the unknown.

She passed the bank of phones and continued beyond Snak Shak, crossing the central plaza, Green Zone, and making her way to the nearest Customer Utilities Concourse (toilets, telephones, cashpoints, parent and baby room). She went into one of the phone cubicles and dialled directory inquiries. Engaged. She tried again. No listing for a pub called the Man in the Moon. She gave the operator the name 'Ruskin'.

'Business or residential?'

'Residential.'

'D'you have an initial?'

'W.B.'

'D for delta?'

'No *B*. B for . . . banana.'

'D'you have an address?'

'No.'

'I'm sorry, nothing listed for Ruskin W.B. or W-anything.'

Constance hung up. Just a hunch. One of her hunches, that was all. Shit. Try to think, try to *think*. She rested her notebook on the small shelf next to the phone and studied the message again. What was the Man in the Moon if not a pub? And if it *was* a pub, what then? A meeting there? What time, what day? Or would you simply go in and ask for Ruskin? In any case, no pub of that name in Hallam. Perhaps it was a 'who', a reference to a person? Or a song. R.E.M., off *Automatic for the People* – a Christmas present from Howard. Constance began humming the tune to herself, trying to recall the other lyrics to see if they contained a clue. No, it was *on* not *in*, 'Man On the Moon'.

She preferred *Everybody Hurts*, on side one; though she'd not been able to listen to it since they'd split up. What *split*? Since he *left* her. Anyway, the moon. The moon. You looked at the moon, at a full moon, and it was like a face; the blue-grey patches of shadow – the lunar seas or whatever – could resemble the features of a face. The pattern was there for those who saw it. The Man in the Moon was something mams and dads told their children about – a make-believe figure, a story, a figment of the imagination; like Father Christmas and the Tooth Fairy. *Yesterday upon a stair, I met a man who wasn't there. He wasn't there again today; I wish that man would go away.* So where did that get her? Nowhere. Absolutely nowhere. What about Ruskin? '. . . *visitors should let Ruskin put them in the picture . . .*'

A man was tapping a coin sharply against the plexiglas wall of the kiosk. Constance became suddenly aware of the mall engulfing her with its commotion – a blur of noise and bustle all around her, seeping into the telephone cubicle like a rising tide of floodwater. It was as though she'd regained con-

181

sciousness after fainting to find herself gazing up into a swirl
of unfamiliar faces all talking to her at once. The man rapped
the plexiglas again. His voice, muffled, *Tha mekkin' a call, or
what?* She gathered up her belongings, trying to conceal her
irritation as she stepped out of the booth to allow him in. And,
in the process of being distracted, it came to her.

The Inky Path
*A journalist must know a little about a lot, and a lot about a
little. If he does not have the necessary information at his
fingertips, he must know whither to go in search of it. For the
best resource of any reporter – and of any man – is his own
resourcefulness.*

Nine o'clock. The building wasn't due to open for another
hour. It had been shut when she'd gone there the previous
afternoon (half-day closing), and she cursed herself for failing,
at least, to check the opening times before making a return
visit. *Basics.* How could you be a journalist when you had the
concentration span of a goldfish? Constance sat on the steps,
waiting; when it began to rain she sought shelter in a nearby
café. She chose a table away from the window – wouldn't do
for someone from work to see her here, with a pot of coffee
and a copy of *Hard Times.* The book was annoying her. She'd
bought it second-hand from a shop at the university and,
evidently, it had once belonged to a literature student. Many
of the pages were defaced with handwritten annotations in
the margins; certain sentences, sometimes entire paragraphs,
were overlaid with orange marker pen. Occasionally, an
exclamation mark or question mark stood alongside a section
of text, or there would be a cross-reference to another page.
Constance found herself unable to read the novel itself for
being distracted by the annotations, her eyes repeatedly drawn
to the pencil markings and luminous highlights rather than the
neat black typeface. Or she'd weigh her own reading of key
passages against the comments, criticisms and observations

made by the book's previous owner – spending more time pondering that person's words than those written by the author. And, to complicate matters, she now had Stan's critique of Dickens-as-socialist ringing in her ears like a whispered mantra.

She folded over a corner of the page and closed the book. Nine-forty. She replenished her cup from the stainless steel pot and added milk, messily, from two small and – deliberately, it seemed to her – inaccessibly foil-sealed plastic cartons. She licked her fingers clean and mopped up the rest of the spillage with a serviette. If there was a knack to unpeeling these things, she'd yet to discover it. Howard reckoned it was a psychological rather than physical problem, a catch-22: she couldn't open the cartons because she *believed herself* incapable of doing so. Howard. Howard this, Howard that. If she couldn't even put milk in her coffee without being reminded of him, what was there left of her life for him to infiltrate? *Blot him out*, had been Milly's advice. *What with, Mill? Time? Someone else? Hallucinogenic drugs?* Her friend had shaken her head and replied: *With yourself.* Easy as that. Constance got up abruptly from the table and was almost out of the café before realizing she hadn't paid her bill.

The Ruskin Gallery and Museum opened promptly at ten, the uniformed attendant apparently disconcerted to find a visitor waiting outside the entrance as he slid back the bolts on the heavy wooden doors, which swung inwards noiselessly and with surprising ease. Much of the space was taken up with a temporary exhibition of South American needlecraft, but – directed by the attendant – Constance made straight for the Guild of St George Collection, a montage devoted to John Ruskin. This permanent display presented an outline of the man's life and works, chronicling his connection with Hallam and the patronage which founded a museum, later to be relocated from the outskirts of the city to the present site. She made a brief study of the photographs, paintings and sketches before opening her spiral-bound pad to note down the accompanying inscriptions. Two panels in particular attracted her attention, and she took care to copy every word.

Ruskin and the Pre-Raphaelite Brotherhood

A secret society of artists founded in 1848 as a reaction against 19th century art's predisposition, stimulated by Raphael (1483–1520), for 'romantic realism'. The brotherhood searched for qualities in Italian art which pre-dated Raphael, finding inspiration in the early medieval period. Their aim was to paint directly from nature or life. Ruskin, one of the prominent thinkers of the Victorian age, greatly influenced the group. His belief in 'truth to nature' became the foundation of Pre-Raphaelite painting.

Ruskin the philanthropist

Ruskin was greatly concerned with social problems, espousing his views in his writing and dedicating some of his wealth to educational enterprises. Ruskin College at Oxford, the first residential college for working people, was named after him. In 1875, he founded St George's Museum for the working people of Hallam ('the workers in iron'), choosing the city for its beautiful surrounding countryside, and because of his admiration of the skill of its metalworkers. The intention was to awaken a visual awareness of 'what is lovely in the life of Nature and heroic in the life of Men'.

On her way out of the museum, Constance saw a notice on the wall by the exit: 'Please remember to sign the visitors book!' And, with a thrill of unease, the wording of the saboteur's message came back to her. The visitors book lay directly beneath the notice, secured by a chain to a small table. Each page was divided into columns for name, address and comments; no entries had been made under that day's date. Turning back to the previous page, she cast her eye over those for the preceding day. More than thirty people had taken the trouble to record their visit to the museum – their remarks, the predictable assortment of *v.interesting, informative, fascinating* . . . ; their home addresses ranging from Aberystwyth to York, Bordeaux to Zurich. Five lines from the bottom of the page – between *Gordon Barber, Leeds, smashing exhibition*, and a group of entries in what looked like Japanese – was one that stood out. In red pencil, written with the exaggerated clumsiness of an adult attempting either to imitate the disjointed scrawl of a young child or to disguise his own hand.

W. B. Rage   *Hallam, England*   *Well Done!*

Two days later, Constance would receive a postcard at the office – addressed to her, but containing no message. The postcard was purchased from the museum shop, its picture depicting one of the paintings she'd seen alongside the panel on the Pre-Raphaelites. The subject was a solitary female figure in circumstances of elemental dishevelment and bearing an expression of dreamlike, beatific rapture. The young woman, her perfect pale complexion radiating a diaphanous beauty, was graced with long flowing curls of luxuriant hair of a rich auburn hue that fused – and was infused with – the vibrance of a flaming sunset, an earthy mellowness of autumn leaves.

Among the press releases to spew from the Mall Link printer while Constance was Ruskin-hunting were two from Warren Bartholomew, head of Mall PRO, which awaited her attention when she returned to the office. The first, a formal announcement that bids were to be invited for the Mall Secure contract when the present in-house agreement expired at the end of the year. The second, purporting to be a statement from Mall Manager Roy Dobbs, warned of the iniquities of the minimum wage and European Union edicts on workers' rights and employment conditions in member states. Under the heading Mall Chief Hits Out At Threat To Jobs, was a diatribe against a perceived assault on *management's right to manage* – political moves which, if adopted in Britain, would force employers, especially those in highly competitive sectors such as the retail trade, to *downsize their human resources costs*. What aroused Constance's curiosity about the press release was that she'd been sent a draft copy, in error, rather than the final version; the statement evidently having been drafted by Mall Admin's parent company in London for each of its shopping centres up and down the country to issue locally. For, wherever a paragraph in quotation marks required attribution, it was followed by the instruction [insert your mall manager's name here]. William Boyce had attached a note to the release suggesting Mall PRO's blunder was worthy of exposure to ridicule in the diary column.

When Constance phoned Warren Bartholomew, he was in no mood to be ribbed about the error. Nor did he appreciate, it seemed, her observation on the remarkable fact that not only did all six Mall Build UK managers share *identical* views on these issues but they chose to express their opinions in *exactly* the same words.

'You never make mistakes, of course . . .'

'Oh come on, Warren, where's your sense of humour?'

'You're never under so much fucking pressure you cock things up?'

'*Warren.*'

He apologized. He said he was well out of order. *It's been one of those days – one of those weeks, actually.* The phone call resumed a more normal pattern, the public relations officer handling her questions on both press releases with something approaching his usual deft professionalism. But she could tell by his tone of voice – a flatness, a lethargy, a distractedness – that Warren was semi-detached from their conversation. He sounded, as Mam would've phrased it, as though he'd *lost a pound, then lost another one*. If he was especially ill at ease while discussing the Mall Secure privatization plan, Constance put it down to his embarrassment at having played down this

186

angle when she challenged him on the story a couple of weeks earlier.

'You OK, Warren?' she said, before terminating the call.

'Yeah, I'm fine. It's just . . . work, you know how it is.'

Send In The Clones, was the headline on the diary piece about the mall manager's statement. The *Crucible* also carried a news story – based on a reissued version of the press release, and reproducing the Roy Dobbs quotes as though they were his. Justifying the decision in a leader column, the editor said he regarded it as a *valid and timely contribution to the general debate on employer/employee relations*. He concluded: *It doesn't matter who said what, it's what is said that matters most.*

'You've had the tape for *two* days, and you came across the entry in the visitors book *yesterday*.'

'The editor wanted to make sure we got first bite at any story.'

'The editor.'

'OK, *I* wanted to as well. I wanted to check it out for myself. I mean, I was the one he—'

'I must've missed your name on the list of new recruits to the department.'

'Paul, I . . .'

'This is not a *story* – it's *crime*. And you aren't a detective, you're a reporter. I've got a team of investigating officers who've been deprived of vital pieces of information because you took it upon yourself . . .'

'I know, I know. I'm sorry.'

'You could be done for withholding evidence, you know that?'

'. . .'

'I'll send someone over. D'you have the tape with you now?'

'Yes. And . . .'

'What?'

'And a postcard.'

187

'A postcard?'

'He sent me a postcard. It came this morning.'

'What sort of postcard?'

'A Pre-Raphaelite painting.'

'Tying in with the Ruskin connection?'

'Yes. I think so.'

'Could we have that as well, d'you think? The postcard. If it's OK with you.'

'There's no message on it, but there might be fingerprints or something.'

'Have you dusted for prints already, or would you like us to do that for you?'

Constance liked to go behind the scenes at Urbopark, beyond doors flagged with signs that read: NO UNAUTHORIZED PERSONNEL. She liked to explore the mall's dirty, dark places – its labyrinth of hidden walkways and passages, rooftops and gantries, stairways and ladders, delivery bays and stockrooms – where the subterranean machinations of mass shopping were made to function out of sight of those who shopped. As a reporter – as a person – she liked to delve beneath the surface. And few surfaces, she thought, were more gleaming and glittery than that of Urbopark's in casting a comfortingly familiar gloss over its workings. A mall offered guarantees: no eating, except in designated places; no litter; no violence; no crime; no dogs (no dog mess); no beggars; no drunks; no homeless folk sleeping in shop doorways; no loitering; no running; no rollerskating; no skateboarding; no weather; no traffic; no traffic fumes; no traffic noise; no graffiti; no vandalism; and – above all – no darkness, no dark places. A mall liberated shoppers from darkness. As a journalist, with her privileged access, Constance got to see the places they were not permitted to see except through her eyes, her stories. She had never been behind the scenes at a beauty contest, but she imagined a parallel contrast between on-stage (toothy smiles, sparkling costumes) and backstage (partially clad contestants quarrelling and weeping and pissing and shitting and waxing their stubble and applying make-up and expelling yellowy gobbets of snot into Kleenex).

This notion occurred to her as she made another of her occasional forays into the out of bounds, observing the goings-on in a service bay at the rear of Fruits of the Churn, Red Lower (feature assignment: *a fascinating step-by-step guide to how food gets from the farm to your shopping basket*). A refrigerated lorry was backing down a concrete ramp to the accompaniment of an electronically synthesized declaration: *This vehicle is reversing, this vehicle is reversing* . . . The corporate logo on the flanks of the truck depicted a stream running through a lush meadow dotted with Friesians, beneath the legend: 'Fruits of the Churn – dairy freshness, every day'. A man in overalls sat at the controls of a fork-lift, ready to unload pallets laden with industrially packaged consignments of milk, butter and cheese. Constance watched, making notes, as each load was manoeuvred with an electric hum through a curtain of clear-plastic strips into a cold-storage area of floor to ceiling metal shelving. When she had seen enough, her escort – the shop manager – steered her to his office so that they could conclude their interview over coffee and biscuits. It was her custom to take summary notes in shorthand while simultaneously taping the entire conversation on a miniature cassette recorder. *Belt and braces school of journalism*, according to William Boyce. It was while she was inserting a blank cassette and testing the equipment to ensure it was working that the manager's telephone rang. A message for Constance.

'You've to return to base immediately,' said the shop manager, smiling, as he replaced the receiver.

'Did they give a name?'

'Gary someone or other on newsdesk. Nice chap. He said, "Tell her, fuck the cheese feature and get her arse back to the office." '

'Jesus, I'm really—'

'It seems the, um, *Mall Madman* has struck again.'

189

The Life and Times of a Hallam Saw Grinder
(a Dramatic Reconstruction in Many Parts)

August 1859

They followed James Linley through the streets of Hallam: from home to work, from work to public house, from public house to his home. Should he venture out to the shop for tobacco, they would not be far behind. Were he to visit a friend, he would unwittingly proceed them there and back. So familiar were they with his movements that they might have drawn up a schedule of them each morning before he had set foot outside his door. However, if the earlier shooting had put him on his guard, the explosion during his residence with his brother-in-law had made Linley more cautious yet in the months that followed. Seldom would he wander abroad unaccompanied; the places he chose to frequent were those where he enjoyed the protection of numbers. And, all the while, Samuel Crookes and Thomas Amory – either singly or in union – had gone about their pursuance. Moreover, though Linley might have expected to be done sooner or later, the pair had not once alerted their quarry to the fact that he was being shadowed. Yet, in all those days, he had afforded them no opportunity when it would have been practical or sensible to execute their plan. It was not the getting of him, explained Crookes, so much as the getting away with it. That was the rub.

Royal Commission of Inquiry (sitting at) Hallam Town Hall Thursday 20 June 1867 (Thirteenth Day)

Witness: William Broadhead, Secretary, Saw Grinders' Union.
  Q. Had you any personal quarrel with Linley?
  A. No. I have no personal quarrel with any man.

Q. What induced you, then, to hire Crookes to shoot at him?

A. Linley was doing a great amount of harm to the Society and to the trade.

Q. Did Crookes tell you that he proposed to shoot Linley?

A. Yes.

Q. Did he say that he intended to kill him?

A. No.

Q. You say that he proposed to shoot Linley but not to kill him?

A. Yes, that was the understanding between us.

Thomas Amory was washing at the kitchen sink after spending a day on his allotment. He was stripped down to his undergarment – a one-piece cotton affair, the top portion of which he had lowered to the waist to leave his upper body exposed. The mat of ginger hairs on his forearms and chest glistened with soapy water. Frances, aided by their daughter Agnes, had made two trips to the yard to fetch water; though the girl – just eight years old – spilled much of what she carried and left a trail from the standpipe, down the jennel, along the pavement, across the floor of the day-room and into the kitchen. Two chores at once, remarked Thomas when his wife scolded the girl – fetching water and washing the floor into the bargain.

While the water was heating, he had sat on the front step and scraped his boots clean under the watchful eye of his youngest son. In recent weeks, Jasper had taken to following his father wherever he went about the house – pursuing him from room to room, even outside to the privy middens. Six years old, face set in a permanent frown as though he was trying to solve some intricate riddle. Thomas accepted the irony that, in a period when he was preoccupied with the pursuit of James Linley, his own son was unknowingly aping his behaviour – trailing after him like a conscience. It was as though the lad had an uncanny inkling of what he was up to. Of course, as Frances observed, Jasper was merely

191

fascinated with having his father about the house so much more now that he was laid off. And there he was again, his freckly face serious with concentration as he watched Thomas gouge the damp mud from his boots. And again, traipsing into the house after him to take up position on the low stool beside the sink.

'Int theer owt else worth doin' but watching thy old man at his 'blutions?'

Jasper shook his head solemnly.

'Thou shalt get thysen wet.'

Thomas cupped his hands in the basin, scooping warm soapy water in the air. His son leapt from the stool, too late to avoid having his shirt-front soaked and a flop of coppery hair plastered to his forehead. He stood dripping, giggling delightedly. This, a prelude to fisticuffs – Jasper punching his father's thigh with all his might, before being wrestled onto the flagstone floor and pummelled with tickling fingers.

'Da', stop it! Stop!'

It wasn't the lad's pleas which caused Thomas to leave him be, but a sudden coughing fit that had him doubled up over the sink. When it was ended he stood for a moment, hands braced against the stone trough, heaving breath in and out of his lungs.

'Don't be bothering thy father.'

Thomas turned to see Frances standing in the doorway. 'He's all right.'

'Go on.'

Her tone was stern, insistent. Jasper ducked past his mother, but her raised hand never landed and, once he had fled into the day-room, she let her arm fall to her side as though unable to recollect why it had been held aloft to begin with. Thomas took a towel from a peg beside the sink and dried himself with brisk, vigorous strokes.

'Off out again?' she said.

'Aye.'

He pressed the towel to his face, glad to conceal himself

192

from her gaze for fear that his expression might betray him. He told her he was meeting Robert Smith, from the allotments. He named the Green Man, in West Bar. It was impossible to gauge her reaction to this information because he did not look at her, even when he restored the towel to its peg and reached for his shirt. The shirt was grubby and sweat-stained from his gardening, but it was the only one he had that was not Sunday best or hanging on a line in the yard. Trousers next, nearly losing his balance as he pulled them on; still managing to avoid catching her eye. Frances filled the kettle and placed it on the stove.

'Wilt thou want owt to eat?'

'Leave us summat, will thee?'

He hesitated, unsure whether or not to embrace his wife. It was not customary for them to kiss goodbye but he felt an urge to do so. He decided against it. Casting a glance at her as he went through to the day-room, he saw that Frances – busy mopping the mess he had made around the sink – did not look up to watch him go.

Witness: Samuel Crookes, Unemployed Saw Grinder, No.28 Furnace Hill, Hallam.

Q. I have to warn you that you face grave charges if you do not choose at this point to disclose, truthfully, all that occurred. You cannot obtain your certificate of indemnity unless you do. Do you understand?

A. Yes.

Q. Now then, it is for you to say, did you do that deed or not?

A. Yes, I did.

Sammy was standing in the doorway of a disused building along the street from Linley's house. He said not a word when Thomas arrived, merely withdrawing into the recess to make room for him. The two men still had not spoken when, some time later, Linley emerged from his house and hurried off in

193

the direction of the town. It was uncommon to see him abroad unaccompanied and, as if conscious of putting himself at risk, he walked with greater haste than usual. This, in turn, caused Sammy and Thomas to abandon the casual gait they customarily affected when following him.

'The Crown,' said Sammy.

'Aye.'

Linley turned into Scotland Street and went into the afore-mentioned public house – one of several he was known to frequent between, and often during, working hours. It was his preference to sup in the back room. Sammy and Thomas took the passage alongside the building and into a cobbled yard at the rear. The sun had set, leaving the yard in semi-darkness apart from a slanting strip of yellowish light cast by an open window. From the shadows, the two men peered into this window – searching among the smoke haze and the muddle of drinkers. They spied him carrying a pot of ale over to a table where a group of men greeted him with little fuss, shuffling along a narrow pew to accommodate him.

'If we shall not do him now, we s'll not have us another shot like this,' said Thomas, speaking in a whisper and inclining his head towards Sammy's.

The other man expressed his concern that they might not be able to escape in safety, reluctant for them to flee back along the jennel into Scotland Street – a thoroughfare that would be too busy at that hour for them to retreat in haste without being recognized or drawing attention to themselves. Together, they explored the deeper recesses of the yard, searching for a gate or a wall that they might scale. In the farthest corner they discovered another narrow passage by which they could gain swift access to a network of ill-lit backstreets and alleys. Returning to their earlier vantage point, Sammy unbuttoned his poacher's overcoat. As he unhooked the air rifle clumsily from its home-made harness, the barrel clinked against a wall. The two men were transfixed as one of the drinkers at Linley's table glanced out of the window.

Although they were pressed into the darkness, he appeared to be looking straight in their direction. However, he presently returned his attention to the boisterous conversation in which he had been participating with his fellows.

'Get it ower with,' said Thomas.

'Too many folk.'

The back room had become yet more congested even in the time the pair had been outside. Voices and laughter spilled into the night air and, from another room within the ale house, came the plink-plonk of a piano. A group next to Linley's was playing dominoes, the staccato clicking of pieces perforating the general babble.

'Thou sees him, can thee not?'

The whole of Linley's upper body and head were exposed in profile as he sat two seats in from the open window, raising the pot to his lips at intervals. His face was waxen in the light of an oil lamp, greasy with sweat. Sammy raised the rifle to the firing position and took aim, lowering the weapon again. He shook his head.

'Give it here, then.'

Sammy refused to let go and, for a moment, the two men were engaged in a silent struggle for possession of the gun – a contest from which Thomas shortly withdrew for fear that they would surely alert those inside the pub.

'If thou dost the shooting,' hissed Sammy, 'we s'll be lucky if the pellet goes in t'window, never mind hitting owt.'

The man's breath was warmly malodorous, spraying the side of Thomas's face as he spoke. Thomas, at that instant, disliked his accomplice almost as much as he did their quarry, so many days had they spent together in fruitless pursuit. He restrained himself from bashing Sammy's head against the wall, instead gripping his lapels and pulling him into yet closer proximity.

'If thou dost not do him, I s'll do thee.'

Sammy shrugged himself free. He stood silently for a moment, facing Thomas – though it was too dark now for either man clearly to make out the other's features. He turned once more towards the open window, raising the rifle and pulling the butt into his shoulder. Dipping his head so that his cheek was pressed flat against the side of the weapon, he closed one eye and aligned the metal V with the sight marker at the tip of the barrel. His index finger was poised. Thomas switched attention from gunman to target, anticipating the crack and the blossom of blood on the man's shirtsleeve. It was then, in the split second when Sammy squeezed the trigger, that James Linley leaned forward – lowering his head slightly – to talk across the table to one of his companions.

Witness: Samuel Crookes (cont.)

Q. How was it that you came to shoot him?

A. I did not intend to do as I did.

Q. You did not want to shoot him but he [Amory] compelled you to shoot. Is that what you are saying?

A. No, I did not intend to hit him where I did.

Q. What do you mean?

A. I wanted to hit him in the shoulder . . . he was bending forward this way (*witness describing the same*) and I was shooting at the shoulder.

Q. You are renowned, are you not, for your marksmanship?

A. I tried to get it just into the shoulder, not into his head at all. He had his head down talking. I did not want to hit him in the head.

Q. So you are saying, are you, that you did not intend to kill him?

A. I did not.

For some days afterwards, Thomas had merely to shut his eyes to bring to mind the appalling image of Linley's head, snapping backwards and sideways as though he had been jolted from his seat by the powerful blow of a man's fist. He tried to picture him in the moment before the shot was fired – his greasy, smiling face; the mouth and eyes animated as he talked and supped and smoked. But all he could see was Linley, having been jerked upright, tilting slowly forwards again in the manner of a drunken man slumping into stupor; lolling asleep, face pressed against the wooden tabletop. And he could see the blood. A coin of crimson, growing a tail – a thin ribbon of a tail, twisting down the side of the man's face; issuing with dreadful persistence from the dark puncture just above and in front of his ear, below the receding hairline.

Chapter Seven

SHOP TALK
The shopping center is today's extraordinary retail business evolvement . . . The automobile accounts for suburbia, and suburbia accounts for the shopping center.

US Urban Land Institute, 1957

Store loses thousands as deadly computer bug puts cash tills in a spin

Mall Madman wreaks havoc

by Constance Amory and William Boyce

A department store at Hallam's giant Urbopark complex is counting the cost today after a deadly computer virus brought trade to a halt.

The sabotage is thought to be the work of the 'Mall Madman', responsible for a spate of attacks in recent weeks.

In the latest incident, Home Zone was forced to close for three hours when a 'bug' was found in its high-tech cash tills.

The virus had already 'eaten' hundreds of till transactions before it was discovered. All sales on credit cards were wiped from the computerized system's memory and customers paying cash were undercharged by up to 20 per cent due to a defect in the barcode scanners.

Temporary closure of the store meant further business was lost while software boffins tried to track down and destroy the bug.

Network

The store was linked to a new till network – Mall Sys – launched last month by Urbopark in co-operation with Hallam Metropolitan University's Information Technology unit in a pilot scheme to speed up the checkout process.

The breach of security raises a question mark over plans to expand Mall Sys throughout the mall as part of a proposed £5m investment.

Meanwhile, police are working closely with the computer experts in a bid to discover how the saboteur managed to infiltrate the highly sophisticated checkout system.

Det. Ch. Insp. Paul Pink, of Hallamshire CID, told the *Crucible*: 'Whoever did this must know what they are about where computers are concerned.'

Credit Card

'The nature of this act of sabotage would appear to place it in a different league to the previous incidents of criminal damage at Urbopark. But, for reasons I am unable to go into, we believe there to be a connection.'

A Home Zone spokesman said the cost to the store in lost business was estimated at 'several thousands of pounds'.

He added, 'The saddest, though not entirely surprising, part is that not one of the cash-paying customers pointed out to checkout staff that they had been undercharged.'

The store is appealing for customers who paid for goods by credit card to return with their receipts so the transactions can be processed again now that the tills have been debugged.

●●● 'Store Wars', page 10
●●● Comment, page 11

The following facts were withheld from the article at the request of the police: a) at the moment when the *computer boffins* located the virus, screens throughout Home Zone's Mall Sys network displayed the word RAGE in scarlet 48-point Century Gothic against a tangerine background; b) the network was not hacked externally but corrupted via rogue software introduced directly into the computer system; c) on the morning of the sabotage, the department store's manager received a cryptic letter – anonymous, word-processed – inviting him to *contemplate the wages of sin*.

These and other related matters were discussed when Paul Pink and Constance Amory met in the chief inspector's office for an off-the-record briefing. *A frank exchange of opinions, hunches and information*, as he'd described it when he phoned to ask her to *drop by*. A newspaper lay on his desk, open at the crossword; much of the grid was filled in. She identified the paper by its typeface as the *Independent*.

'When I joined the force,' he said, as though intuiting a query in the direction of her gaze, 'senior officers were . . . expected to read the *Telegraph*. When you were up for promotion there'd be a question on the form about which papers you read. Beyond a certain rank it was an unwritten rule: no tabloids, no *Guardian*.'

'And the *Independent*'s neutral enough to be acceptable, is it?'

'I buy it for the rugby coverage. And the crossword.'

'I can't get my head round crosswords. Cryptic ones, I mean.'

He nodded. 'It's a matter of familiarity. You get inside his head after a while, the compiler. Of course, most papers these days have more than one, so you've to get to know them all.'

Constance leaned back, then remembered his warning about the chair's instability and sat bolt upright again. One of those pieces of orthopaedically adjustable office furniture that become decreasingly comfortable and increasingly precarious with age, as though its moving parts – the very fact of its adaptability – were its undoing. She was reminded of her childhood dolls – how those with working limbs were always the first to break, while their fixed and rigid sisters survived for years. She shifted her weight. The upholstery was coming unstitched in places to expose tufts of foam padding, and the lever had jammed so that the seat was permanently in its most elevated position. Her feet, as a consequence, were dangling several inches above the floor. The rest of the inspector's office was in a similar state of decrepitude: a venetian blind wedged diagonally across the window – one corner lowered, the other raised; carpet tiles curled up at the edges or mended with thick tape; the veneer surface of the desk peeling away like the flapping sole of an old shoe; a wooden coatstand with two of its prongs missing, apparently snapped off. The walls – green where they'd not been patchworked with maps, notices and framed photographs of rugby teams – hadn't been painted in years. The only new-looking items in the office were the DCI's suit (charcoal; vivid pink tie and matching handkerchief) and a computer terminal that occupied half the desktop and trailed a pot-noodle of cables into a stainless steel panel in the floor at the spot where Constance's feet would have rested, if they'd reached.

'You called it "the force",' she said. 'I thought, these days, you lot referred to it as the police *service*?'

'Aye.'

His eyes, the set of his mouth, emphasized the disdain in his voice. It was uncertain, however, whether he was expressing disapproval of the term *police service* or of her implicit inclusion of him within the phrase *you lot*. When it became plain that he was uninterested in pursuing this topic – or any other, unless she prompted him – Constance asked, 'So, what d'you make of the Ruskin clue? How significant is it, d'you think?'

He almost smiled. 'That depends whether things signify in themselves, or because we . . . attach significance to them.'

'But surely he – the saboteur – must've had a reason for giving us the clue in the first place. Giving *me* the clue, I should say. It really spooks me, you know, the idea of him . . .'

The inspector tilted his head from side to side in a curious shaking motion.

'You think I'm being paranoid?' said Constance.

'Catarrh. It's as though we're talking underwater.' He inserted a little finger in his right ear and rummaged around. 'Pardon me. What I think is, you're taking it too personally.'

'It's *me* the saboteur is homing in on.'

The inspector swivelled his chair towards the computer, pressing keys with a painstaking precision reminiscent of William Boyce's two-finger typing. He said nothing by way of explanation. She waited for him to finish, unsure whether his rude retreat from conversation signified another change of subject. If she got up and left the room, she wondered if he'd even notice.

'Haven't the faintest with these things,' he said at last. 'This latest incident – the virus – I'm in the hands of our software boys on the technicalities. There.'

He clicked the mouse with what, for him, was a flourish. The printer, perched on a separate table alongside the desk, chattered into life, setting up a vibration in the rickety metal legs that drowned out the hum of the inkjet mechanism. When it had finished, he removed two pages from the tray.

'We've been checking out your list of . . . suspects.' Reading aloud, he continued: 'A total of ninety-two people have been successfully prosecuted for theft from shops at Urbopark so far this year; fifty-eight have previous convictions for shop-lifting, and three of those – two men and one woman – also have a record of carrying out criminal damage against stores which prosecuted them. There have been sixty-one sackings and redundancies at the mall this year, any one of whom could bear a grudge. An average of one shop closes every three weeks in Hallam city centre, more than double the rate of closure that existed prior to Urbopark being built – we're running checks on the proprietors. Two firms of architects and four developers made unsuccessful bids for the mall contract – one of the development companies has since gone into receivership.' He paused to glance at her over the top of the paper. 'An extremist – what they call "direct action" – environmental group staged a sit-in during construction of the mall in protest at out-of-town developments; one of its main activists was jailed for – among other things – assaulting a police officer. He emigrated to Germany after his release, where he has, I'm informed, been similarly engaged in "green" issues. According to Home Office intelligence, he is now believed to be resident in the UK once again.'

Constance studied his impassive features.

'As you can see,' he said, 'we've been busy.'

'Can I use any of this?'

'No.'

'Police are pursuing a number of lines of inquiry, then?'

DCI Pink laid the document down on the desk. His only response, a familiar extension of an upturned palm to imply that she'd summed up the position perfectly.

'Why bother telling me?'

'The saboteur – for whatever reason – is, as you say, in direct contact with you; you share that information with us. *Eventually.*' A half-smile. 'It's . . . helpful. You think about this case, you come up with ideas. In return, I tell *you* things. I keep you informed.'

'Crime, Together We'll Crack It.'

'Aye, summat like that.'

'Even though I can't use the information.'

DCI Pink reached into his drawer and brought out a packet of Extra Strong Mints, popping one into his mouth. 'I thought *you lot* thrived on "background briefings". Besides, if I were you I wouldn't be so hasty to put a value on information according merely to its utility . . . or lack of.'

Constance's eyes fell on a wallchart setting out a local rugby club's fixtures for the season. The score of those matches already played was written in by hand, although the figures were too small for her to read. The inspector's voice reclaimed her attention. He was offering the second printout. Her chair tilted alarmingly as she reached forward to take the page from him, causing her to steady herself against the desk with the heel of her hand. She straightened up, carefully. Two words were floating, centred, in an otherwise blank page: *Warren Bartholomew*.

'Warren?'

'I'm talking hypothetically, you understand.' He itemized the points. 'Access to the computer system; intimate knowledge of, and access to, the mall site; awareness that the security cameras were dummies; a . . . working relationship with a female journalist who seems to have become something of a focus for the saboteur.'

She stared at him across the desk, at the growth of black hairs that caused his eyebrows almost to meet in the middle.

The room was stuffy, overheated, and the man's expanse of exposed scalp was resinous with perspiration.

'I've known Warren for, what, more than a year,' she said. 'Since I moved from head office to the mall. Even if he had the opportunity . . .'

'Motive? How about: Mall Admin plans to wind down its in-house PR unit and put the whole operation out to tender, to have it run by a private public relations consultancy? How about: Warren Bartholomew – annual salary £29,000 plus company car, married with one child and a second on the way, and a thumping great mortgage – is leaked a confidential memo about a proposal which would cost him his job?'

Constance said nothing.

'Timing? How about: the memo finds its way into his possession a week before the first of the sabotages? Additional evidence? How about: his initials are W.B.? As in "W.B. Rage" in the museum visitors book, as in "beloved of W.B." in the In Memoriam dedication to Constance Hyde.'

'OK, if it's the *mall* he's after – or, at least, Mall Admin – why target specific stores? Home Zone. HypaCenta. Red Leather, Yellow Leather.'

'By breaching Home Zone's pilot scheme, he threatens the whole Mall Sys investment. *Five million.*'

'And the other two shops?'

'Mr Chapple, the foodhall manager, is a co-opted member of Urbopark's management committee. The committee, incidentally, which met in private to discuss the . . . reappraisal of Mall Admin's public relations operation. As for the criminal damage at Red Leather . . .' DCI Pink spread his hands. 'Not sure.'

'I take it none of this is for publication, either?'

'Naturally.'

'So . . .'

'I was hoping you might be able to tell us a bit more about our friend Mr Bartholomew.'

'*Me?*'

Constance recalled with a creeping sense of unease the evening, three months earlier, when she and Warren had kissed in the cloakroom at the Urbopark Staff Summer Ball – she, immediately post-Howard; he, claiming coital deprivation due to his wife's difficult pregnancy; both of them pissed. A kiss, a grope. All over in less than a minute, and no consequences other than an embarrassingly awkward refusal the following day of his invitation to spend a weekend away with him at some conference or other. He was *married*, for Christ's sake; his wife was *pregnant*. And he had left it at that. They both had. In their work-related dealings since then, they'd continued as though the incident had never occurred. She pictured Warren's boyish face and his fine fair hair; she tasted the white wine on his lips.

'No,' she said, shaking her head. She felt Paul Pink's eyes on her. 'There's nothing between me and Warren, if that's what you're getting at.'

'From your point of view, or from his?'

'Mine.'

'You don't socialize with him outside of work?'

'I don't see what that's—'

'Does he know where you live? Your home address?'

'I . . . no. No, I don't think so. Not from me, anyway. Paul, what is this?'

The chief inspector took back the piece of paper containing Warren Bartholomew's name, crumpled it and dropped it into a bin. As he spoke, she could glimpse a segment of white peppermint moving about in his mouth.

'Our friend seems to have gone missing.'

'How d'you mean, missing?'

DCI Pink explained that the mall's senior PRO hadn't gone home the previous night, nor had he shown up at work that morning. None of his family, friends or colleagues had seen him or heard from him in more than twenty-four hours. He was, to all intents and purposes, a missing person. A detective constable, on finding the door to Mr Bartholomew's office to be locked, had been admitted by the secretary with the aid of a spare key. Everything was in place, as far as she could tell – except that a copy of the Bible lay on the press officer's desk. *Born again*, the secretary had whispered. The holy book lay open at Romans, the constable observing that a mark in blue biro encircled chapter VI, verse 23. The chief inspector, referring to a small leather-bound notepad, read aloud to Constance the relevant quotation: *The wages of sin is death.*

The Inky Path
The journalist is not like the author, who spins a web of creation from inside himself. The journalist is an objective writer, he seeks to record and review what other men are saying and doing. The words he employs – at least, those which are not direct quotations – may be of his own composition, as with any 'story'-writer, but his subject matter is not. This is not to say that an author's medium is 'fiction' and a reporter's is 'fact', and never the twain shall meet. While facts may comprise the latter's raw material, the tools he uses – i.e. words – are bound up with the creation of fictions. For a report of an event is, at the very least, one step removed from what occurred – it is not the event, but a representation of it. The journalist, while remaining diligent in faithfulness to the facts, ought to be conscious of this difference. By so doing, he will learn not to have an inflated opinion of the importance of his reports; and he will learn that events occur irrespective of whether or not they are written about.

It was the third time she'd washed her bedding in six days – since the night Howard stayed – though no amount of detergent seemed to erase the smell of him, or of sex, or of the wine they'd spilled. *Your imagination*, said Milly. *Bung your brain in on a boil-wash and see if that gets rid of him.* Constance carried the freshly laundered sheets, pillow-cases and duvet cover to her room and remade the bed. She'd intended to spend the evening catching up with her background reading in preparation for Stan's class the following night. But books, the thought of being shut away in her room, bored her. What she craved was company, chocolate and a dose of TV soaps. She opened the window to air the bed and went downstairs. Milly was eating off a tray, still in the smart clothes she wore at the university library but with her jacket over the back of the sofa and shoes kicked off in the middle of the room. The television was on. Constance heated some tinned tomato soup and joined her housemate. They watched the regional news: a short item on the discovery of a young man's body (fuzzy mugshot of him wearing a sombrero; scene-setting shot of the railway line where his dismembered corpse had been strewn). With an inquest pending, the word 'suicide' was avoided, but the coded phrasing, and a reference to the deceased's recent release from a short-stay psychiatric unit after treatment for depression, would leave viewers in little doubt that the man had not stepped in front of a train by accident.

Milly lay her tray down on the floor. 'Not nice. Horrible, in fact.'

'*Twenty-two*.'

'It's all so final with men, isn't it? So black and white.'

Constance looked at her. 'How d'you mean?'

'He was depressed, right? A woman gets depressed – *that* depressed – she spends months, years, fucking herself up over it – mental and physical self-torture. You know, maybe she will or maybe she won't end up killing herself. With a feller it's all so dramatic: "Depressed? Life in a mess? Right, fuck it, I'm off." '

'What, you think men are more decisive than women?'

'Suicide's not a decisive move. It's a failure to face up to decisions – the *complexity* of decision-making. Life's full of grey areas and men can't handle grey areas so they make everything simple; only, when they can't do that any more – life fucks up on them or something – the ultimate simplification is "no more life".'

'*Mill*, what're you going on about? You're the one who's simplifying things. I mean, what do we know about suicide – why people do it?'

'Like, in a relationship, you have a row . . . a *problem*; you'll discuss it, the two of you, and the feller'll think that's it: discussion over, problem sorted, draw a line under it. The woman will maybe want to talk about it again and again – the next day or the next month or whenever – because, basically because nothing's ever so conclusive, so uncomplicated. You've said it yourself, about Howard.'

'It's not the same thing.' Constance finished the soup, setting her tray down on a small wooden coffee table cluttered with magazines and old newspapers.

'Con, you've got orange lips.'

She searched in her handbag for a tissue.

Milly went on: 'And they never stop to think about the people they leave behind. Partner. Kids. Parents. Friends. Sometimes they even do the kids in as well. *Unbelievable*. You can't tell me suicide isn't the ultimate in selfishness.'

'My first boyfriend threatened to kill himself when I said I wanted to finish with him.'

'How old were you?'

'Fifteen. He was seventeen.'

'And did he?'

'No, he came round one night – three o'clock in the morning – and threw empty milk bottles at the front of our house, calling me all the names under the sun. Dad ran after him in his pyjamas.'

They laughed. Milly picked up the doofer and channel-hopped. 'It's all to do with heroics, isn't it?' she said. 'Heroic gestures.'

'I think Dad was just angry.'

'*Suicide*, Con.'

'*Joke*, Mill.'

Milly ran her fingers through her short dark hair so that it punked-up on top. Her complexion, in the harsh living-room light, was shiny after her day's work and the long walk home from the library. She didn't drive and would only take the bus when it rained or snowed, or if she was late – because, she said, the slower you moved the more time there was for thinking. Two miles there, two miles home. If surgeons ever perfected the calf transplant, Constance would have herself named as beneficiary on her friend's donor card. Milly, perversely, hated her legs. *Muscle-bound.* She also disliked having to buy a new pair of shoes every couple of months. *Where does all that leather go? You look at the pavement and you can't see any scuff marks, yet hundreds of people are walking up and down all day long wearing out the soles of their shoes. Weird.* This was the sort of thing Milly thought about on her walks.

The ads were on. A talking car . . . a unicyclist juggling apples in a supermarket aisle . . . a couple repairing their marriage with frozen pizza . . . Constance found she knew the script of the commercials almost by heart and was silently playing their dialogue and jingles in her head. *Coronation Street.* Milly doofed up the volume and the two women nah-nah-nahed in time with the signature tune.

'D'you remember that fling I nearly had with Warren?'

'Warren wotsisname, Barlow?'

'*Bartholomew.* Press officer at the mall.'

'Wanted to whisk you away on a romantic weekend for two at a conference on – what was it? – oh, I remember: Press Releases, Double-Spacing or Single-Spacing? A Strategy for the Millennium.' Milly laughed at her own joke. 'Brighton, wasn't it?'

'*Bridlington.* And the conference was on media relations and the Internet.'

'What about him?'

Constance hesitated. 'Nothing. I was just . . . his name came up, at work, and I was just thinking about him, that's all.'

'*Con.*'

'Not like *that*.'

'He's married, isn't he?'

'He's also not my type.'

'Nice feller, then? Caring, considerate, supportive, dependable. All the qualities you don't go for.'

'*Milly*.'

'Russell . . . Rick . . . Howard. I rest my case.'

'You never even *met* Russell.'

'Feels like it, sometimes.'

'Well, I'm sorry for boring you with my past.'

'Sense of humour, Con.'

She laughed, despite herself. 'Jesus.'

'And now Stan the Man.'

'Hardly.'

'You went for a drink with him.'

'And look how *that* evening ended up.'

'I quote: "He seems nice, but I don't quite know what to make of him." Soon as I heard that, I thought here she goes again.'

'Are we watching this, or not?'

'You must admit you're a sucker for unfathomability. Enigma with a captial E. You act like you want to know what it is you're getting into, but secretly I think you'd run a mile if a feller ever—'

'What, I wear a sign round my neck saying: "Man wanted – only complete bastards need apply"?'

'Not bastards. You want someone a bit . . . perplexing, someone with more to him than meets the eye. Nothing wrong with that. Christ, if they're going to put their things inside us we're entitled to expect them at least to be *interesting*.'

They fell silent, watching *Corrie*. Constance disliked Milly when she was in one of her strident moods. No she didn't. It wasn't Milly she disliked, but stridency itself. She felt herself withering under the forcefulness of her friend's opinions, cowed not so much by argument but by confidence of expression. It wasn't even stridency she disliked as much as her own propensity to be diminished in the face of it. It was *herself* she disliked, actually. Sometimes she felt the urge to shake herself and shout: 'For Christ's sake speak up!' *You've a tongue in your head, haven't you?*, as her mam would say, when she wasn't admonishing her for being *lippy*. Throughout her adolescent and adult life, Constance had sensed that what she said was out of synch with the unspoken words forming in her head and with the expectations of whoever she happened to be talking to. If she wasn't saying too much or too little, she was talking crap. Ken Barlow, in the Rovers. Barlow/Bartholomew. A coincidence.

Notes

Hallam's steel output: 1751 8 tons

1835 10,000 tons

1873 100,000 tons

By 1843, H. contributed 90 per cent of UK's crucible steel output and almost half of Europe's 1858: Henry Bessemer introduced the 'converter' to H. – giant machine producing 20 tons of steel in 30 minutes.

Bessemer Converter: process was to pour liquid pig-iron into a huge bowl, or converter, then blast cold air through vents in the bottom. The air reacted with the molten metal and burnt off any impurities ('WHOOSH! with a great flame and shower of sparks, like the mouth of an erupting volcano' – Prof. S. Bell).

QUOTE (anonymous): 'A thick pulverous haze is spread over the city which the sun is unable to penetrate, save by a lurid glare, and which has the effect of imparting to the green hills and golden cornfields in the high distance the ghastly appearance of being whitened with snow.' (Not Krakatoa, 1883; but Hallam, 1861)

By 1864, large manuf. companies set up in the town. An army of labour reqd. to run these new operations, firms employing thousands rather than hundreds.

Labour

In contrast with the 'light' trades (i.e. tool-making, cutlery etc.), trades unionism in the heavy steel industry was slow to develop. No appenticeship – boys taken on when a vacancy occurred, their pay found by fellow workers. No collective bargaining. Few common tasks and activities to unite the men by common interest. At this time, most steelworkers remained unorganized and attempts to form unions failed. This meant they had little or no welfare support during recurrent periods of unemployment or when they were unable to work through sickness or injury.

Prof. Stanley Bell's Physical, Metaphysical and Philosophical Glossary of Metal

steel: in its simplest form, an alloy of iron and carbon. Being harder than iron, steel sharpens better, won't break easily and can be made springy. Steel, in achieving strength through combination, demonstrated greater political consciousness than the men who produced it.

STAN. STANLEY. STANLEY BELL.

The professor spoke twice to Constance during class – typical teacher pupil exchanges, nothing more. Whenever they made eye contact, he smiled at her; but he dispensed smiles indiscriminately among his students. As the group filed out of the building at the end of the session, he did not approach her or draw her aside. He didn't speak to her at all, not even to say goodbye – other than to include her among several of her fellows in a general *cheerio-see-you-next-week*. When one of them called out, inviting Stan to join them at the Tongs, the professor declined apologetically. *Things to do*. Constance, also, did not go to the pub – which surprised the others, as she'd previously indicated that she'd love to. As she set out alone on the walk home, his car overtook her. He bibbed the horn as he went by and, when his indicator began to flash, she quickened her pace in anticipation that he was pulling over to offer her a lift. But the car didn't stop. It slowed down at the end of the street and turned left, in the direction signalled by the blink-blink-blink of the indicator. She watched him go.

The night of the evening class was the night she first heard voices in her sleep. Men's voices. Specifically: Howard, Stanley Bell, Dougal Aitken-Aitken, Gary, Paul Pink, Dad, Granddad, William Boyce. All talking to her at once, yet she could distinguish and identify each as clearly as if they'd been speaking in turn. Another voice, fainter and requiring greater concentration, underlay the others. It was the voice of Warren Bartholomew. At one o'clock in the morning, Constance reached over to switch on the bedside lamp, shutting her eyes against the sudden orange light. As soon as she awoke, the voices ceased. She found that she was unable to recall a word they'd said, despite a strong and strange sensation that their words, easily audible just a moment ago, had been indelibly imprinted on her memory.

She lay on her back, one bare forearm across her brow. Her face was clammy. With her other hand she clawed the duvet away from her throat. She was so tired. So bloody, fucking tired. Exhausted. Her body ached for rest, but she wouldn't sleep now; too alert, her mind was awash with fragments of dream. No way to remember what the voices were saying – just a jumble of meaningless, disconnected syllables; vague cadences. Her neck was tense and stiff, as though she'd been lying at an awkward angle. The bedding – newly washed and remade – was already clingy with perspiration, impregnated with her own odour. She brought her arm down beside her with a slap, gripped a handful of duvet so tightly her knuckles hurt. She let go. Pins and needles. *Ninsy peedles*, Mags used to say – when they were little. A girlhood nightmare came back to her: waking abruptly in a shadowy bedroom with the absolute certainty that little creatures – plastic figures from her dolls house – were climbing the curtains. On with the light; no figures, just the curtains, patterned with tiny flowers, rippling in the breeze from the open window. Mags, sitting bolt upright in the other bed. Her sister didn't ask what was wrong, she simply stared across the room at Constance for a moment then laid her head back on the pillow and fell instantly asleep.

Bewilderment. That's what it was – then and now – the faintly nauseous feeling of bewilderment and disorientation. Warren Bartholomew. Constance went downstairs, naked, to ensure that both doors were bolted and all the ground-floor windows had been secured. She drank a tumbler of water, refilled the glass and went back to bed. On the bedside table was a book she'd borrowed that day from the library, a biography of Ruskin. She would read herself to sleep – craving that familiar drooping of the eyelids, reading the same sentence over and over until the book slipped from your hands to be found among the sheets when you awoke at some deliciously late hour the following morning. There, within that volume, might be a clue to the *why?* of it all. Why *Warren? Why*, Warren? She read the dustjacket blurb, the contents page, the preface and introduction; she turned to the first chapter. She didn't fall asleep. She continued reading through the night, breaking off only to go to the toilet, to raid the fridge for Snickers, to make a flask of coffee and to fetch a pad and pen.

At work the following morning, Constance – in a dazed state of suspended sleep (*Your eyes look like pickled eggs,* William Boyce) – typed a memo to Paul Pink:

Read a biog of Ruskin last night. *All* night. Have some 'blob pars', as we say in the trade:
- Elizabeth Siddal, the beautiful young model for many of the Pre-Raph pictures, was the daughter of an optician and cutler from *Hallam* (p111, line 20)
- Ruskin declared his atheism to Holmun Hunt – there was no Eternal Father, therefore man (and, presumably, woman) was his/her own helper and resource (p174, lines 11–14)
- As an art instructor, Ruskin would leave demonstration sketches half finished 'as if to point up the impossibility of perfecting the artistic process' in capturing truth to nature (p202, line 9)

214

(Did you know, W. B. Yeats's early poetry was influenced by the writings of the Pre-Raphaelites? Coincidence, do you think?)

I'm rambling. I'm too tired for this. I suppose what I'm trying to say is (i) the saboteur directed us to the Ruskin line of inquiry; (ii) if *our* W.B. is the saboteur then you would expect his views on 'truth to nature/nature of truth' to coincide with Ruskin's. At first, I thought: hang on, Ruskin was an atheist, W.B. is a born-again Christian. But the more I think about it, the more I can see a connection. Ruskin believed it was necessary to strive for truth to nature, even though it was unattainable; Christians must strive for Christ-like perfection even though they are prevented from ever attaining it by Original Sin (we – human beings – are tainted by Adam; i.e. by our history).

I was talking to W.B. once about his decision to leave newspaper journalism for public relations, and I said to him (as a wind-up): 'Why did you swap fact for fiction?' I remember, he replied: 'I didn't, I swapped one form of fiction for another.'

The point is, Paul, the attacks on the mall and all the cryptic clues seem to me to add up to a lot more than just revenge for the loss of a job. Which means (a) we've yet to find W.B.'s real motive; or (b) we've yet to find the real saboteur. What do you think?

The Life and Times of a
Hallam Saw Grinder
(a Dramatic Reconstruction in Many Parts)

Royal Commission of Inquiry
(sitting at) Hallam Town Hall
Friday, 21 June 1867 (Fourteenth Day)

Witness: William Broadhead, Secretary, Saw Grinders' Union.

Q. In addition to being Secretary of the Saw Grinders' you are, are you not, proprietor of The Royal George Hotel, Carver Street, Hallam, and treasurer to both the Hallam Trades Council and the UK Alliance of Organized Trades?

A. I am.

Q. Is it true that you are a well-known figure in trade circles in Hallam?

A. That is not for me to say.

Q. We have heard it said in this inquiry that you are known as Old Smite 'Em. From where does this nickname originate?

A. I cannot say.

Q. You know that you are called this name?

A. Yes.

· Q. And what do you have to say of it?

A. People may call me what they will.

Q. You have no opinion?

A. It is my opinion that a name such as this says as much about the men who utter it as it does about the man to whom it refers.

Q. You know the meaning of the word 'smite'?

A. I know also the meaning of the word 'old', and I would willingly smite any man who called me that to my face.

(*laughter*)

Q. Now, you have been questioned already about your involvement or otherwise in some of the specific incidents under examination in this inquiry – and you shall be so

216

questioned again. For the present, however, it would assist the commissioners if you could apply your knowledge and experience to more general matters.

A. I am glad to oblige.

Q. You yourself were a saw grinder by trade, is that so?

A. I was. And that remains my trade.

Q. It is said that a saw grinder is stronger, healthier and better paid than many of his fellows in other trades, indeed in other branches of grinding. How comes this to be so?

A. The grinding of saws requires a deal of physical strength, it is true. I am unable to say whether strong men are attracted into the trade because of this or become the stronger for their labours. Certainly, wages of £4 and £5 per week are not uncommon.

Q. And this is considered to be a high wage?

A. Not by a Queen's Counsel, I imagine.

(*laughter*)

Q. Relative to men in other trades, is what I meant by my question.

A. Yes. I should say, though, that these higher wages have made saw grinders the more vulnerable to the introduction of machine grinding and to encroachments upon their work.

Q. How so?

A. A manufacturer who is more concerned with cost of production than quality of workmanship will seek to have the job done more cheaply – either by machines or by jobbing grinders and others who are not apprenticed in the grinding of saws.

Q. And your union or society seeks to combat this?

A. Wherever possible we take outsiders and their apprentices into the trade so that they cannot undercut rates of pay by remaining out of union. The more men we keep in union the better we are able to maintain wage levels and to regulate the supply of labour according to demand.

Q. How does this regulation occur?

A. When trade is slack, we keep men on the box.

Q. What do you mean by 'on the box'?

A. Of the 190 or so members, we might keep between 50 and 80 out of the labour market for a number of weeks or months by paying them sufficiently generously from the union's funds so that they would not prefer to seek work.

Q. From where does the union acquire such funds?

A. From all of its members.

Q. Does it not require high contributions to maintain such a system?

A. Up to four shillings in the pound would not be an uncommon deduction from a man's weekly earnings.

Q. And members are content to pay these sums?

A. Men know that the pay is better for being in union than out of union, and that they will be the better protected from hardship during times of unemployment or poor trade.

Q. That was not my question. My question was, do the men pay their due without quibble?

A. Some do not. Some default on their payments and others would leave rather than pay their natty money, placing a greater burden on those members who remain in union. Then there are those who are happy to be kept on the box for months, only to leave the union once trade picks up again.

Q. What is the union's opinion of the men who do this?

A. There are words for these men I would not care to use before this assembly.

Q. How else do you seek to regulate the supply of labour into the trade?

A. During slack periods, men will limit their hours to make the work go round; or the union will levy a high charge on those wanting to enter a trade without formal apprenticeship, or refuse them altogether.

Q. It is the case, is it not, that each union – be it Saw Grinders', Fender Grinders', File Cutters' or whoever – jealously guards and upholds its rules, taking whatever action it deems necessary to bring miscreants into line?

A. Not only the union, its members also.

Q. What do you mean by that?

A. Supposing three men are in a beerhouse talking of trade matters and, in conversation, it is found that one of the three is in arrears with his natty money. In such a case, trades unionists would not be surprised to hear of that man's tools or bands being taken without the knowledge or involvement of any official or anyone outside of the three men.

Q. Rattening, then, is as likely to be the act of one man against his fellow as it is a matter of union interference?

A. I know of at least one incidence in Hallam of a man being rattened by his own son.

Q. What is your opinion of rattening?

A. My impression is that rattening has existed in every trade before any of this assembly here was born.

Q. All the trades in Hallam have adopted it, is that your evidence?

A. The way it has been adopted has been the way it is described, not by the order of the Society, but members – as a matter of course – taking it upon themselves to roll up another's bands until he ceases to be obnoxious to his trade and due payment has been made by him to the ratteners for their expense.

Q. This inquiry has already heard that, most commonly, rattening occurs in the grinding trades. Can you say why this is so?

A. The reasons are various. In the first place, the stealing of bands from a grindstone is a relatively simple matter; but it is also true that the work of other trades would be equally disrupted by a cessation of grinding.

Q. Each trade being dependent on the continuation of others in the chain of production. Is that your meaning?

A. In the case of my own trade, the manufacture of a saw requires the work of the forgers, the grinders, the tooth cutters, the glazers and the handle makers. All of these men form separate branches of the saw trade and are in separate unions, though the unions are amalgamated together for mutual

219

support. If any member in any of the branches should be in default or breach of rule – or in the case of a dispute with the masters – the grinders' tools would be abstracted as theirs are the easiest so to do.

Q. So, even if the nub of the issue lay with the handle makers, say, the course commonly adopted would be to ratten the grinders – as a cessation of grinding stops the whole of the saw trade?

A. Yes. And the other branches will compensate the grinders for their loss of time and for the expenses incurred.

Q. Such moneys being recovered from the man or men in default?

A. Or from the master.

Q. Even if the master is not party to the dispute?

A. It is my view that an employer in such an instance ought to have compelled his workmen to comply with the rules of the union.

Q. As a man of experience in trade matters, have you found throughout the trades that, where rattening would not succeed, stronger measures have been resorted to?

A. They have occurred.

Q. Acts of violence against persons and property?

A. Yes.

Q. This commission will gather evidence of such matters in the course of more specific inquiries. For the moment, we would ask what justification do you find both for rattening and for more extreme measures in enforcing the rules of a union?

A. As I have already said, the connection between trades union organization and the wage level is well-known in Hallam as elsewhere. It is the duty of a union to work for the benefit of all members.

Q. Even if that 'work', as you call it, involves authorizing of and complicity in criminal behaviour – acts of theft, intimidation and violence?

A. I would answer your question, if I may, with one of my own: criminal in whose terms?

Q. In terms of the laws of the land.

A. What authority is carried by a set of laws applied to a population largely without franchise – laws, moreover, drawn up by a Parliament hostile to the rights and interests of trades unions and working men?

Q. Trades unions are not illegal in this country, nor have they been since the Combination Acts were repealed some forty years ago.

A. Trades unions might not be illegal, but their normal and necessary activities are certainly made so by legal sanction. Not six months since, the lord chief justice declared unions to be in restraint of trade; and there is another ruling that makes trades unions liable to prosecution for criminal conspiracy.

Q. What are you asking, that the rights of masters, owners and employers be extended to workmen? That there should be equality before the law for these two groups?

A. What I am saying is that if the one group enjoys legal powers which are being denied to the other, then it should be no surprise when that second group takes whatever measures are necessary to rectify this injustice.

Q. Is it your opinion, then, that in all trades – whether at Hallam or otherwise – unions and their members will, from not having legal means of enforcing the payment of contributions or the means of enforcing their rules, resort to rattening and the like?

A. Yes, sir. And I believe this: that if the law would give trades unions some power to operate without recourse to rattening there would be no more heard of it.

Chapter Eight

SHOP TALK

... Arians, being impulsive, fill their wardrobes with ill-considered purchases ... an extravagant Leo goes out for stockings and returns home with a new dress ... the Sagittarian is a haphazard shopper, browsing for hours without a clue as to what she wants ... Capricorns' caution makes them reluctant to part with their money ...

Stars In Their Aisles, by 'Carrie'
Arcadia (incorp. Mall Monthly)
vol.IV no.5, June 1996

New code, new mnemonic. Tighter security at the mall – the issue of a new type of magnetic swipe card, the alteration (*every week*) of personal i.d. codes – was testing Constance's capacity for memorizing numbers. Five digits instead of four, though she failed to understand why this was a better safeguard against breach of security. This week's number, at least, was easy to remember – 30454 – ironically spelling out the word CODED, according to her numerical alphabet (if you translated zero as the letter O). The installation of a more sophisticated computerized security system throughout the Urbopark site was designed to make unauthorized access more difficult. It also enabled Mall Secure to monitor the movements of every legitimate cardholder, with each swipe electronically registering the user's i.d. code by time and location. If the saboteur was a non-cardholding outsider, this system limited his activities to the public areas of the mall between Doors Open and Doors Close – exposing him to risk of capture on CCTV (new cameras, real film) or by increased numbers of uniformed and undercover Mall Secure patrols. If it was an inside job, the perpetrator would be similarly restricted for fear of being electronically 'tagged' to the scene of any sabotages committed out of hours or in restricted-access areas.

Four facts, three of which were reported in the *Crucible* and one of which was not: Mall Admin had spent £175,000 on upgrading security since the series of attacks began; the mall's 250 commercial occupants were losing an estimated £25,000 a day between them in reduced sales; Urbopark visitor numbers were continuing to decline; the personal i.d. code of Warren Bartholomew, senior press officer at Mall PRO, had not been recorded at any swipe point for forty-eight hours (nor did anyone of his acquaintance claim to have seen him in those two days). A fifth fact, to be published in the next edition of Hallam's evening newspaper under a Constance Amory byline: Mall Admin received a word-processed letter, signed 'W.B.', advising that *not until the 'victims' cease their crimes against man, shall I cease mine against Mammon.*

Constance let herself into the office. Among the usual assortment of post was an oddity – a small flat package, thin and hard and surprisingly light, neatly wrapped in brown paper. Her name and the office address had been inscribed, in red, in childlike capitals. The postmark was incomplete and badly smudged. She sat down at her desk to open the package, using the point of a pen to work loose the tightly taped flap. Inside was a 3.5-inch computer diskette; nothing else, no note, no label on the disk to indicate its contents. She turned it over in her hands, as if that would yield any clues. Switching on her terminal, she slotted the disk into the drive and ran the

223

anti-virus check before opening the file. A message appeared on the screen – a typical preface to shareware games programs, inviting the user to send a $15 registration fee to an address in the United States. *Press R to print Registration Form or hit any key to continue.* She hit a key. The screen filled with a multicoloured graphic welcoming her to *Spending Spree – the Game for Shopaholics.* A list of playing instructions appeared. The object was to manoeuvre a figure – a little redheaded woman (remarkably similar to Wilma, in the *Flintstones*) with a shopping trolley – around a labyrinthine mall, buying as many goods as possible along the way. Numerous hazards, meanwhile, conspired to thwart you – fire-breathing monsters, collapsing ceilings, sudden chasms, psychopathic shoppers, explosions, floods. If you made it safely to the exit, your score was determined by the time taken to complete the course and by how much money you'd managed to spend. Constance began to play. She was on her fourth attempt – engrossed – when the distinctive aroma of fishpaste alerted her to the presence of William Boyce, half-eaten sandwich in hand, peering over her shoulder.

He nodded at the screen, spilling crumbs on to her cardigan as he spoke. 'Tonight's lead? "Woman Drowns in Shopping Tragedy".'

'Every time I get her out of the first shop, she's swept away by a tidal wave.'

'What you've to do is step out of the shop – that triggers the wave – then step back sharpish into the doorway and wait while the water goes past.'

Constance turned in her chair. 'How . . . how d'you *know* that?'

'My grandson. He's not so keen on that one 'cos the little woman can't kill any of the monsters or owt, she can only take evasive action or use her trolley as a shield.'

'Nice lad.'

'Ten, he is. None of this trying to outwit the enemy, just zap!' William walked round to his desk, removing *Death of a*

Salesman and a foil-wrapped supply of sandwiches from his briefcase. Gesturing at her terminal, he said, 'Quiet news day?'

'This isn't *fun*, believe it or not. It came in the post, no note with it or anything to say who it was from or why they'd sent it.'

'Mr Rage?'

Constance shrugged.

'Happen a cryptic message comes up on screen if you get to the end,' her colleague suggested.

She broke off from the game – drowned, again – and took their mugs over to the drinks counter. Both were ingrained with grime, the once-white insides stained by frequent hot beverages and infrequent washing up. She rinsed them under the cold tap.

'Tea or coffee?'

'Aye, smashing.' William peered between the computer terminals at the mess on Constance's desk. 'Have you the envelope?'

'There, by the phone.'

He reached across for the torn scrap of brown paper, putting on a pair of reading glasses to examine it. His face creased into a frown of concentration.

'*Which*, tea or coffee?'

'Urboprank,' he said.

'What?'

'Urbo*prank*. He's written "prank" instead of "park".'

'Show me.' She reread the address. 'Jesus, I must've looked at that three times – the handwriting, I mean. I just read it as Urbopark.'

'Aye, well, your eyes see what you expect them to see. If you'd ever done any subbing, you'd know that.'

The day of the picnic was the first without rain for a week, prompting Constance to remark that *someone up there must be smiling on us*. Stan asked if she really believed that. And she said no. She said she supposed it was pure chance that the

225

weather had complied with their wishes. He nodded – relieved, it seemed, to know she shared his atheism. *If there's a God, how come Hallam City are a division above United?* he asked. Stan was dressed in knee-length shorts, navy-blue sweatshirt and walking boots, and shouldering a small knapsack. A 'snapsack', as he described it, because it contained their lunch. Constance had charge of the OS map and the book: *Circular Walks In And Around Historic Hallam*. The outing had been Plan B; his suggestion, when they discovered that her next free Saturday did not coincide with Plan A, a United home match. The deal was, he would make the sarnies if she organized a route. At the end of the call, she'd yanked the phone clean off the table – tripping over the flex in her hurry to tell Milly the news.

The walk began at a stone bridge over one of the city's five rivers, where it coursed along a densely wooded valley that fetched the water down from the high hills to the east of Hallam. They headed upstream on the riverside path, past paddling pools and a children's playground before skirting an area of land given over to allotments. As the track narrowed into the woods, the autumn sunlight was mottled by a canopy of leaves and the ground became muddier underfoot. Single file. Constance, wearing trainers, picked her way through the coarse grass at the path's edge. Stan strode ahead in his boots, heeding her directions as she plotted their route. Already, his bare calves were flecked with mud. Beyond another bridge was a triple weir, then an overgrown dam cluttered with sycamore and young oak. It was cool, beneath the trees, their voices deadened in the green hush of wood and fallen leaves. Reading aloud, she said, 'Look out for a spring which rises in the Ringinglow coal seams above and is bright orange in colour from the iron minerals deposited in the water.'

They couldn't see a stream, orange or otherwise.

'Are you sure we're going the right way?' asked Stan.

'D'you want to take over the map-reading, Professor?'

He laughed. 'Hey, we've not gone half a mile and we're quarrelling already.'

As they continued, Constance drew attention to the site of numerous industrial remains, some dating back to the eighteenth century when, according to *Circular Walks . . .* , 170 water-powered mills and workshops were huddled along a three-mile stretch of the river. Many of the buildings had been reduced to mossy clumps of foundation stone and rusted metal engulfed in vegetation, or so reclaimed by nature that the only trace was a misshapen earth embankment or a faint rectangular depression in the woodland floor. They paused beside one of the more intact sites: Nethercut, the last working Wheel of the valley, where cutlery and scythes were made for more than two hundred years before production ceased in 1934. *All the water control mechanisms are well-preserved and you can still pick out the weir and wheel pit.* Stan and Constance looked at the seized sluices and cogwheels and eroded building blocks, strewn among the undergrowth like postmodernist statuary.

'Is it time for lunch?'

'*Stan.*'

'What?'

'It's not even eleven o'clock!'

They ate soon after midday in a grassy clearing where the route of their walk began the long loop back towards its starting point. Removing their waterproof cagoules from Stan's knapsack, they spread them on the damp ground as a make-shift picnic blanket and – facing one another, cross-legged – arranged the cling-filmed parcels of food between them. There were two rounds of cheese salad and two of tuna and sweet-corn mayonnaise, boiled eggs in their shells, two apples, two oatmeal flapjacks, two packets of crisps and two bottles of still mineral water. Constance could feel her face pinking in the autumn sunshine.

'I love this time of year,' she said. 'When the leaves are turning.'

227

'It's so quiet here. You'd not think we were so close to the city.'

Constance listened to the passage of the river and to the birdcalls. She gestured in the direction of the woods through which they'd walked. 'Can you imagine the noise when all these mills and wheels were in full swing?'

'Can you imagine the colour of the river?' said Stan.

She took a bite out of a sandwich. 'My ancestors might've worked here, for all I know.'

'You reckon?'

She studied the tutor's face, unable to tell whether his expression was one of curiosity or amused scepticism. 'I was asking my granddad about it, our family tree. *Generology*, as he calls it. He was a bit hazy, but he said his father and grandfather were both steelworkers and he remembered something about great-grandfather Jasper having been in one of the big crucible works.'

'When would this have been?'

'Well, I know granddad's granddad – if that makes sense – was born in 1879. So *his* father would've been of working age around that time: the 1870s or 80s, or thereabouts.'

'Just when there was a shift in employment from the light trades to the heavy.' Stan nodded, as if by way of affirming his own statement. 'So it's quite possible your grandfather's great-*great* grandfather could've been a cutler or toolmaker or grinder of some sort.'

'That would make him my . . . no, hang on . . .' Constance used her fingers to count off the generations. 'My great-great-great-great grandfather.' She beamed at Stan. 'He could've eaten his snap *right here*, on this very patch of grass.'

'Odds are he was at one of the Wheels in the town,' he said. 'That's where most of the work was concentrated.'

She faked a scowl. 'Oh Stan, where's your sense of romance?'

After lunch, her companion compounded his lack of the romantic by laying on his back and falling asleep. Constance occupied herself by reading the blurb in the walks book, then went for a stroll along the river – spotting a dipper, two blue tits, and a vole making off along the bank with a wild mushroom the size of its own head. Finally, she returned to the picnic spot and watched Stan while he slept. When he began to snore, she woke him by lobbing dandelion heads at his open mouth.

'Sorry, must've drifted off,' he said, sitting up, disoriented.

'C'mon, we've another 3.7 kilometres to do.'

That afternoon, when he dropped her off at the house, Stan asked what she was doing the following day. *Sunday dinner at my folks*, she said. *Three-line whip, I'm afraid*. He nodded. *How about in the evening?* he asked. She shook her head, barely able to suppress a smile. *Seeing my History tutor*.

A consequence of the visit to Mam and Dad that Sunday was the temporary hospitalization of Fifi, impounded after Dad had given the Fiesta the once-over. *There's more chance o' United winnin' t'Cup than you gettin' back safely in that contraption*. He gave her a lift home in his van and promised to have the car returned in a few days, fully serviced and fitted with a new set of brake pads and two new tyres. When she protested that she couldn't afford the repairs, he gave her a wink.

'Dad, for God's sake, I'm a grown woman.'

'What's that got to do wi' owt?'

'Oh, you know: independence, self-reliance . . .'

'Dictionary words, them.'

Monday morning, Fifi-less, Constance made her way up the hill to the bus stop. Dawn. A terrace of shuttered and unlit shops stood black against a lightening autumnal sky. Only the newsagent's was open, its lemony-white window spilling brilliance into the street. She bought a paper. The pavement was littered with last night's blood-splat pizza boxes and empty burger cartons; someone had puked in the doorway of a derelict shop. The chipboard panels over the windows were plastered with flyposters, some ripped or peeling away to expose jagged patches of other, older posters. This fascination of hers with the overlaying of what went before; she . . . A bus came into view, windows translucent with illuminated condensation, suggestive of warmth and cosiness on a cold morning. She fiddled in her purse for change. An analogy occurred to her of overlapping relationships: each man – Russell, Rick, Howard . . . Stan, possibly – replacing his predecessor, yet remnants of each resisting erasure. Her love-life, fly-posted. People would look at you and you would seem whole, and wholly present – *in* and *of* the present – yet, inside, you were flooded with yesterday's ghosts. Only as she boarded the bus did she realize she'd left her house keys on the hall table.

On the newsdesk schedule that morning, the initials C.A. were marked against a story about the proposed introduction of automated checkouts at HypaCenta. No cashier to run every tin, packet and jar past the barcode sensor as they rolled off the conveyor belt – indeed, no conveyor belt, nor any need for the customer to unload the trolley. Instead, the prices would be tallied by a scanner which 'read' a microchip sealed into the packaging of each item. A digital display screen would flash up the total bill, the customer's payment (cards only, no cash or cheques) would be swiped, and a barrier released so the trolley could be wheeled through. Subject to successful trials, three-quarters of the supermarket's tills would event-ually be converted. Benefits to customer: speedier processing of purchases, reduced queuing time. Benefits to HypaCenta: *downsizing of the checkout personnel base* (Mr Chapple). When Constance queried the benefits for those who were to be made redundant, the manager argued that many more jobs would be jeopardized if the company – any company – failed to minimize costs in a competitive market sector. When she asked if customers preferred to be served by scanners or human beings, he accused her of being a Luddite.

She ran off a printout of her report for William, who had

been asked to produce an opinion column on the topic of automation. It was common for Mr Aitken-Aitken to delegate this responsibility. Ostensibly, those entrusted with the task were free to express themselves without interference over what 'line' to take. In practice, the writer would have such ingrained awareness of the editor's (therefore, the *Crucible*'s) opinion on any given issue that he would espouse a view in keeping with the traditional tone and editorial position. The leading article would invariably read as if Dougal had written it himself. *Leadership*, he stated in one of his own opinion pieces, *is about instilling in your followers a willingness to be led*. On the day of the HypaCenta story, however – with the editor away, the chief sub off sick, and the deputy editor too busy to proof-read the leader page – William broke rank.

Checked Out of a Job

Most of us, if we bother to think about the subject at all, have mixed feelings about automation. At home, we enjoy the convenience of our washing machines, microwave ovens, electric lawnmowers, video recorders – once luxury items, now commonplace 'necessities'. Yet despite these time-saving appliances, the modern lifestyle seems more frantic than ever. And, at work – while many jobs are made quicker and easier by advances in technology – which of us does not fear that our role will be usurped by the latest gadget? This is the prospect facing till staff at Urbopark's HypaCenta food-hall, where – as we report on page six tonight – the introduction of unsupervised, automatic checkouts could lead to redundancies.

Ambivalence towards automation is not new. Since the start of the industrial revolution, machines have been hailed as the means by which mankind might one day be freed from labour for a life of leisure. But for many men and women, work is a justification of their existence – bound up with ideas of self-esteem and of making a worthwhile contribution to society. 'Freedom' from work can mean unemployment and hardship.

Hello
Two centuries of industrial growth have done nothing to ease this tension between technological 'progress' and the anxiety that goes with it. Indeed, as we prepare to

enter the next millennium, there is a marked loss of faith in Utopia-through-automation; instead we share a vision of technology rapidly depleting the planet's resources, poisoning our environment. There is also the fear that Man may be enslaved by the very machines which promised freedom, becoming 'automated' ourselves through an increasing dependence upon them.

In arguing the case for unstaffed tills, Mr John Chapple, HypaCenta's manager, asks, 'When did you last see a check-out operative smile or say hello?' Perhaps the already highly mechanized, repetitive nature of their work has begun the process of turning these men and women into automata? Or perhaps – paid a pittance for working long hours for a company that seeks to protect its multi-million-pound profit by cutting jobs – the 'operatives' find little to smile about?

She met William in the Cutler's Arms, Yellow Lower. He was in the public bar, reading the financial pages of a newspaper, a near empty pint in front of him and a roll-your-own smouldering on the lip of an ashtray. He looked up, startled – it seemed – by her breezy greeting. She apologized for being late.

'What'll you have?' he said, folding the paper away.

'It's OK, I'll get them.'

After a brief dispute, William fetched the drinks while Constance went to the food counter. She offered to order him something as well, but he became furtive, patting the side of his jacket. Sure enough, during their lunchtime session he would – at precise twenty-minute intervals – sneak another fishpaste and cucumber sandwich from pocket to mouth, eating with discreet squirrel-like movements to avoid detection. She indicated the stock market listings in his newspaper.

'Checking your portfolio?'

'*Me?*'

'Oh yeah, I forgot.'

Constance recalled a furious argument in the pub after an NUJ chapel meeting, when William had berated two fellow union members (*so-called socialists*) for buying shares in a newly privatized public utility. *Wait while the bastards start sacking folk and cutting services just so there's enough profit for you lot to get a dividend.*

232

She smiled. 'Buying into the capitalist conspiracy?'

'Aye, well.'

The bar was noisy with conversation, jukebox music and the sporadic kerchung-kerchung of a fruit machine. Men in Mall Clean overalls played darts, two youths patrolled the pool table. Several folk had carrier bags of shopping stowed beneath their tables, like small dogs curled asleep at their feet. Despite the din, a man sitting alone in one corner – his back towards William and Constance – was reading a paperback, held out in front of him at shoulder height. How could he *concentrate*?

'I usually go in the other bar, if I come here at all,' she said. 'The *lainge*.'

'More comfy, that's all.'

William was smiling, semi-serious. 'If you're going to be leered at, you prefer the men to be smartly dressed?'

'And you, presumably, are drinking in here to affirm working-class solidarity?'

'First rule of journalism, Constance: never presume.'

A barman shouted her order number, bringing the toasted sandwich to their table. White bread, she'd asked for brown. No matter. 'I still have that book, *The Inky Path*.' Avoiding eye contact, she added, 'You taught me everything I know about newspapers.'

William laughed. 'Bugger your luck, then!'

Constance resumed eating, self-consciously, trying to make as little mess as possible. Good move, choosing mushroom instead of tomato – impossible to bite into a cheese-and-tomato sandwich without trailing gunk down your face. The jukebox started up again. William was concentrating on rolling another cigarette. She searched his face for clues to his mood, before asking, 'How'd it go with Dougal?'

'HypaCenta have pulled their ads for the rest of the week.'

'*Shit*.'

'Ten grand.'

'Jesus. What did he say?'

'Written warning. Indefinitely relieved of leader-writing duties.'

'*Bastard.*'

'Aye.' He smiled, releasing smoke simultaneously from mouth and nostrils. 'Got my opinion column printed though, didn't I? He can't do owt about that.'

'I bet he was hopping.'

'More surprised than angry. I've written leaders his way for so long he'd forgotten what my politics were. Waved the page under my nose and said, "It's not as if you actually *believe* this guff".'

'Sounds like Dougal.'

Gazing out of the window into the mall, watching shoppers stream by, she observed how the tinted glass reduced the colours of their clothing to a sepia monochrome. William's voice reclaimed her attention.

'History class tonight, isn't it?'

She shook her head. 'Half-term.'

'Oh, aye. My grandson's off this week.'

'The cyberkiller.'

'That's him.'

She noticed his glass was almost empty. 'Can I get you another?'

'Go on then. Just a top-up.'

Constance went up to the bar. As she turned away with the drinks, she saw the corner table where the man had been reading was now unoccupied, the seat pushed back untidily and an empty pint glass standing in a puddle of spilt beer. Next to the glass was the paperback, face up, its title and the name of the author embossed in stark red letters. Wilbur Smith. *Rage*. The book had been left at an angle, pointing towards the bar, as if to ensure anyone passing by would notice it. As if to ensure *she* would notice it. Protruding from the pages was a slip of pink paper – a sheet of notepad, folded in half and serving as a bookmark. She tried to recall the man who'd been sitting there. He'd had his back to her. Broad shouldered. Denim jacket? Blueish, anyway. And he'd been wearing a hat of some sort – a baseball cap. That was all she could remember. Constance became conscious of standing transfixed beside the table, a drink in each hand, staring at the abandoned paperback. Beer was dribbling from one of the glasses. People were looking at her. *William* was looking at her, from across the room.

'Anyone know the feller who was sat here just now?'

Was sat. She hated it when she did that, tailoring her accent to suit the audience. Her words weren't addressed to anyone in particular but to those in the immediate vicinity. Blank faces, a shrug, a shake of the head. Those who didn't look away, studied her with mild curiosity. The barman called out that he'd seen the man leave a few minutes ago. He indicated another doorway, an exit Constance hadn't noticed before. She hesitated. Setting the drinks down, she picked up the paperback and removed the bookmark. It contained the following, in barely legible red pencil:

> *potatoes (2lbs)*
> *bread (white, med. slice)*
> *teabags (PG)*
> *margarine (Flora)*

The Inky Path
Journalism is a profession where disappointments are many and frequent, where frustration and disillusionment are common, where the kicks are often more numerous than the ha'pence. The good journalist should no more dwell on yesterday's mistakes and mishaps than should this week's newspaper print last week's news.

'What was *that* all about?' asked William.

They were walking along the arcade from the pub to one of the plazas, her colleague at last able to raise the subject which

235

had lain unspoken between them as they'd finished their drinks. She shook her head.

'Just me, going off at a tangent.'

'I thought you were after thieving the book.'

'I really know how to show myself up, don't I?'

'Well, you've baffled me, lass.'

They reached a broad hexagonal plaza, drenched in natural light from the atrium; glass-sided escalators rose to the upper level from an oasis of potted palms and shrubbery. An artificial waterfall divided the 'up' and 'down' stairs. Here, the mall's constant soundtrack – muzak impregnated with a bustle of movement, of hundreds of people talking at once – took on an airy quality, dissipated by the sudden expanse of open space beneath a high, glass ceiling. Being half-term, the usual whorl of shoppers – that sense of permanently being in a busy railway station concourse at rush-hour – was blurred still further by children congregating in knots of raucous animation. Teenagers, hanging out. *Milling around*, Mam called it. Constance recalled long evenings spent on the bench outside the parade of shops on the estate: ciggies, smoked brazenly; the sharp nasal fizz of Diet Coke; salty, vinegary chips; and talking of . . . what? Of nothing. She could remember nothing of those conversations. William checked his watch, reached into his pocket for a sandwich. Wouldn't he get indigestion, eating on the move? His digestive system, he replied, was so attuned to being fed at twenty-minute intervals that all other considerations were secondary to this *dietary deadline*.

'First rule of journalism,' he said. 'Never miss a deadline.'

'Exactly how many first rules of journalism are there?'

'Only one: the one you're being told to obey at any given moment.'

As they passed the 'teeming' statues – the mall's meeting place and orientation point for lost shoppers – Constance saw that one of the three bronze figures had the dismembered head of a mop draped over his pate like a stringy wig. A gang of youths was huddled a discreet distance away – pleased enough with the practical joke to have been its perpetrators rather than mere spectators after the event.

'The "teemer",' said William, following the direction of her gaze. 'Bewigged. Looks like a character in a Restoration bloody comedy.'

'We've done this in our evening class, the crucible process.'

They paused beside the statues, depicting three men in boots and work clothes, pouring molten steel. A plaque bore a dedication to Benjamin Huntsman, steelmaker, who *allowed no portrait of himself to be made, but the crucible method has remained a testament to him.*

William indicated the team, towering blackly over them. 'Go on then, show us your credentials as industry correspondent in waiting.'

'No way.'

'Go on.'

Constance laughed. 'All right, how's this: the teemer – or gaffer – is holding a crucible pot in a set of long-handled tongs balanced across his knee. He's pouring the molten steel into a mould, to make an ingot. You can see where he's protected by swathes of wet cloth strapped round his arms and legs. He's to do it quickly and cleanly. Can you imagine it? I mean, the heat, the weight of the pot and having to be so strong and steady-handed, so *precise.* The mouth of the mould is, I don't know . . .'

'Two and half inches square.'

She looked at him. 'Anyway, that second feller, with the long rod – OK, OK, very funny – he's drawing off slag from the molten steel in the pot before it enters the mould. And him – number three, with another pair of tongs – he's holding the dozzle. There. A sort of hollow square that goes into the neck of the mould towards the end of the pouring to make sure enough of the molten metal is directed into the centre.'

He gave her a pat on the back. 'Well done. I'm impressed.'

'Patronizing sod.'

'No, seriously.'

'Like I say, we did it in class. And I've been to Hallam Island a few times. I'm only telling you what someone else has told me, or what I've read in books and that.'

'Aye, well, if knowledge were restricted to things we'd learnt first-hand we'd all be walking round in total ignorance most of the time.'

They moved away, in the direction of the *Crucible* office. William was reminiscing, unprompted, about his coverage of the installation of the teeming statues when Urbopark opened.

'Here's a curious fact,' he said. 'They're supposed to commemorate Hallam's industrial heritage – metalworking capital of the world, a name synonymous with craftsmanship. Right? Wave the flag, Rule Britannia. Well, them statues were made by a *Canadian* sculptor, living in *Italy*.'

'Really?'

'Interviewed the lad. Wouldn't know tongs from a dozzle if you shoved them up his proverbial.'

Snak Shak. She slowed. *My dealer*, she said, as they paused outside the kiosk. 'Talking of curiosities,' she added, 'did you realize that the teeming statue is Urbopark's official meeting point – and "teeming" is an anagram of "meeting"?'

Constance was working on a piece for the Our Gal at the Mall column, William was out on his rounds. In another part of the shopping complex, a woman triggered a tape marked 'chimes' then spoke into the mouthpiece of a mall-wide public address system. For once she was not reminding Urbopark customers of the latest bargains, nor advising them to meet their lost loved ones at the statues in Market Street. What she said was: *Paging Mr White, paging Mr White . . . would Mr White please go to the Red Zone car-park*. The message reached Constance as she tappety-tapped at her computer terminal. She ceased typing, raised her head. After a moment's reflection, she reached for the phone. She knew there was no Mr White. 'Mr White' was a coded signal to the head of Mall Secure, issued when attempts to make radio contact had been unsuccessful.

238

'Car-park' was an Urbo-code instruction for him to contact Mall Admin; 'Red Zone' denoted a Category A security alert. The system was designed to enable sensitive messages to be broadcast without alarming customers or alerting *unauthorized accessees*. But Constance knew, because it was her business to know.

The incident which triggered the security alert occurred in Mall Admin, Blue Upper. An overalled Mall Clean operative trundled a trolley of cleaning paraphernalia towards a door marked 'Ladies'. A crudely fashioned sign hooked over the handle declared the toilets to be Temporarily Out Of Service. The cleaner paused, a puzzled expression on his face. His supervisor had made no mention of there being a problem with this washroom; in any case, the 'out of service' sign was not of the official type. He parked his trolley. After a moment's deliberation he twisted the handle and entered a short, ill-lit, narrow passage with a mirror along the whole of one wall and another door giving access to the washroom proper. Someone was stooping, wedging a barrier of unravelled roller-towel against the foot of this second door. The linoleum floor was wet. The figure – a man, judging by his build – rose abruptly on the appearance of the cleaner in the outer doorway. His head was covered in a black woollen balaclava, with slits for eyes and mouth. The cleaner was in the process of demanding to know what was going on, when his sentence was truncated by a blow to the face. Recoiling, he collided with the door jamb. The masked figure – taking advantage of the other's momentary disorientation – tried to escape from the narrow passage. But the cleaner recovered his senses sufficiently to envelop him in a bear hug. The two men wrestled, wheeling one another round and lumbering against each wall in turn with such force that the mirror was dislodged and crashed to the floor. They became ungrappled. A second punch staggered the cleaner, pitching him backwards; there was a crack as his head hit the skirting board. The assailant fled into the corridor, shutting the outer door to the toilets and hurrying towards a sign marked Exit To Mall. As he let himself out into the arcade, he pulled off the balaclava and stuffed it in a pocket. The corridor was empty, nobody saw him go. No-one glimpsed his newly revealed features in the instant before the door closed in his wake with a rude belch of displaced air.

Constance and DCI Pink stepped aside as two paramedics heaved by with a laden stretcher. The patient was semi-conscious, making childlike noises that seemed to issue from his nose rather than his mouth. His clothes were soaked, his head lolled to one side. The blood appeared purple against the black skin of his scalp, matted in the tight curls of greying hair behind his ear.

'Will he be all right?' she asked, watching the stretcher-bearers depart.

'He'll not want to listen to loud music for a while.'

'You think he caught the saboteur in the act and got a whack for his troubles?'

'Let's wait till he comes round and we can speak to him, will we?'

The chief inspector had come to meet her at the blue-and-white police tape which marked off a section of corridor to either side of the ladies' washroom. The uniformed WPC, who had prevented her from going any closer to the scene of the incident, remained at hand – as though she suspected the reporter might still try to breach the cordon, despite DCI Pink's looming presence. The carpet – lavender, patterned with the mall's pale blue 'U' motif – was stained burgundy with a tongue of dampness that reached almost to where they stood. The detective's shoes had made a sucking sound as he'd approached. He asked how Constance came to be there so promptly, answering his own question with a raised hand: *I don't want to know*. He was busy. Forensics had hardly started. Not much he could tell her.

'You could tell me about the water.'

'He turned all the taps on full blast – put plugs in all the washbasins and left the taps running. Blocked the door – there's an interior door – with roller towel.' DCI Pink gestured at the soiled stretch of carpet. 'As you can see, a fair bit seeped out.'

'And the rest?'

'Our friend on the stretcher must've been out for quite a while, judging by the build-up.'

He explained that customers had reported water streaming down the walls of an arcade adjacent to the main plaza in Blue Lower, directly below Mall Admin's staff washroom. Security officers were in the process of tracing the source of the flooding when the ceiling gave way. A shopper, passing beneath the point of collapse, was knocked off her feet in the deluge. Cable ducts in the space between floor and ceiling had also been penetrated, causing a short-circuit that blew the electrics in half the mall.

'It was the weight that did it – the sheer weight of so much water,' said the chief inspector. 'Have you spoken to any of the folk down below?'

'Two or three. One of them gave me a good quote, actually.' Constance flicked back through her notebook. 'Here it is, Gemma Ritchie, thirty-one: "It were like summat out o' t'*Poseidon Adventure*. It were like a bloody great tidal wave".'

Paul Pink looked at her.

She smiled. 'I think we can say the computer game was more than just a gift from an anonymous admirer.'

'We're still checking it,' he said. 'Can't say any more than that.'

Constance turned to a fresh page. 'It's strictly cardholders only in this section, isn't it? Have you checked the swipe-card data?'

The detective glanced over his shoulder in the direction of the scene of crime, as though anxious to terminate the interview and resume his investigations. He ran the palm of his hand over his pate, smoothing down the stray wisps of hair. He nodded.

She lowered her voice. 'I wondered if . . . you know, if his i.d. code came up?'

DCI Pink looked at the WPC and at a group of Mall Admin staff who had gathered a short distance away to spectate. He raised the tape and ushered Constance through, leading her along the corridor. The carpet was sodden. He cleared his throat.

'Warren Bartholomew didn't do this.'

'No i.d. code?'

'I'm not talking about swipe cards.'

'I don't follow.'

The chief inspector held her gaze. 'Mr Bartholomew's body was found in his car at an isolated country park near Hallam this morning.'

Constance didn't say anything.

'Engine running, hosepipe – usual story.'

'Oh, fucking hell.'

'No note.'

She swallowed. She tried to remember when she'd last seen Warren. It was that time she'd returned to the office to find him and Paul Pink examining the contents of Mam's shopping bag. Surely they'd met since then? No. Spoken on the phone a few times, run-of-the-mill press inquiries. She'd last heard his voice . . . when, last week. They'd spoken last week and now he was dead. He was dead. You talk to people, innocent conversations . . . you'd think death would cast a shadow so that, sensing its presence – its imminence – you wouldn't be so chatty, so trivial; you wouldn't take the conversation for granted because it was going to be the last you ever had together. He'd kissed her. He had kissed her, and now he was dead; had died, *today*. On the last day she'd seen him, he'd been holding a pair of sling-backs her mam had just bought.

'Here.'

The detective removed the pink handkerchief from the breast pocket of his suit jacket and handed it to her. Scented.

Eucalyptus and menthol. She blew her nose and the vapour made her sneeze three times in rapid succession.

'My wife scents them with aromatherapy oils, for my sinuses. Of course, my colleagues refrain from taking the piss. One of the joys of being a police officer.'

Constance couldn't help laughing. Then the amusement subsided. 'Was it because of his job, or what?'

DCI Pink shook his head. 'He'd already lined himself up with another one. Made good use of the leaked memo to . . . dig himself an escape tunnel. Same status, similar salary – give or take a couple of grand. A job, anyroad.'

'Then, *why*? I don't understand why he did it.'

'I met Mrs Bartholomew this morning. Elizabeth. Liz. She came in for the identification. Seven months gone. Very distressing, it goes without saying.'

Constance looked away. 'I've never met her.'

'I asked if she'd any idea why her husband might've wanted to kill himself. *Take his own life*, was how I phrased it.' The inspector paused. 'Mrs Bartholomew informed me that, three days ago – on Sunday evening – she'd told him he might not be the father of the baby she's expecting.'

She waited for him to continue.

'They'd been watching a play, on the telly, about a woman being unfaithful to her husband. Mrs Bartholomew, up to that point, had intended keeping her own . . . infidelity a secret – the affair was over and her husband accepted the pregnancy, unplanned though it was, as a happy mishap. She'd have got away with it.'

'Was it guilt, d'you think? The play . . .'

'A *television* programme.'

She shrugged. She didn't know. She didn't know what to think about a man, a born-again Christian, who would gladly have committed adultery – with *her* – while his wife was pregnant; a man, too, who would kill himself rather than live to see his wife give birth to a child who might not be his. A man for whom the wages of sin – his? his wife's? – were death.

243

'I actually checked,' said DCI Pink. 'Would you credit that? After she'd gone, I got hold of a *Radio Times* and looked up the listings for Sunday evening to make sure there'd been a play on BBC2 about an unfaithful wife.'

Constance was folding his handkerchief into a neat square, not speaking.

'You know what she said to me, Mrs Bartholomew, when I asked her why she'd confessed to her infidelity? Sitting in that rickety chair you sat in, in my office. She said, "I couldn't live any longer with the burden of what I'd done, so I handed it to him." Her exact words. *I handed the burden to him.*'

Constance and the chief inspector disagreed. He believed it to be a coincidence – extraordinary, uncanny, but a coincidence nevertheless – that the 'wages of sin' quotation appeared in a warning letter to Home Zone's manager and, ringed, in a Bible left open on the press officer's desk immediately prior to his disappearance. She wasn't so sure. *What if one prompted the other? What if Warren heard about the letter and adopted the wording as his suicide note?* Paul Pink offered no opinion on this theory, though she knew him well enough by now to detect in his expression a hint of reluctant concurrence. One fact upon which they definitely concurred was that if Warren Bartholomew wasn't the saboteur then someone else *was*. Someone with a capacity for violence and destruction. Someone who'd handed Constance the task of plotting a path into the maze of his rage.

The Life and Times of a
Hallam Saw Grinder
(a Dramatic Reconstruction in Many Parts)

November 1861

Robert Smith was known at the Friendly Society gardens as
Whittler, for his habit – between his labours – of sitting on an
upturned crate, paring away at pieces of wood. When he was
not thus occupied, he was to be seen honing the blade of his
clasp knife on a leather strop. The rasp of steel against hide
was so familiar a sound that men on neighbouring plots had
absorbed it into the natural background of bird calls and of
the breeze in the trees that formed part of the allotments'
boundary. A fender grinder by trade, it was said by many –
though not by himself – that he had missed his vocation, that
he might have been better apprenticed as a woodworker.
However, function was not a consideration for Robert Smith.
He had no interest in fashioning new handles for gardening
implements nor in making shoehorns, clothes pegs, wooden
spoons and other objects of domestic utility. What he cared to
do was to carve for the sake of carving, for the feel of the
wood in his hands and the action of the metal against its
yielding surfaces, for the transformation in shape he effected
by skilful manipulation. He would work with any wood – from
the chocolate hue of walnut and brown oak to the pale blond
of hornbeam, from the satiny texture of elm or yew to rougher
grains of larch and silver birch. If some woods lent themselves
less readily to being sculpted, this was not to their detriment;
rather, they presented a set of difficulties that made his task
the more stimulating. The finished pieces (if they could be so
described, for complete and incomplete carvings were hard to
tell apart) he would place upon the shelves of his toolshed, or
take home to ornament his house or to offer to his children
as playthings. They were best pleased with those most closely

resembling human figures, though any likeness was accidental. Their father's sculptures were abstract in form, representative of nothing; indicative only of his mood at the time of their creation and the properties of the wood from which they were made. Whenever asked about this resistance to functionality, he would reply to the effect that whittling – for him – was an antidote to the practical nature of his daily work at the grindstone. He whittled to please himself.

For all the time he devoted to his hobby, Robert did not neglect his allotment. He was a knowledgeable and efficient gardener who achieved as much in an hour as others would accomplish in half a day. His advice on matters horticultural was in demand – dispensed over tea or a bottle of ale. Even so, his choice of crop was a source of consternation to his fellow allotment-holders. For his plot was given over entirely to flowers. The growing of flowers in itself was not uncommon, though few would omit vegetables altogether, as he did, nor persist in nurturing nothing but pretty blooms when money for food was scarce. So it was that, in addition to his being nicknamed Whittler, an apocryphal rumour was cultivated that – during periods of slack trade – the Smith family was nourished by a diet of chrysanthemums and fuchsias.

Robert's eccentricities earned him the amused and unconsciously envious fond regard of his more conventional fellows. It was not out of disrespect that jokes were made at his expense, but out of affinity. And if the gentleness of his pursuits was taken for weakness of character, or his independence of spirit for aloofness, it was by people who knew him insufficiently well. Tall and angular, with an ill-attended swathe of black hair, he cut a singular figure. Close to, it was his eyes which captured the attention – as much for their intensity of gaze as for the peculiar yellowish-brown of the irises. He appeared more youthful than his thirty-five years. Seated beside one of his companions at the gardens, they looked to be of similar age – though, in fact, Robert enjoyed five years' seniority. The other man – carrot-haired and ruddy

246

of complexion – was pouring tea from a flask into two tin beakers. Setting aside his latest carving and folding away the clasp knife, Robert accepted his drink.

'Tom, I swear theer's more rum than tea in this.'

'Thou hast only to swallow the one and spit out t'other if it's not to thy taste.'

The pair laughed. By the sudden cough and the watering of his own eyes, it was apparent that the supplier of the drink had also been caught unawares by the strength of its fortification. Robert had known Thomas Amory for years, relishing the time they shared in breaks between work at the allotment. Even if neither was in talkative mood, it was pleasant merely to sit in silence together. Another contemplative man, like himself; another man of creativity, for Thomas – to hear him talk – invested as much craftsmanship in the grinding of saw blades as did Robert in his whittling. Another man, too, who performed unsavoury duties for his union out of a sense of justice rather than for financial reward or for the gratification of violence.

'I hear theer's trouble at Hoole's,' said the saw grinder.

'Aye.' Robert studied his companion's expression, gauging whether this was idle conversation or an invitation to be taken into confidence. 'Aye, theer is.'

Thomas nodded. He was sitting on an upturned pail, his drink cupped in both hands to warm the fingers. His hands were ingrained with soil, scarred here and there with the blemishes of work.

'He will not lay off the men he's taken on,' said Robert. 'Nor take back those of us he laid off.'

'That's what I heard.'

'Thou heard right, then.'

'Canst thou not roll them up?'

'Hoole has watchmen posted night and day.'

'And the knobsticks will not be bought off?'

Robert shook his head.

'Nor frighted off?'

247

'Robertson and Kenworthy were asking likewise in t'Corner
Pin last night.'

Thomas coughed. 'What dost thou think?'

He did not answer. He inhaled steamy fumes of tea and rum,
the warm vapour forming beads of condensation on his face
and causing his eyes to sting. An insect was struggling on the
surface of the drink. Robert fished it out with his middle finger.

Royal Commission of Inquiry
(sitting at) Hallam Town Hall
Tuesday, 2 July 1867 (Twenty-second Day)

Witness: John Robson, No.51 Chester Street, Hallam.

Q. You are, are you not, an official of the Fender Grinders'
Union?

A. I am not.

Q. You say you are not?

A. I believe you are mistaking me with a man by the name
of James Robertson.

Q. And your name is?

A. John Robson.

Q. My apologies. (*chairman issues instruction to clerk of the
commission*) I see, now that I have the correct papers before
me, that you were manager of H.E. Hoole's Works, Green
Lane, Hallam, from 1861 to 1862. Is that correct?

A. It is.

Q. What was the nature of the business undertaken at
Hoole's?

A. The manufacture of stoves, stove grates and fenders.

Q. How many men were employed there?

A. I would say between eighty and one hundred.

Q. A number of these men would have been employed at
grinding, would they not?

A. There were two groups of grinders, those in the heavy
Wheels and those in the light Wheels – according to the nature
of the grinding.

Q. Within which group was the dispute with which this inquiry is to concern itself?

A. The heavy grinders.

Q. Can you tell us the origins of the dispute?

A. They would not work with non-union men.

Q. How was it that non-union men came to be engaged by Hoole's?

A. It was on account of the fact that those in the heavy Wheels had been neglecting their work and drinking for a considerable time, for more than a week.

Q. How many of the men had been drinking and neglecting their work?

A. Several. I do not recall how many.

Q. And non-union men were recruited to replace them. Is this so?

A. Mr Hoole asked the foreman, John Sibray, to find other men.

Q. What were the names of the men he found?

A. There were about half a dozen in all, I think. Richard White, George White, William Hulse and George Wastnidge were among them. I do not recollect the names of the others. They all came over from Masbrough, as I recall.

Q. What happened when the men who were in the union knew of them being taken on?

A. When they came into the Wheel to find the non-union men there they refused to work. Not only that, they got the light grinders to cease work in support of them. The following day, a letter was sent to Mr Hoole.

Q. From whom was the letter?

A. There was no name on it.

Q. What was the nature of the letter?

A. That he had better lay off the men not in the union and take back those that were.

Q. Did Hoole act upon this?

A. He did not take the men back, if that is what you mean.

Q. What occurred next?

A. Some days afterwards, the union sent a number of men to see me at the works to ask the same thing.

Q. What did you say to them?

A. I told them no.

Q. What did they say to that?

A. They said nothing more. But I heard later from the non-union men that they were offered £5 per man to leave the firm.

Q. What was their response? Did they accept the money?

A. They did not. I believe they said they would not go for less than £20.

Q. The union would not pay them so much?

A. It would not. One or two of the men, I believe, said they would join the union if they could keep their jobs; but the union would not allow this.

Q. Is it true that Hoole himself induced the union men to offer the non-union men money to leave?

A. It is not.

Q. You are saying he did not do that?

A. He did not do any such thing. I do not know who is saying he did, for he did not.

Q. Did the non-union men continue to work at Hoole's in defiance of the union?

A. They did. And they paid a price for it too.

The route the knobsticks took from Hoole's to their lodgings at the end of each working day was well-known to the union men, having followed them along it often enough. A ten-minute walk from the works in Green Lane carried them along Russell Street into Spring Street, as far as Hollis's Hospital. Here, they would separate – one heading along West Bar, another pair up Snig Hill and the remainder – the White brothers and Hulse – following Bridge Street to the turning into Water Lane. This being the less populous and least adequately illuminated of the three roads, it was deemed a suitable place to lay an ambush. Robert Smith and two others concealed themselves in the mouth of a jennel, a fourth man sat on the steps of a house across the street. When he stood up, it was to be the signal.

Robert's two accomplices in the alleyway had equipped themselves – one with an iron bar, the other with a short wooden stave that would subsequently have been confiscated for the purposes of whittling had it not become irreparably fractured and bloodstained. Robert himself had a small sack filled with stones from his allotment and knotted about his fist to form a bludgeon. He knew the knobsticks by sight but had never spoken to them, not being party to the fruitless negotiations which had been undertaken to induce them to cease working at Hoole's. It was therefore of little matter to him which of the trio he waylaid, whereas his fellows had marked their favourites – one being especially eager to have his go at Richard White for certain derogatory remarks in respect of the combination of working men. His chance would come soon enough, for the lookout was raising himself up.

By the features of the non-union men, it was evident that their initial alarm at being confronted in the street gave way to a calculation of their prospects – being three against four. It was clear, too, that they were none of them unduly daunted by such odds. The fear in their faces only became apparent when they saw that their opponents were armed, and that they were not four in number but six (two more having followed them thus far before making their presence known). Nevertheless they gave good account of themselves, exchanging blows for a minute or two before coming off so much the worse that they had little option but to protect themselves as best they could against the continuing onslaught. Robert took a punch or two from the man he knew to be Hulse before catching him about the ribs with his sack of stones. Hulse, winded, staggered a little and put out a hand to prevent himself from falling to the ground. In such a state he would have been easy prey to the next blow had he not managed to grasp Robert around the thigh so that the two were engaged in an ungainly

251

wrestling match. Unable to get a clean swing at him, Robert was reduced to tugging at the man's arm in an effort to free himself. Another of the union men was kicking repeatedly at Hulse's buttocks and legs, occasionally catching the one he was supposed to be helping, so confused was the struggle. All about them was a cacophony of hobnailed boots scuffling on cobbles, and of grunts and groans and the exclamation of assorted expletives; arms and legs flailed on all sides as various bouts of fisticuffs erupted in such close proximity that any observer might have been hard pressed to state how many were involved or who was attacking whom.

At last Hulse was made to release his grip, drawing himself up to his full height only to be knocked down altogether by a smart smack to the ear with Robert's trusty bag. Lying hopelessly on the ground, he drew his knees into his chest and covered his head with his arms, inert as a sack of potatoes as Robert and his co-assailant set about him. The other knob-sticks were soon similarly cowed, one slumped bloodied and dazed against a flight of stone steps as though struck down in the process of trying to crawl to safety. The third, Richard White, was so insensible as to have ceased to protect himself, sprawled in the gutter like a drunkard. His attacker, continuing to hit out viciously and often with the splintered stump of his stave, would in all probability have caved in the man's skull had not Robert and another of the union men hauled him off.

Chapter Nine

SHOP TALK

If you believe yourself to be impervious to product brand names or to the colour and design of their packaging, visit a supermarket in a foreign country and see how disconcertingly unfamiliar everything is.

I Shop, Therefore I Am: Essays in Mall Culture
eds. Jeremy Nicholls & Barbara Cutteslowe
(Hallam Metropolitan University Press, 1991)

'Listen, what're you up to this evening?'

'This evening?'

'Yeah, United are playing and I've got a couple of tickets and I was wondering whether – tell me if this is a crazy idea – but I thought you might like to go.'

'I . . . well, I don't know.'

'Short notice, I know.'

'OK. Yeah, why not?'

She smiled into the mouthpiece. Could people at the other end of the line tell when you were smiling, would it transmit itself through your voice or the sound of your breath or the quality of the silence between words? Whatever, she sensed that Professor Stanley Bell was smiling too.

'Shall I pick you up?'

'If that's OK with you, only Fifi's still in hospital.'

'Fifi?'

'My car.'

'Oh, yeah. Right.'

'Anyway, what time? Don't make it too early – I'll be late finishing tonight, and I've to take the bus home and get changed and have tea and everything.'

'Let's say, seven-oh-seven.'

She laughed. 'If you've not turned up by eight minutes past, there'll be big trouble.'

The Inky Path
The translation of an actual event into a news report is as much to do with editing as it is to do with writing. A reporter worth his salt will appreciate that all 'news' is summary – decisions about what to omit from a story are as essential as those about what to include. No sub-editor (nor reader) would thank the football correspondent, for example, whose account of a match took ninety minutes to read; nor the court reporter who transcribed verbatim every word of evidence in a six-week trial. If the aspiring journalist is prompted to remark that accuracy and faithfulness to the facts of an original incident are compromised by the editing process, then he will have begun to grasp a fundamental paradox of his chosen profession: that selective omissions of fact are integral to the pursuance of 'truth'.

Jeans, not a skirt. Not her best jeans because the seats would almost certainly be grubby. She put on her scruffiest pair and stood in front of the full-length mirror on the inside of her wardrobe door. Constance took off the jeans and tried on another pair, black ones she'd bought with the money Mam gave her instead of a birthday present. If she wore these, it would mean a change of top. Black top, black jeans: she'd look like a bloody Goth or something. Off with the top and on with a long-sleeve white shirt. It would be cold at the football.

254

Jumper or cardie? Jumper. The green roll-neck. She got it out of the drawer, then put it back again without trying it on and chose a cobalt-blue one instead, round-neck. Lovely. So soft you could hug yourself. Collar inside or out? She tried both, settled for inside. A look in the mirror, then: shoes, earrings, make-up, hair (up or down?) and perfume.

Milly, watching from the foot of the bed, said: 'What time's he coming?'

'Seven-oh-seven.'

'*When?*'

'Seven minutes past seven.'

'And you're going to a football match?'

'*Milly.*'

'I just hope he notices the effort you're making, that's all.'

'I'm dressing for my benefit, not his.'

'Oh, please.'

'What?'

'Nothing.'

'*What?*'

'*Nothing.*' Milly swallowed another mouthful of tea. 'Anyway, they usually notice without realizing what it is they've noticed.'

'There's nothing for him to notice.'

'Sure.'

'Mill, you're going to make me late.'

At precisely seven minutes past seven, Stan pulled up outside the house in his Austin Metro. *A statement of support for British workers*, he insisted, despite having bought the vehicle second-hand in a transaction which would be of no benefit to those on the assembly lines at Longbridge. (When Constance raised this point, he accused her of lacking *a sense of the symbolic.*) He climbed out of the car to let her in the passenger door, letting her out again at the end of the road so she could run back to fetch her gloves. He held the door ajar a second time, steamy breaths escaping from his beard into the cold night air like gasps of smoke from a campfire.

He was wearing a coarse black duffel coat, red-and-white scarf and matching bobble hat.

Her seat was red, his was white – one of those that made up the 'U' of 'United' spelled out along the bank of plastic seating. The pitch appeared unnaturally green beneath the white glare of the floodlights. Stan was sipping Bovril, Constance drinking weak, scummy tea that bore a faint tang of beef – her taste buds confused, it seemed, by the overwhelming aroma emanating from her companion's drink. The teams were out, warming up – the line-ups displayed on an electronic scoreboard, a computerized image of each player's face alongside his name and shirt number.

'Your granddad here tonight, is he?'

'Spect so. Hasn't missed a game in God knows how long.'

'How come he's United, rather than City?'

Constance shrugged. 'Runs in the family, I suppose.'

'Last time I came here, they were still sharing with the cricket.'

She'd forgotten that. The ornate wooden stand, like a cross between a cricket pavilion and a Victorian railway station; the wide swathe of grass separating fans from touchline – extraneous to the requirements of football, but essential to accommodate the greater dimensions of a cricket field. Bramall Lane, home to Hallam United FC in winter and Hallamshire CCC in summer. Cricket had once had this ground to itself, now it was gone; the old grandstand had also departed. Indeed there was no seating at all along one side of the pitch, a new structure delayed for another season. Hoardings had been erected to prevent the ball from disappearing into the wasteground of an aborted building site where the pavilion had stood, lending the incomplete stadium a curiously muted atmosphere. An image occurred to Constance of the void of the past absorbing the cry of today's crowd, transforming it into a ghostly echo.

She surveyed those sides of the ground which were occupied

– more than half full already, and fans still streaming in. Cup tie. There was a fizz of expectation. For the last fifteen minutes, the away supporters – from Grimsby, massed behind one goal – had been waving black-and-white inflatable fishes above their heads and chanting an insistent chorus of 'Barmy Army', the two words repeated over and over. The United fans, after a brief rendition of 'Sing when you're fishing, you only sing when you're fishing . . .', were now responding with 'Who the fucking hell are you?'

'I love all this,' said Stan.

'What, the singing?'

'Just the atmosphere, all these people. I think that's why I got into Aussie Rules when I was in Melbourne. Huge crowds at some of those games.'

'They don't get so many at United these days. If it's crowds you're after, you'd be better off going to Urbopark.'

'The new working-class Mecca.'

'Is that Mecca as in bingo hall, or Mecca as in betting office?'

Stan gave her a smile. He took another swig of Bovril, the ends of his moustache glistening as he lowered the plastic cup. His glasses had steamed up. He handed his drink to Constance while he wiped the lenses with a handkerchief. She watched him – stripped of his spectacles – recalling the flush-cheeked sleepiness of his face on the afternoon of the picnic, as he dozed in a meadow, oblivious to her scrutiny. When he'd finished cleaning his glasses, she handed back the beaker of Bovril. He thanked her. Another smile, even warmer than the last.

He said, 'I'm so pleased you said you'd come tonight.'

'Why, worried your spare ticket would go to waste?' She smiled, too, to take the unintended edge off of her remark, to buff away the snideness.

'What spare ticket? I bought it specially for you.'

'I'm honoured. Grimsby Town and a cup of Bovril.'

He laughed. 'That's *tea*.'

'It *tastes* like Bovril.'

He went to say something else, only to be drowned out by a roar from the crowd. Kick-off. They turned their attention to the pitch – barely speaking again during the first half, apart from occasional comments related to the play. As soon as the whistle went for half-time, Stan stood up and excused himself, said he'd to use the loo. The *lav*. Did she want another drink or a meat-and-potato pie fetching back? No, thanks. She remained in her seat during the interval; nothing to read, he'd taken the match programme with him. The scoreboard was displaying half-times from other matches around the country, a cheer greeting news that Hallam City were losing. At the side of the pitch, a presentation was taking place – a stainless steel tankard, handed to a stalwart United fan who'd not missed a game since 1946. As she watched, her gaze was snagged by a banner being paraded along the front of the stand. Fashioned from white cloth, it bore the message 'JOHN, II:13–16'. Born Again. *God Botherers*, as Dad called them. Or one of those prophets of doom you saw at sporting events: *The End of the World is Nigh. Prepare to Meet Thy Maker. Repent of Thy Sins.* Usually outside rather than inside the stadium, and bearing sandwich-boards or a printed placard rather than an amateurish square of cloth. She thought, fleetingly, of Warren Bartholomew. The person carrying the banner was obscured from view from the waist up by the cloth itself and from the waist down by folk sitting in the front row. All she could make out were glimpses of dark trousers and white knuckles. Few of the fans around her appeared to be paying him any attention. He continued slowly to the end of the section of seating before making his way up the aisle to her right, still hidden from view. Then she lost sight of him altogether in the crowds heading back to their seats in time for the second half. Fanfare over the PA, heralding the return of the players. Applause. She saw Stan shuffling along the row, causing each spectator in turn to stand up so he could squeeze by. He held a pie wrapped in greaseproof paper.

'Bloody queues, Jesus!' He sat down, adjusting his duffel

coat one-handed where it had pulled tightly across the bulk of his belly. He caught her watching him. 'OK, stop making me feel guilty.'

She produced a Snickers from her pocket. 'Does this make us even?'

The game resumed. United were trailing one-nil and, as the second half wore on, the home fans grew increasingly impatient. Then, ten minutes from full-time, an equalizer. Pandemonium. Stan and Constance were out of their seats, cheering; he grabbed her in a bear-hug, lifting her off the ground and performing a jig. In the excitement, his bobble hat came off. She sat down, breathless.

'Sorry about that!' he said, surfacing, red-faced and clutching the woolly hat triumphantly. 'Didn't hurt you, did I?'

She laughed. 'I think every one of my ribs is broken.'

'Jeez, I'm really sorry.'

Her boob was sore from where she'd been crushed against him. But it was OK. It was fine. It was nothing, really. And it was fun. *This* was fun, being at the football with him and seeing him so happy over a goal, being happy herself. When the crowd started chanting she found that she and Stan were joining in, rising from their seats along with everyone else whenever United went close to scoring a winner. But the match ended in a draw, with no further goals during extra time.

'Penalties!' said Stan.

The players gathered in the centre circle, some standing, others sprawled on the grass having their legs massaged or taking swigs of fluid from plastic bottles. The two managers were moving among them, distributing encouragement. After noting down details of those nominated to take the kicks, the referee ushered the goalkeepers towards the penalty area at the home end.

'Five penalties each,' Stan explained, leaning close to the side of her face to make himself heard. Whiff of gravy and pastry. His beard tickled her cheek, causing her to shiver involuntarily.

'And United are the ones in red-and-white stripes, are they?'

'OK, OK.' He was laughing.

They watched the penalty shoot-out, having to stand to see over the other spectators. The refusal of some to *fuckin' siddown!* had caused those behind to stand as well, until everyone was on their feet. Constance had to go on tiptoes, straining to peek between the rows of male heads obscuring her view. Ninsy peedles in her toes. Her calves and the backs of her knees, even her neck, ached from holding the position. Once or twice she lost her balance and put a steadying hand on Stan's shoulder. He seemed not to notice, transfixed by events on the pitch. Grimsby, 1–0; United, 1–1; Grimsby 2–1; United 2–2 . . . As he made his run-up, each Grimsby penalty-taker was assailed with boos, cat-calls and shrill whistles from the United fans; when the ball hit the net, the din ceased as though by the flick of a switch. The process was reversed for each of the home team's penalties: hear-a-pin-drop silence as the player prepared to shoot, then a collective roar of YESSS! Of their allotted five, the visitors scored four; United – having missed their third – were on three from four, with one to come.

'If he doesn't get this we're out,' said Stan.

The player wiped the ball on the front of his shirt, placing it carefully on the penalty spot. As he stepped back to begin his run-up, his own goalkeeper approached him and made a show of offering last-minute advice – pointing to the left-hand side of the goal, as though instructing his team-mate where to aim the shot.

Tickly beard. Stan, speaking into her ear. 'Trying to psyche out their keeper.'

'How d'you mean?'

'Make him think: bluff, or double bluff?'

Hush. Grimsby's goalkeeper swayed slightly on the goal-line, shifting his weight from one foot to the other, knees bent, clapping his gloved hands once, twice. The United penalty-taker approached the ball and struck it firmly towards the bottom left-hand corner, where his team-mate had pointed. But the opposing keeper guessed correctly. At full stretch, he managed to deflect the shot one-handed around the post, the ball bouncing against an advertising hoarding before spinning to a stop on the perimeter track. The United player sank to his knees on the turf. Grimsby's keeper sprinted towards the halfway line to be engulfed in celebration by his team-mates. Three sides of the stadium were silent, a distant noise echoing from the bank of supporters at the farthest end. Plastic fishes, waved aloft. Stan turned to Constance, forming his face into a study of disappointment. She reciprocated. But their expressions contained a self-awareness of fraudulence, both of them – she sensed – conceding the regular Unitedites' prior claim to the true dejection of defeat. First time either of them had been to a game for years, who were they to be upset?

'Shouldn't have taken any notice of his keeper,' said Stan. He pronounced it 'tekken': flat, hard Hallam. Football-speak. 'Heebie-jeebies. Looked like he changed his mind half a dozen times in the run-up. No way to take a penalty, that.'

On the way home, Stan – his buttoned-up duffel coat bulging either side of a diagonal strap of seat-belt – enquired into the health of Fifi. Was her condition . . . *serious*? he asked with due gravity. Constance shook her head. The exploratory op had revealed nothing terminal, she replied. *Which ward is she in?* She looked at him, straight-faced. *You thinking of visiting her?* Stan hesitated. *I thought, maybe . . . some flowers*. Constance nodded. *She'd like that.* They sat in companionable silence for a while, the car stranded in a single file of traffic ribboned with spectators streaming away from the stadium on foot. The interior of the Metro reeked of warm wool, from where he'd stashed his bobble hat over one of the dashboard heater vents. A relic from his days as a student in Hallam, he said; the scarf, too. *Half those players out there tonight weren't even born when I first wore these.* Hand-knitted, by his mother. His *mam*. Constance smiled, recalling the countless pairs of

261

ill-fitting mittens her own mam had made for her and Mags and which seldom survived a week without being mislaid or chewed beyond repair. The roads became less congested the further they got from Bramall Lane. As they passed the Tongs, she was on the point of suggesting they call in. But, as if reading her thoughts, Stan discounted the possibility. Busy day at the university tomorrow, an early start preparing for a nine o'clock lecture. And what with there having been extra-time and penalties . . . It was OK, she said. She wouldn't mind an early night herself. More silence, though of a markedly different quality. Constance watched the night-time streets slip by. Conversation became stilted, sporadic – another of those abrupt and, to her, unaccountable losses of intimacy that seemed to characterize their – what? – their *outings*. She wanted the Stan who, moments ago, had indulged her anthropomorphic concern for a Ford Fiesta. Instead, she had the Stan who made polite discourse: his job; her job; the next evening class; the alterations to Hallam's road system. When at last they drew to a halt outside the house, she let herself out of the car with a friendly but brief farewell. He apologized for the result, as though it was his fault. She shut the passenger door, opening it again to retrieve her gloves. It was then, as she leaned in, that Stan placed a hand over hers and gave her a brusque, bristly peck on the side of the face. In withdrawing from the kiss, he banged the rearview so hard with his head that the mirror was dislodged from its mounting and fell into the footwell.

The following day, the back page of the *Crucible* carried a report of the match beneath the huge headline: 'IT'S GRIM!' A strapline read, 'United pay the penalty as Grimsby grab Cup glory'. On page one, meanwhile, was a report on the latest development in the sabotages saga. Another byline for Constance's scrapbook.

'Hate' mail link to Mall Madman, say police

by Constance Amory

Local companies have received 'hate' mail for trading with Hallam's giant Urbopark shopping centre.

Envelopes containing razor blades and threatening letters were sent to managers at two firms in what police believe to be the latest twist in the spate of attacks by a mystery saboteur.

Finger

The letters were opened by secretaries – one of whom suffered a cut finger. A third firm, with no apparent connection to Urbopark, received a similar letter.

Yoghurt

The three firms were:
- Fruits of the Churn – a dairy company contracted to supply butter, milk, cheese, cream and yoghurt to the HypaCenta foodhall;
- CZZ (Chemicals) Ltd – a firm supplying industrial-strength hygiene products to the Mall Clean in-house cleaning unit; and
- Guard Rite – a security firm employed at various sites in Hallam, including the town hall and university campus, but claiming to have no link to Urbopark.

Police are not divulging details of the letters, though a spokesman described them as 'generally abusive' without making any specific threat or warning. Urbopark was not named, but each letter contained a codeword used in connection with attacks on the mall.

This is the fist time the 'Mall Madman' – whose motive remains unclear – has targeted firms outside the shopping complex.

The 'hate' mail follows an assault on a cleaner who was trying to stop a masked man escaping from the scene of the latest sabotage.

Ceiling

In that incident, a serious flood resulted in the partial collapse of a ceiling in a Lower Mall arcade and left half the mall without electricity for several hours.

A spokesman for Fruits of the Churn told the *Crucible*

turn to page 2

The smallholdings could be reached on foot via a snicket descending from the edge of a housing estate. The path, zigzagged by metal barriers, was so steep that Constance – making the mistake of looking down from her vantage point above the patchwork of allotments – came over dizzy. She shut

263

her eyes until the feeling passed. Carrying on down the snicket, she chanced another look – hoping to make him out. But the only discernible movement was that of plastic carrier bags, fastened to stakes as bird-scarers and being agitated by a stiff breeze. She went through a gate leading onto a track treacherous with mud. No wellies. She wasn't even wearing her oldest work shoes, but the brand-new ones: Footsies, Orange Lower, £29.99. She skirted the worst of the wet ground. A man, repairing the roof of his shed, broke off to give directions, making vague signals with the aid of a claw-hammer. Navigation in the network of narrow paths was complicated by a shantytown of toolsheds and towering wig-wams of runner beans that obscured her view. She heard him before she saw him, the familiar deadpan voice claiming her attention as she prepared to step over a low fence constructed of corrugated iron. *Over here. No, here.* Paul Pink was standing among what looked like a row of small shrubs, some thirty metres away.

'Hi!' She waved. 'How do I get to you?'

'There's a gate,' he called, pointing back along the track. 'Stick to the path or you'll be up to your ankles.'

In shite, by the smell of it. Not shite, compost – a makeshift enclosure of wooden slats was stacked with rotting vegetation. She let herself through the gate and made her way towards him. Off-duty: green overalls, sleeves rolled back at the wrist; wellies; cloth cap. He'd resumed his work. The shrubs, she could see now, were Brussels sprout bushes. DCI Pink was squatting, reaching beneath the leaves to get at the sprouts and snapping them off one at a time with a sharp downward tug. He tossed the pickings into a bright red plastic bucket and removed any yellowed leaves and an occasional sprout into a bowl similar to the one her mam used for washing up.

'Blown,' he said, holding up one of the rejects for her inspection. 'See, all open and loose. A good Brussel should be firm and tightly packed. More flavour.'

'What causes that, then?'

'Wrong soil or incorrect planting, if it happens to someone else's crop. Poor weather, if it happens to yours.' He stood up, battering the palms of his hands together. His wrists were thick, the coarse black hairs matted with mud. 'I've to finish off while there's some light left. Them tall buggers over there want staking out.'

'Need a hand?'

He looked at her. 'I've an old shirt and a spare pair of boots in the shed.'

The afternoon light was beginning to fail by the time they sought the shelter of the hut, her host pouring coffee from a thermos flask and producing a packet of fruit biscuits from a tin. A stool and a wooden bench provided the only seating and occupied most of what floor space remained among the sacks of organic fertilizer, boxes, buckets, a coiled hose and assorted gardening equipment. Forks, hoes, rakes and spades hung from long nails hammered into the wooden walls, and sets of shelves were piled with smaller tools and empty flowerpots. There was a transistor radio (*for the rugby*), a disorderly stack of gardening magazines strewn across the surface of the only workbench and half a dozen Raymond Chandlers supporting an open jar of what smelled like turps. The hut stank of unidentifiable odours, masking the aroma of coffee as Constance brought the steaming beaker to her lips. Inhale and drink, inhale and drink; warmth was absorbed into her cupped, mud-caked hands. Something was triggering her asthma, probably the turps. Or paint. Was there fresh paint in here?

'I'm sorry for just turning up like this.' A wheeze, as she spoke. He must've heard it too. One sleeve of the man-size shirt had come unrolled, causing her hand to disappear within the flapping cuff. Her feet were lost inside the wellies he'd lent her.

'Your wife said you'd forgotten to take your mobile. It took me ages to find this place. I mean, I'm sure there was nothing wrong with her directions, just my—'

'I didn't forget my mobile, I left it at home so I'd not be disturbed.'

'Like I say, I'm sorry . . .'

DCI Pink sniffed suspiciously at his beaker. 'This taste all right to you?'

'Yeah, fine. Why?'

'Last time I used this flask was for tomato soup.'

'Seems OK to me.'

'My imagination then,' he said. 'Autosuggestion. D'you ever do that, where you imagine you're biting into a lemon or an orange and your mouth starts watering?'

'Is that autosuggestion, though? I always took auto-suggestion, you know, to imply an *absence* of conscious thought.'

He drained his drink and placed the beaker on the work-bench. She watched two ants investigating a scattering of biscuit crumbs. They would return to the nest with their find and, before long, the scarred and stained wooden surface of the bench would be alive. The chief inspector leaned forward, brushing the ants to the floor with the flat of his hand. He offered her the packet of biscuits.

'Have another. Go on, they've to be eaten before they go soft.'

He took one himself and ate it whole, cheeks bulging. She was reminded of a cartoon character's throat assuming the shape of whatever it had swallowed. Tom and Jerry. Tom, swallowing a dustbin lid.

Paul Pink said, 'What've you got for me?'

'How d'you know I wasn't hoping to get something from *you*?'

'You look pleased with yourself, is how I know.'

She laughed, covering her mouth with her hand. 'Give away, is it?'

'Don't ever take up poker.'

Constance searched in her bag for the folder she'd fetched with her from the office, producing a document. She explained

266

that it had been obtained by her colleague, William Boyce, from *one of his sources*. This was a photocopy, the original having been returned to the place from where it was borrowed. Silence while the detective inspected the document. When he'd finished, he glanced up at her.

'There *is* a connection,' she said. 'Guard Rite is bidding to take over from Mall Secure when the security operation at the mall is put out to tender.'

'OK, so all three firms who received hate mail have links with Urbopark.'

'But, you see, the security bid isn't public knowledge. The saboteur must be privy to that information – either someone at Guard Rite or within Mall Admin.'

'Could be someone related to – or friendly with – an employee at one or the other.' DCI Pink paused, unsmiling. 'Or someone who overhears something in a pub. Or someone who knows someone who knows someone else who—'

'OK.'

'You get my point?'

You see. That had been her mistake. She'd patronized him, and now he was shredding her. Don't sag, don't look away. Constance picked at the edges of the folder, not once taking her eyes from his. He was the first to break eye contact, turning his attention to the breast pocket of his overalls. He got out a box of matches and lit three candles positioned around the hut, each mounted on a saucer encrusted with old wax. It wasn't until the wicks began their shadow show that she realized how gloomy it had become – the light defining the darkness.

'I've got something else as well,' she said. 'Some cuttings from the *Crucible*.'

She retrieved several photocopies from the folder, watching his features flicker in the candlelight as he read them. Finally, he set the pages down on his lap.

'Enlighten me.'

'I went through our files on each of the stores targeted by

the saboteur – Mall Admin, as well. I wanted to see . . . I suppose I didn't really have an idea what I was looking for, *specifically* – I was just after something that might connect them.'

DCI Pink nodded, glancing again at the cuttings as she continued.

'There were quite a few connections, actually – but only one that applied to all of them: industrial relations.' She leaned forward in her seat, counting off each point. 'HypaCenta was named in a survey as paying its staff less than any other supermarket in the region, *and* it plans to get rid of checkout workers by installing automated tills; Home Zone is cutting weekend pay rates from double time to time and a half; Mall Admin is privatizing the security operation . . . and, if you take the firms who received hate mail: CZZ has derecognized trades unions at its plant; and Fruits of the Churn is being taken to a tribunal over its working conditions, employing people at excessively long hours and in breach of health and safety rules.'

'What about Red Leather, Yellow Leather?' asked the chief inspector. 'I don't have a cutting here . . .'

Constance produced another page from the folder. 'We didn't carry this story, but there was something in the *Guardian*. Here. The company started as a workers' co-operative, with just one branch in London. Over the years, a chain of more than fifty shops has been built up all over the country – and now, the founders have sold the business to one of the big multinationals. No more workers' co-operative.'

'And Guard Rite, by negotiating to take over mall security, would be party to Mall Secure employees losing their jobs.'

'*Exactly.*'

DCI Pink exhaled. 'So how does all this tie in with the . . . incidents?'

'Look at the dates. Apart from the security privatization and the HypaCenta low-pay report, every sabotage occurred *within a few days* of a corresponding story about the "victim". About their "crimes against man", to quote Mr Rage.'

She studied him in the unreliable light cast by the candles as they guttered in the draughty hut. The misshapen, elongated shadow of his head was repeated in triplicate on the wall and the slanting underside of the roof. They sat in silence for what seemed like several minutes. When, at last, the detective spoke, he said only one word. *Rain.* A discreet pattering on the roof, wind-blown droplets at the solitary cobwebby window. DCI Pink raised the sheaf of papers and asked if he might keep them. She nodded.

'I've to be home by six,' he said. 'Shepherd's pie of a Thursday.'

'*Every* Thursday?'

'Without fail.'

Change of subject, discussion over. No idea whether he was impressed by her investigations, or by her theory. His retention of the documents was as much as she'd receive by way of recognition. Fine. That was fine. She trod the boots off at the heel. Her own shoes felt insubstantial by comparison; dainty, like a ballerina's. She removed the borrowed shirt and put on her jacket. The inspector was extinguishing the candles, pinching each wick between wetted thumb and middle finger. Smells of smoke and hot wax. She followed him outside, waiting in the drizzle while he padlocked the door. They walked along a track to a dead-end road she'd failed to find from Mrs Pink's directions. He was carrying a sack filled with sprouts, holding it one-handed by the scruff of the neck and adopting a lopsided stride to accommodate its weight. Vehicles were parked on a grass verge. He placed a hand on her shoulder, guiding her.

'I'll give you a lift back to your car.'

'Is this road marked on the map?'

'How old's your map?' She produced the street plan from her bag and opened it for him. 'Out of date,' he said. 'Look.'

The cul-de-sac, built to serve the allotments after the

construction of a dual carriageway, was unmarked. They got into his red Mondeo. *A plain-clothes police car*, as Mam once remarked during an episode of *The Bill*. DCI Pink cleared a copy of The *Independent* from the passenger seat and slung it in the back along with the bag of sprouts. While they waited for the heater to clear the windscreen, he switched on the interior light and opened the map to display another section of the city.

'I'll show you summat else. There.' He pointed to a triangle of land formed by three roads close to Hallam City football ground. A cluster of rectangular buildings were indicated as 'works'. 'D'you know that part of town?'

'Yeah, it's near where my granddad lives.'

'Which works is that?'

Constance tried to match the map's two-dimensional image with her recollection of the neighbourhood. 'There *isn't* a factory on that side of the road, is there?' She glanced at him. 'Isn't that where Valu-Land is?'

'Spot on.'

Granddad refused to shop at Valu-Land, preferring to give his custom to several smaller shops in the area – butcher, baker, grocer, greengrocer – even though the supermarket was more conveniently located and sold its produce more cheaply.

'So why's it marked as a works site?'

'D'you remember what used to be there before they built the supermarket? Years ago, I'm talking about.'

'The old barracks, wasn't it?'

DCI Pink nodded. 'All the old maps of Hallam show the barracks as "works". National security.'

'Security against *who*?'

'Russia, at one time. And terrorists – the IRA. There's always an enemy.'

'Funny, isn't it?' she said. 'I mean, there are people – kids – who'll only ever know of it as a supermarket.'

DCI Pink shook his head. 'Those Brussels – a year ago, I had carrots growing on that strip. And lettuce the year before

270

that. Crop rotation. You've not to grow the same type of veg – brassicas, roots and so on – in the same place year after year or you'll . . . encourage pests and upset the balance of nutrients in the soil.'

'Yeah, yeah – and there was something there before the barracks were built and there'll be something else after the supermarket has gone. I know all that.'

Christ, *she* was the historian – not him; she wasn't doing anything more than remarking upon a curiosity of . . . what? Of perspective. A curiosity of perspective. Constance sat back heavily in the passenger seat, staring straight ahead and biting back her irritation. Jesus. The windscreen was partially demisted, two irregularly transparent arcs gradually encroaching upon the film of condensation. The car's bright red bonnet was visible, as well as a patch of muddy verge whose unkempt grass had been flattened and dishevelled by the repeated passage of vehicles. The remainder of the view was still draped in a milky haze. She rarely had the patience to allow the heater to clear Fifi's screen, wiping with the back of her hand or a grubby chamois pad. *You'll only smear the glass*, Howard would say. She'd do it to annoy him – still did, even though he wasn't around any more to be annoyed. Imaginary conflicts. She was doing it now, continuing the argument with Paul Pink inside her head; saying nothing. What argument? There was no argument. It was just her, failing to make herself understood. As per. He produced a packet of Extra Strong Mints from the glove compartment, took one for himself and handed the packet to her. *You'll spoil your tea*. Mam. They sat in silence, save for the hum of the engine and the hairdryer blast of heater vents, the rubbery fart-fart of the wiper blades. She watched the windscreen clear fraction by fraction, allowing herself to be lulled by the soporific warmth, waiting for him to set the car in motion. When he spoke, his voice startled her.

'We've had a profile of the saboteur compiled by a criminal psychologist.' DCI Pink adjusted his rearview-mirror. 'This is for you, not for umpteen thousand *Crucible* readers. Nor for

271

your editor. I'm telling *you*, because our friend is in communication with you and it's . . . necessary for you to know who you're dealing with.'

Constance didn't say anything.

'There's a marked escalation, both in activity and intensity – the acts of sabotage, the cryptic clues. A build-up. The psychologist says the pattern of behaviour conforms to type – to a certain type of obsessive criminal activity. There'll be more incidents, he believes, and they will become more . . . physical in nature.' The detective paused. 'It's his opinion that, ultimately, the saboteur has the potential to kill.'

The Life and Times of a Hallam Saw Grinder
(a Dramatic Reconstruction in Many Parts)

November 1861

The first time Daniel Amory became intoxicated was on the occasion of his twelfth birthday, when his father permitted him two glasses of beer. This allowance was made not in celebration of his birthday, as such, but to mark the commencement of the boy's apprenticeship as a saw grinder. The beer, home-made to a traditional Amory family recipe, had been brewing in an assortment of containers in the cellar at No.11 Garden Street for some weeks, lending the house a pungent aroma. Each evening in the week preceding Daniel's formal initiation into his father's trade, a crate of ale would be loaded on to a sack-barrow and wheeled to the home of a neighbour or relative for communal consumption. On the birthday night itself, the Amorys (Thomas, Frances, Daniel and his younger siblings, Agnes and Jasper) visited the Smith family. Robert Smith was Thomas Amory's closest friend, while his wife Mary – a midwife – had brought each of the Amory children into the world. Their own two offspring – William and John – had been playmates of the other three since they had been able to crawl.

The Smiths lived in Glossop Road, near the public baths which Daniel's father frequented during winter, on days when the standpipe in the yard was frozen. This custom did not prevent him, whenever the subject of bathing was discussed, from declaring: 'Cleanliness is next to Godliness, I allus say. Missen, I bathe regular – once every twelvemonth wi'out fail, whether needed or not.' He made this joke again on the occasion of Daniel's apprenticeship celebrations. The womenfolk were in the kitchen, preparing food, the men were in the day-room waiting for the ale to settle after its journey

273

in the barrow. Daniel, who had been forbidden to drink during the previous outings that week, knew that this evening heralded his turn to join the supping.

'Thou wilt not make the ale any less lively for gawping at it, son!'

Daniel felt himself redden, having been caught out in his impatient scrutinizing of the bottles. They were arranged on a table in a corner of the room farthest from the hearth. A fire, newly replenished with coal, was casting an orange glow over the faces of those assembled. Thomas and Robert were standing either side of the fireplace, discussing work and the latest spate of rattenings. Daniel had heard the word for the first time a few months earlier and had enquired as to its meaning. When his father had prevaricated, the boy asked if it was anything to do with rats. Thomas had chuckled at this, replying, 'Aye, thou couldst say so.' Jasper and the two Smith boys were sitting cross-legged on a rag-rug in the centre of the flagstone floor, playing a game with small pebbles. Jasper – at eight years old, the youngest of the players – had managed, in his excitement, to scatter his pebbles about the room. One came to rest by Daniel's foot. He picked it up, hesitating as he did so – tempted, momentarily, to join in the game. He resisted; he was to begin his apprenticeship in the morning and was, as a consequence, too adult to be bothering himself with such childish pursuits. Instead, he pressed the pebble into his brother's hand with the air of an uncle giving a shiny new farthing to a favourite nephew. Daniel withdrew to the fireplace to keep company with his elders, so perfectly aping his father's manner of standing with feet apart and hands clasped behind his back that the two men burst out laughing. The boy blushed again, despite himself, turning away from the hearth and striding from the day-room. He tried to slam the door on his departure, but – being warped and ill-hung – it merely screeched against the floor, closing with a shudder rather than the dramatic bang he had intended.

Royal Commission of Inquiry
(sitting at) Hallam Town Hall
Tuesday, 2 July 1867 (Twenty-second Day)

Witness: John Sibray, stove-grate manufacturer, No.9 Ship Hill, Rotherham.

Q. Were you employed at the works of H.E. Hoole, Green Lane, Hallam, in 1861?

A. From April to November of that year, I was.

Q. What was your position there?

A. I was a foreman in the stove-grate department.

Q. Were all the men at Hoole's members of their respective unions at that time?

A. They were when I commenced my work with the firm.

Q. We have heard from another witness that non-union men came to be engaged in the heavy-grinding Wheel. Is this so?

A. It is.

Q. Can you say how this came about?

A. One of the union men was drunken and unsatisfactory in his work. Mr Hoole asked that I find a man to replace him.

Q. You say that one of the men was drunken. It was not more than one?

A. It was not.

Q. Yet we have heard from this other witness that more than one of the men was drunken at his work and that you were asked by Hoole to find several new men.

A. I was asked to find more than one man, but not on account of drunkenness.

Q. How, then?

A. I hired one man, a man by the name of Charles Taylor, to replace the worker who was drunken. When the others saw Taylor at his trough they would not work with him.

Q. Why would they not work?

A. Because Taylor was not a member of the union.

Q. What happened then?

A. When the men would not work, Mr Hoole asked me to find others who would.

Q. Is that how there came to be more than one non-union man in the Wheel?

A. It is.

Q. And you say that the union men, with the exception of one, were not drunken as a rule nor unsatisfactory at their work?

A. They were not.

Q. Why did you hire non-union men? Did you not know it would cause trouble?

A. I hired them because Mr Hoole needed men to do the work, and because I knew that no union man would take another union man's job from him.

Daniel avoided the kitchen, from which were issuing the sounds of women's voices and smells of hot food, choosing instead to climb the narrow staircase to the first-floor chamber. From previous visits, he knew this to be where William and John slept. The room was cold, illuminated by a moonlight that bathed the plain walls and lent the patchwork cotton bedspread a faint luminescence. He went to the window. The rear courtyard was enclosed on three sides by houses and on the fourth by a small forge which, during the day, made conversation impossible with its clatter and prevented the women of the terraces from pegging out their washing for fear of smuts. The muddy ground was rutted with footprints, overlaid by the moon's snow-like sheen. This illusion of a wintry aspect was enhanced by the moonlight reflecting in the still surface of a dozen puddles so that they resembled sheets of ice. Before daybreak – before the sky lightened and the yard became busy with dogs and chickens, and children, and people fetching water or going to and from the privy middens, before the lad came to light the furnaces in the forge, before William and John woke to the smells and sounds of their mother making breakfast – before all of this, Daniel Amory

276

would walk from his own home to the Union Wheel with his father to begin his first day at grinding saws. Leaning on the window-sill, he pressed his forehead against the glass. His exhalations made ovals of condensation which expanded and contracted with each breath. He picked at the window frame, dislodging flakes of paint with his fingernails as he listened to muffled voices and laughter below.

From the weight of the footsteps, it was not one of the adults who had come to find him. The chamber door opened. It was William Smith, a year his junior, bearing news that a glass of ale was stood on the table for him downstairs. Daniel neither turned round nor moved away from the window.

'Hast thou been crying?' asked William, drawing up alongside.

'Shut thy mouth.'

'Hast thou?'

'If thou dost not I shall shut it for thee.'

The younger boy hesitated. 'I cry sometimes. When Da takes his belt to me.'

Daniel made no reply. He wiped his face on his sleeve. The pair continued to stare silently into the night. William breathed deliberately on the glass, finger-writing a 'W' in the condensation. Daniel reached across and used his thumb to erase it, making a breath-mark of his own and drawing a 'D'. William laughed, breathing again on the window and repeating his own initial. When Daniel went to obliterate it a second time, the two fell into a fight made ludicrous by both boys being so enfeebled through mirth. The struggle ended with their distraction by the sight of a figure emerging into the yard below. It was Robert Smith; the unruly mop of dark hair would have identified him even had not the moonlight exposed his tall, long-limbed angularity. They watched him pick his way to the privy, letting himself into the wooden cubicle without troubling to close the door behind him. The splashing of urine was audible to the boys, both of whom were endeavouring not to giggle. Presently the man reappeared, looping his braces back over his shoulders and buttoning his fly. He gave a tuneless whistle as he retraced his steps across the yard. The whistle appeared to halt him in his tracks, which struck the boys as odd; though it was not until another figure stepped out of a darkened corner that they realized it was not William's father who had made the sound but this stranger. The other man approached and a moment's furtive conversation ensued, too hushed for the eavesdroppers to catch what was said. At its conclusion, the stranger withdrew into the shadows from whence he had come and Robert returned indoors. A door closed and they heard his footsteps in the kitchen. The yard was silent and empty again; so desolate and seemingly undisturbed it was as if the scene the boys had witnessed had not taken place at all but had been a figment of their imaginations.

Witness: John Sibray (cont.)

Q. On what night did the assault occur?

A. November the fifth, as I recall.

Q. At what time did it take place, to the best of your recollection?

A. It would have been between six and half past. I was going home from my work.

Q. Whereabouts were you assaulted?

A. About the head.

Q. That is not what I meant. What I meant was, whereabouts in Hallam?

A. In Alma Street, outside the old workhouse and across from the Union Wheel.

Q. Is that far distant from Hoole's works?

A. It is not. Green Lane gives way to Alma Street there, by Hallam Island.

Q. Could you say how many men attacked you?

A. There were two men.

Q. Did you recognize either?

A. I did not see them properly.

278

Q. How was this?

A. It was a very foggy night, as I recall. And they approached me from behind.

Q. You did not see their faces?

A. I turned when I heard their footsteps, but that is when I was struck and I do not remember much else after that.

Q. What did they do to you?

A. One gave me a stroke with his hand and I staggered a little towards the other one.

Q. What did he do?

A. He ran away. He went up by the side of the workhouse.

Q. The man who struck you, what did he do?

A. I did not see where he went.

Q. With what did he strike you?

A. I do not know what he had in his hand.

Q. He had something in his hand, you say?

A. I cannot say.

Q. You cannot say whether he had something in his hand, or you can say that he had something in his hand but you cannot say what it was that he had?

A. Can I ask that the question be put again?

Q. Did he hit you with his hand or with something else?

A. I cannot say. All I know is that he struck me.

Q. Was it a bag full of stones?

A. I never saw a bag full of stones.

Q. We have heard others from Hoole's give evidence that when they were assaulted they were struck by a man in the habit of carrying a bag of stones for the purpose.

A. That may be so, but I cannot say that I was.

Q. Nor can you say that you were not.

A. I did not see fit to ask him what it was he had struck me with.

(*laughter*)

Q. This is a serious matter, John Sibray.

A. Let me tell you, it is more serious still if you are the one who has been struck.

Q. On what part of your head did he strike you?

A. On the mouth.

Q. Did it knock you down?

A. No. It staggered me a good deal.

Q. Did it draw blood?

A. Yes. I went to a doctor the same night.

Q. Were you otherwise injured?

A. I thought that I would lose a tooth, but I did not; it was only loosened.

Q. Is it the case that, as a result of this assault, you left your job as foreman?

A. It is not the case.

Q. You say it is not the case?

A. I was working off my notice at Hoole's at the time of the assault and I left four days afterwards, as I had agreed already with Mr Hoole.

Q. Why did you leave your job there?

A. On account of being sent threatening letters.

Q. By the union?

A. I cannot say who the letters were from.

Q. The letters were sent anonymously?

A. They were signed 'Tantia Topee' or 'Tid Pratt' or some such names.

Q. Can you say whether or not it was union men who assaulted you that night?

A. No. I cannot say that.

Chapter Ten

SHOP TALK

What I hate is when you're in t'queue for t'checkout and you've only one or two items and t'person in front's got a trolley load and they waint let you go first. I hate that, me.

Michelle Hibbitt, 21, mother of one, beauty consultant

William Boyce took the message. He answered with a gruff *Hello*, declining even to state the title of the newspaper never mind follow the corporate courtesy style for dealing with incoming calls. He pulled a notepad towards him, cradling the receiver between ear and shoulder while he found a blank page. *Who is this?* It was his tone of voice which made Constance take notice. He hung up.

'Problem?'

'Told me to give this to Ms Amory. "A cryptic clue," he said.'

He handed her the note, written in shorthand and transcribed underneath into longhand. It read: 'Praise the Lord – the bells are ringing, for me and my gal.'

Constance sat down. 'He say anything else?'

'When I asked who it was, he said "Mr Age".'

'Mr Rage?'

'I thought he said Age. I'm sure he paused between the Mr and the Age.'

William picked up the phone again and dialled. *Nothing*, he said. 'Mr Age' must have prefaced his call with the digits which meant there would be no way of tracing his number. Constance repeated the names over and over in her head, testing each variation – Mr Rage, Mr Age, Mr Rage, Mr Age – until they merged into one word, Misterage, like a mantra; until it became impossible to distinguish one from the other. She couldn't be certain her colleague had heard correctly – although, being privy to the codeword, surely he'd have been more likely to assume the name to be Rage rather than Age? She turned her attention to the message itself.

The Chapel of St Dunstan – Pink, Lower – was intended as a sanctuary for spiritually inclined shoppers. Alternatively, according to cynics: a sop to those opposed to Sunday trading. *Pray as you pay*. A vicar of the parish which included Urbopark was responsible for ministering to mall users' needs and for conducting a weekly service. His duties increased when a joint initiative by Mall Admin and the diocese saw the chapel combine with the Urbo Suite function rooms to offer wedding, christening and memorial packages. (After the first marriage ceremony at the mall, the *Crucible* carried a page one picture of groom wheeling bride away in a shopping trolley.)

Admission to the chapel, in an arcade adjoining the Pink Zone car-park, was gained via a pair of pine-effect doors, one of which bore a highly polished brass cross. Above the door lintel was a crest, depicting a figure in pontifical robes and carrying a pair of pincers in his right hand. An inscription read: 'Dunstan, patron saint of goldsmiths and metalworkers'. Constance pushed one door, which was bolted, then tried the other. It opened stiffly, admitting her into a large artificially lit vestibule, its walls adorned with church notices and a framed photograph of the Queen. Set into an alcove was a row of wooden lockers where visitors could stow bags of shopping. She scanned the noticeboard before going through a second set of doors, into the chapel proper. The silence was so total it created the illusion of a ringing noise in her ears. Outside in the mall, thousands of folk bustled about the shops and arcades in perpetual, gregarious clamour; here, she was alone, isolated. The world she'd left on entering this place could have ceased to exist for all she knew. There was a sudden creak of hinges, of a door being eased open. Constance started as though someone had crept up behind her and popped a paper bag. Someone was in the vestibule. She turned towards the doorway through which she had just come, waiting for whoever it was to appear. Nothing. No noise, no footsteps. No-one. After a moment's hesitation, she went back into the lobby and saw that it was empty; the creaking sound – it dawned on her – had not been caused by the opening of the outer door but by its prolonged closure following her own entry. She let out a laugh. This was stupid, coming here on her own. Jesus, he'd *directed* her to this place. And she hadn't even told William or Sally or newsdesk where she was; she'd just gone. Basics of personal safety. But she was here, the building was deserted, and somewhere inside – according to one of her hunches – she'd discover the reason for her being here.

The chapel was long and narrow, unusually low-ceilinged for a place of worship, and illuminated by a sequence of geometrically patterned stained-glass windows. Wooden chairs were arranged in rows either side of a narrow aisle, the end of each row decorated with floral displays that complemented the chapel's pink-and-white colour scheme. The altar was also decked out with flowers, the only adornment to its simplicity: a table draped with heavy white cloth, a plain brass cross standing on a wooden plinth, a lectern, a board displaying hymn numbers. To one side of the altar was a font, to the other a wooden pulpit. Constance studied her surroundings, strolling around the perimeter of the room and pausing to read the biblical inscription above each of the stained-glass windows.

The opposite wall was windowless, mostly filled with artwork by pupils from a local primary school. She examined each painting, each collage, each illustrated poem; she read the names and ages of the children. She made a note of the hymn numbers on the board. The lectern was bare, so was the altar table. On her last visit – the previous Saturday – the chapel had hosted the marriage of a young couple who'd met through the *Crucible*'s lonely hearts column. Caption story. 'The paper that's all ♥!' *Wedding bells were ringing for this happy pair thanks to . . .*

Now, there were no guests, no bride and groom, no vicar, no organ music (taped). She surveyed the rows of empty chairs. She let her gaze wander, catching momentarily on the shiny rhubarb-and-custard spines of the Bibles and hymnbooks stacked on shelves at the back. Red leather, yellow leather. Not leather, probably, but synthetic; leatherette. Another Bible caught her attention: fat, its pages edged in gold leaf and fanned out, reflecting the pale pool of light from an anglepoise lamp. Going over to the pulpit, she made her way up the spiral steps, the heels of her shoes clunking on varnished wood. At the top, she stopped, holding the wooden rail rather than bringing her clammy palms into contact with the delicate, ornately decorated pages. Mingled smells of paper, old leather and wood polish. The Bible lay open, its pages cambered by their own weight, a thin silk bookmark draped down the cleft. The text was set in an attractive serif typeface unfamiliar to her, suggestive of a bygone age of printing. The Gospel According to St John, chapter II. Four verses were highlighted in pink marker:

13 And Jesus went up to Jerusalem,

14 And found in the temple those that sold oxen and sheep and doves, and the changers of money sitting.

15 And when he had made a scourge of small cords, he drove them all out of the temple, and the sheep and the oxen; and poured out the changers' money, and overthrew the tables;

284

16 And said unto them that sold doves, Take these things hence; make not my Father's house an house of merchandise.

Constance noted down the verses verbatim, checking what she'd written against the original. 'There' instead of 'those', line 14; she scribbled a correction. What was a scourge of small cords? She recalled this passage from her schooldays, R.I. Religious Instruction. *Religious Indoctrination*. A whip. It was a whip. As she studied the verses again, she noticed a mark in the margin – small, neatly handwritten. It said, p1,867. She searched through the gold-edged leaves, carefully opening the Bible at the appropriate page to find a slip of paper. A word, made up of individual letters of varying sizes cut from a newspaper – the *Crucible*, judging by the typeface – and pasted haphazardly to spell 'JEROME'. Beneath this was a sentence, similarly constructed:

Tell the merchant of worshipful homonym to beware the poisoned chalice.

'Can I help you?'

A yelp, like a small dog. She almost sent the Bible clean off its stand – just managing to rescue it before it disappeared over the edge of the pulpit. Covering her face with both hands, she exhaled into the palms.

'So, sorry.' The vicar was standing at the foot of the pulpit steps, looking up at her as she turned and lowered her hands. 'I didn't mean to make you jump.'

Constance laughed, relieved, one hand pressed against her breastbone. She laughed again. Recovering now, she said, 'Where *on earth* . . .?'

'Ah, St Vincent, originally.' He smiled, gesturing beyond the altar in the direction of a door. 'Just now, I was in the vestry.'

Her notebook and pen, and the cryptic message, had fallen by her feet. She bent to retrieve them, zipping them away in

285

her bag. Looking down into the vicar's amiable, upturned face, she said, 'I really shouldn't be up here, should I?'

He returned her smile. 'It's a lovely Bible.'

'Yes. Yes, it is.'

'Miss Amory, isn't it?'

'That's right.'

'You were here on Saturday, with your photographer.'

'We were trying to be as unobtrusive as possible.'

'Please.' He beckoned her to come down from the pulpit, extending his hand in greeting as she descended. 'Mike Beverley.'

They shook hands. Reverend Beverley. *Rev Bev*, as he was known. 'I thought the chapel was empty,' she said. 'Otherwise I'd have . . .'

'I heard footsteps and thought: either a worshipper, or a very big mouse!'

She hesitated. 'I'm afraid someone has defaced your Bible.'

Revd Beverley sat across the desk from her. His black shirt was unbuttoned at the throat, the stiff strip of dog-collar had been detached and lay curled on the blotter pad in front of him. In one hand he held the piece of paper, in the other a mug. The vestry was impregnated with an aroma of hot chocolate. Constance sipped from a glass of tap water, watching him. He was young, under forty; short receding hair, his throat was chafed by shaving rash – the black skin encrusted with white powder. For all his Caribbean features, the accent was Home Counties. He laid the message on the desk and picked up the quotation she'd noted down. Then he set that aside as well.

Big brown eyes, the whites slightly bloodshot. 'Curiouser and curiouser.'

'Whoever it was must've been here this afternoon, not long before me.'

'We had a christening at noon and I've been cooped up in

286

here since about half-twelve, twenty to one. Catching up on my paperwork.'

Constance looked at her watch. 'Hour and a half. You didn't hear anything?'

'Not a dickie.'

'He couldn't have tampered with the Bible before, could he? I mean, earlier on this morning.'

The vicar shook his head. 'I gave a reading during the christening. I would have shut the Bible afterwards – I always do. Excuse me.' He stood his drink on a coaster and began gently fingering the closed eyelid of his right eye. 'Contact lens. Every now and then it goes for a wander. There.'

She indicated the message. 'So who's Jerome?'

'Well, now, you're not really asking the right person.' *Arksing*. He blinked several times in rapid succession. 'Vicar, I may be, but I'm no authority on sainthood.'

'Jerome was a saint, was he?' Constance reclaimed her notebook and turned to a blank page. 'D'you mind?'

'Is this for the paper?'

'No. Not necessarily. I mean, this may not make a story at all and, even if it does, I won't be quoting you or anything.'

'Because, like I say, I'm no authority.'

'Sure.' She wrote 'St Jerome' at the top of the page, and underlined it.

'I have a book here somewhere.' He reached over to a set of volumes between bookends at one end of his desk. Running his index finger along the spines, he pulled out a large paperback. She couldn't make out the title as he flipped through the pages. 'Jerome, Jerome . . . here we are, St Jerome. D'you want me to read it out?'

'Please.'

'Tell me if I'm going too fast.' He cleared his throat. ' "A father of the Western Church, and compiler of the Vulgate (c.340 to 420). He is usually represented as an aged man in a cardinal's dress, writing or studying, with a lion seated beside him. St Jerome's Day is 30 September." That's all, I'm afraid.'

287

'What's the Vulgate?'

'Now, I do know this. The Vulgate was a Latin translation of the Bible, originally intended as a sort of standard text, if you like. It was revised a few times in the centuries that followed. It comes from the Latin, *editio vulgata*, which was the, um, common edition of the Bible sanctioned by the Roman Catholic Church.'

'What, the authorized version? Like a definitive text, you mean?'

'Ah, well.'

Constance smiled. 'Sorry, I'm not really . . . you know, religious or anything.'

'No, no, I wasn't intending to be critical. It's just that the very notion of a *definitive* text, with regard to the Bible, is something of a grey area. So many versions and translations, you see. As soon as you convert anything from one language into another, you are into the realm of interpretation of meaning. Quite apart from disputes over which books should be, um, considered canonical or legitimate in the first place. The Vulgate is a case in point, actually.'

'How d'you mean?'

'The Vulgate included certain non-canonical books of the Old Testament which were not usually to be found in Jewish or Protestant texts. Our friend Jerome referred to these as the Apocrypha, implying that they were, um, of doubtful origin or in some way spurious. As in, "apocryphal".'

Revd Beverley closed the book and replaced it, selecting a large hardback dictionary. As he did so the remaining volumes toppled sideways, propelling a bookend towards the edge of the desk. He stopped it one-handed, a rapid reflex action that caused Constance to jump. He stood to straighten the books, then sat down again.

'Research is so addictive,' he said, thumbing through the dictionary. 'Here we are: apocryphal. "Of doubtful authenticity. Applied to a story or anecdote, especially one concerning a well-known individual, to indicate that it is *in*

288

character, but fictitious." Etymological roots: *apocryphus*, Latin, meaning "secret"; *apokryphos*, Greek, meaning "obscure" or "hidden away". See "crypt", it says here.'

He looked up, beaming. White teeth and excessively pink gums. Flakes of the powder on his throat had speckled his shirt, like dandruff. The sight of his shaving rash made her own skin itch. He found the page, reading to himself for a moment, then aloud. 'Crypt comes from the Greek *kryptein*, "to hide"; or *kryptos*, "hidden". A crypt, therefore, is "a chamber (e.g. a vault) wholly or partly underground, especially in a church".'

'What about "cryptic"?' Constance asked. 'Does that have the same root?'

'See, now *you're* doing it!' The vicar ran a finger down the page. 'Yes. "Cryptic: intended to be obscure or mysterious, serving to conceal, making use of cipher or code".'

'D'you have a crypt here, at St Dunstan's?'

'Ah, 'fraid not. Nothing underneath us at all. Apart from foundations, of course, and soil and rock and whathaveyou.'

'I suppose you're a bit too modern to have a crypt – the building, I mean.'

'Well, we're not entirely without our, um, relics you know.'

The vicar half-turned in his chair to indicate something hidden from her view by a tall coatstand. Leaning forward, she saw an iron bell mounted at head height – its slightly tarnished surface dully reflecting daylight from a window in the opposite wall of the vestry. Beneath the bell was a plaque, partially obscured by a rope cord suspended from the clapper. Unable to make out the inscription, she stood up and went over to have a closer look. The legend on the plaque stated simply that this was the ship's bell for the first HMS *Hallam*, cast by the local firm of Bayfield's.

'We used to have it hanging in the vestibule where everyone could see it,' said Revd Beverley, who had joined her to stand in admiration of the bell. 'But at weekends and during the school holidays, certain young lads liked to amuse themselves by sneaking in to give it a good ring. Usually during a service.'

'What's the connection with St Dunstan's?' asked Constance.

'None, as such. At least, not directly. For about twenty years the bell used to hang in Bayfield's entrance hall. Then when the firm closed down in . . . 1984, I think it was, it was donated to the city as a museum piece. When the mall was built, the council decided to move the bell here, to the chapel.'

'What, because Urbopark was built on the former Bayfield's site?'

'That's right.' The vicar went to a shelf and took a selection of glossy leaflets from among several stacks. 'If it's history you're after, you might find these helpful.'

Sir Robert Bayfield (1858–1940)

Founder, in 1888, of **Bayfield's Steel Foundry Co.,** which grew – by 1919 – to become Hallam's largest employer and the biggest special alloy steel manufacturer in Britain, with a workforce of 15,000. **The East Winsley Works,** where **Urbopark** now stands, was constructed on cornfields in 1897.

Bayfield was autocratic and dictatorial, yet he still inspired loyalty in his workforce and was among the more liberal employers of his times. He was one of the first to shorten the working day to eight hours, and labour problems were virtually unheard of until the strikes of the 1920s.

The company declined between the wars; even so, Bayfield's still employed 6,000 by the outbreak of the **Second World War** and was one of the largest steel foundries in Europe. In the 1960s and 70s the firm went through a series of mergers and takeovers and was the scene of ugly picket-line clashes in 1980 when its workers defied a **national steel strike**. In 1981 the workforce at East Winsley was reduced to 700 and steel production ceased altogether by early 1984. In April of that year the plant closed, ready for demolition.

Robert Bayfield became a **Master Cutler** in 1899, was knighted in 1908, was made a baronet in 1917 and was given the **Freedom of the City of Hallam** in 1939. He died on September 30, 1940.

The leaflet included a plan of the shopping mall superimposed over a diagram of the former Bayfield's works. Where Hypa-Centa now stood, had been the site of a ten- and fifteen-ton ingot gantry; electric arc furnaces were situated on land now occupied by Home Zone; a smithy and a forge had made way for the Red Zone car-park . . .

As he was escorting her out of the chapel, Revd Beverley paused by the outer door from the vestibule to the arcade. He placed a hand on her arm. 'That note, the reference to the poisoned chalice . . . and the quotation from the Book of John.'

'What about them?'

'St John the Evangelist is usually represented bearing a chalice with a serpent issuing from it – an, um, allusion to the story of his driving the poison from a cup offered to him to drink.' He looked at her. 'Just a thought, for what it's worth.'

The editor instructed her to confine her coverage to the facts. *Report what happens, when it happens, and leave the theories to the police.* She argued that: a) HypaCenta was a likely target for another sabotage because the *Crucible* had carried a story about the sacking of a shopworkers' union official there; b) the foodhall's manager, John Chapple, shared the first name of the saint from whose gospel the saboteur had quoted; and c) his surname was a homonym for the place where the clue was found: *a chapel.* Dougal Aitken-Aitken laughed like a drain.

The Inky Path
Newsworthiness does not depend on an absolute standard of what is, or is not, news. The first edition lead might, by second edition, be relegated to an inside page by the occurrence of an event of more importance. An incident given prominent coverage today might, on a busier news day, merit no more than

a few paragraphs. Similarly, a 'big' story in a local weekly may warrant scant coverage in a regional daily; the regional daily's lead, in turn, may find no home in one of the nationals; and what is of vital consequence to readers in one country will be of little or no interest to those elsewhere in the world. These are necessary lessons for the young reporter, in his life as well as in his work. From them, he will learn that all things are relative; that significance is not inherent but derives, always, from context and circumstance; that what matters to him may not matter a hoot to anyone else.

She'd no sooner come off the phone from the editor than it rang again. She picked up the receiver. DCI Pink, sweeping aside her conversational pleasantries.

'I am fucking furious with you.'

'*Me?* Why?'

'How long have you got?'

'I don't—'

'After hanging on to it for twenty-four hours, you finally get round to arranging for one of my officers to collect the note from our friend. Covered, by now, with your fingerprints and those of Reverend Mike Beverley. And when I speak to the vicar, he tells me he found you prowling around the chapel. Alone.'

'Did he say I was prowling?'

'If you were a fish, the angler wouldn't even have to bait his hook – you'd just jump right out of the water and land in his lap.'

'Anyway, the vicar was around.'

'He was there when the message was planted as well – didn't see or hear a thing.' The chief inspector paused. 'Did you speak to the vicar first? No, you just turned up. As far as you knew it could've been just you and Mr Rage.'

'I . . .'

'Had you told anyone where you were going? A colleague or someone?'

She hesitated.

'You didn't think it might be a *police* matter rather than a journalistic one? You didn't think to tell *me*? Eh?'

'All right. *Jesus*.'

'Don't you fucking Jesus me. I get that from my daughter, and she's fifteen.'

'*Paul*.'

'Right, how did this come about – you going to the chapel?'

'I told your—'

'I want to hear it from you.'

Constance exhaled. 'I got a call – that is, William took a call from a Mr *Age* – without the R. He gave a cryptic clue, basically, directing me to St Dunstan's.'

There was a moment's silence, apart from DCI Pink's breathing and a faint rustling of papers in the background. Constance pushed her hair back from her forehead, gripping a handful in her fist and tugging at it until her eyes watered.

'I told you to be careful.'

'I know.'

'I've also warned you before about withholding evidence.'

'I know you did.'

'If you want to put yourself at risk, that's up to you. But I won't have you impeding my investigation.'

'Paul, I'm *sorry*. I don't know what else you want me to say.'

'I'm sending a DC over this afternoon to take a formal statement from you.'

'OK.'

Another pause. When the detective spoke again, his voice had lost some of its sternness. 'The biblical quotation about throwing the merchants out of the temple – John: chapter II, verses . . .' another shuffle of papers '. . . thirteen to sixteen.'

'Yes?'

'You say in your note they *may* – underlined – be the same as the ones you saw on a banner at the football. Is that right?'

'I'm not sure. The banner definitely mentioned John, but I

293

really can't remember the verse numbers or the chapter. It was all over in a few seconds.'

'You didn't get a look at the person carrying the banner?'

'No.'

'And it's *possible* the verses were the same as those highlighted in the Bible?'

'Yes, it's possible.'

'If they were exactly the same, it's too extraordinary to be just coincidence, wouldn't you say?'

'Yeah.'

'How many people knew you were going to be at the match?'

She hesitated. 'Quite a few.'

'Who?'

'Friends. Family. Colleagues. It was so long since I'd been to a game, I was blabbing off about it beforehand to anyone who'd listen. *You*, for one!' She laughed, he didn't. 'Look, I can't say for sure the two passages were the same – I mean, you get these religious types at football.'

'You see what I'm getting at, though, Constance?'

'If the saboteur was the one parading the banner, he was doing it for *my* benefit. Which means he *knows* me.' She held the receiver away from her face for a moment, then moved it back into position. 'And I must know him.'

It was a day of telephone calls. She rang the *Crucible*'s football correspondent and culled a name and number from his contacts book. She called photographic, to speak to Howard; she hung up after two rings. She phoned Stan, at the university, to invite him to supper after Tuesday's class; he reversed the invitation by asking her to his place – not this week, but the following one. He asked if she was a vegetarian, she said she used to be but she wasn't any more; he asked if there was anything she couldn't eat, and she said, *plastic carrier bags, carpet tiles and soap*. They laughed a lot about that. It felt good to laugh, though she stopped herself from telling Stan so. She also refrained from saying she wanted to see him sooner than they'd arranged – that she wanted to see him tonight, tomorrow night and the night after that. When they came off the phone, she dissected the conversation – what he'd said, what he hadn't said, the subtle inflections of voice, mood, laughter – for signs that he couldn't wait to see her either, even though he'd been the one to put her off for a week. She called Mam, to let her know she had a bag of sprouts for her, courtesy of Detective Chief Inspector Pink. A spoonerism: she pronounced it 'defective' with an 'f' instead of a 't', and 'chiet' with a 't' instead of an 'f'. They talked for half an hour at the paper's expense. The final call was from Constance's source at HypaCenta. He informed her that John Chapple had received an anonymous letter giving him twenty-four hours to announce, publicly, that the foodhall would: 1) reinstate the sacked union official; 2) abandon plans for automated checkouts; 3) improve pay and conditions. Failure to comply, the letter said, would *incur the wrath of the enraged.*

By the following day, Constance was able to stand the story up. Paul Pink confirmed that the police had been notified of the warning letter and were subjecting it to forensic examination; Mall Secure confirmed that it had been requested by HypaCenta to increase security in and around the foodhall. John Chapple, however, refused to talk to her, on or off the record; nor would he even confirm the existence of the threatening letter. But she had enough substantiation; a simple *Mr Chapple declined to comment*, tacked on to the end of the story. And, though she couldn't get him to say so, the heightened security gave her grounds to speculate that Hypa-Centa had no intention of acceding to the blackmail demands. When she rang newsdesk, Gary was enthusiastic. *Fucking excellent, Con.* 'Splash' written all over it, he said. She filed in good time for city final. But, when copies of the edition arrived at Urbopark on the van from head office, her story was not to be found on page one, or anywhere else.

*   *   *

'What's going on, Gary?'

'Can't talk now, Con, I'm off into conference.'

'Where's my HypaCenta splash?'

'Look, let me buzz you back after . . .'

'I want to know what happened to my story.'

'. . .'

'*Gary.*'

'Pulled.'

'What d'you mean, *pulled*?'

'The editor. Said we couldn't run it without quotes from Chapple.'

'That's crap, though! The police and Mall Secure—'

'*We're not in the business of scaremongering.*'

'I don't believe this.'

'I'm only telling you what Dougal said.'

'You said yourself it was a brilliant story.'

'I'm not the editor, Con. And nor are you.'

Notes

Traditional handicraft basis of Hallam metal trades began to be undermined in 1860s and 70s, with gradual mechanization of more & more processes.

Separation between 'light' and 'heavy' trades pronounced during 2nd half of 19th C. Heavy industries' huge growth in H. created by several expanding markets: springs, axles and rails for railways (UK & o'seas); materials and components for steam engines, ships, machines and machine tools, cranes etc.; guns, shells & armour plate for UK & foreign govts. Discovery and development of large-scale methods of making steel provided the metal for these markets.

QUOTE: 'Quantity City 1 Quality Utd 1, after extra-time. Quantity wins 4–3 on penalties.' (Prof B.)

Labour

The prospect of the workhouse kept labour costs down, for it placed a premium on finding and keeping a job whatever the wage.

Prof. Stanley Bell's Physical, Metaphysical and Philosophical
Glossary of Metal

Hallam Plate: a way of making 'pretend silver'. In 1743, by combination of accident and design, Thomas Bolsover developed a
method of hot-plating copper with silver so that finished articles could
be made from sheet plate rather than laboriously adding silver to the
finished base article. The result was that attractive pieces of 'silverware' were able to be manufactured more quickly and in greater
numbers, this at time when the market for dining-room ware (as
opposed to kitchenware) was expanding. Hallam Plate, and therefore
Hallam, had literally become a household name – the city's reputation
enhanced by virtue of a product that was, essentially, masquerading
as something else.

The class adjourned to the refectory during what their tutor
referred to as the *tea 'n' pee break*. Hot and cold drinks were
dispensed in plastic cups by a vending machine, hot and cold
snacks were similarly available – served on disposable plates,
consumed with the aid of cutlery fashioned from moulded
plastic. A man sitting next to Constance was prompted to
remark, as a fork prong snapped against a piece of pie crust,
that the cutlers of Victorian Hallam would be gyrating in their
graves.

'Where does the word cutlery actually come from?'

The query, by a woman at one end of their table, caused all
eyes to turn to the tutor. Stanley Bell was trying to peel the
cling-film wrapping from a Scotch egg, elbows propped on a
surface patterned with dried tea stains and unidentifiable
fragments of food. He had a biro behind one ear, tilting his
glasses out of alignment.

'From the Latin,' he said, preoccupied. 'I don't have any
nails.'

'Here, let me.' Their hands touched as Constance took the
Scotch egg from him and unwrapped it, setting it back down
on his plate.

'Ta.' He made an incision with his knife. '*Culter*, "l" before

297

the "t", was a knife or ploughshare. In Middle French, this became *coutel*: knife. Or *couteau*, in modern French. In English, of course, cutlery encompasses forks and spoons as well.'

He cupped a hand beneath his mouth as he ate. His nails, she noticed, were bitten down to the quick. Bitter aloe. As a teenager she was made to paint her fingertips with it, only she became perversely partial to the flavour. The hairs on the backs of Stan's hands glistened with reflected light. His skin was still tanned, though the colour had faded in the months since he'd left Australia; the once obvious white line where his wedding ring had been was now so faint as to be almost indiscernible.

'Hello, are you receiving me?'

'Sorry?'

It was the *gyrating cutlers* man. Smiling, a flake of pastry stuck to his lower lip. He was originally from South Africa and had become known behind his back as the Crashing Boer, for his frequent mind-numbing conversational sieges.

'I was just saying "Constance" is a nice name. Unusual.'

'Sorry, I was daydreaming.'

'Is it a family name?'

'One of my grandmothers, on my Mam's side. I never knew her.'

'So, are you a Con or a Connie?'

'Er, both, I suppose. Constance, mostly. I mean, it all depends on who—'

'Con Amory.' His smile broadened. 'Like the Italian: *con amore.*'

'Pardon?'

'*Con amore*. It means: "with love". In Italian.'

'Oh, right.'

'Ah, but are you constant, Constance?'

She forced a laugh. Stan. Stan was engaged in a discussion with the woman at the end of the table. What were they talking about? He was telling her an anecdote relating to his work at the university. He'd lost weight, it seemed, in the weeks she'd known him. Less bulky around the midriff. And his face appeared to be thinner, or maybe it was the way his hair and beard had been trimmed. She wished it was just the two of them, talking. Here, or in the Tongs & Dozzle, or at one or other of their homes, or anywhere where there weren't half a dozen people squashed together – all elbows and knees, and intruding voices – around a table. Someone else was asking him a question. *Shut up. Shut bloody up.* OK, he'd smiled (warmly? yes, warmly; breezily) and said hello to her when she came into the classroom. *Hi, Constance.* But he smiled at everyone. *How're you doing?* She'd said she was doing fine. That was all. Anyway, what more could they have said in front of the group? Here, in the refectory, was no better. He was sitting diagonally opposite her, which would've required them to converse across two of the other students. What could they have talked about? Nothing. Just crap, idle chit-chat. Shop talk. The *tea 'n' pee break* was little more than an extension of the class itself. Stan's voice, louder; he'd been saying something – not to her, to all of them – and she realized she'd not taken in a single word. Everyone was laughing. A joke, a witty remark. She smiled at him even though she'd no idea what was so funny. His eyes held hers as his gaze swept along the row of appreciative faces. A wink? No. This was farcical; she was behaving – not behaving, *thinking* – like an infatuated teenager. They were adults. Professionally: he was her tutor, she was his pupil; *one* of his pupils. Privately: they'd been out a few times, they'd arranged to have dinner together at his place the following week. One clumsy kiss on the cheek. *Tummy butterflies*, Mam called them. She had tummy butterflies. Even on the way back to the classroom, as the students streamed along the narrow corridor, their random pairings seemed to her to be a conspiracy to keep her from him.

Midnight. Alone in the semi-darkness of her bedroom. She'd been talking to Stan, on the phone. She shut the door behind her and leaned back against it, fastening her dressing-gown more tightly. Her hair was loose, strewn about her shoulders. After a moment, she went to the window and drew open the curtain to expose a night-time view over a great sweep of inner suburb. Rooftops and roads and streetlights, the gaping black chasm of a park – its treetops indigo against the yellowish-grey city-haze of the horizon. The phone call. Stan had called to say goodnight; to say he'd enjoyed going for a drink with her after class; to say she'd left her handbag in his car; and to say that, he supposed, they'd have to meet up again – the following evening, perhaps? – so he could return it to her. They'd agreed this would be an unavoidable nuisance. At length, she turned from the window. Smiling to herself in the dark. She didn't get into bed, but bounced up and down upon it as though it were a trampoline.

Mall Madman injected contaminant into drinks cartons – police

Poison attack puts thirteen in hospital

by Constance Amory, Urbopark Reporter

Police are stepping up the hunt for the Mall Madman after an outbreak of food poisoning at Hallam's giant Urbopark complex left 13 people in hospital.

Six children and seven adults – including five pensioners and a pregnant woman – were taken ill after consuming drinks and other products bought from the HypaCenta foodhall.

They all suffered severe vomiting, diarrhoea and headaches and are being treated in the Royal Hallamshire Infirmary, where the condition of one elderly woman is giving doctors cause for concern.

It emerged today that the incident occurred despite heightened security at the supermarket following a warning – purporting to be from the saboteur – that an attack was imminent.

HypaCenta manager, John Chapple, said, 'We treated the matter very seriously and informed the police and Mall Secure immediately. But there was no indication of what form any sabotage might take and it's difficult to know what else we could have done to prevent this, short of closing the store down altogether or turning it into a fortress.'

Asked why the threat to the store had not been made public at the time, Mr Chapple said, 'The saboteur is intent on damaging business at the mall – we felt that causing widespread alarm among our customers would have played right into his hands.'

Cough Mixture

Detectives investigating the spate of attacks on Urbopark were immediately suspicious when the first cases of food poisoning were reported. Food and drinks containers at the victims' homes were found to show traces of contaminant, and minute punctures – of the sort made by a hypodermic needle – had been made.

Cartons of milk, yoghurt, tomato juice and grapefruit juice were all affected, as well as plastic bottles of cough mixture, lemon squash and lemonade. The contaminated products were traced back to HypaCenta and had been purchased within the previous 48 hours.

'The toxic substance was injected into the tops or necks of the containers to avoid leakage and to make detection difficult,' said Det. Ch. Insp. Paul Pink, of Hallam CID.

'With each incident, the perpetrator is showing increasing disregard for the safety and well-being of innocent members of the public,' he added. 'We are doing all we can to put a stop to his activities.'

Gardening

Forensic experts have analysed the rogue substance and believe it to have been made up of a cocktail of hazardous fluids obtainable from any DIY or gardening shop.

Police say it is probable the saboteur tampered with the containers on the supermarket shelves rather than when they were in transit or storage. Any shoppers who saw anything suspicious are asked to come forward.

HypaCenta has withdrawn all 'at risk' products – chiefly drinks and other liquids in penetrable containers – and has appealed to customers to return any similar items purchased in the past two days. Anyone who has already consumed such produce is advised to see their GP immediately if they feel unwell.

Mr Chapple said the cost – in terms of withdrawn stock, customer refunds, compensation and loss of consumer confidence – was 'impossible to calculate'.

One man's campaign
of hate – page 9

The Life and Times of a
Hallam Saw Grinder
(a Dramatic Reconstruction in Many Parts)

November 1861

It was not customary for Jacob Stringer – proprietor of the
Ball Inn, in Green Lane – to collect the empty tankards, a
potman being retained in his employ for such duties. Indeed,
it was uncommon for Stringer to venture out from behind the
serving side of the counter in anything other than exceptional
circumstances – even the ejection of drunkards, rowdies and
ruffians was most often delegated to one or other of his
barmen. So it was a matter of no little consternation to the
men gathered at a corner table to find their conversation
interrupted by the proprietor himself reaching amongst them
to retrieve their spent glasses. As they fell silent, Stringer –
addressing his remarks to the two most newly arrived
– declared that he would have appreciated them choosing
another venue for the conducting of Society business.

'If thou hast a committee room available upstairs, Jacob, we
should be glad to have use of it,' said one, a Fender Grinders'
official by the name of James Robertson.

'That's not the sort of Society business I mean, as well thou
knowest.'

'We are but half a dozen men supping and talking around
a table.'

'Aye, and I mind the consequence of such talk.'

Robertson laughed. 'Jacob, there s'll be no heads broke here
today.'

'Thou canst break as many heads as thou wilt – my concern
is with the glasses and tables and chairs that become broke
into the bargain.'

The landlord carried the empty pots away – returning to his
sanctuary behind the counter, from where he kept an eye on

proceedings at the corner table. As for the six seated there, the arrangement of chairs symbolized the division between them – the two Society officials set apart from the four non-union men from Hoole's. Three of these – the White brothers and Hulse, still sporting the bruises and scabrous wounds of a recent beating – drained what ale stood in front of them. They took their leave of the inn, deaf to the offer of Robertson and his companion, Bill Bayles, to replenish their pots. The fourth of Hoole's men, George Wastnidge, told his mates he would rejoin them at the works once he had been to the privy. However, having relieved himself, he returned instead to his place at the table with the two union men.

'Thou hast more sense than those three together,' said Bayles.

'I would sup with them afore thee any day o' t'week.'

James Robertson raised his hand in a gesture of reconciliation, silencing the pair before tempers became irreparably frayed. He despatched Bayles for more ale, awaiting his return for the resumption of the negotiations that had been disrupted by the landlord's intervention and by the abrupt departure of Wastnidge's fellow grinders.

'Thou sayest thou wilt not have ten pounds, then what wilt thou take?' asked the union official. 'Those three with their talk of twenty pounds – thou knowest the Society cannot pay so much as that.'

Wastnidge sipped at the freshly drawn beer, belching for want of allowing it time to settle. He made no acknowledgement of the generosity of those who had supplied him with his pint. His hair, blond in the summer months, had already reverted to the colour of damp straw now that an especially inclement autumn was bracing itself for the onset of winter. He was fatigued from another night's disturbed sleep, his lad's earache being the latest ailment to unsettle the household since the move from Masbrough. At least there was money for the necessary remedies, though Harriet had jested that the union was somehow fostering the child's various illnesses so the

303

wages from Hoole's would be frittered away on doctor's fees.
If he was tired already, the ale was not helping to sharpen his
wits. Wastnidge fixed his attention on Robertson.

'I do not want paying off,' he said. 'I had not worked for
many a long month before old man Hoole took me on.'

'What dost thou want, then?'

'I want to work, that is all.'

'Even if the work thou hast belongs of right to another?
That other being a member of the union of that trade, thrown
out with his fellows by such as Hoole – who cares not whether
he employs knobsticks or whoever so long as his pockets are
filled.'

'I have nothing to say against the Society,' said Wastnidge.
'That is what I want to say to thee now, that I will join if thou
wilt have me.'

Robertson shook his head. 'There is little enough work to
go round without bringing yet more men into the union. There
are men drawing scale – Hallam men at that; fender grinders
like thyself, only they've paid their natty – who ought to have
work ahead of thee if there is work to be had.'

'Thou wilt not have me?'

'I have said no.'

'And thou wilt not find me another situation were I to do
as thou sayest and give notice to Hoole?'

'No, I cannot.'

'Then I cannot leave. Not for ten pounds or anything.'

'Then thou hadst better enjoy that sup, for the next thing
thou hast from the Society shall not taste so well.'

Royal Commission of Inquiry
(sitting at) Hallam Town Hall
Tuesday, 2 July 1867 (Twenty-second Day)

Witness: George Wastnidge, Fender Grinder, No.2 Tummon
Street, Masbrough.

Q. What did you take him to mean by that?

A. I found out soon enough.

Q. How so?

A. I was walking a few days later with a man by the name of Cooper, in Dun Street I believe it was, when some men came out of a pub and assaulted us.

Q. Cooper was another of the non-union men at Hoole's?

A. He was.

Q. Were you seriously assaulted?

A. No. We got away to where I was living at that time and shut ourselves inside.

Q. Did you recognize any of the men who assaulted you as being those formerly employed by Hoole?

A. No.

Q. Did you continue to work at the firm despite this attack?

A. I regret to say that I did.

Q. Why 'regret'?

A. For the dreadful consequences of my doing so.

Robert Smith was of the opinion that one lie required the telling of a second to conceal the first and a third to conceal the second; that once you began lying there was no end to it. He discussed this matter with Thomas Amory one day at the Friendly Society gardens, his friend making the observation that the best way to avoid the telling of lies – at least, the telling of significant lies – was to conduct your life in such a manner as to make lying unnecessary. Yet, they agreed, experience had taught them the difficulty of leading a life so virtuous as to be shorn of the need for dishonesty. Examining this dilemma over beakers of tea laced with rum, the two men concurred to the effect that the definition of 'virtuous behaviour' was the nub of the matter. For what some might consider to be fit and proper, others would hold in reproach. Nor was it enough simply to abide by the laws of the land or the dictates of the Bible, when the former were replete with injustice and the latter purported to be the Holy Writ of a creator in whom neither man believed. However, if you dispensed – even in part – with the rules of others, you had to assume for yourself the awesome responsibility of deciding between right and wrong, between good and evil.

'Thou must do what thou believest to be right,' said Thomas.

'But if what thou dost is against the law or against the beliefs of others, then thou hast to hide what thou hast done by the telling of lies,' replied Robert.

'Aye, right enough.'

'By which, thou art true in deed and untrue in word . . . shamed by a deed even though thou believed it to be proper.'

Thomas reflected on this seeming contradiction before answering with one of his own. 'So, even in right there is wrong?'

That notion silenced them. It was a notion which was to recur in the thoughts of both men over the years to follow as they deceived their wives and children time and again, concealing the illegitimate activities they pursued in the causes of their unions. Theirs was a general deceit – lies of omission rather than commission – necessitated by the leading of a double life; this invisible edifice of untruth being shored up when occasion demanded by the telling of specific falsehoods.

Such a lie was uttered by Robert Smith to his wife Mary when, during the course of stitching a rent in his coat, she discovered a canister of gunpowder in the pocket. The powder had already required one false statement. In response to a suspicious enquiry by the shopkeeper in Snig Hill, Robert had said the explosive was to be used for 'fishing' – it being common practice, among men impatient with rod and line, to stun dozens of fish at one go by lobbing a charge into the river. This lie would not suffice for Mary, who had never known her husband to go fishing – by methods conventional or otherwise – in all the years of their marriage. Besides which, he would have to sustain the falsehood by coming home with a batch of fish. Nor would feigned anger at her for going through his pockets serve as anything other than a temporary diversion; a tactic, moreover, which would surely exaggerate her suspicion.

So, when confronted with what she had found, he assumed a nonchalant air. He had bought the gunpowder, he said, for the sinking of a well at the allotments. This, the prelude to an elaborate technical exposition on how the task was to be achieved – combined with a reassurance that he would not be out of pocket, because the men at the gardens had collected the money between them and entrusted it to him for the acquisition of the explosive. Whether or not Mary believed him was uncertain, though she gave no indication that she did not.

Witness: Robert Smith, Fender Grinder, No.67 Glossop Road, Hallam.

Q. Who gave you the money for the gunpowder?

A. Bill Bayles.

Q. How much did he give you?

A. Half a sovereign.

Q. Where were you when he gave you the money?

A. At Joe Green's.

Q. Is that a public house or the home of a man of that name, or what kind of establishment is it?

A. It is a public house.

Q. Was this money Bayles's own to give you?

A. I believe he got it from James Robertson, of the Fender Grinders'.

Q. Did he promise you further payment?

A. He said I would have six pounds.

Q. What was it that you were expected to do for your six pounds?

A. I was to blow up the home of a man who was wrong with the trade.

Q. What was the name of that man?

A. George Wastnidge.

Q. And you say you were to blow him up at his home?

A. That is what Bayles told me. He gave me the half-sovereign to buy gunpowder.

Q. This inquiry has heard from James Robertson that Wastnidge was to be given a beating and that the money was a downpayment. What do you say to that?

A. If Robertson said that, then he is a liar.

Q. Why would he lie?

A. To save his own neck.

Q. As the perpetrator of this mischief, are you not the one who has greater cause to lie, having regard – as you say – to the saving of necks?

A. If I am to get my certificate from you, I have the greater cause to tell the truth.

Q. Is that the only reason for speaking truthfully, so that we might indemnify you from the consequences of your deed?

A. My indemnity will not stop folk from pointing me out in the street. Nor will it stop them from saying 'there is that b----- wretch who . . .'

Q. I would remind you, sir, that there are ladies present in this assembly, and ask that you mind your language.

A. I cannot see how I can cause greater offence to a woman than I have already done.

Taking the can from his pocket, he lit the fuse – a simple matter complicated by the cold that befuddled his fingers and by the failure of the first two matches to ignite. When, at last, the fuse was alight, he stepped out from his hiding place and strode along to No. 24. The cellar grate, as he had known it would be from his reconnaissance the previous night, was too secure to be levered off. Retreating several paces into the deserted street, he took aim at the front of the house and hurled the canister directly into the first-floor chamber. There was a great crashing of glass that caused him as much fright as if the breaking of the window had been an entirely unexpected consequence of his action. Transfixed for a moment where he stood, he finally regathered his wits and made off full tilt into the beckoning pitch-black of a snicket.

Chapter Eleven

SHOP TALK

Vegetable producers are under intense pressure to comply with the demands – with regard to price, delivery time, quantity and quality – of the major supermarket chains. Vast armies of casual workers are employed during the picking season, compelled to work excessively long hours at low rates of pay so that the growers remain within cost. This has inevitable consequences for the health of these workers, with the disabling effects of Repetitive Strain Injury (RSI) becoming increasingly commonplace.

Profit and Loss: The Economics of Health
by Campbell MacGregor.
Industrial Research Publications, 1990

You've heard of Tennis Elbow and Housemaid's Knee, well wacky doctors have now come up with a new ailment to add to the list . . . Sprout Picker's Wrist!

The Daily Blurt – 30 September, 1990

A doodle: her own name, the letters filled in with blue cross-hatching and decorated with flowers. Constance Amory. *Con amore.* Con, meaning 'with'; amore, meaning 'love'. Chilli con carne, chilli with meat; chilli sin carne, vegetarian chilli. *Sin amore*. Without love. Love the sinner, hate the sin. *He who is without sin among you, let him cast the first stone*. My name is Constance Amory, I am without love. I am without, not within. *The wages of sin is death*. She ripped out the page, screwed it up and dropped it into a wastepaper basket.

The Bible. Fact: the passage marked in the Bible in the pulpit at St Dunstan's Chapel was the same (probably) as that emblazoned on the banner being paraded at Hallam United. Conjecture: the person who defaced the Bible was the person carrying the banner. She trawled her memory, but could recall nothing other than brief glimpses – hands, trousers – which the banner itself had not concealed. She couldn't even be certain, thinking back on the incident, that it was a man – although that had been her impression at the time. And how would he have known which part of the stadium she was in? Process of elimination: the section behind one goal was restricted to Grimsby fans; the Kop end was chiefly the preserve of The Lads; and one side of the ground was awaiting redevelopment. Which left one stand, the one in which she had been sitting with Stan. All the saboteur had to do was parade his banner slowly along the front in the hope that she would spot it. More conjecture. Constance drew up a list of everyone who knew she was going to attend the match.

Mam	Paul Pink
Dad	Gary
Granddad	Dougal Aitken-Aitken
Stan	William Boyce
Milly	Howard

Dad knew because he phoned her at home that evening, with news about Fifi's repairs, and she told him she was in a rush to get ready for the football. Dad would've told Mam, and Granddad was having his tea with them before going to the match himself. Stan knew, obviously, because he was the one who'd invited her. Milly chatted to her about the match while she was getting changed. She mentioned it to DCI Pink, casually, on the phone. The editor knew because Gary asked her at short notice to cover a meeting and she said she couldn't because she'd already arranged to go to Hallam United. He told the boss, who refused to give her a bollocking – she discovered later – on the grounds that watching United would be punishment enough (Dougal being a City fan). William knew, because he was in the office when Stan phoned. And Howard knew, because she mentioned it to him when they went out on a job that afternoon; he was going to the match himself, taking pictures for the *Crucible*.

The Inky Path
The would-be journalist will need a quiet persistence coupled with the ability to make a nuisance of himself in a courteous way. Without this tactful tenacity the beginner will fail to get a story where others succeed.

Dougal Aitken-Aitken had taken to wearing red braces, slipped off the shoulders to dangle from the waistband of his trousers. Every now and then he would amuse himself mid-conversation by flexing an elasticated length of strap between thumb and index finger to form a makeshift catapult, firing pellets of paper at a waste bin. The corner of the room where the bin stood was littered with fallen missiles.

'Eighteen per cent success rate.' He fired another shot. The pellet hit the rim of the basket and landed on the carpet. 'One in five, for headline purposes.'

Constance looked across the desk at him.

'We do that, don't we?' he went on. 'Round things up, round things down. Everything has to be simplified, in newspapers. Why is that?'

'We don't credit readers with the intelligence to cope with complicated issues.'

'Symptomatic. Our simplification of statistics is symptomatic

311

of our simplification of life as we know it. As we *report* it.' He seemed pleased with this. The editor eased his braces back on and swivelled his chair in her direction. 'Ever feel as though you're just scratching the surface? Complex story, awash with pros and cons, plenty of nitty-gritty; ten pars. Two hundred words, two-fifty max.'

'That's the challenge, I suppose, to condense a—'

'Bite-size chunks of news. Soundbites. We dabble in superficialities, all in pursuit of a high story-count – each page packed with snippets to tickle every palate.' He pitched his voice lower, producing a resonant bass. 'We don't dig deep any more.'

She sought signs of irony in his expression. The era of the high story-count at the Crucible had dawned with Dougal Aitken-Aitken's appointment, an early memo setting out *story quotas* and *word ceilings* required by the redesign from broadsheet to tabloid. *If it can't be told in ten pars, it ain't worth telling.*

'Though, naturally, some of us dig deeper than others.' He pronounced 'us' in mock-Hallam – with a short flat 'u', and a 'z' instead of an 'ess'. White teeth. He stretched his arms, clasping the hands behind his head and tilting the chair backwards. 'Some of us just go on digging, even when we've no idea what we're digging for.'

'Meaning me?'

'Your theory about the saboteur's motive . . .'

'It's not just a theory. I mean, he specifically listed his demands in the warning letter to HypaCenta.'

'Only got your word for that. I should say, your contact's word.' He talked over Constance's objection. 'John Chapple denies it . . .'

She shook her head. 'He wouldn't confirm *or* deny—'

'And the police won't divulge its contents. Nor will Mall Secure.'

'Dougal, I—'

'You seen the letter?'

She hesitated.

'Have you actually seen it with your own eyes?'

'No. No I haven't.'

'But you'd be happy for us to publish those "demands" as if their existence was an accepted fact?'

'What about all the cuttings – the coincidence of the sabotages following soon after we carried articles . . .?'

'Coincidence. Your word, not mine.' He looked at her. 'And as for all that historical and religious mumbo-jumbo.'

The editor broke off to search among the papers in his tray, retrieving a print-out she recognized as the background briefing she'd produced for him. He removed a slim leather pouch from his shirt pocket and took out a pair of reading glasses.

'Got them this week.' He put them on. 'Optician made me read one of those charts. She said to me, "Can you read the fourth line down, Mr Aitken-Aitken?" And I said, "Can't make out the letters, but I can tell you they're twenty-four-point Helvetica bold." '

Constance didn't smile. She crossed her legs, aware as she did so that the editor's eyes flicked from her face to her legs and back again.

'It's an old one,' he said, enjoying his own joke. 'One of what my wife refers to as my "apocryphal anecdotes".'

Apocryphal. Odd, the way he held the pages – three fingers supporting the bottom sheet, thumb and index finger tucked in over the top sheet like pincers. How would she hold them? She recalled the football match, the fists gripping each end of a banner. *Normally.* Nothing out of the ordinary. Hirsute? Rings? Long or short fingers, thin or chubby? Couldn't remember. She couldn't remember anything apart from two sets of whitened knuckles. She opened her eyes at the sound of his voice.

'Can we substantiate any of this?'

She hesitated. 'Not yet.'

'As in: "no".'

313

'No, not yet.'

He flopped the papers onto the desk, a cushion of air causing them to glide towards her over the polished wooden surface as though propelled by an unseen hand. 'Can we attribute?'

She shook her head.

'So it's *you* who's saying this. One of your infamous hunches.'

'The thing is, I'm still trying to piece together all the—'

'Substantiation and attribution. Basics, Con. The basics of good journalism.'

She indicated the print-out. 'You asked for background.'

He slumped in his chair, producing a farting noise from the upholstery. The braces were half on, half off. Functional, or a fashion accessory? Granddad wore braces – trouser cuffs high on the shin to expose his socks; waistband hoisted to his navel. *Not a belt man, me. Only belt I ever 'ad were round t'ears from me dad.*

The editor looked at her over the rim of his glasses. His tone became pedantic. 'We are a provincial evening newspaper, not *The New York Times*. Urbopark is not Watergate. You and William Boyce are not Robert Redford and Dustin Hoffman.'

'Woodward and Bernstein.'

'What?'

'Woodward and Bernstein were the reporters, Redford and Hoffman played them in the film, *All the President's Men*. And it was the *Washington Post*.'

'A stickler for facts, all of a sudden!' The editor laughed, nodding in the direction of her notes. 'Shame you don't always adopt that attitude.'

'There were plenty of facts in the piece you pulled about the warning letter to HypaCenta.' She watched his face harden. His expression said, *You've pushed it far enough*. Well, sod that. 'We had more than enough to stand that story up.'

'Constance—'

314

'I'm not talking about *motive*, I'm talking about the fact that HypaCenta increased its security in response to a specific threat. I'm talking about why we didn't even run a story saying the letter *existed*, when the police and Mall Secure both . . .' Slow down, slow down. She eased back in her chair, relaxing her grip on the armrests. 'Dougal, you knew as well as I did there was a warning letter.'

He smiled. 'Connie, if you ever get to be editor, you'll—'

'What? I'll learn how to suck up to major advertisers who are shit-scared we're going to publish something they don't like?'

The editor leaned forward. He removed his glasses and laid them on his blotter pad with excessive care, continuing to stare at them for a moment before looking up at her. 'You know,' he said, still smiling, 'I read somewhere that women think in block capitals and talk in italics. Other way round in your case, isn't it?'

She ignored this remark. 'I even had the line about the "poisoned chalice". The saboteur more or less *told* us what he was going to do to HypaCenta, *and* why he was going to do it. And you pulled the story. You and John Chapple, between you . . .'

'What did we do?' No smile now, nor even a hint that there ever was one. 'Did we poison people? Did we give the saboteur – what was Maggie T's phrase? – the "oxygen of publicity"?' He paused. 'Or did we hurt your feelings?'

William asked, tentatively, how the *summons* had gone.

'I kicked his ass, and he kicked mine,' she said, mock-American.

Her colleague smiled, as though infected by the exuberance of her grin. 'I reckon this is the first time Dougal's ever been held to a draw.'

You're in a good mood, said Paul Pink, on hearing her voice. *Someone tried to make me cry today, and I wouldn't let him.*

She didn't say that. What she said, was: *Yeah, well, you know . . . it's better than being miserable.* She asked if he'd had any more luck than her in getting information out of sports desk's contact at United.

'Yes and no,' said the chief inspector.

'What: yes, she'd talk to you; no, she wasn't any help?'

'They only have records of tickets paid for by cheque or credit card. I'll get you a printout of all the names off the club's computer – just in case – but I wouldn't expect him to have bought the ticket in a way that could be traced.'

'How about the crowd surveillance?' she asked.

'That's why I'm ringing. The SIU got back to me just now . . .'

'The what?'

'Soccer Intelligence Unit. They've trawled through summat like twenty hours of footage and our friend doesn't appear on it once, not from any angle.'

'Always a long shot, I suppose.'

'Even longer shot: Hallamshire TV were there, for the highlights round-up. Apparently, there was a presentation at the side of the pitch during half-time – some fan who's not missed a match for fifty years. They filmed it for their news programme.'

'Yeah, I remember. It was right in front of where I was sitting, so if they've caught him at all it'll only be with the banner obscuring his face, same as I saw.'

'No, the TV gantry is on the opposite side, where they've not got round to building that new stand.'

'So, if he was in the background at the time . . .'

'There's a possibility we might have ourselves a rear or side view of him – maybe enough to get an i.d., if we're lucky. Anyroad, they're getting back to me.'

Before they concluded their conversation, DCI Pink informed Constance of two other pieces of evidence, newly come to light. Firstly, police had eliminated from their inquiries all security swipe-card owners logged as having been present in

Mall Admin prior to the flooding. With one exception. A Mall Clean cleaner initially claimed his card had been lost when his wallet was stolen; after further questioning, he admitted selling it for £50 to a man in a pub. The deal, struck one lunchtime in the Cutler's Arms, was made on the understanding that the cleaner would not report the card as missing for twenty-four hours, delaying the erasure of its magnetic recognition code from the mall's security system. He was helping a police graphic artist to compile a portrait. However, the detective confided that the man's recollection of the suspect's appearance was *next to useless*. The second item of new evidence concerned the computer virus in the Mall Sys tills at Home Zone. Officers had established that the bug was introduced via rogue software installed during the system's trial. Mall Data technicians and members of the university's information technology team, who had been working together on the project, were now *helping police with their inquiries*.

Fred Amory's grey-haired figure loomed, fragmented in the frosted-glass panel of the front door, as he made his way along the narrow hallway.

'Hi, Granddad.'

She was carrying a copy of the *Sunday Mirror*, two lottery scratch-cards, a pack of bacon rashers and a pint of milk. Granddad was always out of milk, and he'd never have a proper cooked breakfast if it was left to him. They kissed on the lips. His face was shiny-smooth and smelt familiarly of Old Spice and salt.

'Here, give us that.'

He helped fetch the things through to the kitchen, where two slices of rough-cut toast were about to catch. While he rescued the bread from the grill, she hurried in after him and pulled the door shut before the smoke could trigger the alarm in the hallway. Dad had fitted smoke detectors a few months earlier, after a chip-pan fire broke out while Granddad dozed in his armchair.

317

'Don't be frettin' thissen about that,' he said. 'I've tekken battery out.'

'*Granddad.*'

'Bloody thing goes off bleeping at owt. I tellt thi dad it were a waste o' money. Nobbut a scrap o' plastic wi' an Ever Ready inside. Japanese.'

He took a knife from a drawer and scraped the scorched slices of toast. Constance went to the fridge. No margarine or butter, only lard – sitting in a saucer, like a lump of misshapen white soap. She melted some in a pan and opened the pack of bacon, laying all four rashers to cook. Granddad busied himself with more toast. Whenever she visited him at home he seemed smaller and older than he did at work, somehow more shambling. It was as though the exchange of his museum attendant's uniform for *civvies*, and the corresponding diminishment of responsibility, effected a loss of presence as much mental as physical. Her theory was that he unconsciously equated being at home with being laid off, a psychological throwback to the years of unemployment following the closure of the steelworks. It was all to do with a reduced sense of self-esteem. *Self-importance more like*, Dad had said in reply to his daughter's observation. Mam reckoned it was on account of his being widowed. *Pop's lonely, that's all. While he's at work, he's not having to sit theer at home with his memories.*

'Wheer d'tha get them rashers from?'

'That place on the main road, by the lights.'

'Paki shop?'

'Bedi's.'

'Sugden's is cheaper. Better cut an' all.'

'Sugden's isn't open of a Sunday morning.' Ten minutes in his company, and she was saying 'of' instead of 'on'.

'Tha could read t'paper through that, they slice it so bloody thin.'

Constance turned the rashers, stepping back from the cooker as a spit of hot fat stung her cheek. When they were done, she lifted them straight from the pan onto the slices of dry toast which Granddad had arranged on two plates. The kitchen table was laid with place mats, cutlery, salt and pepper, brown sauce, English mustard and a pot of tea covered in a home-knitted cosy. Granddad poured. They ate their bacon butties in silence. He read the football pages while she flicked through the colour supplement, greasy fingers leaving translucent smears. The smell of mustard from his sandwich was making her eyes water. He closed the paper.

'D'you go yesterday?' she said.

A shake of the head. 'They were away.'

'How'd they go on?'

'Two-nowt.' His tone, the set of his face, made it plain United had lost rather than won. 'I can see 'em goin' down, missen.'

After breakfast, they replenished their mugs of tea and went through to the sitting room. The decor hadn't altered from her memories of it as a child, coming to play at Gran and Granddad's. Carpets, curtains, wallpaper all patterned in rich oranges, browns, reds and yellows that gave the room a dated, oddly psychedelic, ambience. Framed black-and-white photographs of old Hallam adorned the walls, and the furniture comprised a tan draylon three-piece suite with threadbare armrests, a television set and a polished wooden sideboard, its glass doors revealing Granddad's collection of pewter tankards. The sitting room was drenched in daylight despite the dense net curtains. A clock on the mantelpiece had stopped at five past twelve. He bent to ignite the gas fire mounted in what had once been an open hearth where Constance and Mags, as children, used to toast muffins on a spindly iron fork. Just thinking about it now, she could taste the melted butter dribbling down her chin.

Granddad took his usual armchair, she the two-seater sofa which was firm at one end and sagged at the other – testifying to the years Gran had spent sitting there, knitting or watching telly or dozing with an open book face down on her lap. There was a photograph of her on the mantelpiece, standing in front

319

of the Rovers Return during a sixtieth-birthday outing to the set of *Coronation Street*. Granddad lit a cigarette and spent a moment on the scratchcards Constance had given him, rubbing with the edge of a 2p piece until his lap was speckled with silvery dust. He squinted at the cards, then handed them to her.

'Ave I won owt?'

'Fraid not.'

'Can't retire just yet, then.' He looked across the room, his eyes slitted against an exhalation of smoke. Then he pinched the tip of the cigarette. 'Sorry, duckie.'

'What?'

'I can hear tha lungs from here.' He replaced the cigarette in its packet. 'It'll save while later.'

'It's these cold mornings, going in and out of doors. Sets me off.'

It was the gas fire, and the cigarette smoke, and the damp. This house had always been damp, she could detect it in her breathing as soon as she stepped inside. It had been worse still in the days when they had a dog. Chappie. Hairs everywhere. Even now – years after he'd died – she imagined she could smell him, as though the carpets, the draylon suite, the very air, were impregnated with him. She glanced at her handbag.

'Don't be embarrassed on my account,' he said.

She flushed. She got the inhaler from the zip compartment, removed the cap and took two squirts of Ventolin.

'Used to be a condition known as grinder's asthma,' she said. 'Hundred and odd years ago, this is. Grinder's disease. From all the dust and particles of stone and metal they breathed in, working on the grindstones.'

'Aye, clogs up the bronicles. Theer were jobs at our place as'd do for your lungs if tha stayed at 'em too long, like.'

'Silicosis, they call it nowadays.' Her breathing was easing already. 'We've been studying industrial hazards in my evening class – you know, injuries and diseases, and that. Those Victorian workshops and factories . . .'

320

'Oh, aye. Even in my time. It were t'heat more than owt, I mind some local bigwig – mayor or alderman, or summat – doin' a tour of our place and sayin' to t'foreman, all posh like: "Doesn't the heat damage the men's brains?" And t'foreman says to 'im: "If they 'ad any brains, your worship, they'd not be workin' 'ere!" '

They laughed.

'Wouldn't you dehydrate or something?'

'Me first day – I'd 'ave been fourteen – I worked four 'n' afe hours straight off before we went outside for us break. And I sat on them steps and cried my bloody heart out. The heat were unbelievable.' He paused, knocking scratch-card debris off his lap as though puzzled at how it came to be there. 'It's surprising what tha gets used to. I could go up to summat, an ingot – one thousand four hundred degrees – and I'd stroke it and not get burnt because my 'ands were that hard. The skin, like.'

Half of his face was etched with daylight from the window. The temperature of the ingot rose with each telling of this anecdote.

'Couldn't do it now.' He inspected his palms. 'Soft as owt. Spent too many years punching tickets and doffing me cap to American tourists.'

'Stan – Professor Bell, our tutor – he wants to take us to Hallam Island; sort of like a group outing. So you might be seeing us all traipsing round.'

'Oh, aye?'

'Don't know when. It'd have to be a weekend because a lot of the students have jobs. I think he's quite interested to meet you, actually.'

'Who?'

'Stanley. Stan. Our tutor.'

'Young chap, is he?'

'*Granddad*.'

'And what does your lad mek of all this? That Harold.'

'His name's *Howard*.' What was it with her family and

321

names? She took a sip of tea. 'We split up. You *knew* that. Not that it's got anything to do with anything.'

'Aye.'

'Industrial history is his . . . specialist field, I suppose. Stan, this is.'

'It weren't industrial history while I were theer, it were still goin' on.'

'Oh yeah, I didn't mean . . . you know, I'm just saying – that's his field.'

'Field, aye.'

They lapsed into silence, Granddad finishing his tea and standing the empty mug on the floor beside his feet. For a moment he appeared to be nodding off, then she realized he was narrowing his eyes myopically at the mantelpiece. He stood up, rewound the clock and put it back without bothering to reset the hands. He sat down again, stiffly, protective of his knee. An industrial injury, he claimed – years of strain imposed on the joint from all the *lifting and carrying*. His GP reckoned it was plain old arthritis, probably a legacy of Granddad's footballing days – midfielder for the works team, Bayfield Albion. But what did doctors know? There were discrepancies, too, over how he came by the various small scars on his hands – each anecdotal explanation at variance with previous stories. One scar, at the base of his left thumb, had no fewer than four causes to Constance's recollection.

'Any news on the funding wrangle?' *Wrangle*. She was starting to use journalese in everyday speech now.

'Come sniffing round for a story, eh? A *scoop*?'

'Yeah, yeah. I normally have to stop you talking about the place, never mind wheedle tip-offs out of you.'

'Aye, well just let me know when I get boring.'

She watched Granddad's gaze shift momentarily. 'Oh for God's sake, have a fag if you want one. It's your house.'

He removed the partially smoked cigarette from the packet and placed it between his lips. The tip was charred, and flattened from where he'd extinguished it earlier. After a moment, he took the cigarette – still unlit – from his mouth and lay it on the armrest of his chair.

'I'd a gift from one on 'em, t'other day.'

'From who?'

'American tourist. Leastways, I think he were American – I'm not so clever on accents. We get all sorts: Japanese, Spanish, New Zealand.'

'And he gave you a gift?'

'We're not s'posed to accept pre-requisites, like, but I showed t'gaffer and he said it were summat an' nowt, so why not keep it?'

Pre-requisites. What was he talking about? Mags was better at deciphering Granddad's idiosyncrasies of speech. Bronicles and pre-requisites, she'd have to remember to share these with her sister – additions to the family lexicon.

'D'you mean "perquisite" – you know, as in "perk"?'

'Aye, perk.'

Constance tried not to smile. 'So, what was it he gave you?'

'I'll fetch it.' He raised himself out of the armchair and went over to the sideboard, opening one of the drawers. Searching unconvincingly among some papers, he eventually produced a shallow leather-bound box about six inches square. He handed it to her. 'Go on, open it.'

She lifted the lid. Inside, mounted on purple mock-velvet lining, was a horseshoe – pitted and rusted with age, misshapen where its edges had worn thin and crumbled away in places as though nibbled by rodents. She ran her fingers over the crusty metal, tracing the holes where the nails would have been driven in. The folds of the lining were peppered with flakes of rust. Also in the box was a coin – a Victorian penny, blackened and worn so smooth the monarch's head was barely distinguishable.

'He give you that as well?'

'The coin? No, I've had that since I were a lad. Fambly heirloom. I put it in t'box for safekeeping. I were telling t'American feller – we got talking, like – it were all I've got left of me dad's. Not worth owt, o' course.'

'Sentimental value.'

'Aye.'

'So the two of you were getting nostalgic together, were you?'

'Said he were a blacksmith, back home, and wanted me to have the horseshoe as a *token of his esteem* for showin' 'im round t'museum. Nice chap. Interested, like.'

'It's certainly different.' She studied the horseshoe a little longer, out of politeness, before snapping the lid shut and returning the box. 'Good luck charm.'

'Like I say, summat an' nowt.'

'Shouldn't you nail it up over the front door or something?'

'Tha grandmother were t'one for superstition.' He placed the box back in the drawer. 'Rabbits' feet, St Christophers, lucky colours – you name it. God rest. Tha mother's the same.'

'Tell me about it.'

'To me, a horseshoe's a horseshoe. Nobbut a lump o' metal.'

Constance left Granddad's house twice that morning: once without her handbag, once with it. They kissed goodbye a second time and she could see him diminishing in her rearview-mirror as he stood on the doorstep to wave her off. An anonymous handwritten note had been left under her wind-screen wiper: *This is* resident's *parking*. The note was now crumpled in the passenger seat footwell, along with the usual detritus of empty Lucozade bottles, crisp packets and Snickers' wrappers. She turned left, then right; she cruised the radio stations for a decent reception then gave up, fishing blindly for a tape from the door pocket. Pulp: *Different Class*. She removed the tape from its box one-handed while steering and pressed it into the cassette slot. Simply Red. Right box, wrong tape. Or: right tape, wrong box. At the next red light, Constance made a hasty search of the door pocket – retrieving a jumble of empty cassette boxes, loose tapes, and boxes which

324

may or may not have contained the cassettes advertised on the inserts. She slung the whole lot on the passenger seat, scrabbling through them for the Pulp album. Did it have to be Pulp? Yes. Someone was papping their horn. Shit, green light. Fifi lurched, then stalled. Shit. Shit. *OK, OK, stop papping for Christ's sake!* Constance restarted the engine and pulled away from the lights at the second attempt, one hand raised in apology to the driver behind.

Her route took her past a swathe of derelict land strewn with rubble that had, until a few weeks earlier, been high-rise flats. Now, despite the security fencing, the site was pock-marked with stray cats, a group of children playing, and men apparently scavenging for scrap. She recalled the photos in the *Crucible* the day after the demolition – a sequence of before-during-and-after shots showing one of the blocks imploding. Half the shops on the opposite side of the road were boarded up, To Let signs secured to the frontages like bedraggled bunting left over from a long-forgotten street party. Most of the neighbouring factories were also derelict – overgrown acres of wasteground, or windowless and roofless shells awaiting demolition. Some remained in production, red-brick Victorian facades dressed up in smart blue or cream cladding inscribed with bold corporate logos; other sites had been infilled with light-industrial units and warehouses, or turned into pay and display car-parks. Constance tried to visualize this area in its heyday: a thriving ribbon of land adjoining two parallel roads following the course of Hallam's main river. Huge steel mills and factories; before that, the smaller metal-working and toolmaking workshops of the last century; before that, the craftsmen's cottages. And before that? Fields, probably. Lush watermeadows where herdsmen brought their cattle to graze; cart-tracks where the roads now lay, routes by which folk fetched their produce to market in what was now a busy city centre and was then the hub of a small town surrounded by hills and open country and woodland and tiny hamlets. A hundred years from now the razed flats, the empty shops and the defunct factories – even those still in business – would themselves be buried beneath something else. All traces of their existence expunged from the surface of the city. The buildings – the folk that lived and worked in them – would be the preserve of archaeology and of historical record. And, like the neighbourhood she was driving through, Constance would also have been reduced to dust.

Instead of going home as intended, she headed northeast out of the centre. A spontaneous, spur of the moment decision. An impulse. Was she impulsive by nature? She was being impulsive *now*, at least. What happened was: she'd approached a set of lights, meaning to turn right; but the lights had been red, and in the time it took for them to change she'd chosen to go left. The reason: a traffic direction signpost. Not that the sign itself constituted a reason, but it planted the idea in her head. And so she found herself, unexpectedly, breaching the vast arches of the Wicker viaduct and heading out on the road to Urbopark.

She parked as usual in Green Lower and switched off the engine. The car-park was nearly full, the approach to the mall entrance clogged with shoppers reminiscent of seaside day-trippers toing and froing at the beach. URBOPARK: SHOPPING IS LIBERTY was emblazoned above the automatic glass doors, the neon strips that comprised each letter reduced, in their unlit daytime state, to a uniformly dull green – the second P of 'shopping' no longer blinking on and off. She noticed new Customer Services posters: Mall Care – Help Us To Serve You Right! Being a Sunday, the *Crucible* office was closed. The grey shapes of its unlit interior loomed out of the multi-coloured patina of the plate-glass frontage like shadows on the floor of a swimming pool. She found her keys and let herself in, locking the door behind her and leaving the lights in reception switched off as she went through to the back. No Sally, no William. The phones were silent, there was no background hum of air conditioning, the office equipment – photocopier, computers, Mall Link printer – stood in states of dormant disconnection. Once she'd shut the door between front desk and editorial, even the gush of noise from the arcade diminished almost to nothing. She hung up her coat. The off-white ceiling and walls, each pooled in its own lemony spotlight, seemed to resound with silence. The room had that lonely, sleepy, three o'clock in the morning atmosphere which workplaces acquired at hours when people were not supposed to be at work. And she knew, then, the reason for coming here. Sanctuary. Somewhere to think, undistracted. Somewhere to be alone. Had she locked the door to the mall? Constance went back into reception to check. She had. There seemed to be plenty of give when you pushed. She shot the bolts into place, top and bottom. That was better.

Her colleagues, who'd both been working on Saturday morning, had left messages on yellow notelets gummed to her computer monitor or scribbled on an open notepad that lay across the keyboard. She'd leave them; if she'd not come in, the messages would've had to wait until Monday so where was the harm in ignoring them? She'd ignore them. She made herself a coffee then sat down at her desk, gathering the memos into a pile and reading them in turn. Nine, in all. Most were not urgent. She put them in her in-tray, sorted into order of priority; some, she binned (the three relating to calls from Mam). Two messages remained. One, timed at 10.40 the previous morning and written in Sally's unmistakeable flowery script, was from Paul Pink – asking Constance to ring him. The other was from William, also dated Saturday, in barely legible Teeline. His outlines were too large, too far apart and imprecise – strikingly similar to her own, the difference being that she was accustomed to making sense of her own shorthand. She made a painstaking transcription into longhand, using context to hazard a guess at those words she couldn't decipher.

Constance,
Please excuse the cryptic [form] of this message! I've been doing

some digging around re HypaCenta and came up with something [that might be] of use. In January last year, the supermarket cancelled its [long-standing?] contract with a local producer, Hallamshire Poultry Supplies – worth £275,000 per annum. HPS asked Mall Admin to [exert pressure] on HypaCenta to adhere to Urbopark's [declared] policy of using local suppliers where possible. Mall Admin refused. HPS laid off 10 workers as a direct result and [subsequently] had to make another 6 redundant. In September last year, the firm went into receivership – a year to the day before [the first] of the sabotages! The boss of HPS – Donald Moss – was unemployed for months after his business collapsed, finally taking a low-level managerial job in the poultry section of a livestock distribution company, Wainwright & Babcock (Meats). And – get this! – Moss's son, [Michael? Mitchell?], is a junior systems analyst with Mall Data. *Take no action on this until we speak.* I'm off on Monday, but you can ring me at home. Yours,
William

A smudge disfigured William's original note. Constance examined it, held it beneath her nose. Fishpaste. She also saw that the first line of shorthand had been written over a thin film of Tipp-ex. She held the page up to the light.

I've been doing some digging

So, he'd begun the message in longhand before changing his mind, obliterating the first few words and starting again in shorthand. Fair enough. Constance reread her transcription then lay it aside. She rang William at home. He wasn't in. His wife said he'd be at the town hall all afternoon, taking part in the amateur dramatic society's first dress rehearsal. *They open next Friday*, she said. Death of a Salesman. Next, she rang CID. DCI Pink wasn't on duty. She dialled his home number. No answer. She tried his mobile. Disconnected. Snickers time. Constance consumed a bar with her mug of coffee, eating and drinking one-handed while she switched on her terminal and logged on. Shit, semi-colon instead of an 'L'. The machine bleeped at her. *Invalid Password.* She typed again: C-U-R-L-E-W. Access. She began trawling the system, keying in the file names and calling up the stories she'd scrolled through the previous week to make sure she hadn't missed anything. The 'HypaCenta' file revealed nothing new. This time she added the filenames 'Hallamshire Poultry Supplies' and 'Donald Moss' to her search request, confirming much of the information in William's memo. There was, however, no reference to HPS's failed attempt to get Mall Admin to intervene over the termination of the contract. If this had been known at the time, the *Crucible* would have run a story – so the information had to be new, and therefore must've come from one of William's sources rather than from the files. As a long shot, she ran a cross-reference check on each of the stories under 'HPS' and 'Donald Moss' – a laborious process that required her to scan through 'company failures', 'livestock (poultry)', 'food industry', 'employment (redundancies)' and 'animal welfare (transportation)'. One cross-reference caught her eye. She typed in the filename 'letters', with a search name of 'Donald Moss'. What she found, that William hadn't, were two letters from Moss to the *Evening Crucible*, around the time of HypaCenta's decision to switch poultry suppliers. The first letter set out the dire consequences for his business – and for local jobs – as well as Moss's belief that the supermarket was in breach of Urbopark policy. It also criticized Mall Admin for failing to intervene. The second letter, dated ten days after the first, accused the editor of keeping the story out of the paper for fear of antagonizing two of its biggest advertisers: HypaCenta and Urbopark. Both items of correspondence contained an identical footnote beneath the name of the signatory: NOT FOR PUBLICATION. NO REPLY. (D. Aitken-Aitken).

The Life and Times of a Hallam Saw Grinder (a Dramatic Reconstruction in Many Parts)

Royal Commission of Inquiry
(sitting at) Hallam Town Hall
Tuesday, 2 July 1867 (Twenty-second Day)

Witness: Mrs Harriet Wastnidge, No.2 Tummon Street, Masbrough.

Q. When it exploded, what happened to you?

A. I do not know.

Q. You were very much burnt were you not?

A. I do not know how I got into the garret again, but I did.

Q. Did you immediately become insensible?

A. Yes, I went off.

Q. You do not recollect anything afterwards until you found yourself in the infirmary?

A. No, I do not.

Q. Were you very much burnt?

A. Yes.

Q. Were you blinded at the time?

A. Yes.

Q. Do you feel injury from that now, after all these years?

A. Yes, I do.

Q. What is that?

A. My right knee fails me, and I have no use in my right hand.

Q. Your knee was hurt in the fall, was it, or how did you come by that injury?

A. I believe it must have been in the fall.

Q. How long were you blind?

A. I daresay about a fortnight.

Q. Do any of the marks from the fire continue about you now?

A. Oh, yes, fearful.
Q. About your body?
A. Yes.

November 1861

The house at No.24 Acorn Street was arranged on four floors: a semi-basement cellar, a parlour and kitchen on the ground floor, a bed chamber on the floor above that and another in the garret. George Wastnidge, his wife Harriet and their small son Charles slept in the uppermost chamber while their lodger, an Irishwoman by the name of Bridget O'Rourke, had the first floor. The household had been retired for three hours when George was jolted awake by a crashing of glass that seemed – in his confusion – to have occurred in the very chamber where he lay abed. He sat up, dimly conscious of his wife – a ghostly figure in her cotton chemise – hastening to the window.

'What is it?' he demanded.

'Someone hast broke a window down below.' Harriet Wastnidge – a light sleeper – explained that she had been disturbed by the sound of footsteps in the street a moment before. 'There! I can see him running off!'

In the time required for George to disengage himself from the bedclothes, his wife was already halfway down the steep stairs leading from the garret. He caught up with her in the first-floor chamber, where Bridget O'Rourke was out of bed and holding an object emitting a shower of sparks. Harriet screamed at the younger woman – seemingly paralysed by fright – to throw the device back whence it came, out of the shattered window. Broken glass was all about and, with his faculties addled by somnolence and confusion, George found himself altogether disregarding the fiery missile in his concern that the two women should take care where they trod. He was on the point of issuing a warning to this effect when the object, being passed at that instant from Bridget to Harriet, exploded. The blast framed the pair in a corona of brilliant white.

331

Standing in the doorway, George staggered back a step – made to flinch by a sudden wave of heat and an incandescent glare that momentarily dazzled him. When he was able to look again, he saw that both women were on fire. The lodger reeling about the room as though drunk, his wife running towards him in a state of hysteria with her chemise ablaze like a cloak of flame. He tried to catch hold of her but she propelled herself past him and back up the stairs to the garret, tearing at the garment in a frantic endeavour to free herself of it. Coming to her aid, George – half choked by the pulverous smoke – managed to keep her steady long enough that he might rip away the last fragments of burning cloth. She stood before him, her hair smoking and her body odorous of scorched flesh. Her face was quite blackened.

Witness: George Wastnidge, Fender Grinder, No.2 Tummon Street, Masbrough.

Q. You were once again in the garret at this time?

A. We were.

Q. And where was Miss O'Rourke?

A. I do not know whether she had fled her chamber or what she had done.

Q. The house was burning, was it?

A. The stairs were alight and everywhere was thick with smoke.

Q. How did you make good your escape?

A. My wife was the first out.

Q. How so?

A. My little lad had got out of bed and I was afraid of his being stifled. I picked him up – he had got under the bed – and before I could get to the window my wife was out.

Q. She had nothing on her at all, had she?

A. No.

Q. Was she perfectly naked?

A. She was.

Q. And she had jumped, you say, from the garret window?

332

A. I did not see her do so, I only saw that she was out and the window was open.

A crowd had gathered in the street, folk from neighbouring houses who had been disturbed in their sleep by the explosion. A voice called to George to throw down the small boy. Charles, coughing fit to burst his lungs and with his eyes streaming, clung to his father's neck as though he would surely die if he were ever made to let go. But let go he did, his skinny limbs prised off one by one. Dangling his son by one wrist, George lowered him as far as he dared before releasing his grip to watch the boy plunge safely into the upraised arms of two men attendant some twenty feet below. Some other men, he saw, had fetched a ladder and were standing it against the front of the building. Vivid flames from the first-floor window licked at the rungs, though this escape route was the lesser peril than remaining a moment longer where he was – the floorboards beneath his feet being well alight now and searing his legs. The ladder was too short to reach the top storey, however, requiring George to climb out and try as best he could to jump onto it so that the rungs might at least break his fall.

Witness: George Wastnidge (cont.)

Q. Where was your wife at this time?

A. They told me she and the boy were being cared for in a house across the street.

Q. What did you do then?

A. I went back inside with some others to seek Miss O'Rourke.

Q. The house was still burning, was it?

A. The upper floors were burning, downstairs it was mostly smoke.

Q. Did you find the woman?

A. She was in the cellar.

Q. How came she to be in the cellar?

A. I do not know. I think she had tried to escape the house

333

and had got herself in a confusion what with the shock and the smoke and with her being all burnt.

Q. In what state was she in when you found her?

A. She was dreadfully burnt.

Q. I believe Miss O'Rourke had all her nightdress burnt off, is that so?

A. She had.

Q. So she would have been quite naked?

A. That is so.

In the two weeks after the gunpowder attack, George Wastnidge had become a familiar and popular figure with the nurses at the infirmary. Having been in their care for several days himself, he was now a daily visitor to the ward where his wife continued her recuperation. Always ready with a smile or a kind remark, he had impressed the nurses not only with his consideration for their work but also with his facility to raise his wife's spirits – as beneficial to her recovery, they said, as any amount of medical attention. Moreover, they admired the fact that he always found time to look in on Bridget O'Rourke, even though she had failed fully to regain consciousness and was largely in a feverish state of incoherence on the rare occasions when she did awaken. However, although he was not oblivious to the fondness with which the nurses welcomed his visits, George believed it to be due to him invariably arriving with his son in tow. Charles, when he was not filling the wards and corridors with his boisterous mischief and peals of childish laughter, would follow his favourite nurses about their rounds like a devoted puppy. And, at the sight of one of the doctors, the boy would assume a solemn and melancholy expression of self-pity – coughing pathetically and stating aloud, feeble of voice, that he really was 'quite poorly'. Such were his transparent and consistently unsuccessful attempts to have himself readmitted to the children's ward, where he had had such fun in the days following the fire.

What George Wastnidge found most difficult about his visits

334

was the necessity he imposed upon himself not to burden Harriet with his own troubles. His wife's convalescence was delicate enough without him giving her cause for further anxiety. It was a consolation, though an odd one at that, that – being temporarily blinded – she was unable to see his expression; for George had never been able to conceal his moods from her. Even so, she knew him with sufficient intimacy that a mere inflection in his voice was enough to disclose to her that all was not well.

'What is it?' she asked, during one of their bedside conversations.

'What is what?' he replied, averting his gaze from her face even though she could see nothing, so she said, but indistinct shapes and shadows.

'George, I s'll wheedle it from thee ere long, so thou wouldst do as well to speak now.'

'Whatever it is, it is no concern of thine.'

'It is always the same thing with thee.'

'I am working again, if that is what thou means.'

'Full time?'

He did not speak.

'Part time, then,' said his wife. 'Where art thou working?'

'Part time is all I am able.'

'Back at Hoole's?'

'Aye.'

'And what was he paying thee whilst thou wert in here?'

'He paid me some.'

'Paid or loaned?'

'Loaned.'

'And now thou art on a part-time wage?'

'Aye.'

'When hast thou to pay him back?'

'I am paying him back already. He is stopping from my pay each week.'

Harriet considered this for a moment. 'And I daresay thou hast said to him that this is a fine and dandy manner to reward

335

a man who was nearly killed along with his wife and son for the sake of working there in the first place.'

'I've said so, though not in the words thou hast used.'

'And thou hast had him come to Acorn Street to see the state of the house?'

'I've told him of it, aye.'

'And thou wilt go on working for this Hoole?'

'I must repay the money I borrowed, that is all.'

How much longer Mrs Wastnidge might have pursued this argument would never be known, for at that moment a doctor approached. To begin with, George thought he was being summoned to retrieve Charles from yet another scrape elsewhere in the infirmary, but by the doctor's expression he knew that it was a matter more serious than that. Excusing himself from his wife's bedside, George followed the doctor to a small room at the end of the ward.

'What is it? Is it concerning Harriet?'

The doctor shook his head. 'Your wife is as well as might be expected.'

'What, then?'

'I regret to have to say to you, Mr Wastnidge, that the young woman – Bridget O'Rourke – has, not one hour since, passed on.'

'She is *dead*?'

'I regret to say that she is.'

Robert Smith, having fled the scene of the explosion, concealed himself nearby by climbing the railings of Ebenezer's Chapel and laying himself down for some moments in the chapel yard. After a time, deeming it safe to return to Acorn Street, he saw that a crowd had gathered. The house was well ablaze in its uppermost storeys and thick black smoke belched from all of its windows, the glass – he presumed – having exploded in the heat. Among those assembled, he saw a man he recognized as George Wastnidge. He was burnt about the shins, and staggered somewhat on account of having just leapt from the garret window onto a ladder which broke beneath him. As soon as Wastnidge had satisfied himself that his wife and child were being cared for, he raised the alarm that there remained a woman trapped inside the building. Three men went in through the front door to find her: Wastnidge and two others. He urged that they go up at once to her chamber, but a faint cry from the mouth of the cellar stairs alerted them to her whereabouts. Choked by smoke and at peril from flaming missiles descending about them from the storeys above, the three men hurried into the basement. Bridget O'Rourke was slumped against the wall beneath the cellar grate, shorn of her clothes and – even in the gloom – evidently marked by horrific burns. Her hair had been scorched entirely from her head. Between them, the men managed to raise her up the stairs and carry her into the street. They set her down. Wastnidge and one of his assistants stood up, racked by a fit of coughing. The third man continued to tend to the mutilated woman. His eyes wept copiously, it seemed, from being irritated by smoke; his chest and throat heaved with sounds that might have been mistaken for sobs had it not been obvious to onlookers that he was in difficulty breathing. When at last he let go of her, his hands came away with morsels of the woman's burnt flesh adhering to the palms like gobbets of roasted pork. That man was Robert Smith.

Chapter Twelve

SHOP TALK

In the past two decades more than 750 superstores have been built in the United Kingdom and 10,000 small independent shops have closed.

Urban Planning Quarterly Review
Spring 1995

After she left the office that Sunday, the phone rang. The answering machine cut in, and a voice – male, neutralized by disguise – left a message that sounded as though it was being read from a script. This message would remain unattended to until Constance replayed the tape on arrival for work the following morning:

'Hello, Ms Amory. This is Mr Rage. The Mall Madman, as you prefer. I thought we were friends but when I impart information, you do not print it. I do not like that. Look in yesterday's *Crucible* and you will see something that might reignite our friendship before it is too late. In the meantime, guidance on where to dig can be found in the opening pronouncement of the saint symbolized by an eagle.'

*   *   *

While the message was being recorded, Constance was parking Fifi in the street outside her mam and dad's house. A crimson Ford Mondeo occupied the drive. She paused beside it to peer through the lightly tinted glass of the front nearside window: smoke-grey velour interior, fancy radio, the *Independent on Sunday*, a half-finished packet of Extra Strong Mints. Vegetables. He'd come on his day off to deliver vegetables from his allotment. She walked round to the front of the car and pressed a hand against the bonnet. Cold. Surely not Sunday dinner? How could he have become this friendly with Mam and Dad without her knowledge? It would explain why she'd not been able to contact him earlier. All along, she'd been looking in the wrong place, because here he was – right under her nose. Detective Chief Inspector Paul Pink, of Hallam CID, at 'home'; sitting down to Sunday roast. Jesus Christ.

Lamb, judging by the aroma. Mint sauce. Roast potatoes. She should've phoned, she shouldn't just turn up unannounced like this. Three o'clock, probably too late for dinner anyway. And she was ravenous; she'd not eaten since the bacon butty at Granddad's. Oh, and a couple of Snickers at the office. Mam's roast potatoes were, without fail, mouth-wateringly crisp – though not according to the woman who cooked them. *Dry. Too salty. No flavour.* She'd a way of denigrating her meals from the first mouthful as a pre-emptive strike against compliments. Same whenever she dressed up posh to go out: *Do I look awful?* So that any response, no matter how flattering, was reduced to a solicited reassurance and, therefore, of dubious sincerity.

Constance called out, her voice echoing in the hallway. 'Only me!'

'That you, duckie?'

She found Mam on the upstairs landing, showing off one of her framed Impressionist jigsaw puzzles to a tall, slender woman in a pale green two-piece. A large brooch in the form of an owl perched on the lapel – one eye closed, the other open. The woman's hair was the same vivid ginger

339

as Constance's, but straight and cut in a bob. Her freckled throat was adorned with a small silver crucifix on a chain.

'I were just showing Christina me latest Monet.' Mam rhymed the artist's name with bonnet. 'Finished it t'day before yesterday.'

The woman smiled. 'You must be Constance.'

'Hello.'

They shook hands self-consciously.

'Your mother just gave us the most wonderful lunch.'

'Joint were in too long.'

'Nonsense.'

'Tough as old boots.' Mrs Amory hung the picture back on the wall. 'Paul's in t'garden with your dad. If it's dinner you're wanting, there's some meat left and I've a few tatties and a bit o' veg put by. It'll want warming, mind.' Turning to her guest, she added: 'I've a Cézanne above t'bed – fifteen hundred pieces.'

Paul. As she followed Mrs Amory into the bedroom, Christina smiled again at Constance and mouthed *see you in a minute*. Baby owl earrings, to match the brooch. She was younger than her husband by about five years. What did she do? Teacher? Constance couldn't recall. Green eyes, and a voice like velvet. What was life like, married to Paul Pink?

The detective was squatting beside a flower-bed, caressing damp earth between thumb and middle finger and giving a complicated appraisal of soil-type. Dad, nodding intently. Their discussion was moving on to matters of fertilization and suitable species of bedding plant, when the two men noticed Constance. They stood up. She gave her dad a hug and said hi to Paul, her outstretched hand declined.

'You'll not want to get mucky,' he said, displaying his mud-stained fingers. In his chequered V-neck sweater and beige slacks, he reminded her of a TV quiz-show host. David Coleman, minus the relaxed bonhomie. Not so much off-duty as on standby. 'Not quite winter yet and your dad's already planning for next spring.'

'Been picking his brains.' Mr Amory gestured at the flower-beds. Putting on a nasal voice, he added, 'He's been *helping me with my inquiries.*'

They laughed, Dad loudest and longest.

v. H'Centa	**v. Mall**
graffiti	graffiti
dead chickens	bomb hoax
drinks contamination	leather/fur goods
	cash tills (Donald Moss's son?)
	flooding (son, computer game tip-off?)

Notes/Queries:

1) W.B. (= Wainwright & Babcock, Moss's new employers? Why?)
2) Man in the Moon?
3) Ruskin/Pre-Raphaelites? (What the hell has this got to do with anything?!)
4) Biblical quote (re: merchants in the temple). Why?
5) United v Grimsby? How would he (D. Moss) know I was there?
6) Why most sabotages directed at mall, not HypaCenta?
6a) Why *me*? *Crucible* connection/failure to publish letters?
7) Ship's bell/Bayfield's on U'park site. Clue, or not?
8) Rage? (also, 'Mr Age') Why 'rage'? WHY RAGE?

'So, what d'you think?'

DCI Pink didn't reply, not even a nod or shake of the head. He continued to stare at the uppermost page of a sheaf of papers arranged on his lap. They were sitting in Fifi. The car was stationary outside the Amory house, its heater – unreliable at the best of times – issuing alternating blasts of hot and cold air through the vents. Mam, Dad and Mrs Pink were indoors, on their second pot of tea. Constance had managed to contain her impatience for nearly an hour before finally asking him if he would cast his eye over William's memo and the other notes she'd fetched from the office. *Taking advantage*, Mam called it. *Whatever it is, can't it wait while Monday?* But Paul, as far as you could discern his feelings about anything whatsoever, seemed not to mind. Afternoon was yielding to evening, the sky dulling from aluminium to pewter. A light was on in a neighbour's living room, though the curtains weren't yet drawn and you could see him moving about. DCI Pink raised his head. In profile, his misshapen nose sat in the centre of his face like a potato.

'Or don't you think anything at all?' added Constance, exasperated.

'If you ask Christina, I'm the way I am because I was born with Saturn in the ascendancy. Says I've a tendency to be gloomy, surly and sullen. Stern.'

'I wouldn't say you were surly or sullen.'

He inclined his head towards her. 'How about gloomy and stern?'

She laughed. 'Serious, I'd say. Maybe solemn, on a bad day.'

'Anyroad, according to her, Saturn was a god in ancient Roman astrology – portrayed as a bent old man with a stern disposition. People born while Saturn's on the rise are supposed to . . . inherit some of his characteristics.'

'Hence the word "saturnine", presumably.'

'Aye.' He sounded impressed. 'Aye, saturnine. Being gloomy, I head northeast to follow planet. Nine letters.'

'Did you just make that up?'

He shook his head. '*Independent*, a week ago last Tuesday.'

Constance leaned forward to tinker with the heater controls, to no obvious effect. Surely the engine had been running long enough by now? It was cold in the car, and she wanted the loo. The lad from next door – Bert and Dorothy's eldest – was standing beside his Escort, wiping his hands on a rag. Hot air. She clicked the fan onto maximum, flustering the loose pages on DCI Pink's lap. He'd spent some time poring over them without comment, occasionally breaking off to jot something down in his pocketbook. Her own notes – the table of sabotages and the list of queries at the foot of the page – had claimed his attention longer than any of the other documents. She wanted his verdict, like a child awaiting teacher's approval for a piece of schoolwork. She *felt* childish, beside him. Immature. Perhaps that was what it would be like to be married to him. Unless you were cool and confident, like Christina. Or perhaps you *became* cool and confident, as a protection against succumbing to the notion of your inferiority. She didn't know. What did she know? She didn't know anything about marriage to Paul Pink, or anyone else.

'You know what he was god of, Saturn?' he said. 'Agriculture. Appropriate, what with me being an allotment holder. Maybe there's summat in it after all.'

'Paul, the thing is . . .'

'So if I come across as being gloomy, it's not because I'm . . . uninterested in all this.' He patted the sheaf of papers. 'I am. I'm excited, as a matter of fact. You'd not know it to look at me, but I'm excited.'

She studied his face, which was as devoid of excitement as it was conceivable for any face to be. She suppressed a smile. 'Tell me, when you played rugby did you jump up and down and punch the air whenever you scored a try?'

He looked indignant. 'I've never scored a try in my bloody life.'

Fire bombs go off at shopping mall

by Constance Amory, Urbopark Reporter

Fire bombs exploded in the car-parks at Hallam's giant Urbopark shopping complex this morning, moments after a mass evacuation.

A dozen incendiary devices – placed in litter bins around the mall site – ignited following a coded telephone warning.

Mall Secure officers had just enough time to move shoppers and motorists out of the car-parks before the first of the devices went off.

Fire crews were on hand to douse the series of small fires that ensued, though several cars parked next to the bins were badly damaged.

Curtain

Mother-of-two Samantha Wilcox, 28, of Burston, said her Austin Metro was 'burnt out' after she left it in the Blue Zone car-park.

'I'd only popped into Home Zone for some curtain material,' she said.

Police say the attack is the latest by the Mall Madman, who has been terrorizing Urbopark.

Det. Chief Insp. Paul Pink, of Hallam CID – the man leading the hunt – said the fire bombs were probably planted between 9 and 10 a.m.

'These were small devices, each one of which would have been easy to place in a litter bin without drawing attention,' he said. 'But, given the number and their distribution, it could not have been done quickly.

'I would ask anyone using the car-parks this morning to come forward if they saw anything remotely suspicious.'

Material

DCI Pink said forensic tests were under way to establish the materials used to make the devices, but he added that the nature of the blasts suggested a 'degree of expertise' on the part of the saboteur.

'This is the worst of the sabotages so far, and a very worrying development,' he said.

The attack occurred despite tougher security at Urbopark, where stores and administrators have been trying to restore the confidence of shoppers driven away by the saboteur.

Mall manager, Roy Dobbs, said, 'Business is suffering already and this won't help at all.'

Police are studying film from newly installed closed-circuit television cameras in the car-parks to see if the perpetrator was recorded in the act of planting the devices.

They are also examining a coded message left two days ago on an answering machine at the Urbopark offices of the *Evening Crucible*.

Constance made a copy, allowing a scenes of crime officer to take the original. She replayed the tape, paying close attention to the rhythm and patterns of speech. Accentless. The disguise was so complete it wasn't possible even to say whether the caller was a native English-speaker. If the voice seemed irritatingly familiar to her, it was – she was sure – because she'd listened to it so often on previous recordings. The over-stressed 'z' of 'Ms', the erratic pauses – too short between some words, too long between others – the quality of someone giving dictation. She made a verbatim transcription, breaking it down into its component parts like a crossword clue.

'Reignite': a forewarning of the fire bombings, the word spoken with clumsy emphasis. Obvious, in retrospect, but too obscure for the exact nature of the sabotage to have been anticipated. And the reference to Saturday's *Crucible* was infuriatingly oblique. Page ten, single column: Mall Admin was to use (unpaid) volunteer gangs of school pupils to collect litter at the Urbopark site, under a Children in the Community scheme to promote environmental awareness and good citizenship. The move would result in the loss of fifteen jobs at Mall Tidy, a sub-unit of Mall Clean. This tied in with her earlier theory, but she couldn't square it with the Donald Moss vendetta. And how could you connect the word 'reignite' with a story about redundant litter-pickers, to predict the blowing up of a dozen rubbish bins? As for *the opening pronouncement of the saint symbolized by an eagle* . . . If Mr Rage wanted stories about the *why* rather than simply the *what* of his sabotages, he'd have to give her more than this to present to the editor. She replayed the tape. So, they were no longer friends. He didn't like that. Nor did she. It wasn't the loss of friendship she mourned – *what* friendship? – it was the tone of voice. As though, somehow, she'd disappointed him. He was giving her another chance with the fire bombings – some chance, twenty-four hours to decode his warning and turn it into copy. She'd let him down again.

While she was analysing the message, Gary – on newsdesk – rang. One of the London-based agencies had issued a syndicated feature chronicling the sabotages and speculating as to the motives of the Mall Madman. A copy spewed from the fax. She read it. Littered with inaccuracies and distortions, the article evidently cobbled together in a hurry in the wake of the fire bombings. Predictably clichéd, too. *As if life wasn't depressing enough in the grim northern city of Hallam, shoppers at a glitzy mall now tread the aisles in fear after a spate of* . . . Much of the background had been plagiarized from Constance's own stories, some passages lifted more or less verbatim. Where the agency writer bothered to disguise this by paraphrasing, he got things wrong. He tagged animal rights extremists as the most likely culprits. No reference to an alternative political agenda. Nor to Donald Moss or Hallamshire Poultry Supplies. For the time being, the *Crucible* had this line to itself – even if Dougal would print nothing until every gap in the story was plugged and every potentially defamatory or erroneous fact double-checked.

The next phone call brought good news and bad. Paul Pink, informing her that Hallamshire TV had supplied film from its coverage of the half-time presentation at Hallam United. A special screening had been arranged for her – as a potential i.d. witness, *not* as a reporter. Friday, oh-nine hundred hours. DCI Pink also told her the latest sabotage could not have been perpetrated by Donald Moss or his son, Michael, as both men had been in custody all morning being questioned by detectives.

The Inky Path
A reporter starting out on a provincial weekly might expect to earn £10 a week. If he is disgruntled about this he ought to look elsewhere for a living, for the true journalist measures his remuneration not in pounds, shillings and pence but in column inches. This is not to say that trades unions do not exist in the newspaper industry, nor that they have no role to play in defending the wages and conditions of their members. However, he who derives greater pride from disrupting production of his newspaper than he does from espying his byline on the front page has no place on the inky path.

The cuttings library at head office was a curious juxtaposition of Dickensian fustiness and high-tech modernity. Ranks of floor to ceiling shelving crammed with fat envelopes of yellowed clippings that protruded here and there from split seams, like tufts of stuffing from an ancient sofa; towering cases of reference books, some so infrequently used that their spines were coated with a greyish-brown film; bound editions of the

Evening Crucible dating back to the last century, the year of publication tooled into each leather binding in gold leaf. Separated from this by a frosted-glass partition was a small open-plan area clinically laid out with new desks and chairs, photocopiers, microfiche monitors, CD-ROMs and computer terminals, their clean angles and reflective screens gleaming. To enter the rear section – sepia-lit, smelling of wood polish and leather and dust – you'd to pass through this minimalist reception room. It was necessary to write your name in a ledger by the connecting door, and to sign for borrowed items on exit. The chief librarian – holder of a masters in Information Technology, and enthusiastic advocate of electronic storage and retrieval systems – had pinned a notice outside the *inner sanctum*: Greetings, Time Traveller.

Constance wrote her name in the ledger and went in. The reference books appeared to be in no particular order. Choosing one of the more up-to-date editions, she hauled the tome onto a desk which looked like (and was) a relic from a pre-war schoolroom, complete with inkwell holder – minus the inkwell. She opened the encyclopaedia at the appropriate page and began taking notes.

Eagle: In Christian art, the eagle is the symbol of St John the Evangelist (him, again!), to whom one of the four gospels is ascribed. Gospels: First four books of the New Testament. Exact authorship uncertain. First three (Matthew, Mark, Luke) are called Synoptic, as they are very similar in nature and style, while the fourth – John – 'stands apart as the work of one mind'.

Constance set the volume aside and found another with a section devoted to a biblical glossary.

John: One of the disciples with Jesus on the mount of transfiguration (?, look this up). John, Gospel According to: Characterized by long philosophical discourses, in contrast to the short pithy sayings or vivid parables in the first three gospels. Despite recasting Jesus's teachings into a more overtly theological form, it remains concerned with adherence to historical truth (contradiction in terms!?). The author was clearly a man of great intellect and deep reflection. It seems dubious that John, disciple of Jesus and humble Galilean fisherman, wrote the gospel (i.e. too working class!) – though he may have been the source of the author's historical information.

She leaned back in her chair, stretching her arms above her head with the fingers of each hand interlocked. A bone in the base of her neck clicked. John. What was it with the saboteur and John? And which John: 'umble fisherman or intellectual philosopher? This was like being an undergraduate all over again: the more information you looked up, the more you needed to look up. Cross-references, everywhere. She'd been in journalism too long – a reporter's eagerness to wrap up the story, tempered by a historian's patient fascination with digging up facts for facts' sake. *Digging*. Christ, she was even beginning to adopt his terminology. She stood up. There were several versions of the Bible, shelved between an achronological series of Whitaker's Almanacks and Rothman's Football Yearbook, 1971. She selected a copy of the New Testament and turned to the first page of the Gospel According to St John. What did 'opening pronouncement' mean? First verse? What if it contained three clauses – were these to be taken as one pronouncement? *In the beginning was the Word, and the Word was with God, and the Word was God*. Or did the clue refer only to the initial clause? *In the beginning was the Word*. Yes: first clause; first *idea*. She made a note:

IN THE BEGINNING WAS THE WORD

Lastly, Constance consulted a dictionary: transfigure: (verb) to give a new appearance to; to transform outwardly.

* * *

348

The day of the fire bombings, DCI Pink held a press conference. Reporters and photographers from some of the nationals attended, interest whetted by the agency story. One of them, a features writer from the *Guardian*, had spent an hour at the *Crucible*'s Urbopark office gathering background. Constance and William were helpful, friendly; they told him nothing he couldn't have found out for himself from the police or from back copies of the paper. (In the piece the *Guardian* was to carry the next day, she would be misquoted twice and have her surname spelt 'Armory'. They would also get her age wrong – twenty-nine, instead of twenty-five.) At the conference, the chief inspector announced that Donald Anthony Moss, forty-nine, of Old Station Way, Baversedge, near Hallam, would make a preliminary appearance before city magistrates the following morning charged with the theft of an unspecified quantity of poultry from Wainwright & Babcock (Meats) Ltd, Hallam, and on various charges relating to the deposit of said poultry at HypaCenta, Urbopark. With a court hearing pending, DCI Pink hoped the press appreciated his inability to discuss the case further. In anticipation of the journalists' next query, he stated that Mr Moss and another man had been questioned at length in connection with the so-called Urbopark sabotages and had been eliminated from police inquiries. The detective was 'entirely satisfied' that the poultry incident, while coincidental with the first of the attacks, should now be treated as a separate and unrelated matter. He declined to comment on one reporter's remark that the dead chickens were, in fact, a red herring. With regard to the sabotages investigation, DCI Pink confirmed that officers were pursuing several lines of inquiry. Quizzed about motive, he refused to lend credence to any of the reporters' various speculations. (The *Guardian* would describe him as 'saturnine'.)

Constance waited for her fellow journalists to disperse before making her approach. Paul Pink ushered her into an anteroom – used for training, to judge by the neat rows of desks facing a flip-chart perched on a tripod. He lowered the blind over the glass panel in the door. They crossed the room, standing side by side at a window overlooking a parking compound at the rear of the police station. Their breath made patches of condensation on the glass, his the larger and slower to evaporate.

'I can't tell you anything you can use, Connie.'

'How about some of the things you didn't tell *them*.' She nodded in the direction of the other room. 'About Donald Moss and his son, for instance.'

'You know as well as I do—'

'I'm not going to prejudice his trial. It's background I'm after – I mean, we were the ones who put you on to Moss in the first place.'

DCI Pink didn't answer.

'Sorry. I shouldn't have said that. It's just . . .'

'Alibis. Cast iron, for just about any of the sabotages you care to mention – they were both on holiday in Ibiza when some of them took place. Forensic have been through their homes, their offices, their cars, their clothing – and come up with nothing. And the voice analyses from the tapes don't match, nowhere near.'

'But—'

'Donald Moss had a grudge against HypaCenta over the cancellation of the contract – he admits that. But the dead chickens was the extent of the revenge. A stupid one-off, performed while under the influence, to mark the first anniversary of his business going bust.'

'Will he plead guilty?'

'Oh, aye. Lose his job and all, I shouldn't wonder.'

Constance made a mark with her finger in the haze of her own breath, leaving a smear on the window. When she exhaled again the blemish could still be detected beneath the new film of vapour. Three floors below, two uniformed officers were climbing into a patrol car, the clunk-clunk of the doors echoing off the surrounding walls. She watched them drive out of the compound, her forehead pressed against the cold pane. Despite indicating right, the car turned left.

'What about the incendiary devices?' she said. 'Anything there?'

The detective blew his nose on a salmon-pink handkerchief, releasing a strong fragrance of menthol. 'We've had thirty suspicious persons sighted in the car-parks – most likely folk who were lost or tying their shoelaces or waiting for the wife or wiping their nose. As for the descriptions . . .'

'Eyewitness Syndrome?'

He nodded. She used to stand like this at the bedroom window, watching for Dad to come home from work. Only there'd be a net curtain – *lace* curtain, Mam called it – between her forehead and the glass.

'We've had two people come forward *claiming responsibility* for the sabotages. That's just this week. Makes nine false confessions altogether. Never mind those grassing up some poor innocent who's done summat to upset them. One lass shopped her fiancé after a row.'

'You never told me any of this.'

'It's a cry for attention. Course, you've only to ask for the codeword and their story comes apart. I'd do them for wasting police time, but it's help they need.'

'Can we use this stuff? You know, "Police are being hampered in their search for the mall saboteur . . ." type of thing. Might even make a background feature – go into the psychology, and that.'

'And hand the idea to every other nutter who hasn't already thought of it?'

The window vibrated against her forehead, a reverberation caused by the slamming of a door in another part of the building. Her skin was damp, from being in contact with the cold glass and from the condensation. It was making her queasy to look down. She leaned back, away from the window.

'You OK?' he asked.

She studied his semi-transparent reflection: teeth, eyes and shiny pate. 'I should be off. I've the press conference to write up, and there's a chapel meeting.'

'I'd no idea you were a believer.'

'*Union* chapel.' She turned to look at him properly, detecting a suggestion of amusement – in his eyes rather than his lips. There were smiles to be found in Paul Pink, if you knew where to seek them. 'Very funny.'

Coincidences. The dead chickens had *coincided* with the start of the sabotages, but were no longer considered to be linked. A red herring. Serving, at the time, to cause a connection to be made with the daubing of blood over the doors of the mall. But the blood, like the connection, had proven to be synthetic. More significant even than the nature of the 'blood', perhaps, was the word spelled out in its misleading redness. Why 'rage'? All this time spent contemplating Crime, Opportunity, Motive – the mind of the perpetrator, the trail of clues – when the most significant clue of all might be contained in the codeword itself. Rage, French for 'rabies'. Conclusive proof – according, all those weeks ago, to Dorothy's Bert – that the graffiti attack was the work of animal rights activists. Constance consulted a dictionary, finding that beneath the contemporary structures of each word – rage, rabies – were common etymological foundations. Both were rooted in madness. Another co-incidence: while she was at the chapel meeting Constance got out a notebook, ready to record the minutes, and a leaflet fell from between the pages. It was one of those on St Dunstan's Chapel, handed to her by Revd Beverley. She'd forgotten it was there. Reading the leaflet, she learnt that the patron saint of goldsmiths and metalworkers was usually represented carrying a pair of pincers. According to legend, the Devil asked Dunstan to shoe his single hoof – whereupon, Dunstan seized the Devil by the nose with a pair of red-hot tongs and refused to release him until he promised never again to enter a place where he saw a horseshoe displayed. So, an additional co-incidence: a reference to the legendary origins of the 'lucky horseshoe' shortly after she'd seen the one presented to Granddad by a grateful museum visitor. On their way back to Urbopark from the union meeting, Constance mentioned the legend of St Dunstan to William. New one on him. He'd read somewhere that the horseshoe was considered to be a protection against evil because it was made from iron, and Mars – an alchemical symbol for iron – was the mythological enemy of the God of Witches, namely Saturn.

An aroma of cooking: a tomatoey, oniony, meaty smell impregnated with a subtle though not immediately identifiable blend of herbs and spices. Music was playing, though Constance was insufficiently familiar with classical works to name either composer or composition. She surveyed the semi-basement flat; little more than a glorified bedsit – the narrow kitchen separated from the lounge only by a breakfast counter. The lounge itself was divided into 'sleeping' and 'sitting' areas, not by any partition but by the strategic arrangement of furniture – two armchairs, an occasional table, a CD player, a desk upon which a word processor sat, various potted plants and a tall standard lamp – positioned in such a way as to create the illusion of screening off that part of the room from the double bed which stood against the farthest wall. Two doors led off from this bedsitting room. One, with items of outdoor wear hanging from hooks, was the front door; the other, she presumed, gave access to a bathroom. Constance, perched on a high stool at the counter, sipped from a glass of red. Stanley Bell stood at the cooker, stirring the contents of a saucepan.

'D'you like Chopin?' he said.

'Not especially. All those crowds, and I always spend more than I should.'

'*Chopin*, not . . . oh, OK . . . right. OK.' Not laughter so much as a guttural explosion; a great belch of amusement. 'Walked right into that one!'

The wine was good, as far as she could tell. Not too acidic

or vinegary, unlike the reds she usually bought if she bought wine at all. She chose drink according to price. *Tell me, Connie, do you have a favourite wine?* Howard's mam – mother – had once asked at the dinner table. *I like two forty-nines quite a lot*, she'd replied. *Some two ninety-nines aren't bad*. The woman's face had frozen. Stan, too, fancied himself as something of a connoisseur, going by his expression when he removed the tissue from the bottle Constance had brought. Australian white, on special offer – a selection inspired by the professor's Antipodean connection. He'd disguised his reaction well, standing the bottle on the floor beside a full wine rack and suggesting they drink his red – on account of the fact they were having spaghetti Bolognese. Fine by her. There followed a brief anecdote about a German-speaking community in the wine-growing region of South Australia, the descendants of a group of Lutherans who'd fled persecution in Europe. *Barossa Valley, north of Adelaide. You'd think you were stepping back in time – the language, the buildings. Like a small piece of nineteenth-century Germany transplanted into 1990s Oz.* By the time they'd moved on to another topic, her bottle of cheap Aussie plonk had been forgotten.

'I had you down as a beer man.'

'Oh, in pubs, yeah. But with food . . .' He let the sentence trail off. Patting his belly, he added, 'Have to keep an eye on this.'

'Wine's fattening too, isn't it?'

'But it doesn't *feel* fattening. I feel – when I'm drinking beer, I feel like I'm filling up. All bloated. You don't get that with wine.'

He was in brown cords and a blue-and-green striped shirt with one wing of the collar buttoned down and the other sticking out at a right-angle. The trousers bagged, as usual, around the ankles. He looked neater, though – his beard and hair showed signs of a recent trim. Suited him, shorter. Unlike hers, which was an absolute disaster. Nineteen ninety-nine to have your hair set about with a pair of sheep shears by a sixteen-year-old trainee who spent the *entire time* wittering to her colleague about . . . what? About *nothing*. The headscarf had been Milly's idea, fashioned into a thin strip and tied up and over so that all her hair except the fringe was swept back from her face. Constance watched Stan, the casual – almost slapdash – manner in which he attended to the cooking. She made herself more comfortable on the stool, smoothing her skirt. She'd never kissed a man with a beard. Prickly, she imagined. Tickly. One day's stubble was enough, with Howard, to leave her face pink about the mouth like a messy child who'd been flannel-scrubbed after eating too much strawberry ice cream. More wine. If the meal wasn't ready soon she'd be squiffy. Already a little light-headed and becoming chatty, a surge of words backing up inside her.

'Sure I can't help with anything?'

'All under control, thanks. I did the salad before class and bunged it in the fridge.' He glanced up from the pan of Bolognese sauce and smiled, lowering his voice to a conspiratorial whisper. 'And the garlic bread's shop-bought, from HypaCenta.'

'I didn't know you shopped at Urbopark?'

'Spent more time looking for the supermarket and trying to find my way out of the mall afterwards than I did shopping.'

'It does take some getting—'

'Couldn't find the car, either. I forgot where I'd parked it – wandering around Pink Upper when I should've been looking in Grey Lower.'

'There *isn't* a Grey Zone.'

'Green, then; whatever. What happens if you're colour blind?' He laughed. 'There must be dozens of colour-blind shoppers doomed to spend the rest of their lives lost in the wrong car-park at that place.'

Stan switched attention to a pan of pasta on a back ring, adjusting the burner and giving the contents a stir with the same spoon he'd been using for the sauce.

'I love gas,' he said. 'Instant reaction. With electric, you turn the heat down and it takes the cooker two bloody days to cotton on. Meanwhile, major boil-over.'

Constance smiled. 'You didn't get back to find your car on fire?'

'I *saw* that story.' He stopped what he was doing. As he turned to look at her, she noticed that his glasses had filmed over with steam. He removed them, wiping each lens in turn on a tea towel. 'There was something in the *Guardian* as well. One of my students got a mention, young lady by the name of *Ar*mory.'

'Don't know her.'

Stan put his glasses back on. He took two plates from the grill shelf, where they'd been warming above the saucepans, and placed them on table-mats on the breakfast counter. He set cutlery and side-plates and replenished Constance's wine, without asking, as well as his own. Quick slurp. Lifting a large earthenware bowl of mixed salad from the fridge, he peeled off the cling-film cover and put the bowl down between the dinner plates. The pair of wooden servers were hand-carved, he said, their long handles depicting figures from the Aboriginal dreamtime.

'Traditional native Australian craft, making salad spoons for Melbourne's white middle classes.' He held up two bottles of dressing. 'French or Italian?'

She chose French, watching her host pour liberally over the salad before using the servers to rough up the contents of the bowl. A leaf of curly lettuce spilled onto the counter, gleaming with oil. *'Scuse fingers*. He popped it back in and continued mixing. His sleeves were turned back beyond the wrist, folded so tightly that the material appeared to be pinching the flesh. Snagged in the hairs at the base of his right thumb joint was a shred of raw onion no bigger than a fingernail clipping.

'You hungry?'

'Starving.'

He served up the pasta and sauce and retrieved the garlic stick from the oven, drenching the kitchen with its pungent aroma. They ate, sitting diagonally opposite one another to allow room for their knees beneath the narrow counter. No conversation at first, apart from a brief discussion over choice of music when the Chopin concluded. Giuseppe Verdi. *Joe Green*, as Stan called him. He reduced the volume slightly. On returning to his stool, he clicked off the kitchen light so that the only illumination was provided by the softer glow from the wall-lamps in the adjoining lounge.

'You're wearing your hair differently,' he said.

'Yeah, it's . . . I had it cut – today, I mean – and it's . . . well, to be honest, it was a bit of a last-minute salvage operation.'

'Looks nice. Stylish touch, the headscarf. Sophisticated.'

'Oh, please.'

'Seriously.'

She concentrated on her plate, twirling the fork among the mass of spaghetti and testing for stray strands – *dangly bits*, according to Milly – before raising the food tentatively to her lips. Stan, meanwhile, hoisted great tangles of pasta into his mouth, reeling in the loose ends with a series of swift sucks. Every now and then he'd dab at his beard with a cloth napkin. His apparent lack of embarrassment infected her, and she began to eat with less inhibition. Delicious. She told him so. He said any credit was due to his ex-wife, who was Italian. *Taught me to cook, then walked out.* They talked about the former Mrs Bell – referred to only as 'she' or 'her', never by name – and about his children. He didn't volunteer a reason for her departure, Constance didn't ask. She cast an eye around the lounge, seeking in vain for family photographs. Stan opened a second bottle.

'D'you mind me dredging up my past like this?'

'It's your *present* too, isn't it? The children, I mean.'

'Sure. Yeah, sure.' He refilled their glasses. 'Even her, I suppose. You never entirely manage to bury things.'

'No.'

'How about you, any skelingtons in your cupboard?'

357

Skelingtons. She helped herself to more salad, shaking off the excess oil over the bowl. The radishes were sliced so thinly as to be almost translucent; the cucumber too. Which was a surprise, because he struck her as the sort of haphazard cook – the sort of *man* – who'd chop vegetables into rough chunks. The Aboriginal salad servers were heavy, ugly; awkward to use. She didn't look up. She was peripherally aware of him staring across the counter at her, elbows propped either side of his plate and a wine glass cradled in his hands. How long had she taken to answer? Ages. It seemed like ages, though it couldn't have been more than a few seconds; the time it took to transfer a helping of salad from bowl to plate. She cleared her throat.

'Not skeletons, as such.'

'Sorry, I'm prying.'

'No, no. It's just . . . you know, like you say, you can't always bury the past.'

'Yeah.'

'That's why I'm interested in history, I think. Partly. This idea that while actual events may be, I suppose, *located* in the past – you know, over and done with *as events* – their reverberations are still with us.'

Drunk, and spouting rubbish. She glanced up. Stan's face was a blank of concentration, to be interpreted in any way she chose.

'So the past is also to be found in the present. Is that what you're saying?' he said. 'And in the future too, by logical extension.'

'Yes. Sort of.'

'And how long do these past *reverberations* take to fade? To disappear without trace, would you say?'

'I don't know. It depends. I don't know that they ever do, really.'

'Then there's the problem of selection – which bits of the past do we choose to keep alive and which do we consign to the historical dustbin.'

Constance broke off a piece of garlic bread and pressed it

between her lips. Her fingers were greasy, flecked with bread-crumbs and flakes of oregano. 'It's not always a matter of choice, though, is it? I mean, with – like – *people*, people from our past, we can't always control what . . . the extent to which we forget them. They're still there, *here* . . .' She pointed to her temple. '. . . Whether we like it or not.'

Stan nodded, without comment. They both resumed eating. For want of something to say, she paid another compliment to the food. *Too hurried*, he said; she'd have to come again on a night when there was no class, so he would have time to *knock up something special*. They discussed the evening's session, Constance making a joke about the Crashing Boer. The *Con Amore* man, who'd bothered her in the college canteen that time, had provided the talking point of the latest class with a tirade provoked by one of Stan's more blatantly political obser-vations. To everyone's amusement, the student had terminated his diatribe by calling the tutor a *pinko dinosaur* and storming out of the room with a melodramatic flourish. More shocking had been Stan's reaction, hurling a textbook at the door in the instant after it had shut. Stunned silence engulfed the class. The professor became uncharacteristically confused for a moment, eventually going over to retrieve the crumpled book and muttering his apologies. Reminding him of the episode appeared to rekindle Stan's embarrassment. Constance was about to change the subject when she was waylaid by hiccups. Too much talking, combined with an excess of wine.

'Hold your breath and swallow four times.'

She followed his suggestion. By the third swallow, she'd run out of saliva and was gasping for air. Shaking her head, she said, 'I can't.' The 'can't' was split into two syllables by another hiccup – which made her laugh, which made her hiccup. He fetched a glass of water and told her to pinch her nose while she drank.

'Take small sips, and try to hold your diaphragm in.'

How d'you do that? She tensed her stomach muscles and sipped from the glass. The water was cold, with a faint metallic

359

tang. It didn't work. Stan stood up and walked round to her side of the counter, getting her to sit up straight while he thumped her back. Gentle, repetitive blows with the heel of his hand, the way Mam used to pummel her ribs to ease her breathing during an asthma attack. Constance closed her eyes, sensing her body swaying back and forth in synchronization with his hand. He stopped, the flat of his palm spread between her shoulder blades. Not massaging, not moving at all; just resting there without applying any pressure beyond mere weight of contact. She could feel its warmth through the thin cotton of her shirt.

'Gone?'

'I think so.'

She paused, regulating her breathing. No hiccups. She opened her eyes, leaning forward slightly in the instant when Stan withdrew his hand. Where his palm had lain, a lingering impression remained – so real it was as if he still touched her. Christmas Day, you took off your party hat at the end of the meal and, for a moment, you experienced the illusion you were still wearing it. *Daft*, Dad said. *It's just wheer t'hair's been flattened against thi scalp*. Stan continued to stand behind her. She sensed him, she could hear his shallow breaths. If she leaned back again would contact be restored, or had he withdrawn his hand altogether? She wanted to turn round, her face upturned towards his. No she didn't. What she wanted was for *him* to turn her, to place a hand on her shoulder and turn her round on the stool to face him. But in the split second when either of these things might've happened, he moved away. Her back, where it had been warm, became cold – as though chilled in a draught from the open window. She shivered. The loo. She needed the loo. Excusing herself, she got down carefully and made her way across the lounge with the steadiness of someone trying to conceal the impact of drink. Behind her, she could hear him stacking plates in the sink.

The bathroom suite was avocado, to complement the intricately patterned green wallpaper; bath, wash-basin and toilet shining as though recently scrubbed. Undispersed traces of cleaning fluid and air-freshener mingled to give the room its almost overpowering fragrance of floral antiseptic. No window, no natural light or ventilation. As soon as she'd pulled the light cord, an extractor fan had clattered into action in imitation of an ailing aircraft. Constance inspected her face in the mirrored doors of a cabinet above the basin. Waxy. Her eyes looked tired, pouchy; wisps of hair had escaped here and there from the confines of the headscarf. She tilted her head to decrease the prominence of her jowls. Sitting on the toilet, she surveyed the room in more detail. The peach loo roll clashed with the colour scheme, as did the towels draped over a hot-rail – one yellow, one red-and-white striped and bearing a Hallam United insignia. Newspapers and magazines were stacked in the space between the WC and the bath – mostly old *Guardians*, mixed in with the odd *Crucible, New Statesman* and *Private Eye*. A framed John Waterhouse print hung on one wall: an exquisite auburn-haired woman in an evident state of rapture as she inhaled the scent of a rose. A spider plant and two cacti sat on a shelf above the bath. On another wall was a verse in a clip-frame. She couldn't make out the words because of the reflection on the glass. She finished peeing and went over to have a closer look. A rhyme – not a poem so much as a slogan of political protest, which brought a smile of recognition:

> The law arrests the man or woman,
> Who steals the goose from off the common;
> But leaves the greater rascal loose,
> Who steals the common from the goose.

No attribution, but she identified it as dating from the time of the Tolpuddle Martyrs. Eighteen . . . what? Thirty-something. Thirty-four. Yes, 1834. The year the men were transported. Stan had made a passing reference to the agricultural workers' cause in his lecture earlier on, setting the metalworking industries' trades unionism in what he termed its sociopolitical context. *Land*. He'd said the history of *working folk's struggle* was all about *the ownership of land and the ownership of the means of production which takes place on that land*. She'd written it down in her notebook, under the heading QUOTE OF THE WEEK. This remark, and the debate which followed, were to culminate in the scene with the Crashing Boer.

Constance washed her hands. She checked her face again; could do with a wash, but that would mean reapplying her make-up and she didn't have any here with her in the bathroom. She made do with dabbing at the shinier patches of forehead, nose and chin with the dampened corner of a towel. Breath. Her breath reeked of garlic. She used Stan's toothbrush and paste, then opened the cabinet in search of mouthwash. The shelves were crammed with spare bars of soap, tubes of ointment, a hairbrush with a stainless steel comb wedged between its teeth, a bottle of anti-dandruff shampoo, a can of deodorant, talcum powder, a small grey pumice stone, nail scissors, tweezers, nail file, a box of Wilkinson's Sword razor blades, athlete's foot powder and a strip of Elastoplast. No mouthwash. Shit. She cleaned her teeth for a second time.

'You OK in there?'

'Coming!'

She unbolted the bathroom door and stepped outside. Stan was setting a tray down on the occasional table in the bedsitting area.

'No pud, I'm afraid. Unless you want fruit. Fruit meaning "an apple", basically.' He smiled, standing a glass and chrome cafetière on a wicker mat and placing two mugs on coasters. 'Or there's cheese and biscuits, minus the biscuits.'

'Coffee's fine.'

'I thought we'd lost you to the troglodytes.'

'The what?'

'When I was a lad, my mother told me there were goblins living in caves under our house and if I spent too long in the lav they'd climb out the bowl and kidnap me.'

362

Constance laughed. 'It was spiders with my mam. Right up till I went to university I couldn't use the loo without putting the plugs in the bath and wash-basin.'

'Grab a pew.' Stan indicated one of the armchairs. They sat down. He checked if she wanted milk or sugar (yes, no), then depressed the plunger in the cafetière and poured. 'There you go. Nicaraguan. *Not* from Urbopark.'

'Thanks.' The coffee tasted of Colgate minty gel. 'I was reading your Toldpuddle Martyrs thingy, about the goose and the common.'

'I wrote a book about them while I was in Oz. About what happened to them after they were transported.'

'Yeah?'

'Seemed too good a chance to miss, being Down Under and having access to the historical records. Also, there was an *affinity*, I suppose you'd call it. I've always seen myself as something of a transportee, albeit the exile was self-imposed.'

'How come you came back?'

'Ah. Long story.' He slapped the arm of his chair. 'Bugger! We've not had the parmesan cheese. I grated some to have with the spag. bol. It's still in the fridge.'

'Oh well.'

'Buggeration!'

'Stan, the meal was *lovely*. Really lovely, even without the ptarmigan.'

'Ptarmigan?'

'Mags, my kid sister – Margaret – she couldn't say "parmesan". Couldn't say spaghetti either. "Pasgetti".' She smiled at him. '*Skelington* was another one.'

'As in, "skelington in the cupboard"?'

'Exactly.'

'You, um . . .' Stan had removed his glasses and, for the first time that evening, was clicking one of the earpieces between his teeth. He laid the glasses on the table, as though suddenly irritated by his own habit. 'You never did get round to answering that one.'

'I thought I did.'

'OK.' He scratched his beard. 'See, I don't know whether you answered the question you *thought* I was asking or the one I was *actually* asking. By that, I mean the one at the surface or the one beneath the surface. If you follow me.'

Constance had to suppress a giggle. This was like being sixteen all over again. Which was nice. It was *nice* to feel like a sixteen-year-old. The elaborate convolutions of two people plotting alternative routes to the centre of the same maze. *Knowing.* Knowing that the other person knew as well, and knew that *you* knew. She was drunk.

'Yes to the latter, no to the former,' she said.

He laughed loudly. 'Now *I'm* confused.'

'What I'm saying . . . right, OK, we're at the surface: do I have any skeletons in my romantic cupboard? Answer: yes. The question beneath the surface is: is that a problem now? As in here, tonight. Is that the question I *thought* you were asking?'

'Yes.'

'Well, the answer is "no". The skeleton is in the cupboard, where it belongs.'

'For the time being.'

'Which makes us even, doesn't it?'

'Sorry, stupid thing to say.'

'No, it's not.'

It was. It was a stupid, insecure, possessive, immature and very human thing to say; stupid, because it was the sort of thought that usually went unsaid. But at certain crucial moments you could choose to rebuff or to reassure. And she chose to reassure. Momentarily, his years of seniority peeled away and he became the student, the one seeking guidance. Her voice softened.

'It isn't stupid.'

He put on another disc. The CD player and the computer were his but more or less everything else came with the flat, which had been supplied by the university. *Bit dingy, being a semi-basement. But closer to Oz, at least!* He halted, seemingly embarrassed at his own embarrassment. Excusing himself, he disappeared clumsily into the bathroom with an invitation to Constance to help herself to more coffee. Quarter to twelve. She took off the headscarf and shook her hair loose, frisking it with her fingers. Footsteps overhead, someone in the upstairs flat; oblivious to her presence, her concerns, her existence. She got up and went over to the solitary bookcase. Mostly historical works, including several written by her host; another one in progress, a stack of typescript in a wire tray next to the word processor. One shelf was devoted to books on Hallam, its steel and cutlery trades, the history of trades unionism in the metalworking industries. She recognized some from the background reading list he'd handed out at the first evening class. There was also a dictionary, a world atlas, a handful of political biographies (Benn, Attlee, Keir Hardie, Marx); some fiction (Arnold Bennett, Dickens, Orwell, Lawrence). She selected one of his own titles – *Labour Pains: The Birth of Industrial Revolt*, by Prof. S. F. Bell, F.R. Hist. S. – and turned to the dustjacket flap. His middle name was *Francis*. Frank. The mugshot depicted a younger Stan: bearded and bespectacled, but thinner of face and less sunworn. His hair was darker, though this might've been a trick of the light, or a consequence of the black-and-white photography. She checked the date of publication, calculating that the picture was at least twelve years old. She'd have been thirteen when it was taken. Nice smile. *You can tell a lot about folk by their smile*, Mam reckoned. And Stan had a nice smile. Still had. She was about to read the biographical blurb beneath the photo when the author emerged in person from the bathroom. He drew up alongside her. Her knees clicked as she stood up.

'Old bones,' she said.

'Hardly.'

The beard did tickle. And his breath, when they kissed, smelt so distinctly of toothpaste she could scarcely detect any hint of garlic whatsoever.

The Life and Times of a Hallam Saw Grinder (a Dramatic Reconstruction in Many Parts)

October 1866

The stretch of river was little altered in the years since Daniel Amory used to swim there on summer afternoons with his brother and friends. Its course still described a familiar, gentle curve amidst pasture that was prone to flooding in winter but which provided lush grazing for cattle during milder seasons. Cows were cropping at the grass on this day, initial curiosity at the intrusion of two men into their field having given way to bovine indifference. To Daniel's eye they might have been the same herd which browsed here when he was a boy. The grassy knoll where he and his fellows would lounge wetly naked seemed unchanged; the narrow strip of mud-flat where the ground declined towards the water's edge looked as it did then; the weeping willow wept as profusely as ever. And, on the opposite bank, stood the old oak with its overhanging branch from which they would take turns to swing at the end of a rope before plunging in with a great splash. There was no rope now but the outstretched limb remained scarred by a ring of exposed wood, its bark irrevocably chafed.

As he and his father unpacked their fishing tackle, Daniel tried to calculate how many years had elapsed since he was last here. More than five, he estimated – recalling an outing one sweltering day in the summer before he had become apprenticed. Now, approaching his seventeenth birthday, he had returned as angler rather than bather; though seeing the clear water glimmering with chips of reflected sunlight he savoured a momentary temptation to strip off his clothes and leap in. What had surprised him was the length of time they took to walk out from the town, a journey that had seemed so much the shorter when he was a boy. No more than two miles,

following the long straight road that ran parallel to the river
from the hay market, out beyond The Ponds and Pond Forge
and the riverside straggle of works, dams, tilt yards and
sawmills, until – almost imperceptibly – the buildings yielded
to fields and woodland. Yet it must have taken them an hour
to reach the break in the hedgerows, where a farm track cut
a path to this secluded stretch. Daniel had grown accustomed
of late – at home and at work – to his father's debilitation, the
walk to the Wheel or the climbing of stairs sufficient to render
his breathing painfully audible. However, he had been ill
prepared to witness the effects of travelling two miles on foot,
weighed down by fishing paraphernalia. During one of many
pauses along the way, Thomas Amory had remarked in jest
to his son:

'I've the body of a man o' thirty-five . . . and t'lungs of a
sixty-year-old!'

The general commotion of the two men's arrival had caused
a family of moorhens to evacuate to the opposite side of the
river, only the red markings on their heads visible in the gloom
of a grassy overhang. It was possible, during the course of the
day, that they would see reed warblers and dippers, or a
kingfisher; though for the moment the only birdlife in obvious
attendance was a pair of blackbirds who had perched upon a
nearby hedge – apparently fascinated by the boxes of live bait
from which father and son were loading their hooks. Daniel
was first to cast, not out of greater proficiency but for want of
the older man's unhurried manner. Such characteristic predisposition to impatience was a recurring source of conflict
between them – especially at work, where five years under his
father's tuition had so far failed to instil in him an attention
to detail. The frequent charge was that he could not grind one
saw blade without thinking of it in relation to how many others
there were to be done and how many hours there were in
which to do them. Daniel was not unusual in this respect. It
was a constant cause of exasperation for Thomas to hear the
apprentices at their lunch break boasting to one another how

many boxes of saws they had cleared that day, that week, that month. Jasper's temperament would have been better suited to the work, but the younger Amory brother had turned his back on grinding to take a situation as apprentice to a crucible team at the Eagle Ironworks. The boys once heard their father remark that he knew not which was worse: having a son who *could not* grind, or one that *would not*. Daniel had a belt round the ear for replying that, seeing how his father could not decide, he ought to be content to have one of each.

As they sat a few yards apart, Daniel propped his fishing rod on a forked stick. His hands free, he worked away with his thumbnail at the edges of a scab that had formed on the knuckle of the middle finger of his right hand. The cut, turned bad at first, was only now beginning to heal. Challenged by his father to account for the injury, Daniel had explained it away as the consequence of drunken fisticuffs between lads from the Union Wheel and a group of others at the Moseley's Arms, in West Bar. The damage had been insufficiently serious to impede him greatly at his work, so Thomas had said no more about it. It was only now, amidst the tranquillity and companionship of the riverside, that the young man felt inclined to unburden himself.

'Dost thou know a man by the name of Samuel Crookes?'

Thomas looked askance at his son. 'Aye, what of him?'

'A saw grinder.'

'Aye, thou couldst call him that.'

'He had me and one or two more lads do some work for him.'

'What sort of work?'

'We had five shillings each from him for it.'

'Aye an' some other sod got crowned an' all, I should say.'

Daniel smiled. 'Fearnehough.'

'Thomas Fearnehough? The knobstick?'

'That's him.'

'He hast t'other half of that, does he?' asked Thomas,

indicating his son's scabrous cut, weeping now from being picked at.

'Aye.'

How long was it since he had had dealings with Crookes? More years than Thomas cared to recall. He tried to recreate, in his mind, his erstwhile friend's cabbage-like face and comical gait; the times they went rabbiting in the woods. But along with these images came others: Linley, slumped at a table, a hole blown in his temple; Robert Smith, sobbing in the doorway one night with a woman's charred flesh in his hands. Thomas's nostrils filled with the stench of chewing tobacco and raw onion and the oil Sammy used to lubricate the shooting mechanism of his rifle. He studied his son. Seventeen years old. He wanted to make it so that the boy had lived the life of his father, so that he would know the world for what it was without having to find out for himself. He wanted Daniel to be a child again, all spindly limbs and freckles.

'Since when hast Sammy Crookes been using thee for Society business?'

'He hast not, before this once.' Daniel hesitated before adding: 'He tellt me thou hast done union work in thy time and would I want to follow in thy footsteps?'

Thomas turned his face towards the river. The son did likewise. They sat in silence, staring at the dappled surface. Their floats – whittled from cork for them by Robert Smith – wavered in the sluggish current. When at last Thomas spoke, his voice was so hushed that his son had to strain to make out the words.

'There are men in this world worse than Sammy Crookes, and Fearnehough is one such,' he said. 'If thou wilt take part in rolling men up or giving them a smite, then thou art a man now and thou can do what thou wilt.'

'Aye it's bloody well-paid work, an' all!' Daniel laughed. His amusement died in his throat with one look from his father, and when he spoke again it was a blushing embarrassment of apology. 'I'm only sayin', like . . . aye, I know. I know.'

369

Thomas continued to hold the young man's gaze, daring him to look away. 'What I ask,' he said, 'is that thou hast nowt to do wi' shooting or wi' making explosions.'

'Aye.'

'Promise me.'

'Aye, I promise.'

The father's voice hardened. 'And never tell me thou wouldst be a rattener – or owt else – for the mere filling of thy pocket with shillings.'

Royal Commission of Inquiry (sitting at) Hallam Town Hall Friday, 7 June 1867 (Fifth Day)

Witness: Charles Staniforth, Saw Grinder, No.18 Joiner Street, Hallam.

Q. You work, do you not, for a firm by the name of Messrs Hague, Clegg & Barton?

A. I do, and have done so for a number of years on and off.

Q. What is their business?

A. The manufacture of saws and files and machine knives.

Q. Did a man called Thomas Fearnehough work for Hague's as a saw grinder?

A. He did.

Q. At which Wheel did he work?

A. At Rayner's, in The Park.

Q. Why at that Wheel in particular?

A. On account of him being wrong with his union.

Q. Of what consequence was that to Hague's?

A. Fearnehough warned they would be rattened for engaging him, and there was talk of someone wanting to blow him up. So the firm took out troughs for him at Rayner's.

Q. Could he not be as easily rattened or blown up there as anywhere else?

A. Rayner's is less easily got at than The Park Wheel or Kenyon's, where Hague's has its other troughs.

Q. How was Fearnehough wrong with the union?

A. Because he was always in arrears with his natty. He is one of those, when he is in work he pays no money into the Society yet when he is out of work he is happy to draw his scale like the rest of us. Also, he is a knobstick.

Q. How is he a knobstick?

A. While he was at Hague's the handle-makers there were not paying to the trade and he was offered money, I believe, to roll up their bands.

Q. Did he do this?

A. He did not. He told the firm so that they could guard against it.

Q. Who offered him money, was it the Society or who was it?

A. I cannot say.

Q. Was an attempt made to blow up Fearnehough's trough in June, 1863?

A. I believe it was.

Q. Has Fearnehough ever expressed to you at any time his fear of injury being done to himself? Or was he reckless that it might be done?

A. He told me he would not pay any more while Broadhead was secretary, and that he would see him at hell first. It is not very good language, but I tell you what he said.

Q. You were all very angry with Fearnehough, were you?

A. We did not like his not paying and our paying.

Q. Have you ever been at any meeting of the committee where Fearnehough's conduct has been mentioned?

A. It was mentioned when he got drunk.

Q. I did not ask you that. I asked if the men in the union complained much about Fearnehough? Did they call him a 'knobstick'?

A. Yes, and they would call him worse than that sometimes.

Q. What else did they call him?

A. They called him a d----d thief.

Q. Whom have you heard call him a d----d thief?

A. Several of them; they cannot call him a good name.

*　　*　　*

What Samuel Crookes enjoyed about entertaining new visitors at his home in The Wicker was the opportunity it afforded him to brag about the dwelling's status as 'an historical monument'. It was invariably unnecessary to guide the conversation towards this topic – the condition of the day-room being sufficient to provoke anyone entering for the first time to remark upon it unbidden. So it was that Daniel Amory, on being ushered indoors by Sammy one Sunday morning, became the latest to prompt his host into boastful anecdote. Setting foot inside the room, the overwhelming dampness in the air was immediately obvious; but this in itself would not have aroused curiosity had it not been for the distinctive tidemark. The wallpaper, an otherwise unremarkable beige symmetrically patterned with reddish-brown floral motifs, was divided by a thick horizontal line skirting the room at waist height. Below this mark, the paper was faded and stained, irregularly discoloured, and peeling away in numerous places.

'What's the cause of that?' enquired Daniel, unwittingly echoing the queries of every previous newcomer to the house.

Sammy was glad to explain, in the engaging and melo-dramatic manner of a practised storyteller, that his home had fallen victim to the infamous Hallam Flood two and a half years earlier. He drew attention to a point on the wall where he had had someone of more scholarly bent than himself inscribe the date '11 March, 1864' along the line of the tidemark. Daniel knew of the flood, as did every man, woman and child in a town where 250 of its citizens perished and hundreds of homes and buildings were swept away with the bursting of Dale Dyke Dam. Indeed, the Amory boys and their father had stood on Lady's Bridge on the day following the disaster to view the spectacle of The Wicker awash with mud and rubble and dead cattle and the arches of the great viaduct by Victoria Station altogether blocked with flood-borne debris. Daniel listened with fascination as Sammy recounted how – awoken by the thunderous din outside – he had come down from his bed chamber during the early hours to discover the parlour filling with filthy brown water that continued to rise to the level of the window-sill before abating. Unable to quit the house, he had remained in the uppermost storey for several hours watching the dramatic events unfold from the window. The street was a raging river of uprooted trees, timber, building rubble, broken furniture and floating corpses; the blockage in the arches causing the water to rise up so that it broke over the parapets of the bridge itself. In the weeks and months that followed, residents and shopkeepers in the neighbourhood had cleaned, repaired and restored their premises as best they could; but Sammy – apart from replacing sodden rugs and ruined furniture – had left his day-room walls (in particular, the tidemark) as permanent testimony to the flood.

'One day, a hundred years from now, I shouldn't wonder that they turn this house into a museum,' he told Daniel. 'A brass plate on t'wall outside will say: Here lived a saw grinder by the name of Samuel Crookes.'

They laughed at the notion, Sammy – pale and unshaven – giving full rein to a high-pitched snicker that reminded his companion of a whinnying horse. The host gestured at his guest to join him at a table set against the back wall. Daniel, though less than half the other man's age, was a full head taller than Sammy and had to take care not to catch his head on an iron candle-holder suspended from the ceiling. The table was covered with a coarse brown cloth, and cluttered with the detritus of the man's meal from the previous night. Clearing away the plates and cutlery and leftovers, Sammy returned a moment later from the kitchen with a wooden spoon, two paper parcels and an empty metal canister. Seated side by side at the table, the two men measured off a portion of the contents of one of the parcels into the tin. The remainder they combined with the contents of the other packet, with the intention – explained the older man – of selling it on as unadulterated gunpowder; and making a tidy profit for themselves on the sum Broadhead had paid them.

Chapter Thirteen

SHOP TALK

First Woman: We had a thirty-six-hour stopover in
               Singapore on t'way back from our Lawrie's.
Second Woman: Time for a spot of shopping, then?
First Woman: Oh, aye. Well, there's nowt else to do there.

Constance ordered more coffee. Her head ached from too much wine and too little sleep, her eyes were three times too large for their sockets and had been dabbed with pepper or sand or something. She was sore. Chattanooga Choo-Choo. The tune would revolve in her head for the rest of the day, one of those irritatingly catchy melodies with which the Cocoa Foundry liked to drown out the mall's persistent muzak. It was the rhythm of the train, chug-chugging along the line. A logical and irresistible progression from A to B to C, right through to Z. To *Zee*. Like a train of thought. Which, she supposed, was where the expression came from. Only, when did thoughts ever proceed in a straight line? Not often. Not with her, anyway. She watched a Gatsbyesque waitress sashaying swivel-hipped and sexily slim towards her table in time to the music, bearing coffee. She invited Constance to *enjoy*. Christ almighty her head was peeling apart. Eleven-thirty. She'd have to head back soon, for second edition. Good coffee, strong. Ought to be, at one ninety-nine a pot. She rummaged in her handbag for the pack of paracetamol she knew to be in there somewhere but had earlier been unable to find. There it was, wedged among bank statements and a council tax payments booklet. A single, unwrapped, honey and lemon-flavoured throat lozenge had adhered itself to the box of tablets. The powdery aftertaste of the paracetamol almost made her retch. A sudden garlicky flush of saliva in the back of her throat.

She wanted to cry. Why? No idea. No definite idea. Just a general sense of the imminence of tears, a pervasive melancholy of sadness and tiredness and aloneness. She was so bloody, fucking *alone*. Don't blink. Her clothes felt stale and crumpled, though she'd taken care even in her inebriated impatience to arrange them on hangers last night and to freshen them up this morning with his iron. And she'd showered with his soap, drenched herself with his deodorant. *Gillette, the best a man can get*. Still, she felt grubby and unkempt. The possibility of tears must've suggested itself, unconsciously, or else why would she be sitting there drinking coffee by herself instead of brewing up at the office with William and Sally? Nothing to do with tears, it was to do with not wanting to talk to anyone. Not wanting to talk to *them*. About *this*. A glass-walled lift descended from upper mall to lower, disappearing into a jungle of decorative foliage. The sky above the high glass roof brightened suddenly, sharpening the intensity of light in the plaza. Her eyes narrowed, her back prickled with perspiration. How long had she slept? Three or four hours in total, dissected into fragments of slumber that reminded her of long nights spent in overheated, jolting train compartments while she was Inter-Railing round Europe. In the hour before they finally got up, she'd lain awake on her back staring up at the blank expanse of ceiling.

Coffee. She touched her face, her lips, with tentative dabs; seeking evidence of him. Had it been like this after the first time with Howard – an awkwardness over breakfast, a clumsy goodbye, a sense of desolation? No it hadn't, because it had been a Saturday night and they'd spent the next day in bed, not surfacing until late in the afternoon. His place, though. The same sense of unfamiliarity, of newness, of the uncertainty that arises when something – some*one* – is so fragile in its newness you concede the possibility of its destruction. How was it that a beginning managed also to embody an impression of ending? Milly's theory was that the first time you met a man, or slept with him, you glimpsed – albeit fractionally, subliminally – what it was between you that would ultimately cause your division.

The waitress, *her* waitress, was cleaning the adjacent table in a series of vigorous circular sweeps. It was the table Constance and Howard had shared – when? – all those weeks ago; she'd had a tuna sandwich, he'd had chicken. *Fowling In Love Again*. A smile. A mother, father and three children were standing behind the Please Wait To Be Seated sign. One of the children, a boy aged about four, was wearing a replica blue-and-white Hallam City kit. The shirt was out of date, emblazoned with the imprint of the previous season's sponsor and the name of a player who'd since been transferred to another club. The Charleston. They were playing the Charleston now. What Constance wanted was not to be alone, but to be with him. Stan. Stanley Bell. Professor S.F. Bell, F.R. Hist. S. If she could be with him now, talking to him, this feeling of loss would dissolve – resolve itself – into a feeling of gain; because he'd tell her what she wanted to hear. And what she wanted to hear was what *he* felt, what he was thinking, what it meant – what *she* meant – to him. If Stan was here, everything would be transfigured. Her coffee had gone cold. She drank it anyway, grimacing. Looking up, she saw William Boyce approaching her table with evident urgency.

The Inky Path
Journalism does not lend itself to a stereotypical office routine.
The reporter must be out and about seeking and gathering the
news, which is no respecter of meal-times or the demands of the
reporter's private life. Take off your hat and loosen your tie,
by all means, but be prepared – at a moment's notice – to return
to the fray.

Paul Pink was talking to a young woman whom she recognized, though she couldn't recall her name or the connection in which they'd met. Some story she'd written, probably. The woman was sitting at a computer terminal, the chief inspector standing behind her chair. He was peering over her shoulder at the screen. The sound of the door caused the two of them to look up. The young woman's plaits swished with the movement of her head, the multicoloured beads catching the light. She smiled warmly. DCI Pink straightened, extending a hand.

'This is Dee-Dee Johnson; Dee-Dee, Constance Amory of the *Crucible*.'

'Hi!'

Her cerise blouse, rainbow leggings and cherry-red Dr Marten boots contrasted starkly with the detective's grey suit, for all its pink adornments. Her wrists were looped with bangles and bracelets that clinked and rattled as she moved.

'Haven't we met before?' asked Constance.

'You know my mam, Frances Johnson. Effie. She works for Mall Clean. Told me all about you – Connie this, Connie that – like, you're the only celebrity she knows.'

'Effie, yes! She's shown me your photograph. I recognized your – you know, the hairstyle. I didn't know you were called Dee-Dee, though.'

'Daniella. D for Daniella, so Dee-Dee. Like, it's a family tradition. Effie, Jay, Bee, Zee-Zee, Kay, Veefer . . . we're, like, alphabetti spaghetti in our house.'

'Veefer?'

'My brother. V for Victor.' They laughed. 'Sort of a half-brother, really.'

DCI Pink cleared his throat. The two women assumed serious expressions, exchanging glances of suppressed mirth, like girls caught talking in class. Dee-Dee turned back to the VDU, Constance and the chief inspector drawing up chairs and sitting on either side of her. They were in an area of Mall Admin that Constance had visited during an introductory tour after her appointment as Urbopark correspondent. Mall Data – where the shopping complex's electronic information was processed, stored and analysed. This room, designated Mall Data (1/4c) according to the sign on the door, housed three work stations, each with its own terminal. A venetian blind blotted the only window, diffused-light ceiling panels casting angular shadows. The room smelled like the interior of a new car. Dee-Dee's desk was the only one in use, although one of the other chairs had a man's jacket draped over the back and the monitor displayed a screen saver, yellow text traversing a purple background: Sir Vivian Fuchs Off to Antarctic.

'Miss Johnson processes information relating to car-park usage,' said DCI Pink. 'She's been helping us with the latest . . . incident, the incendiary devices.'

As he spoke, Dee-Dee's screen displayed a graphic representation of the Urbopark site. The mall was a series of interconnected blocks surrounded by coloured areas for the adjoining car-parks: blue for Blue Zone, green for Green Zone etc. Clicking the cursor over the blue, she called up an enlarged map of that car-park.

'What she's done is insert a cross at each point where a litter bin was blown up. See, here and here . . .' Paul Pink used a biro to indicate. 'She's done this for each of the car-parks targeted in the attack, twelve crosses in all.'

'OK.' It was making Constance's eyes water to stare at the screen. 'What, you're trying to plot the saboteur's route or something?'

'That was the initial purpose, aye.' Addressing Dee-Dee,

the detective added, 'Can you call up the main plan again?'

The digital map of the mall site reappeared. He explained that the crosses were too small to make out, but it was possible to produce an enlarged printout. Dee-Dee clicked the mouse. The printer emitted a hoarse whine as a single sheet of A3 spewed into the plastic tray. Retrieving the page and laying it flat on the desk, the chief inspector beckoned Constance to look. He smelled of aftershave and peppermint; she noticed a pencil-line of black stubble beneath his jaw where he'd missed with the razor.

'There,' he said, tracing the pattern with the blunt end of his pen.

'Very neat,' said Constance.

'Aye.' He placed a hand in each corner of the page. 'And if we do this . . .'

The chief inspector let go, leaving faint impressions where moisture from his fingers had caused the thin paper to pucker. He leaned back in his chair, turning his head to one side to cough into his cupped palm.

''Scuse me.' He coughed again. 'So, conjecture.'

'The letter "U",' said Constance. 'U for Urbopark?'

'The mall logo.' He pointed to the floor of the computer room, where – in common with the rest of Mall Admin – the corporate identity, a recurring 'U' motif, was picked out in the carpet. 'Question is, why?'

'Confirmation of motive? You know, telling us the mall isn't just a random target for the sabotages, it's fundamental to his motive. Urbopark is a clue in itself?'

DCI Pink nodded. 'Conventional police procedure in, say, a murder inquiry, is to find out as much as you can about the victim in the hope that this gives you some clue as to why they might've been killed, and who by. By whom, I should say.'

'The victim, here, being a shopping complex.'

'And we've done that. We've followed conventional procedure, even though we're dealing with a place rather than a person. We've looked at reasons why someone might have a . . . grudge against the mall, or shops within it, or against Mall Admin.'

'Then this clue doesn't take us any further.'

'*Unless*. Unless our chap is giving us a little nudge.'

'How d'you mean?'

'What if we're overlooking another conventional investigative procedure? Examining the *scene* of the crime. I don't mean letting forensic loose on the individual locations of the sabotages, I'm talking about Urbopark itself. This,' he jabbed the printout, 'might be inviting us to think of the mall in a wider context.'

'What, as in Urbopark's *very existence*? D'you think? As though we've to consider the mall as scene of crime and victim rolled into one.'

The chief inspector sat silently, tapping the edge of the desk with his pen. Dee-Dee caught Constance's eye, forming her face into a *you've completely lost me!* expression. When he finally spoke, his voice was heavy with caution.

'No more than conjecture, at this stage.'

'*Paul*, the pattern of fire bombings is too precise to have been an accident.'

'We were the ones who . . . rotated the thing to make a "U", not him. For all we know, he might've been drawing a letter "n" or a hat or a fucking croquet hoop. If you'll pardon my French.'

'Listen, guys, I'm well out of this,' said Dee-Dee, 'But if you arks me, it looks more like a horseshoe.'

Being seven o'clock on a Wednesday, the lounge bar of the Tongs and Dozzle was quiet. Constance and Milly had a corner alcove to themselves. They were drinking pints, a bag of smoky bacon crisps split open for them to share.

'He hasn't phoned, then?'

'No.'

'Have you phoned him?'

Constance shook her head.

'Why not?'

'Why d'you think?'

Milly appeared to be about to respond, but halted herself. Constance hazarded a guess at the unspoken words Why does it have to be *him* who rings *you*? She helped herself to another crisp. She'd made no fewer than three calls that day to Stan (two to his office at the university, one to his home); each time, she hung up before he could answer. Guilty about lying to her friend, she added, 'I couldn't, Mill. I was going to, but I just couldn't.'

'Yeah, I know.'

Better, nearer the truth. She wondered, to herself, whether he might be trying to ring her now. Had she put the answering machine on? Yes. She was also concerned that the jacket potatoes would be burnt if she and Milly didn't go home after this, their second round.

'I mean, there could be loads of reasons why he didn't ring.'

'There'll probably be a message for you when we get back.'

'Yeah.' She didn't smile. 'Yeah, you never know.'

Constance sat back in her seat, then almost immediately leant forward again – adjusting her position.

'You OK?'

An embarrassed grin. 'I'm a bit sore, actually.'

'So you *did*, then!'

'Of course we did.'

'Protected?'

'*Milly.*'

'Yours or his?'

'You think I carry them around with me, just in case?' The two women laughed. 'He had some in his bedside table. And *no*, I didn't check how many were missing.'

Another lie. At one point during the night – while Stan was using the toilet – she retrieved the pack of condoms and found they'd been purchased that day (the bag and till receipt were still in the drawer; Drugstop: Urbopark, Upper Mall – Pink Zone; £1.99) and the only one of the three that was missing was the one they'd just used. Which she took to mean: a) he wasn't fucking anyone else; b) he bought them specially for her visit, confident they'd make love. Confident or optimistic, or merely wishful? It amounted to pretty much the same thing; and what did that say about her? Her deceit made it impossible to seek Milly's opinion, though her friend would most likely have asked: what does that say about *him*?

'Was it nice?'

'We had a lovely evening.'

'That isn't what I meant.'

'I *know*.'

'I'm starving.'

'We should go after these.'

'I'm going to get some more crisps.'

Constance assumed a shrill voice. 'You'll spoil your tea.'

She watched Milly approach the bar. Bright yellow jumper, extending below the hem of her skirt, which said as much about shortness of skirt as it did about length of jumper. Her legs were bare. Her legs, Constance would die for. Constance herself, having changed out of her two-day-old clothes on arriving home from work, was wearing a denim shirt, black jeans and a delicate silver necklace which she fingered from time to time as a matter of habit. A Valentine's present from Howard. She ran the pendant back and forth along the chain. Despite herself, she made a comparison: Stan was more

382

considerate; less inventive, less robust. Howard was slimmer, smoother. Stan *lasted*. With Stan, she didn't have to fake an orgasm in order to have one; and, in the darkness of his semi-basement flat, there were no wall-shadows to arouse her.

'Weird, isn't it, with someone new?' Milly sat down and opened the bag of crisps. 'Only cheese and onion, I'm afraid.'

'How d'you mean?'

'They *feel* different. Different to the last person you slept with.'

'Yeah, I know. You get used to someone.'

'Not just when they're, you know, *inside* – but the way they touch you. And the way they feel when you touch them. Their body is all wrong.'

'Stan's hands are bigger than Howard's. And he's a bit wobblier round the tummy.' They laughed. 'As for the beard . . .'

'Like snogging a bird's nest.'

'*Milly.*'

'*Joke.*' They paused to sip their drinks. Milly took her purse from the table and zipped it inside the pocket of her jacket, folded beside her on the seat. She added, 'It's, like, your brain knows who you're making love to, but your body's expecting someone else.'

'Strange for them, too, I suppose.' Constance smiled. 'I did my trick with the duvet; you know, the one that pisses – used to piss – Howard off.'

'Sleeping upside down?'

'No, with the duvet. You wake up in the middle of the night and it's sweltering under there with two of you, right? So you turn the duvet over: warm side out, cool side in. It'd always wake Howard up. He hated that, used to get all grumpy.'

'And Stan didn't?'

'No.'

'They don't, do they, the first time.'

'No, I mean he didn't wake up. He didn't even notice in the

383

morning when we made the bed, even though his duvet's got a different pattern on each side.'

'They don't fart, either, the first time,' said Milly. 'And – it's miraculous how they do this, because I always thought it was an involuntary thing – *they don't snore.*'

When they returned home from the pub, Constance checked the answering machine. No messages. She made three phone calls. The first was to a home-delivery pizza restaurant, to order the food they'd have to eat instead of the jacket potatoes that had shrivelled to burnt husks while she and Milly downed a third pint at the Tongs.

Secondly, she called Granddad, to ask if he could remember anything about the museum visitor who'd given him the horseshoe. Granddad couldn't come up with more detail than he'd told her before. He was an American tourist (possibly, though Granddad wasn't hot on accents) who worked as an ironmonger back home.

'I thought you said he was a blacksmith?'

'I never said owt, that were what he tellt me.'

'But, when you told me – *he* said he was a *blacksmith*, not an ironmonger.'

'Aye, blacksmith. I'm only telling thee what he said.'

'D'you remember what day it was he came to the museum?'

'Blimey, now you're asking.'

'Last week some time, wasn't it?'

'Tuesday, I'd say. Or mebbe Monday. It'd not have been Wednesday, cos I were off Wednesday. Aye, it were definitely Monday or Tuesday.'

Granddad was no more helpful with regard to the man's appearance (*white, middle aged, tallish*). He couldn't recall the colour or style of his hair, nor what clothes he was wearing, nor any distinguishing facial features (*might've had a tache, though I'd not swear to it*). Constance thanked him.

Finally, she phoned Stan. She sat at the foot of the stairs listening to the ringing tone until her ear ached from holding the receiver against it for so long. When the pizzas arrived, she ate one slice of hers and gave the rest to Milly.

'No sandwiches?'

'Wife forgot to take the bread out o' t'freezer.'

'I wouldn't stand for that.'

William looked at her.

'Sorry,' she said. 'Wrong side of bed.'

She felt more tired this morning than the previous day, despite an early night and a sleep undisturbed by dreams or sex or the necessity to flip the duvet. Off like a light, too; she hardly recalled undressing and climbing into bed. She yawned profusely. *'Scuse me!* Lowering the paper she'd been reading, Constance called up the morning newslist. Her initials were alongside one story, William's alongside two. No matter how often she saw 'WB' on the schedule, the letters caused her a moment's associative alarm. *You're starting to see clues everywhere.* Paul Pink's latest admonition, prompted by her incoherent theory on the recurrence of the horseshoe motif: the legend of St Dunstan and the Devil; the mysterious gift to Granddad; the pattern of fire bombings in the mall car-parks. *The detective must learn to discern between what is relevant and what isn't.* Substitute 'reporter' for 'detective', it seemed to her, and the DCI's observation could've been plagiarized from *The Inky Path*. She double-clicked on 'print'. William, meanwhile, had completed his morning ritual: the unpacking of the briefcase, the hanging up of the jacket, the arrangement of pens and notebooks. He leaned across the desk, handing her an unmarked envelope.

'Tickets,' he said. 'For Friday night.'

'Oh, right! Thanks very much.'

'There are two. I thought you'd want to bring someone.'

She took out the tickets. Professionally produced, black text on pale pink; reminiscent of tickets for United games. On closer examination she noticed the title of the play had been misprinted. She tried not to laugh.

'I know, I know.' William wasn't smiling at all. 'Three hundred of them, all the bloody same. Printers have waived the fee, of course.'

'I quite like it, *Dearth* of a Salesman.'

'Hopefully, not many folk'll notice.'

'What do I owe you?'

He shook his head. 'They're comps, them. Actually, we were hoping you'd do a little write-up for us. In t'*Crucible*.'

'Isn't someone on arts and leisure covering it?'

'I've squared it with them, and they say if it's OK with you . . . Two hundred and fifty is all they want. You could write it up from t'programme wi'out even going.'

'What, and miss your big night?' She put the tickets in her handbag and made a note in her diary. 'How's the accent coming along?'

'A man's godda do wadda man's godda do.'

'Go on, just a few words.'

'Aye, that's it, you have a good laugh.'

The phone rang. William answered it while Constance retrieved the newslist from the printer tray. Her story was mostly written, just a couple of quotes to tie it up; earmarked for page three. Nothing to be done until the phone was free. She made two coffees, placing one on her colleague's coaster. He gave off a distinctive odour of fishpaste and cucumber even when he hadn't brought any sandwiches. He hung up.

'How'd your *assignation* with Inspector Pink go off yesterday?'

'Oh, OK. Didn't get a story out of it or anything.'

'You mean I ran all the way to t'caff for no reason?'

'That message was half an hour old!'

'Aye, well, I'd to track you down first.' William checked his watch, reaching for the place where his sandwich box would normally stand. He appeared momentarily disoriented. 'Do they do sarnies at Snak Shak?'

'HypaCenta's your best bet – bigger range of fillings. It won't be open while half past eight, though.' *While*. She hadn't used a Hallam 'while' since she was at school. 'Here's the newslist. You're down for one and five.'

He took the schedule from her. 'Summat to do wi' t'sabotage inquiry, was it?'

'Like I say, nothing I can use. Something Paul came across on the fire bombs.'

'Oh, aye?'

'He . . .' She watched him, as he read the schedule and made jottings in his notebook. Interested one moment, then not paying her the slightest attention. 'I mean, just background really; something and nothing. You using the phone?'

William looked up, distracted; seemingly irritated by being made to break off from what he was doing. He pushed the telephone across the desk towards her.

The flowers arrived mid-morning, paraded ceremonially into the editorial room by Sally. A bouquet of vivid scarlet and tangerine, comprising carnations, tulips, marigolds, chrysanthemums and roses. Their combined perfume was overpowering. Stapled to the cellophane wrapping was a small envelope containing a card; a single word: Sorry. The writing was feminine, penned – Constance presumed – by the florist's assistant who'd taken the order. *Sorry*. Nothing else, no sender's name; not even *her* name, though the delivery girl had asked for her at reception. She stood them in a few inches of water in the sink while Sally rooted around for a vase. Sorry for what? Sorry for not phoning. Sorry for ignoring you for twenty-eight hours and thirteen minutes. Sorry for being a bastard. Or, sorry if you thought the other night meant something. Sorry we fucked. Sorry, and goodbye . . . Delete where applicable. Sorry for *what*?

The Inky Path
The aspiring reporter would do well to spend an hour in the production department. There, he will witness letterpress print-ing in operation – the transfer of an inked raised image to paper

387

by direct pressure. It may occur to him that, under such a method, it is possible to produce either solid black or nothing at all. How, then, are the shades of grey in newspaper photographs obtained? An amiable printer, if such a breed exists, might explain to him that the reproduction of photographs is achieved by means of dots. The quality of the outcome depends on the number of dots per square inch, or 'fineness of screen'. The greater the number of dots, the better the result. If he has his wits about him, our reporter might draw two lessons from his time 'below decks'. Firstly, the images in a newspaper photograph are not as solid as they seem; secondly, the more fragmentary the image, the more truthful is its likeness to the original. For it is a paradox of journalism that, while newspapers are printed in black and white, news itself is seldom susceptible to such convenient extremes of definition.

(Friday, 11.03 a.m.)

'Hello, *Crucible*.'

'Connie?'

'Oh, hi, Paul.'

'You all right?'

'Yeah, yeah. I'm fine.'

'You're not on deadline?'

'No, it's OK. I thought you might be someone else, that's all.'

'Sorry to disappoint you.'

'I didn't mean . . . it's just, I've been expecting a call.'

'I wanted to catch you—'

'Don't we have an appointment?'

'Aye, that's why I'm ringing. We've hit a snag.'

'How d'you mean?'

'The tape arrived first thing this morning and I had one of our lads set it up ready for when you came in.'

'And?'

'Hallamshire TV have sent us the match highlights instead of the half-time presentation footage.'

388

'Great.'

'Didn't think you'd want to sit through that penalty shootout again.'

'So, what now?'

'I've sent the tape back. Given them a polite bollocking and told them to get the right one over to us as soon as.'

'Any idea when that'll be?'

'Not while next week now. I'll let you know.'

'*Paul*, this is—'

'They've *mislaid* it.'

'How can you mislay a video tape?'

'The lass I spoke to reckoned it'd been filed in the wrong place. It's a case of trawling through until they find it.'

'Jesus.'

It was dusk when she set off, heater on full blast to clear the front windscreen and the rear view being revealed through the slowly spreading fingers of the demister. She was late. Indigestion, from gulping her tea down and showering and changing in a hurry. The rain was heavy; she flicked the wipers from intermittent to continuous. Her breath. It was her own breath that was clouding up the windscreen. She peered out into the glare of oncoming headlights reflecting wetly off the tarmac and the greasy smears left by her wiper blades. The roads, the air itself, seemed impregnated with a metallic yellow sheen, as though the rain was leaching sulphurous dye from the streetlamps. Ticket! One-handed, searching her purse. There it was.

Driving home via Stan's had been a mistake. It had made her late; it had been a waste of time. Sitting in her car across the road from his flat like – what? – like some stalker or something; like a loopy, obsessed woman. And he hadn't been in. No lights in the semi-basement, no response when she rang the bell, no sounds from beyond the locked door. The couple upstairs said they hadn't seen him for a few days. Constance looked at the dashboard clock, lit so weakly she could scarcely

389

make out the digits. Fifteen minutes. It all came down to how quickly she'd find a parking space – on a Friday night, in the centre of Hallam. Shit. Shit. But what were you supposed to do when he'd not phoned for three days, when you couldn't get an answer from his home number, when you rang him at work and a secretary told you *Professor Bell is on sick leave*, when he'd sent you flowers with a note saying 'Sorry'? He could've been anywhere. The gearbox screamed in protest at her attempted shift from fourth to first, instead of third. She patted the console. *Sorry, Feef.* Ahead of her, a line of cars queued behind a stationary bus, indicators blinking in erratic synchronization as the drivers waited for an opportunity to overtake. *Come on!* So she'd waited outside his flat for two hours. Then she'd written him a note, pushing it through his letterbox. Several notes, only one of which ended up on his doormat – the rest, crumpled and unfinished, in her handbag. 'Hi Stan! Thanks for the flowers, they were lovely! Ring me when you get back. Yours, Connie XXXX* (*P.S. Australians couldn't give a four-X for anything else!)' Exclamation marks all over the place. *Dog's dicks*, William called them. *A typographical device to tell readers when to laugh or when to be startled – as though they'd not the gumption to work it out for themselves.* William. He'd be suffering third-degree stage fright now: sweaty palms, repeated visits to the toilet, dry mouth. Maybe not, maybe he wasn't the type. Seven minutes. That line about Australians not giving a four-X . . . if she could have reached her hand through the letterbox and retrieved the note. He wasn't even *Australian*. She'd sounded silly, juvenile. In trying to be jolly and relaxed and (no-hard-feelings) friendly, she'd made herself sound stupid. As per.

She parked in a pay and display two minutes' walk from the theatre, arriving in the foyer – umbrellaless, soaked – just as the last call to curtain-up was being announced. Enough time to buy a programme, have a pee, take two puffs of Ventolin, and dry her hair as best she could on a roller-towel in the ladies'. The auditorium lights were dimming as an usherette showed her to her seat, which – miraculously – was at the end of a row and required no knocking of knees or treading on toes or muttered apologies to people you couldn't even see. Her notebook. Where was her notebook? In the car. Shitting crap. It was OK, as the stage lit up she saw that an ad on the back of the programme contained sufficient white space for her to scribble a few notes during the performance. She squirmed out of her jacket and laid it untidily on the seat next to hers. The seat where, ludicrously, she'd hoped Stan might've been sitting. Her *guest*. Even now – despite not having seen him since Wednesday morning, despite the fact that he could have no idea she was here or had a spare ticket – she imagined he might appear at any moment, breathlessly apologetic, at her side. She became aware of her own odour: a combination of perspiration, vanilla musk bodyspray and damp wool. The play was starting. Already, she found herself mentally composing the opening line of her review. This frame of mind was to characterize the evening, making it difficult for her to watch without mediating the performance through the words with which she'd subsequently choose to describe it. Or thinking of Stan.

Backstage was mayhem; members of the cast in various states of undress mingling with, and outnumbered by, the amateur dramatic society's behind-the-scenes team as well as friends, family and other well-wishers. The communal dressing room – a narrow, windowless chamber lit by bare lightbulbs and cluttered with stage props, clothing rails and half a dozen tables and chairs ranged along one wall – seethed like a rush-hour railway carriage. The air reeked of sweat and cigarette smoke. Somewhere, a champagne cork popped – triggering cheers and shrill laughter amid the babble of too many people talking at once. Constance stood in the doorway, trying to make out William Boyce. Hot, stuffy. She spotted the lad who'd played Biff, conversing animatedly with two women. He wasn't half as good looking close up as he'd seemed from row K of the

391

stalls. As she crossed the dressing room, she succeeded in jogging the elbow of a man with a full glass in his hand. William saw her before she saw him. His voice, calling her name, drew her attention to a clearing in a corner. He was with his fictional wife and two lads about Constance's age. They were drinking champagne. The lads, all in black, had been responsible for set-changes between scenes. William and the actress were in stage clothes, though looking less authentically fifties American in this setting. His suit jacket and homburg lay on a nearby table; the leading lady had removed her shoes and was, for some reason, holding them one-handed by the heels.

William raised his voice to make himself heard. 'What did you think?'

'I really enjoyed it,' said Constance.

'Aye, but what did you *think*?'

She held up her programme for them to see the patchwork quilt of shorthand notes filling every available space on the back page. 'It's all here.'

'Are you reviewing us for the *Crucible*?' asked the actress. Before Constance could answer, the woman prodded the programme with her shoes and said, 'Make sure you spell my name correctly . . . only kidding!'

William performed the introductions. After a moment's polite conversation, the two stage hands drifted almost imperceptibly into a neighbouring group and the leading lady went off in search of another drink; her parting words to Constance, *Two Zs in dazzling!* Her co-star waited until she was out of earshot, *Aye, and one P in crap.*

'Not exactly Meryl Streep, is she?' said Constance.

'*Three* prompts.' He stood his drink on the table behind him. 'Skipped half a page of script altogether, and called me William instead of Willy, at one point.'

'I noticed that.'

He excused himself, stepping out of the shoes and trousers and changing into others stowed in a battered metal wardrobe.

He removed his braces and tie, but kept on the white shirt. The armpits were stained with sweat and the lower half of the sleeves were creased from having been rolled up. Rubbing at his head with a towel to remove the worst of the hair-oil, he asked, 'Go on, then – how'd I do?'

'Pick of the bunch. And I'm not just saying that.'

'Really?'

'Just the right amount of pathos; you know, at the end.'

'You mean I was pathetic?'

Constance laughed. His hair resembled a wheatfield after a storm. He slung the towel down, knocking the fluted champagne glass over and spilling its contents. While William moved quickly to rescue the jacket and hat, she grabbed the glass to prevent it from spiralling off the table.

'It's gone everywhere,' he said.

'Have you got a cloth?'

The fizzy liquid was still spreading across the surface, dribbling over the edge to form a puddle on the floor. His stage clothes had been spared but a clutter of make-up paraphernalia was drenched. Between them they salvaged the items one by one, wiped them off as best they could and placed them on a dry part of the table. A powder compact and brushes, lipsticks, a tray of assorted eyeshadow, false eye-lashes, eyebrow pencils, a fake moustache, several eyeliner sticks, lemon-scented facial wipes, various hair gels and sprays, a tub of cold cream and half a dozen clear plastic sachets of what looked like tomato ketchup. The mishap seemed to have gone unnoticed, the dressing-room hubbub continuing without interruption.

'What are these?' asked Constance, shaking off the excess champagne before patting each sachet in turn with a cloth.

'Blood. *Fake* blood, that is.' He took one from her and slipped it inside the breast pocket of his shirt. 'You get shot or stabbed, on stage, you clutch your hand to your chest . . .' He demonstrated. '. . . Only, you've got a pin in your hand. Hey presto, a bloody shirt.'

393

Constance picked up another of them, examining the contents. Too fluid for ketchup; more the consistency and colour of the raspberry syrup she and Mags used to adore on ice cream when they were little. Tacky, like wet paint. Your lips would stick together, coming apart again with a moist kissing sound as you opened your mouth.

'Or you get made-up before going on,' he said. 'You've been in a fight or summat, and you've to stagger on stage wi' a bloody nose.'

'What's it made of?'

'No idea. Some synthetic stuff. Very realistic, mind.'

He removed the sachet from his shirt pocket and put it with the rest of the debris on the table. She watched him dry his hands, then use the towel to mop up the last of the champagne; by now, most of it had spilled onto the floor or soaked into the tabletop to leave a dark stain. There was an alteration in the quality of noise in the room, as if her ears had been affected by an abrupt change in air pressure. The background murmur of voices became muffled, distant; indistinct echoes in a tunnel of rushing water. For a moment she thought she was going to faint. But the sensation passed almost as soon as it came, to be replaced by a vague nausea. She was, she realized, still watching William clear up the mess when a male voice penetrated the swooshing sound in her ears. Someone was shouting. No, not shouting; it was a speech. A dozen separate conversations had diminished to allow the director – perched on a chair in the centre of the dressing room – to make an address. William stopped to listen, edging into the circle of people that had formed. His hand was on her elbow, steering her into position . . . *marvellous opening night, I'm sure you'll all agree* . . . Ripple of applause. The director's head was partially obscured by one of the bare lightbulbs that hung from the ceiling by a cord, drenching the whitewashed walls and upturned faces in a sickly light. Laughter, more clapping. Constance found that she was still holding one of the sachets of synthetic blood. . . . *without whose sterling efforts, of course,*

394

none of this would have been possible . . . She kept her hand by her side for a moment, then slowly eased it into her jacket pocket. Keys, inhaler, paper handkerchief; each object immediately identifiable by touch alone. She let go of the sachet so that it fell among these things.

The Life and Times of a
Hallam Saw Grinder
(a Dramatic Reconstruction in Many Parts)

Royal Commission of Inquiry
(sitting at) Hallam Town Hall
Tuesday, 18 June 1867 (Eleventh Day)

Witness: Thomas Fearnehough, Saw Grinder, No.8 Hereford Street, Hallam.

Q. You say you sought to make yourself right with the Saw Grinders'. Why did you?

A. On account of having been done.

Q. What do you mean by that?

A. I was rolled up and had to pay £5 to have my bands back.

Q. You feared you would be rattened again or worse?

A. I did.

Q. How did you go about sparing yourself such a fate?

A. I saw Broadhead at Joe Green's one time.

Q. What did you say to him?

A. I told him I wanted to make myself straight with the union.

· Q. What did he say to that?

A. He said I must pay the £14 I owed.

Q. What did you say?

A. I said I would have two shillings and sixpence stopped each week from my scale.

Q. You were drawing benefit from the Society at the time, were you?

A. I was. I had no work at that time.

Q. And you had not paid your natty money?

A. I was behind.

Q. You were receiving money from the union, then, though you had paid none in?

A. That is why I wanted to make myself straight.

Q. What did Broadhead say to your suggestion?

A. The Society said half the arrears must be paid down at once and I would have the whole of my scale stopped until the rest was cleared.

Q. What did you say to that?

A. I asked what my family was to live on if I had no work and no scale.

Q. Broadhead would not change his position?

A. He would not.

Q. Now, it has been said at this hearing that you have been in the habit of absenting yourself from your work and your family for days at a time, drinking. Have you?

A. I have done so, I ought to tell the truth.

Q. And were you discharged from Hague's for bad conduct?

A. I was not. I gave them a month's warning and left when the month was up.

Q. And when you were at Slack's, did you receive a letter concerning your continuing to work while other men were in dispute with the company?

A. I received a letter, yes.

Q. From whom was it?

A. I cannot say.

Q. By whom was it signed, or was it not signed at all?

A. It was signed, I believe, by The Man in the Moon.

Q. That is a pseudonym, is it?

A. I would say it is, for I have not met anyone in Hallam who goes by that name.

(*laughter*)

Q. What was the substance of the letter?

A. It was in red ink or pencil.

Q. That is not what I meant. What I meant was, what did the letter say?

A. I do not know. I am no scholar.

Q. You cannot read?

A. I cannot.

Q. What did you do with the letter?

397

A. I gave it to the police.

Q. Why did you do that?

A. It is rumoured that some of them can read.

(*laughter*)

Q. No, why did you hand the letter to the police if, as you say, you knew not what it contained? Or had you cause to be suspicious?

A. A letter in red ink can be only one thing.

Q. Such letters are well-known in Hallam?

A. They are.

Q. With regard to your letter, did the police confirm its contents to you?

A. They said I would be done if I continued at Slack's.

Q. Did this make you afraid, or what effect did it have upon you?

A. I did not need a letter to know what would happen to me.

Q. On account of your being wrong with the union?

A. Yes.

Q. Your ilk are not well liked within the Hallam trades. Would you say that is true?

A. I daresay it is. And if there was not us, I daresay men would find others to blow up.

October 1866

At the time of the explosion, Thomas Fearnehough was at Messrs Slack, Sellars & Co., where he persisted in his work despite his fellow grinders having withdrawn their labour. Conscious of the danger to which this exposed him, Slack's found a place for him at Butchers Wheel, its only entry being a gateway that was under constant guard. Samuel Crookes, conscripted by Broadhead to prevent Fearnehough from working, reconnoitred the Wheel. He reported that it would be impossible to disable the man's grindstone or strew explosive among the emery powder in his trough. Further beatings in

398

the street would, in all likelihood, have no more effect than those already dispensed. Nor was it an option to take a shot at him, Crookes having forsworn this method of retribution after the demise of James Linley seven years previously. Thus it was that – in the early hours of 8 October – he and a young accomplice, Daniel Amory, found themselves outside Fearnehough's home in Hereford Street.

Witness: Daniel Amory, Apprentice Saw Grinder, No.11 Garden Street, Hallam.

Q. Now, mind what you are about. If you make a full disclosure, you need not fear any consequences at all. You know what we can do with you if you do not tell the truth?

A. Yes.

Q. If you speak the truth, we will give you a certificate of indemnity from prosecution; but if you do not, very serious consequences may happen. Do you understand?

A. I shall speak the truth.

Q. Now, I will ask you a second time, do you know of any person who ever wanted to do an injury to Fearnehough?

A. No.

Q. Did anybody ever tell you that he was disposed to do it?

A. No.

Q. Were you disposed to do it yourself?

A. No.

Q. Do you know of anyone who wanted to give him a beating?

A. No.

Q. Were you yourself disposed to give him one, or did you ever do so?

A. No.

Q. Do you know of anyone who would blow him up at his home?

A. No.

Q. Were you yourself disposed to do so, or did you do so?

A. No.

Q. You cannot recollect anything of this sort involving yourself or anyone else?

A. I cannot.

Q. Have you heard what Crookes has said? I will remind you that Crookes has been here and has sworn. I will tell you what he says – and I caution you – he swears that you and he were in cahoots. I ask again were you a party to these matters?

A. No.

Q. You say that is false?

A. Yes.

Q. What age are you?

A. I shall be eighteen in November.

Q. You are in the final year of your apprenticeship to your father, are you not?

A. I am.

Q. Are your parents here present, your mother and father?

A. They are.

Q. Where are they?

(*witness indicates*)

Q. And are you answering as you do because of their presence in the chamber?

(*witness hesitates*)

Q. Answer me. Is it for fear of being shamed before them that you say as you do?

A. No.

Q. You persist in denying that you were in cahoots with Crookes?

A. Yes.

Q. It is entirely an invention of his, is that your testimony?

A. Yes.

Q. Then I must state now, Daniel Amory, that I believe you to be committing a gross perjury and contempt. I order that you be taken and held overnight in the cells. In the morning, you will return to answer truthfully the questions put to you; or in the event that you do not do so, the Commission will decide what is to be done with you.

                              *   *   *

The more youthfully athletic Daniel soon left his accomplice
to lag behind as the pair fled from the scene of their atrocity.
He glanced over his shoulder to see Sammy's ungainly figure
silhouetted against gusts of flame. The narrow street reverberated, still, from the cacophonous boom – punctuated, now, by
the cries of those inside the house. At the main thoroughfare,
he – in an exhilarated state of panic and disorientation – turned
right instead of left, every stride carrying him away from the
town. By the time he crossed the bridge over Porter Brook,
Sammy was altogether lost from view. There being no discreet
place to conceal himself, the young man continued as far as
St Mary's, hoping to hide in the churchyard until the commotion had abated. Finding the gates chained, however, he
pressed on up Bramall Lane – intermittently running and
walking, anxious that the road was too commonly frequented,
even at this hour, for him to remain safely upon it. Presently,
he reached the cricket ground where – in their childhood – he
and his brother Jasper would come to watch the play. As on
those occasions, he chose a favourable spot and climbed the
fence.

   In the uppermost row of the pavilion, Daniel was sheltered
from the drizzle. It must have begun raining while he was
making good his escape, for his clothes and hair were quite
dampened. The wooden bench upon which he sat would have
seemed uncomfortable had he not been glad merely to take
the weight from his feet. The excitement of events in Hereford
Street and his subsequent flight had dissipated, and the lesser
thrill of trespassing upon the cricket ground yielded to a
creeping fatigue. He yawned. How odd it was to be in this
place at the dead of night, the terraced bank of seating so
deserted and desolate it was difficult to believe the season was
but a fortnight ended. Not that he had ever been admitted to
the pavilion on match days, making do – as a boy – with
spectating illicitly from the embankment alongside Bramall
Lane. He yawned again. Now that his eyes had become

                                  401

accustomed to the dark, he could make out a sight-screen's ghostly white boards a hundred yards distant, beyond the black expanse of the pitch. Staring at the sight-screen, it appeared to oscillate in the gloom as though disturbed by an invisible presence. He stretched out on the bench. By closing his eyes, he could visualize the players in their whites; he could hear bat on ball and a clatter of applause. He imagined people standing, in recognition of a batsman's innings, so that Daniel, too, had to rise in order to see between their heads.

When he awoke – stiff-limbed, cold – he could not immediately comprehend where he was nor how his bed came to be so narrow and hard. It was not yet dawn and the darkness offered no clues to his whereabouts. Then, as he lay blinking, his memory shrugged itself free from the drug of sleep. He sat up abruptly. What if Fearnehough were dead? Or his wife and children? He was consumed, in that instant, by the absolute certainty that they had all perished in an inferno of his own making. He knew that he must return home at once, so that he might come down for his breakfast without alerting the household to the fact that he had been abroad for most of the night. The prospect of his father intuiting his complicity in some awful deed caused Daniel a moment's dread. And, even if he did not, it would be but a short while before the seeds of suspicion were sown by news of the explosion. The son, compelled to contain within him a guilt that would gnaw at his insides with each innocuous look or word from his father. He must go home. The two would sit together at the fireside, as was their custom, and eat their breakfast in silence while they listened to the comforting sounds of the woman who was at once mother and wife going about her chores in the kitchen. Perhaps she would be humming melodiously to herself. He saw in his mind the dark curls of her hair and the flushed cheeks and the mischief in her eyes that gave her the semblance of a woman half her age; and his own eyes filled up. Daniel wiped his face on his cuff. He would go home, and rise as usual for his breakfast. Listening to his mother's tuneful good cheer, Daniel and his father would break off from their food to catch one another's eye and smile. In due course, they would don their clogs and coats and set off in the rain on their familiar walk to the Wheel. No doubt the men there would be animated with news of the explosion, for hardly a saw grinder in Hallam had not wished to see Fearnehough done. He would take care to give no indication that he already knew of what had passed in Hereford Street. And he would be sure to be as careless as ever at his work, for nothing would more greatly arouse Thomas Amory's suspicion than the sight of his son paying attention to the grinding of saws.

Daniel made his way down from the pavilion and onto the field, stepping out in the direction of the road. He was hungry and faded by exhaustion. The rain had ceased but the grass – lush, he supposed, from having remained unmown since the end of the cricket season – was wet underfoot. He bent to moisten his palms on the drenched turf then cupped his hands to his face, rubbing vigorously to freshen himself. As he repeated the action, his fingers struck something small and metallic in amongst the grass. Too dark for him to identify the object by sight, he picked it up. A coin or a medallion of some description. He weighed it in his palm – judging its size, shape and dimensions by touch alone – concluding that it was almost certainly a penny piece. He traced his thumb over both faces to see if he could determine whether the head engraved upon it was that of Victoria or some earlier monarch; but the surfaces were worn too smooth for him even to distinguish heads from tails. Not until he could inspect it by daylight should he be able to satisfy his curiosity. For the time being, Daniel Amory was content to pocket his find in the knowledge that he was a penny wealthier. He determined, however, never to spend the coin but to keep it on his person at all times as a talisman. Wrapping the penny piece in his handkerchief, he stowed it in his trouser pocket. He wet his face once more, his fingers smelling of grass and of old metal and – indelibly – of himself.

Chapter Fourteen

SHOP TALK

Shopping is a functional activity, a matter of necessity, a chore. This, of course, is problematic. You have only to contrast the contents of two people's trolleys at a supermarket checkout, to contrast the clothes they wear, to contrast the way in which they furnish their homes; and you see that shopping is an expression of individuality. More than that, it is a journey into the Self. To shop implies the question: who am I? To make a purchase implies the statement: this is me!

I Shop, Therefore I Am: Essays in Mall Culture
eds. Jeremy Nicholls & Barbara Cutteslowe
(Hallam Metropolitan University Press, 1991)

Sunday lunch-time. Everything Under the Bun, Yellow Upper. Paul ordered a Gut Buster Special, £3.99; Constance chose fishburger, fries, diet cola. Both were in civvies, the inspector in a chunky-knit cardigan and plain grey trousers (pink socks), while she wore jeans and a bottle-green chenille sweater that had lost its shape in the wash. The cola – mostly slushed ice, and diluted to the point of tastelessness – was so cold it set her teeth on edge. In their window seat, the tinted glass gave a panoramic view over the Place du Marché, where three arcades converged on a circular fountain. The plaza, designed to resemble a village square in rural France, was congested with diners at the dozens of red-and-white chequered tables shared by the food kiosks around its perimeter. With only the window between Constance and the plaza floor thirty feet below, she experienced a surge of vertiginous panic. She lifted her head.

'I can't look down,' she said, in response to her companion's puzzled expression. 'Even on footbridges, I have to stare straight ahead.'

'Christina's afraid of heights.'

'I'm not *afraid* of heights, as such. With me, it's more – I don't know – when I look down from above, I'm up here *and* down there at the same time. If that makes sense. Disoriented, I suppose.' She waved a hand dismissively. 'I can't explain.'

DCI Pink patted his lips with a serviette.

'As a child,' she went on, 'I used to have this recurring nightmare that the floor had given way beneath my bed and I was plunging down and down. I don't remember what it was I was plunging towards, just this . . . *feeling* of falling.'

He ate methodically, careful to avoid mess. Between bites, he set the burger down in one half of the carton with the portion of fries neatly tipped into the other half. Slower eater than her. *Patience of a gardener*, her dad had remarked. Even now, the inspector appeared content for them to share Sunday lunch without displaying the slightest curiosity as to why she'd invited him to meet her on his day off.

'Ketchup?' Constance pushed a sachet across the table.

She studied his face, observing the alteration as the oddness of the clear plastic packet became apparent to him. He picked it up, asking her what it was. She told him. He asked where she'd got it from, and she told him that as well.

'Made in Hallam.' He indicated the manufacturer's name on

the serrated seal: Dramarama Stage & Screen Accessories, Hallam, UK. 'Can't say I've heard of them.'

'We ran a feature a few months ago. One of William Boyce's company profile pieces.' She paused to lick a smear of tartar sauce from her thumb. 'I dug out the file.'

He waited for her to continue.

'It was set up by a group of chemistry postgrads at the university. They produce make-up for TV, film and theatre – fake blood being their speciality.'

'Your colleague's . . . amateur dramatic society being one of their customers?'

'He wangled a load of free samples, as a sort of "thank you" for the publicity. The local TV and radio stations did pieces as well, after it went in the *Crucible*.'

The inspector studied the sachet again, pressing the fluid and air-filled pocket between thumb and middle finger. If he was aware of her watching him intently, he gave no indication. A momentary distraction: a man in an inflatable burger costume – Mr Bun – passed by their table, handing out customer research questionnaires.

'When did you say William Boyce wrote this article?'

'August. Couple of weeks before the first of the sabotages.'

He nodded. 'OK, what else? *Apart* from the fact his initials are WB.'

Constance went to pull herself in closer to the table, but her chair and the adjacent one were moulded together and – like the table itself – fixed to the floor. Palms face down on the table-top, séance style. Hers, not his; he had laid down the sachet of synthetic blood and was smoothing the bald dome of his head with a familiar absent-mindedness. Listening mode. Both were staring at a point mid-table.

'The bells are ringing for me an' my gal. *William* took that call. We've only his word for it that it was the saboteur on the line – I mean, it could've been anybody.'

'The message was from William himself, you're suggesting?'

'Possibly. It's *possible*.' She looked at the inspector before continuing. 'Apart from that one time, he's never been in the office when the saboteur has called, and – far as I can remember – the sabotages have coincided with him being out on his rounds. As for the bomb hoax, he could've made that call from any payphone.'

'Does he keep an appointments diary?'

Constance nodded.

'Simple enough matter to verify any alibis,' he said. 'Dates, times, names.'

'Then there was the computer game, the warning about the flooding.'

'What about it?'

'He *knew* the game. And he made a point of handling the disk and the packaging it came in, so his fingerprints would be on them.'

'His prints already being there, if he was the one who sent the disk.'

'Precisely.' Her palms were ingrained with particles of salt. She took a sip of cola. 'Also, don't forget, he was transferred to Urbopark at his own request. He knows the layout of the mall. And he's been behind the scenes, *including* Mall Data – so he could've easily slipped a corrupted piece of software into Mall Sys.'

'I still don't—'

'And *he* was the one who diverted us towards a false suspect – Donald Moss.'

DCI Pink sighed. 'OK, what about motive or some of the . . . clues?'

'He's union FoC. Father of chapel, it's the equivalent of a shop steward. Ties in with the "chapel" clue.' She outlined her horseshoe theory – the reference to St Dunstan, and Grand-dad's gift from an 'American' tourist. 'William had to learn the accent for his part in the play. And he knew my granddad worked at the museum.'

'What about the other biblical stuff?'

'OK, "In the beginning was the Word". This is a bit vague,

but it could be a cryptic reference to journalism. No, seriously, William's . . . he's always talking about reporters being *wordsmiths*; and, there's a phrase I've heard him use, something about the journalist being a . . . a *craftsman whose raw material is the written word.*'

As she repeated the aphorism, she wondered if she hadn't actually read it in *The Inky Path.* The inspector went to say something, but she interrupted.

'And the banner – he was one of the people who knew I'd be at that game, by the way – the banner referred to the same passage marked in the Bible at St Dunstan's, about Jesus throwing the merchants out of the temple.'

'I don't follow.'

'William's one of those nostalgic socialists who remembers manufacturing in its heyday – when workers belonged to trades unions, and the unions were powerful organizations. He's reported industry for thirty-odd years, he's *steeped* in it.'

'So . . .'

She raised a hand. 'No, let me finish – he's seen the way things have declined. The tens of thousands of men who've lost their jobs. He's always banging on about it.'

'Why Urbopark? Why should he have a grudge against a shopping mall?'

'Because, to him, Urbopark symbolizes this shift – I mean, Hallam's shift from a city that *makes* things to a city that *consumes* things. He can't stand the sight of all this . . . this rampant materialism, I suppose. The mall is a temple to consumerism and, through his sabotages, he's trying to get rid of the merchants.'

DCI Pink shook his head. 'Don't buy that. Pure conjecture.'

'And I've heard him say how shopworkers are the new "downtrodden masses" – long hours, low pay, poor job security, hardly any union representation, repressive management and so on.'

'All right, so he feels strongly about these things.'

Constance smiled. 'Those clues about where to *dig*, seeking the place to start digging. The connection to the Apocrypha, and to crypts – in other words, what lies *beneath* us, buried in the past.' She sensed her excitement being betrayed by her voice, her animation. 'Paul, what stood on this site before Urbopark was built?'

He looked at her.

'*Exactly!*' she said. 'A steelworks. A bloody great steelworks.'

The detective reclined in his chair. His face had regained its composed expressionlessness, the flicker of interest aroused by her last remark disappearing so rapidly and completely that she might have imagined it. The remnants of their meal cluttered the table. For a minute or two he'd been toying idly with one of the questionnaires handed out by Mr Bun. He wondered aloud – deadpan – whether William's dramatic repertoire included dressing up as a burger. *Or d'you reckon I'm suffering from connectionitis?* When she asked what he meant, he turned the paper towards her so she could see the slogan emblazoned across the foot of the page in heavy black type: THANKS TO YOU, OUR BURGERS ARE ALL THE RAGE!!!

On Monday morning, William thanked her for the enthusiastic review of *Death of a Salesman*, which had appeared prominently (with picture) on the arts pages of Saturday's *Crucible*. All three evening performances – as well as the Saturday matinee – had played to full houses, he informed her. Theatrical anecdotes followed, over coffee and during the opening of the post. He seemed not to notice her failure to make eye contact, or to contribute more than monosyllabic punctuation to his monologue of amdrammery. *She entered stage-left, the silly cow, with me looking stage-right* . . . After first edition, her colleague went out. As soon as he was gone, Constance sat at his terminal, switched off his monitor and switched it on again. She followed the log-on procedure, typing in 'William Boyce' and – one of her hunches – hazarding a guess at his password. The cursor moved blankly across the screen as she tapped the letters E-A-G-L-E. After a pause, the computer bleeped. *Password Invalid*. OK, worth a try. She turned her attention instead to his appointments diary – identifying the relevant dates and photocopying those pages. She faxed them to Hallam CID.

Mid-morning, Stan phoned. She felt intuitively that it was him, even though the caller didn't speak. She repeated his name several times into the mouthpiece.

In her lunch break, Constance drove to the industrial museum at Hallam Island. She took with her a head-and-shoulders photograph of William, obtained *en route* from the file of reporters' picture-bylines in the library at head office. She showed the mugshot to Granddad, asking him to examine it for any resemblance to the American tourist. A shake of the head. *What about if he was made up in some way – false moustache, or something?* Another negative. *Feller what gave me t'horseshoe were darker; darker hair, darker skin. Fair bit younger an' all I'd say.* He massaged the lower half of his face. *More stubbly.* Granddad studied the picture a little longer, prompted by her reminder that the man might've disguised his appearance; that men can shave or not shave, that they can wear wigs. Like, the way actors . . . *No, ducks. Different shaped face. Can't alter that, can you?* You could try, with make-up and the cut of your hair; earrings, even a hat for weddings and christenings and the like. The tilt of your head when you looked in the mirror, or when you were talking to someone; the strategic cupping of (jowly) chin in hand. Constance had been trying to disguise the shape of her face for as long as she could remember. Granddad handed back the photograph. There was a note of exasperation in her voice as she asked whether he was *absolutely certain* the American and the man in the picture weren't one and the same. Granddad said he'd never been absolutely certain of anything in his entire life.

'Blood' clue in hunt for Mall Madman

Exclusive Report
by Constance Amory, Urbopark Reporter

Police are celebrating a breakthrough in their hunt for the Mall Madman behind the spate of attacks on Hallam's giant Urbopark shopping complex.

The synthetic blood daubed on the doors to the mall in the first sabotage in September has been traced to a local manufacturer specializing in theatrical make-up.

Drama

A sample of 'blood' produced by the firm, Dramarama, has been found to match the graffiti.

The company, set up by three postgraduate chemistry students at Hallam Metropolitan University, has a small laboratory on campus where a range of cosmetics is synthesized.

Dramarama is co-operating with police inquires and has supplied details of all sales of fake blood to customers in the TV, theatre and cinema industry in the weeks before the first sabotage.

Then begins the pains-taking process of following up each order to eliminate the buyers from the investigation and to see if any of the product has gone astray.

Laboratory security is also being examined and a comprehensive stock-taking operation is under way to establish whether all 'blood' supplies manufactured by the firm can be accounted for.

Pink

Det. Ch. Insp. Paul Pink, of Hallam CID, said, 'This is a significant breakthrough in our investigation.

'Given the quantity of synthetic blood used in the graffiti incident, we are hopeful of finding out how, when and where the saboteur obtained his supplies. Once we discover that, we should be able to narrow the focus of the inquiry.'

Roderick

Roderick Rudd, 23, who co-founded Dramarama, said he was 'shocked and appalled' at the news that their product was implicated in the sabotages.

'I am not aware of any breach of security on our part, and what happens to the supplies after we've delivered them to the customer is hardly a matter over which we have any control,' he said. 'Nevertheless, we will do everything we can to assist the police.'

When she returned to Urbopark, there was a note stuck to the rim of her computer monitor, telling her to ring DCI Pink urgently. The note was signed by William, timed at 13.40. Why the twenty-four-hour clock? He was out, again, but he'd be back because his supply of foil-wrapped sandwiches lay in neat stacks on his desk. She rang Paul Pink right away. He thanked her for the fax, asking if she'd had any difficulty obtaining the photocopies. She said she hadn't. Had she spoken to her colleague, or anyone else, about her suspicions? No, of course not. Good. That was good. His officers had made discreet inquiries to the business contacts William had been with, according to his diary entries, at the time of various sabotages. The questions were carefully constructed, a general: *What were you doing . . .?*, rather than *Who were you with . . .?* or *Can you confirm whether a certain journalist was with you . . .?* Indeed, to safeguard against word filtering back to the suspect, his contacts were asked to supply a full résumé of their activities for the day in question. Checking these schedules against the timing of the sabotages, the police found that the entry 'William Boyce, *Crucible*' was, without exception, consistent with the suspect's own diary. Was it possible, she wondered, for these appointments to have been deliberately cancelled by William at the last minute; *phantom alibis* – the entries relating to meetings which never took place but which hadn't been erased from the respective contacts' diaries? DCI Pink said it had been established to his satisfaction that this wasn't the case.

'He didn't do it, then?'

'Not unless he's perfected the art of being in two places at once.'

'What about all the, you know, the things we talked about? The *clues*.'

'We constructed similar cases against Warren Bartholomew and Donald Moss; same evidence, different motives. Same outcome.'

Constance held onto the phone without speaking.

'Connie?'

'So we're back to square one,' she said.

'Not exactly.'

'How d'you mean?'

'Firstly, the Hallamshire TV tape – the correct one – will be available on Wednesday, fourteen-thirty at Hallam Central.'

'And secondly?'

'Secondly, I think the case you built against William was very . . . convincing.'

'Oh sure, just a shame he . . .'

'That is, I believe you may have got very close indeed to the *reason* for the sabotages. At least, it makes more sense than anything we've come up with so far.'

'What – right motive, wrong suspect? Or do I score another "maybe"?'

'If it isn't William Boyce,' said the inspector, 'it's someone who sees the world in very much the same way. Except, unlike your colleague, he's no longer prepared to confine his . . . political activism to the medium of the written word.'

Constance arranged the slices of Snickers on a plate. She ate them one by one between alternating sips of orange juice. The plate and glass stood within reach on her bedside table while, open on her lap, was the Ruskin biography. It was the first time she'd read the book since it had kept her up all night. Still bugging her, that clue: the message from the 'Man in the Moon', about Ruskin and *the nature of truth*. The more she reflected on John Ruskin's and the Pre-Raphaelites' belief in 'truth to nature' the more confused she became. To be true to nature, surely, required an appreciation of the nature of truth? All of which seemed to her to express an intellectual concern with the process of seeking rather than with what was being sought. Not so much a cryptic clue from the saboteur as an enticement to contemplate the nature of the cryptic itself. Taking up her pen and notepad, she wrote: Resistance To Meaning.

Another piece of Snickers. Beside her on the bed lay a telephone, which she'd been using from time to time during the course of her ruminations. She picked it up again and dialled. Ringing tone. *See, the thing is, whenever I call you at work, that woman – your secretary – says you're on sick leave, only she won't say what's wrong with you or when you're*

413

expected back. And she knows me, she recognizes my voice now. She doesn't like me. I can tell. She's fed up with me ringing up all the time, except it isn't all the time it's just a couple of times a day really, because how am I supposed to know . . . She listened to the ringing tone a moment longer then hung up.

Ruskin admired Hallam and its metalworkers so much he set up a museum here for working folk. She made another note: Preservation Of The Past. According to Granddad, Britain was turning into a theme park. No industry, only industrial heritage. *I made steel for thirty year, me. Now, t'gear we used – tools, machinery an' that – is in glass cabinets for folk to gawp at; and I'm cooped up in a coffin wi' a sliding window, punching tickets all day long.* Was this what the saboteur was getting at, a tension between past and present? Victorian romantic realists drawing influence from Raphael, more than three hundred years earlier; the Pre-Raphaelites, dissatisfied with this approach, casting back even further for inspiration. A blurring, an indivisibility of past and present, dead and living; that which was buried rising up to engulf that which had taken its place. This was her. This wasn't the saboteur, this was the historian in her interpreting his clues to fit her own preoccupations. This was her obsession, not his.

Telephone. No answer, just the familiar ceaseless ringing. *And when I phone your home number, you're never there. Is it her? Have you gone back to your ex-wife in Australia, to your children? Or has she come here, to reclaim you? If you hated me this much for what happened last week you could at least have . . .* The Snickers had softened in the warm room, leaving moist brown stains on her fingers. One more evening class before the end of term. So he couldn't have gone. And the flowers couldn't be goodbye. *The thing is, I don't know where you are. Are you there now, letting the phone ring and ring, knowing it's me? I don't know where you are. I don't know what's happening. I don't know what to think.*

Howard once said he'd been attracted to her because she

414

reminded him of a woman in a Pre-Raph. She'd loved him for
saying that. She had related his remark to Milly, who'd said,
What, he prefers his women two-dimensional? And, reflecting
on this now, Constance remembered the last time she'd seen
a Pre-Raphaelite painting.

The Inky Path
It benefits the aspiring journalist to have a thorough knowledge
of History. Events do not occur in isolation, and for their
implications to be fully comprehended they must be set in their
appropriate context. More important, however, than merely
absorbing the factual minutiae of historical record, the journalist
ought to develop a sense *of history. He must discern between*
the momentous and the significant, the interesting and the
mundane. Moreover, he must appreciate the scale *of history. In*
proportion to the age of the planet, mankind has lived but a
moment, each man for the duration of a blink. Seen thus, events
upon which the journalist reports – be they the barbarities of
war or prize-giving at the village fête – become so fleeting as
almost to disappear without trace. A consequence of such
thinking is that he may begin to question the relevance of himself
and his work in the wider world. This is no bad thing. The
reporter who has not, at some point, asked himself 'Why do I
write?' is as impoverished in his existence as the man who has
never wondered 'Why do I live?'

For the first time since the course began, Constance arrived
early. Two other women were already in the classroom. An
empty vase stood in the centre of the lecturer's desk, which
was otherwise bare. Its chair was tucked in neatly. The
blackboard, inscribed with mathematical formulae, gave a clue
to the room's previous activity. More than the pervasive
coldness, it was an indefinable smell of lingering damp – an
absence of the familiar singed-dust stench of hot radiators –
that drew attention to the lack of heating. Wheezy. A distinct
tightening of the *bronicles*. The hurried walk up the hill, the

apprehension, the classroom's mildewy chill. Would he be there? What would she say to him? Her head was swimming with unanswered questions, her stomach made into a chasm by the gap of his absence.

'Can't make head nor tail of that.' One of the women, addressing Constance, nodded in the direction of the blackboard. 'All that x = y stuff.'

Constance reciprocated her smile. 'I expect it means something to someone.'

'Aye, well, they're welcome to it.'

She went to her desk, draping her coat over the back of the chair and stuffing her scarf and gloves in the pockets so she'd not forget them. Her notepad had lost the newness of that first class, all those weeks ago; dog-eared, crammed with loose sheets and printed handouts, pages puckered from being written on. The pad's spine was creased, its cover tattooed with doodles. She rummaged in her bag for a biro.

'D'you know if Stan's going to be here?' she asked.

The two women looked at her. 'Far as I know,' one of them said.

'Only, I heard he'd been ill.' She placed a hand against the nearest radiator. Tepid, just beginning to warm up. 'Since last week, I mean.'

'They'd have let us know if t'class were cancelled or owt,' said the second woman. 'Leastways, you'd think so.'

Other students were arriving, fetching incomplete conversations into the room with them from the corridor and creating a discordance of footsteps and scraping chairs. Constance sat down, making space for the woman who shared her desk. They exchanged greetings, discussed the weather, the lack of heating; her neighbour lowered her voice to speculate conspiratorially on whether the Crashing Boer would turn up after storming out of the previous class.

'I wouldn't, if it were me,' she said. 'Wouldn't know wheer to put me face.'

Constance smiled. Ought to take a couple of puffs. Too late now, should've done it beforehand – in the ladies', or walking along the road. Ridiculous. Absolutely fucking ridiculous. She dragged her bag onto the desk, took out the inhaler and used it. Once, twice. She put the inhaler away again and set the bag back down on the floor. Her neighbour paid no attention whatsoever. Another smile. The woman offered her a sweet. As the room filled up, the *Con Amore* man's vacant seat was becoming the more conspicuous. So too was the tutor's, Stan usually being among the first arrivals in order to distribute any handouts and to organize his materials in readiness for a prompt start. Those women were right, if he wasn't coming the class would've been cancelled and the students notified in advance. Any moment, he'd walk through the doorway with one of his breezy greetings and an anecdotal apology for being late. She could picture him, dishevelled, breathless; glasses steamed up and clothes in their customary state of baggy disarray. He'd dump his battered leather briefcase at one end of the desk and produce swathes of papers and books, chatting all the while. Making folk laugh. And he would catch her eye. He'd smile at her, and his expression would impart some unspoken signal that she understood to mean she was to wait behind at break-time; so they could talk, so he could explain. Because, the way her mind was working now, she couldn't imagine how he'd even begin to find the words to convince her. Of what? Just to *convince* her. If she saw him, if she heard him speak, everything would be resolved. It would make sense. She wanted to see him so much she was afraid of herself.

A man entered the classroom, rapping self-consciously on the open door to attract attention. Awesomely tall, with prematurely thinning fair hair and blue cravat, thirtyish; clutching a sheaf of papers. He appeared to be blushing.

'Industrial History?' An affirmative murmur. He moved towards the lecturer's empty desk and stood behind it. More confident now, as though bolstered by adopting a traditional

417

tutorial pose. 'Now, I'm afraid to say Professor Bell is indisposed this evening . . . however,' he raised the wad of notes, smiling, 'he hasn't forgotten you.'

As he made his way around the room, passing copies to each student, the intermediary explained: 'Basically, so far as I can gather, they summarize the topics he'd have covered with you himself, if he'd been here.'

Constance glanced at the handout. It was a photocopy of one of the word-processed study sheets Stan produced to impose a semblance of structure on his otherwise informal lectures. Typed at his flat, she presumed, if he hadn't been at the university for the past week. Only, he'd not been at home either. She slipped the page inside her notebook. Some members of the group were expressing disgruntlement at the last-minute cancellation of the class, others were gathering up their belongings. The man in the cravat tendered an apology on behalf of the college, then – having handed out the last of the study notes – excused himself. Constance was still hauling her coat on when she caught up with him in the corridor. He turned, towering above her, his pale face looming spectrally out of a corona of light cast by a strip directly overhead.

'Are you . . . d'you mind me asking, only I was wondering if you were a friend. Of Stan's. Professor Bell.'

'We're colleagues, yes,' he said. 'That's to say, I teach here as well.' He had one hand on a door that gave on to a stairwell, holding the door ajar. Green eyes. A strand of blond hair, combed to conceal his baldness, had flopped forward on to his brow. He swept it back with mild irritation. 'Was there a problem?'

'It's just, I didn't know whether you'd seen him.'

' 'Fraid I don't quite follow.'

'When he gave you his lecture notes.'

'Ah, no. Got those from the office. He dropped them in and muggins here, being in the wrong place at the wrong time, was asked to do the honours.'

'He's been into the office, then? I mean, in the last day or two.'

'When I say "dropped them in", I couldn't swear that he actually delivered them in person. They may have arrived in the post for all I know.' He checked his watch. 'Look, I have a class of my own waiting for me.'

'You've no idea what's wrong with him?'

He seemed puzzled. 'Nothing, so far as I know.'

'You said he was indisposed . . . is he ill, or away, or what?'

'Something of a generic term, "indisposed". "Not here", in ad. ed. parlance.' He opened the door more widely. 'I really can't tell you any more than that, I'm afraid.'

Constance went to say something else, but checked herself. Several students from Professor Bell's class were making their way noisily along the corridor towards them. She said thanks, apologizing for detaining him. He formed his face into another smile and went through the door without a word, letting it clatter shut behind him.

At home that night, Constance read Stan's study sheet – headed 'Week 12: Trades Unions' – making a summary of his handout in her own notebook:

Notes

Main concerns of unions (aka: trade societies) in H. in mid-19th C. were to combat:

(a) introduction of machinery to replace traditional tool-making methods (i.e. beginnings of mass production, threat to quality of craftsmanship and livelihood of craftsmen);

(b) non-union workers undercutting union members (i.e. working for lower rates of pay);

(c) non-union workers undermining industrial action by filling the jobs of those on strike;

(d) non-union workers/employers taking on too many apprentices (i.e. flooding the labour market, forcing down rates of pay, reducing quality/skill factor);

(e) union members failing to pay subscriptions (i.e. benefit without contribution; shortage of funds to support other members during periods of poor trade, unemployment and sickness);

(f) false marking of 'Hallam' as place of origin, use of inferior materials and the practice of marking machine-made products as hand-made.

Rattening

With unions technically allowed to exist but severely hampered by legal restrictions on their activities, the societies in H. had no compunction in taking steps against the above (i.e. points 'a' to 'f'). Rattening consisted of the removal or destruction of the band connecting a grindstone to its revolving shaft, making it impossible for the grinder to work. If these methods failed to halt 'rogue' practices, more direct intimidation was used – including physical assaults on individuals and gunpowder attacks on their workplaces or homes. In 1859, a Hallam saw grinder was shot dead; in 1861, an explosion at the home of a fender grinder resulted in the death of an innocent lodger. A similar attack in Hereford Street in 1866, while not causing death or injury, led to such an outcry around the country that there were calls for a public inquiry into the legal status and activities of trades unions.

Inquiry

In 1867, a Royal Commission of Inquiry was appointed. So serious and unique was the situation in Hallam that a separate sub-commission was set up, with power to grant indemnity from prosecution to those who testified truthfully (deemed necessary to get such a close-knit community to give evidence). Only one witness was placed under arrest – Daniel Amory, an apprentice saw grinder, held overnight for falsely denying his involvement in the explosion at Hereford Street. Facing criminal charges, and certain imprisonment or transportation, the youth – nicknamed Lucky Penny – was eventually persuaded to co-operate with the inquiry when his father visited him in his cell in the hour before his recall to the witness box. Over five weeks, the commissioners – sitting at Hallam Town Hall –

heard evidence of hundreds of cases of rattening and more serious offences. The most notorious orchestrator was the secretary of the Saw Grinders', William Broadhead – known as Old Smite 'Em.

NB: These acts of violence became known as the <u>Hallam Outrages</u>.

QUOTE OF THE WEEK (1): 'All trade outrages, strikes and rattenings are the inevitable consequence of one-sided and unjust laws; and so long as the working classes are treated as outlaws, it is not only their right but their bounden duty to make and enforce such laws as will enable them to maintain their wives and families in comfort by their labour, and in so doing they only obey that law of necessity which overrides all partial and unjust man-made laws.'

Isaac Ironside, 30 September 1867

QUOTE OF THE WEEK (2): 'The only way to do away with trade outrages is to remove the cause, by legalizing trades unions and by placing labour on an equality with capital.'

Spring Knife Cutlers resolution, September 1867

Prof. Stanley Bell's Physical, Metaphysical and Philosophical Glossary of Metal

<u>Coins</u>: Perhaps the most remarkable metallic creation in the history of humankind is the coin. Devoid of practical function and mass produced from stamped blanks of cheap metal, its value derives entirely from its potential as a means of exchange for goods or services. In other words, a coin is worth whatever society deems it to be worth at any given moment. While coins themselves are increasingly marginalized or superseded by paper, plastic and electronic cash transactions, the principle of the superiority of monetary value over inherent value is stronger than ever. Our ability to live is determined by our ability to spend. It is this facility for constructing a society based on an abstract concept of worth that characterizes humankind.

The room was in darkness, blinds pulled down over the windows. Paul Pink and Constance Amory sat in front of a television monitor being operated for them by a police technical officer. As the screen flickered into life, a silvery-blue light illuminated the features of the three viewers. A picture: crowd scene, interior of a football stadium. Paul and Constance leant forward, faces close to the screen; her hair brushed his shoulder. The camera was aimed at a section of pitch inside the right-angle formed by touchline and halfway line. Two people were in the centre of the shot – one holding a microphone and handing a metal tankard to the other, much older, man. They were smiling, exaggeratedly. In the foreground was a photographer (captured on film, capturing the moment on film); in the background was a perimeter hoarding (an advertisement for double glazing) and several rows of seating.

'That's you,' said DCI Pink, touching the tip of a finger against the screen.

She was standing; the seat to her left was empty, as were several others in the vicinity. Most of the spectators in shot were also standing. He indicated a man to her right and asked if that was the *professor chappie* with whom she'd attended the match.

She shook her head. 'He was off getting himself a meat-and-potato pie.'

'The banner man comes into shot any second now, from the . . . right?' He looked for confirmation to the technician, who gave the thumbs-up. 'Our angle means we catch him more or less directly from behind.'

The technician, who had freeze-framed, let the film run on. A figure appeared from the edge of the screen. He was facing the bank of spectators as he paraded slowly along a channel between the first row of seats and the advertising hoarding. Arms raised, supporting a large white cloth. The words could not be seen on the video recording, because the banner – like the man's face – was directed away from the camera. He was wearing a red-and-white bobble hat.

'*There*, hold it there . . .' The picture froze again. 'He turns his head. Only slightly, but enough for us to make out that

422

he's wearing glasses. You see the stem, where it's glinting in the floodlights?'

Constance nodded.

'About five-ten, five-eleven,' the inspector continued. 'Caucasian. Weight? Hard to tell in that get-up.'

The banner man was wearing a black duffel coat and brown trousers. The definition was imperfect, the camera did not zoom in for a close-up. Nor did the subject reveal more than tantalizing glimpses of his face in profile (and then, mostly obscured by his upper arm as he held the banner aloft). His legs, partially concealed by the hoarding, did not come fully into shot until he moved up one of the exit aisles. His trousers were too long, bunching in baggy folds over his shoes.

DCI Pink looked at Constance. 'Anyone you recognize?'

'Is that the only shot we've got of him?'

'Aye. Not much to go on, I know.'

She continued to stare at the picture, freeze-framed in the moment of the suspect's departure. She could see her screen-self in the crowd, head turned to watch him go; the seat to her left remained unoccupied – her companion yet to make a flustered return with his half-time pie. The real Constance leaned back in her chair.

'No,' she said. 'Sorry, but I don't recognize him at all.'

When she arrived home from work, there was a letter on the hall table. Her name and address were written, in red, in an unfamiliar hand; the envelope was postmarked Hallam. She took the letter into the kitchen, where Milly was spooning cottage cheese into her mouth straight from the tub. They said hi. Constance examined the handwriting again before opening the envelope. Inside was a strip of paper – a checkout receipt:

HypaCenta
Urbopark, Hallam
General Store Manager
John Chapple

423

On the reverse, two serial numbers had been written in the same red ink as that on the envelope:

331.88 DOU
823.914 BEL

'Anything interesting?' asked Milly.

'D'you make of this?'

Milly took the strip of paper. 'Shopping receipt.'

'Yeah, but on the back.'

'Book classification codes. Dewey.'

'How d'you mean, Dewey?'

'Dewey Decimal Classification. We use this system at work.'

'Any idea what sort of books? I mean, can you tell from the codes?'

Milly moved over to where Constance was sitting. 'Sorry, I've got cottage cheese on it.' She brushed at the paper, leaving a smear. Pointing to the first of the numbers, she said, 'Right, 331.88 is trade unions, I think. Industrial relations, anyway. D-O-U is the first three letters of the author's surname.'

'What about the other one?'

'OK, literature – my area. Any books in the 800s, basically, come under the general heading of literature. The 820s are English literature, and the 3 in 823 tells you it's fiction rather than, say, poetry or drama or whatever. Does all this make sense?'

'Yeah, go on.'

'And the numbers after the point refer to when the book was written. Here, we've got 91, which means the twentieth century – and the 4 on the end narrows it down to post-1945. Again, B-E-L is the author's name.'

'Bell?'

'Or Bellamy. Or, I don't know, Belper. Could be anything.'

'Do all libraries use this system?'

Milly shook her head. 'The university does, but the public libraries in Hallamshire – the council ones – they use a different one.'

'So I could borrow these two books out of your library, could I?'

'Not without a user's card, which you haven't got – seeing as you're not a student, or staff, and you haven't paid a user's fee.'

'But *you* could.'

Milly frowned. '. . . Yeah.'

Constance looked at her watch. 'Mill, what time does the library close?'

The first volume, bound in green fabric and frayed at the corners, was *Rage & Outrage: Minutes of the 1867 Royal Sub-commission of Inquiry into the Hallam Trades Unions* (Hallam Metropolitan University Press, 1959); introduced by Alisdair Dougvie, Prof. of Political, Economic & Social History. The second wasn't a book at all, in that it was neither a published work nor professionally printed. They came across it in the fiction stacks, shelved correctly according to its author code and classification number between ranks of properly bound volumes. It was a typescript comprising dozens of sheets of A4 between two rectangles of blue card, held together by treasury tags. Milly remarked that *theft* of library books was common, but she'd never known anyone trouble to make a donation. The text was double-spaced in 12-point Times New Roman. The title, pasted to the cover, read: *The Life and Times of a Hallam Saw Grinder (a Dramatic Reconstruction in Many Parts)*, by Stanley Bell.

At home that evening, Constance opened the typescript at the first page and began reading.

November 1857

The children were still asleep when Thomas Amory sat on his fireside stool to eat the breakfast his wife had made . . .'

Friday was Art in the 'Park day. The exhibition was the first in a programme of cultural events devised by Mall Admin to repair the damage done to Urbopark's public image (and to its trade) by the sabotages. An artist living and working in Hallam had been commissioned, according to the press release, to *capture the mall's essence in aesthetic form*. More specifically, she'd been asked to paint a selection of exterior and interior views – *portraying the impressive scale and modern architectural grandeur of the Urbopark site, as well as the vibrant hustle and bustle of the arcades themselves*. Mall Promo intended to use the paintings in a series of posters, postcards and limited-edition prints. A temporary gallery had been set up in the main plaza, where a ceremonial unveiling by the Mayor of Hallam was to take place promptly at ten.

A buzz of consternation emanated from the gathering when he drew back the curtains. Instead of a dozen paintings, there was one – a large oil-on-canvas standing on an easel in the centre of an otherwise empty exhibition area. The subject was a solitary, middle-aged woman peering into the window of a milliner's shop (Hat's Your Lot – Red, Lower). Various items of headwear were visible through the glass, in which could also be seen the woman's face in reflection. The title was:

> Mrs Marjorie Collings, 56, Of Sherwood Road,
> Huxley, Hallam, Seeks
> A Hat For Less Than £50 To Accompany
> The Sky Blue Outfit She
> Has Bought For The Occasion Of Her
> Granddaughter's Christening

As the babble of confusion among the onlookers abated, one of the journalists – an art critic – put a question to the artist, standing beside her work. He wondered whether, by painting just one picture – and by her choice of subject matter – she was deliberately exploiting individuality to symbolize the universality of the shopping experience. *No*, replied the artist. *It's a picture of Mrs Collings, choosing a hat.*

Constance and William, between them, filled most of page one of that evening's first edition: Mall PR Stunt Backfires, Urbopark To Sue Artist Over Exhibition 'Fiasco', Hat's Off To Painter Says Mrs C.; Howard's photographs completed the *Crucible*'s coverage. As soon as the copy had been filed and the pictures despatched to head office by motorcycle courier, Howard invited Constance to join him for a lunch-time pint at the Cutler's Arms. She declined. Because a) she didn't want to go for a drink; and, b) she didn't want to be with him. Two reasons. Three reasons, the third being Howard's comment while they were discussing the mall exhibition story – *If you get paid to produce a range of pictures, you produce a range of pictures. End of story.* It was the sort of remark he'd always have made, but it was only now she'd allowed herself to *notice* it. When you came down to it, she could've spent the day compiling reasons why she didn't want to go for a pint with

Howard. But, when he made the invitation, she simply said, *No thanks*. And he went away.

Alone in the office, Constance resumed her internal dialogue with Stanley Bell. A monologue, really, because Stan's contributions were her words in his mouth. *In the beginning was the word, and the word was: rage.* She'd worked out most of the 'what', 'how', 'when' and 'where', she knew the 'who'; even the 'why' made sense in what she interpreted to be his terms. The time he'd arranged to pick her up for the football had been one of his more obscure clues. 7.07. Which, taking liberties with the twenty-four-hour clock, could be translated as 18.67 (sixty-seven minutes past six); or 1867, the year of the commission of inquiry into the Hallam Outrages. The 'Jerome' note having been concealed at page 1,867 of the Bible in the pulpit at St Dunstan's. And St Jerome's day was 30 September, which also happened to be the date of death, in 1940, of the steel entrepreneur Sir Robert Bayfield, whose factory made way for Urbopark; and the date, in 1867, when Isaac Ironside argued a moral justification of trade outrages; and the date, in 1996, when Stanley Bell told Constance Amory she had a lovely smile. He had a thing about dates. 8 October 1866: Hereford Street outrage, after which (according to *The Life and Times . . .*) an ancestor of Constance concealed himself in a cricket ground at Bramall Lane; 8 October 1996: Hallam United vs Grimsby Town, at a stadium occupying the site where the cricket ground had stood. Stan's midriff bulge, a banner hidden beneath his coat; his beard, tickling her when he spoke into her ear. Stan's beard. Even if she hadn't made a connection with the slashing of the leather and furs and the sending of sabotaged hate mail, she could've kicked herself for failing to wonder why an unshaven man would have razor blades in his bathroom cabinet.

Amory. Good old Hallam name, that. The very first evening class. But the first of the sabotages had already taken place before then – before Stan even knew her, or knew of her connection with Urbopark. So it wasn't because of her. It wasn't *just* because of her. She was a bonus, an added dimension; a fortuitous twist to be incorporated into the plot of his outrages. What was it like, coming back to Hallam after all those years to find a shopping mall where the steelworks had stood? Because it wasn't the first time, was it? That phone call she'd taken yesterday from a journalist in Australia, where a mall built on former industrial land had been the target for a similar campaign. Unsolved. The name of his newspaper, the *Melbourne Age*. As in Mr. So many names you couldn't tell the true ones from the false. The Amorys of his story were *real* – Thomas and Daniel were there in black and white in the official minutes of the inquiry – but were they her ancestors, or was the surname yet another coincidence? She rang Granddad. *Now then, my dad were born in 1904, and his name were Clement; and his dad – my granddad – were born in 1879 . . . Thomas Amory.* No. Too late, 1879; the Thomas of Stan's story would've been born in about 1830. *Was Thomas a family name, d'you know? Couldn't tell thee, ducks – lot o' folk took theer father's name in them days. Or their grand-father's? Aye, mebbe.* Lucky Penny was fact – a family heirloom – though its existence in *The Life and Times* . . . was a fiction, an idea gleaned from an 'American tourist's' gossip with a museum attendant wearing a name badge marked 'Frederick Amory'.

Stan would've approved of the portrait of Mrs Collings, choosing a hat; it would've appealed to his non-conformism and to his penchant for disruptive action. A physical as well as intellectual rejection of officially imposed values. What Constance was less sure of was whether he'd understand the artist's motive or share her perspective. To Stan, she sensed, the hordes of shoppers who visited Urbopark each day were just that – hordes; an unthinking lumpen consumertariat with a herd mentality, enslaved by the guile of marketing and advertising, bewitched by the glittering wonderland of arcadia, consumed by a conditioned urge to consume. Pigs at a trough. *Stan, you wouldn't even* see *Mrs Marjorie Collings looking at the display in a milliner's window – if you painted a picture of the mall, she'd be a tiny anonymous figure among thousands swarming along an arcade.* He wasn't around to hear any of this. At least, he *was* around – the bouquet, the silence at the end of a phone, the till receipt, the library books, the voice in her head – but she had no idea of where he was or how to contact him. Or what he planned to do next. The number of times she'd read his typescript, seeking connections between the outrages then and the sabotages now – finding clues in every reference to blood, leather, floods, fire . . . and clues to other clues: the Eagle Ironworks, the Bible, a chapel, the Man in the Moon. But if he had one final sabotage in mind, she'd no idea what it might be or when it might occur.

A declaration over the mall's public address system interrupted her train of thought. *Urbopark – we put U first.* Which was crap, because what they meant was 'you' second-person plural rather than 'you' second-person singular. *You lot.* Mall Admin weren't interested in Mrs Collings, hat buyer, any more than Stan was. What she should do was pick up the phone and tell Paul Pink. She should just pick up the phone and tell him. She picked up the phone, put it down again. *Why me, Stan? Why choose me for your game of cat and mouse?* And he'd reply: *Because you are a descendant of the men of steel; because you have words at your disposal; because you are the Gal at the Mall. Because you are a traitor to your class, your roots, your history.* Or something like that. She wanted to ask him why he'd fucked her. 'Fucked', or 'made love to'? At the time it had seemed like love-making, now it felt like she'd been fucked. How could that happen? How could an experience – an actual physical experience – be one thing, then become something else? She wanted to ask why he'd fucked her, but she was afraid this might lead her to question why she'd fucked him. And she didn't want to think about that.

Professor Bell, lecturer. *The university's report on low pay at HypaCenta – did you have a sneak preview before it was published? Did one of the Guard Rite security staff at the*

430

campus tip you the wink about the firm's Mall Secure bid? Did your university security pass sneak you into the I.T. centre to infect the Mall Sys software with your virus? And into the Dramarama lab to steal their fake blood? And into the library to conceal your typescript among the books? She could've stumbled across that typescript at his flat; if he'd spent longer cleaning his teeth in the bathroom before that kiss, she might have become curious to peruse the pages stacked beside his word processor. And what if she had? What then? *Why poison innocent people, Stan?* See, if he'd thought of shoppers as 'Stacey Liddle, aged seven, schoolgirl, yoghurt eater', or 'Mr Ernest Jones, 73, retired steelworker, orange-juice drinker' he wouldn't have made them sick. *So why?* And Stan answered . . . She didn't know. To tell the truth, she didn't know what he would say in response to any of her questions.

The connecting door between editorial and reception opened.

'Feller asked me to give this to you,' said Sally. '*Extremely* urgent, he said. I told him, whatever it was, it were *extremely* late for city final, but he—'

Constance stood up, still holding the unopened envelope, and ran out into the arcade. Hopeless. Hundreds of people streaming past in both directions, an eddy of bobbing heads and faces made kaleidoscopic by the patternless whirl of motion, and by the play of light.

'*Connie.*' Sally was beside her, clutching Constance's arm in the manner of a mother grabbing hold of a child at the edge of a busy road.

'You see which way he went?'

'He'd been gone a few minutes before I had a chance to give you t'letter.'

'What'd he look like?'

'I don't know . . . beard, glasses. Forty summat, I'd say.'

Constance, who'd continued to stare up and down the arcade, finally gave up – aware that passers-by were looking

431

at her; aware, too, that she was causing an obstruction. She turned back towards the office.

'D'you know him, then?'

'Yeah. I mean, sort of.'

She went through to editorial, shutting the door behind her. Her name was written on the envelope in red. Inside was a postcard bearing an aerial photograph of Urbopark, showing its coloured roofs and glass domes and atria gleaming beneath an unnaturally brilliant blue sky. The mall resembled a cruise ship, or a luxury hotel, or a palace, or a gigantic theme park, or a futuristic city on the cover of a sci-fi magazine. The mall, captured with such sparkling clarity, might've been constructed of nothing but crystal and silver and stained glass. She turned the card over. On the reverse, signed 'Yours, W(illiam) B(roadhead)', was the message: EXIT, ORANGE & RED.

The Orange exit gave onto an elevated concrete walkway connecting the mall to its appropriately colour-coded car-park; this broad bridge being exposed to the sky and to the biting winds which seemed perpetually to circulate the superstructure of the complex as though generated by the walls themselves. The uninterrupted ebb and flow of shoppers made Constance conspicuous as she loitered by the doors – examining faces for his, or for the approach of some stranger bearing another message from him. Perhaps he'd left a cryptic clue for her to find: a few words of graffiti, a note scribbled on an advertising billboard. But there was nothing and everything; because, how could you seek something when you didn't know what you were supposed to be looking for? Was she supposed simply to wait here, or what? *For* what? She shouldn't be here. She shouldn't be alone. Where she should be was, in her office – talking to Paul Pink on the phone, waiting for him to relieve her of the burden of the message, of its implications and of the necessity to act upon it. She should hand the burden to him. Constance removed a scrunchie from her wrist and fixed her hair against the irritating attentions of the breeze. Why orange *and* red; why both exits? The two colours prompted an association, causing her to search in her bag for the HypaCenta till receipt. Three 'orange' items (orange juice, apricot shampoo, carrots), three 'red' (tomatoes, Red Leicester, cherryade); the colours of the bouquet he'd sent her; scarlet 'rage' on a tangerine screen when Mall Sys crashed. A vanity mirror. Mirror? *Daily Mirror* . . . mirror, mirror on the wall . . . *the cutler must produce a keen cutting edge and make the sides of the blade so even and smooth that they reflect light like a mirror, without distortion* (Industrial History of Hallam, Week 9) . . . mirror, signal, manouevre . . . hall of mirrors . . . *the role of the newspaper is to hold a mirror up to society, so that the reader will see his world from another perspective and be better able to reflect upon it* (*The Inky Path*). Why was there a vanity mirror among the items listed on the till receipt? *For Christ's sake, Stan, how d'you expect me to . . .?* The chief inspector wouldn't find Stan, because Stan – she was sure – wouldn't allow himself to be found by anyone but her. 'Exit, Orange & Red' was for her alone to understand. Which meant he must be spying on her – here, now – to make certain she wasn't leading them to him. Constance moved away from the doors so that she was fully exposed in the centre of the elevated walkway. Here was a panoramic view from Orange over the adjacent Red Zone car-park, sprawling below her. Queasy. She braced herself with both hands against the parapet, gazing out across hundreds of vehicles arranged in compliance within the grid's perfect symmetry. Trees and landscaped shrubbery alleviated the urban harshness of metal and glass and asphalt. Beyond the car-park was one of the peripheral roads which encircled Urbopark, and beyond that lay the black hulk of a disused rolling mill soon to make way for another of the mall's overflow parking zones. A flash of light, then another and another in rapid succession. If she was only subliminally aware of the first, the other two enabled her to take a bearing. The source of the flashes was a tall free-standing structure silhouetted on the horizon beside the abandoned works. A water tower. Something at the top of the tower was glinting with erratic frequency, catching what light there was in the anaemic November sky. Too far away to make out what it was, though the sequence of coruscations seemed too contrived to be the result of mere chance.

To reach the water tower, she had to go back inside the shopping centre, down a flight of escalators to the Lower Mall, and out again into the car-park through the Red exit. She traversed the car-park briskly, her view of the tower obscured now by trees lining the perimeter road. It wasn't until she'd crossed the carriageway that the structure became visible again – looming above her at the brow of a steep grassy bank. Four legs supporting a great square tank of blackened and corroded metal, made accessible by a ladder enclosed within a tubular safety frame. Constance was prevented from scaling the slope by a fence of spiked palings more than twice her height. Following the fence, she came to a point where the road looped round the end of the derelict factory and under a bridge. Here, she would leave the reassuring familiarity of the mall site behind altogether and disappear into an industrial wasteland of empty buildings and deceased streets and clearance sites; no cars, no people. She hesitated. *Why me?* And he answered: *Because you must be made to bear the weight of your history.* His words, in her mind, were spelled out in red: the colour of the ink on the envelope containing a HypaCenta till receipt; the colour of the writing on the postcard of Urbopark; the colour of the anonymous warnings to the men who were about to suffer at the hands of their enraged fellows. *You are the Mall Madman, Stan, but are you mad? Are you mad* enough? She saw a bloodstained cleaner on a stretcher; a blazing car; a book flying through the air to crash against the newly closed door of a classroom. And she felt the gentleness of his touch as he cured her hiccups; she heard the warmth of his laughter, and the softness of his voice the time he phoned to say goodnight. One or other or both of these Stans was beckoning, but the path was hers to choose. Turn around. Just turn around

434

now, while you still can; go back to the office and phone Paul Pink. Or, go ahead. Constance made her choice.

The gates of the abandoned mill were imposing, fabricated more than a century ago from wrought iron. They guarded the entrance to what would have been a delivery yard in the days when steel was still manufactured here. Partially blocked from view by one of the factory outbuildings was the tower – seen, now, from the opposite angle to her first glimpse of it from the mall. A fat chain coupled the gates, fastened by a padlock the size of a man's fist. There was a placard: DANGER – KEEP OUT. It was only when she took a closer look that she saw the chain had been severed, as if by bolt-cutters – the dull greyish-brown skin of one of the links shorn open to expose its shiny innards. When Constance pushed against the gates, the chain unravelled and fell noisily to the ground.

Her footsteps reverberated off the blank brick walls of the buildings, each sharp sound multiplied so that the echoes themselves spawned echoes. Over one of the doors, a painted sign, faded and flaking, said 'Goods Inwards'. The door was padlocked, the lock apparently seized with rust. In the far corner of the delivery area, a narrow passage afforded access into a second, smaller, yard overgrown with weeds that had forced jagged fissures in the concrete. It was here that the water tower stood. She looked up, seeking a figure. There was none. For the first time, she called his name; no response other than the ricochet of her own voice repeating the solitary syllable. She called his name again, with the same consequence. *Have I sinned against the past?* Silence. *If I am a sinner, what are the wages of my sin?* Silence. *Do you have that potential?* Silence, the unuttered questions pulsing in her head. Her neck hurt from looking up. The vast tank was etched black against the sky, the drifting passage of a cloud creating the illusion that the tower itself was moving – toppling over – and would, at any moment, crush her beneath a tangle of dead metal. Her shirt, the thin material dampened with perspiration, clung to her beneath the prickly wool of her jumper. The only sounds were a muted backdrop of traffic and, overhead, an almost imperceptible creaking, as though the long-neglected water tower was muttering in protest against the assault of the elements and of its own old age. Or, perhaps its ancient joints were betraying whatever it was that lurked unseen within the black tank. Constance swallowed, leaving a bitter aftertaste. *Did you anticipate this, Stan; that I wouldn't be able to resist? That, despite the fear and the dread, I would have to* know? *I am afraid, if that's what you want; but I've no idea whether I'm afraid of you or of me or of fear itself.*

It wasn't until she began to climb the ladder that she noticed the wind, tugging at her clothes as she ascended out of the sheltered enclosure of the yard. Look up. Whatever you do, look up, don't look down. The rungs were encrusted with rust, one or two missing altogether or so obviously corroded that she knew not to tread there. But most were sturdy, supporting her weight. Her palms, where she gripped the sides of the ladder, were ingrained with sweat and reddish-brown streaks of dirt. She wanted to shut her eyes, but she couldn't; she had to focus on the next rung, and the rung after that. Five, ten, fifteen . . . She had to concentrate on the minutest detail of each step without once permitting herself to think about the consequences of their accumulation. Twenty, twenty-five . . . Her arms ached, her breathing became laboured. Despite keeping her eyes fixed on what she was doing, she couldn't help but become peripherally aware of the ground receding beneath her and of the air's invisible expansion above and all around her, until the urge to look down became almost irresistible. She stopped, closed her eyes. No. This was worse, engulfing her in a swimming nausea; she opened her eyes again and continued to climb. Thirty, thirty-five, forty . . . Her legs were heavy, her hands and feet reduced to clumsy lumps of meat at the ends of her limbs. She allowed herself to glance up, expecting to see his face staring down at her from the rim of the tank; but she saw only sky.

What could he do? Close down the mall and construct a

factory on its ruins? Teach shoppers and shopworkers to make steel? One by one, bring back to life all the other long-dead works that gave Hallam its name of Steel City? Then what? Transform the rolling mills into toolmakers' wheels; turn steelmakers into cutlers and grinders? Would he, then, replace the workshops with craftsmen's cottages and the cottages with fields; would he turn the city into the town it once was, its marketplace drawing in folk from miles around to spend, spend, spend on things they themselves had not produced? Could ore be extracted from metal and restored to rock? Could the hands of time be made to run anticlockwise? If he had answers to these questions, she could not hear them in her head. She was angry with him, now. She was furious at the implied assumption of her complicity in his historical perspective – his insistence that she should see the world as he saw it, or not at all. Having fucked her body, he was trying to fuck her mind. Only, she would not be fucked in this way. Her mind had been penetrated, but penetration wasn't the same as fucking; she wouldn't permit herself to be fucked there. She refused to become a character in history, in *his* story. *I don't exist in the past, Stan. Here and now is where I dwell. My history is not alive, it is dead. It is yesterday's news.* The past was to be found only in memories and in the visible traces of what remained, yet to be buried. *Thomas Amory, saw grinder, is dead. Daniel Amory, saw grinder's son, is dead.* Crookes, Linley, Fearnehough, Robert Smith . . . all of them. Stan could not revive them by writing a story of their life and times, no matter how he balanced the truth and the fiction of it. *I am alive. You may have manipulated and manoeuvred me with your clues, your words, your emotional and physical violations – but I am not dependent on you for my existence. I am* alive. He could no more control her life than he could remake the world to suit him. The moment he'd chosen to effect change through terrorism, he had relinquished creation in favour of destruction; he could not create, he could only consume. *So, will you consume me, Stan? Will you destroy that which you*

437

*cannot control? Will you kill me? How? Push me from this
ladder? Or, having led me here, will you watch me become so
petrified that I fall like a stone to my own death?*

At the top, the ladder described an inverted 'U', descending
briefly inside the water tank to be bisected by a narrow
platform. As she went to raise herself over the rim of the tank,
Constance was buffeted by a gust of wind that yanked her left
leg free of its foothold. Her shoe came off, spiralling to the
ground in a shower of rusty fragments. Her yelp of alarm
reverberated in the yard below. She brought her foot back
into contact with the uppermost rung and swung herself over,
clambering hurriedly down the other side. She stood on the
platform, rooted; her hands continued to grip the rails so
tightly her knuckles whitened and, if she ever let go, her fingers
would surely be seized in claw-like deformity. The metal
beneath her feet was cold and abrasive against her bare skin
where the sole of her tights had been torn. Jesus. She shut her
eyes again. And, when she reopened them, she looked down
into the tank. Empty. Dry, save for puddles of stagnant
rainwater that had formed in the hollows of its misshapen
floor. Here and there, she could see chinks of daylight. More
rungs continued to the bottom, but the floor looked unsafe
and, in any case, there was nothing to see but fallen leaves,
drinks cans, the corpse of a starling, an empty paint tin, two
tennis balls, shards of fractured glass. No Stan, nor any sign
of him. She began to wonder whether the sequence of flashes
she'd seen from the car-park was imaginary; or whether they
hadn't been signals but had, after all, been the result of light
reflecting randomly off some semi-detached part of the tower's
structure. A laugh escaped from her. She let go of the rails at
last, cupping her hands to her face and exhaling into the palms.
Her fingers smelled of rust and sweat. Stan wasn't here. He
hadn't been here at all. He . . . Then, among the detritus in
the tank, she saw what appeared to be a perfect round hole
directly beneath her at the base of the ladder. Peering down,
she was startled by a fleeting sight of flesh and hair, an eye, a

nostril. In that shocking instant, she believed it to be him standing beneath the tank, looking up at her through the hole. But what she'd seen, she realized, was not *his* face but a fragment of her own; what she was looking at was not a hole but the reflective glass of a brand-new vanity mirror.

From her vantage point, she looked out over the rolling mill, and beyond to the city skyline pockmarked with high-rise housing and bright office blocks. And, in the opposite direction, she saw the mall, dominated by its central glass dome; beyond that, the elevated section of motorway and twin cooling towers in the shadow of which she parked at the commencement of each new working day. All of this, made miniature beneath the uninterrupted vastness of the sky. From here, Urbopark resembled an architect's model for a proposed development, with tiny plastic trees and toy cars and inch-high people. The mall. Was that his intention? Was there to be a final outrage – not against her, but against Urbopark itself. It occurred to Constance, in a moment of overwhelming dread, that he had lured her here not to harm her but to ensure that she would not be harmed by whatever was about to take place. As she gazed out over the complex, she anticipated the deadened boom of an explosion from within its walls, and great belches of flame and smoke bursting through the shattered glass of its atria. She pictured people disgorging from the exits in panic, their screams – and the awful cries of those still trapped inside – carried faintly to her on the wind. And she visualized the scene inside the mall: men, women and children shredded by flying glass, blown apart, burnt alive; their dismembered and charred and bloodied corpses scattered about like so many mannequins. She saw her mam, naked and blackened with soot, leaping from a window in the Upper Mall.

There was no explosion. Nor, she sensed, would there be one. The idea slipped from her imagination almost as soon as it had appeared. Watching the gleaming edifice of the

439

shopping complex reflect the last light of a dying afternoon, Constance felt the panic ebb from her. This wasn't to be his ending. As she pieced together the puzzle of Stan's parting gesture, she became calmer; she reassured herself. He was gone, she was sure of that. He had been, and now he was gone. Professor Stanley Bell had said all he wanted to say and done all he wanted to do; everything of his was laid out in word and deed for others to pick over in their own search for meaning. The fierce flames of the furnaces had been extinguished, the flag of trades unionism had been lowered; after one vivid final flare, orange and red had made their exit. Stan, too. His ultimate clue – his farewell – had been the mirror. He'd guided her here, she believed, for no other reason than to make her see the mall and all of Hallam as she hadn't seen them before. He had offered her a perspective, a pause for reflection. Having done that, he'd departed. Instinctively, Constance looked down into the yard and across to the gates of the derelict factory and into the street beyond. She sought him – a last glimpse of him, escaping from the scene of his concluding act – but he wasn't there. Her pressing and powerful desire to *see* him – to know where he was and how she might find him – would gradually yield to the vague unease of unfulfilled curiosity; in time, she knew, this too would give way to resignation and, eventually, indifference. Stan would fade into her past. This was her story, not his; that was the other message symbolized by his parting gift. What she saw most clearly of all from her new vantage point was not him, but herself. He had provided the mirror; but it was her reflection, and her eyes which looked upon it. He had brought her to this lookout, but she was the one who looked out. And, having looked, she would never see in the same way again. *I create. I make something out of nothing: I fill blank screens with my words, I fill silence with my voice, I fill space with my presence. And, by living – by constantly transforming my past into my present – I make something out of that which already exists. This is me.* Talking to herself, now, not to Stan. Or to anyone else. The

440

wind was potent here, dishevelling her hair and her clothes and causing her eyes to stream. The warmth of her exertion in scaling the ladder had dissipated, the sweat turning cold on her skin. She shivered. Soon, she would have to descend from the tower and explain herself. She would have to fashion these events into a story to be published under her name. She would have to continue to exist, transfigured, on the endlessly shifting terrain of herself. *It is no more stable down there than it is up here*. She smiled. For now, Constance was content to be alone; to savour the unfamiliar sensation of occupying a high place and of being unafraid to look down.